A WISH UPON A STAR

What Reviewers Say About Jeannie Levig's Work

Threads of the Heart

"What a beautiful and moving story about five women learning invaluable lessons about love, self-awareness, cause and effect, consequences, betrayal, trust, truth, relationships, friendships, family...and life."—*2015 Rainbow Awards*

"[The main characters'] individual stories were interesting on their own but the interaction between the characters really makes this novel great. ...The steamy scenes were so well written and extremely hot—in fact the best I've read in a long time. They were very varied and inventive. I thoroughly enjoyed the book and was so sad to finish it. I wanted it to go on and on!"—*Inked Rainbow Reads*

Embracing the Dawn

"*Embracing the Dawn* by Jeannie Levig has to be considered one of the best books of 2016 and one of the best audiobooks of 2017. We also see a lot of the relationships with secondary characters, and how important those friendships are to the growth and happiness of our main characters. Levig handles all of these relationships with a deftness that is truly a joy to read, and reread. The story is well plotted, the characters have depth, and the story sucks you in and keeps you turning pages."—*The Lesbian Review*

"*Embracing the Dawn* was written beautifully and it has slipped straight into my Favorite and Must Read Again shelves. It was so raw and honest. The story was very believable and I think that's what has stood out from most books I've read recently. Bold Stokes Books have really upped the ante recently with their authors. This was a fantastic novel. I was gripped from the beginning."—*Les Reveur*

"Seldom have I read such a passionate and insightful love story as this. Ms Levig's novel flows like a magnificent river, sometimes roaring other times meandering but always effortlessly and impressively moving gracefully on."—*Inked Rainbow Reads*

Into Thin Air

"Two things are apparent to me after reading Jeannie Levig's three novels. 1. She is an absolutely fantastic writer. 2. She is anything but formulaic. Every single one of her books has been good, but all so different. This writer knows how to drawn emotion from her readers. …Levig challenges you with this book. This story is like a pendulum of emotions, so well crafted that you can't stop. This is a really fantastic book, you haven't read anything like this one, I promise."—*The Romantic Reader*

"Jeannie Levig created such a poignant story that drew so many intense emotions out of me. Each of her characters were so realistic with their flaws and unique personalities traits and I felt so close to each of them. …This story surprised me on so many levels because it is one of the few books that I have ever read that threw all of my expectations out of the window. I have cycled between delight, outrage and sorrow throughout this story and I loved every word of this book because it sends several messages and it is so worth the read."—*The Lesbian Review*

A Heart to Call Home

"Can we please all pause and celebrate the fact that both of these women are in their mid to late 40s? Because there are so few in lesfic and it's refreshing to see! *A Heart to Call Home* is beautifully written. It has so much angst and tension that works well alongside the chemistry and pull between Jessie and Dakota. Even though I knew it's a romance and that they would have a happily ever after, their crisis still brought tears to my eyes."—*The Lesbian Review*

"What a fantastic novel! Jeannie Levig continues to blow me away with her beautiful story telling. Jeannie Levig writes conflict between protagonists better than many authors. You can feel the tension coming off the page that added another element to this wonderful novel."—*Les Reveur*

"Jeannie Levig knows how to develop a character. She weaves her story around her protagonists and draws you right into the amazingness of her stories. I'm never sure where I am going to go, what I'll read and I can never predict the ending. Levig keeps me guessing throughout the whole book and I love her for it. …Levig definitely doesn't play by the rule and loves to add a curveball here and there. Levig does it again with bringing you an amazing story that grips you to the last page."—*The Romantic Reader*

"The main characters embark on a soul searching journey which is moving, poignant and sometimes heart-breaking. The reader joins this emotional rollercoaster suffering and enjoying along with the characters. It is one hell of a ride."—*Lez Review Books*

Visit us at www.boldstrokesbooks.com

By the Author

A WISH UPON A STAR

by
Jeannie Levig

2018

A WISH UPON A STAR

ISBN 13: 978-1-63555-274-4

THIS TRADE PAPERBACK ORIGINAL IS PUBLISHED BY
BOLD STROKES BOOKS, INC.
P.O. BOX 249
VALLEY FALLS, NY 12185

FIRST EDITION: DECEMBER 2018

CREDITS
EDITORS: VICTORIA VILLASENOR AND CINDY CRESAP
PRODUCTION DESIGN: SUSAN RAMUNDO
COVER DESIGN BY MELODY POND

Acknowledgments

As always, I want to begin by thanking my best friend and First Reader, Jamie Patterson, for being with me through every word I write—and so much more. Thank you for your love, your friendship, your support, your research skills, and your critical eye. You make it all a lot more fun…except maybe in those moments when I'm sick to death of a scene and you say, "But what about…" But then the scene turns out better, so it's all good. :)

This book brought me my first experience of working with a beta reader, and a heartfelt thank you goes to Victoria for making it so wonderful and educational. Thank you for all of your input and feedback, and especially for sharing your expertise on autism and helping me give an accurate representation of the challenges and joys of Siena and Erica's relationship. You are deeply appreciated.

Thank you always to my family and my spiritual circle for loving me through everything, whether it be another book and the crunch of a deadline or simply a frustrating day. I couldn't do any of it without you.

And always, my deepest acknowledgment and gratitude to all the amazing folks at Bold Strokes Books. To Radclyffe for creating this supportive space in the world where creativity is so richly nurtured and writers are encouraged and assisted in their growth. To Sandy Lowe for always being there with answers, suggestions, and ideas, and for always taking the time to talk them through. In particular, thank you for your guidance on this book. I couldn't be happier with how it turned out. To my incredible editors, Victoria Villasenor and Cindy Cresap. Vic, what can I say but "YEAH! I got to stay with you!" Ahem…and thank you for always making my books better and for making it such an enjoyable experience. I love working with you and hope we'll have many more books to work on together. To Cindy, who…woman, I don't know how you keep all the stuff in your head that you do. I'm grateful that I can fully trust that when my work has gone through copy edits with you it is squeaky clean. And thank you for all you do as the production manager. And finally, to all of the many behind the scenes people at BSB, from the cover artists to typesetters to proofreaders and more. Thank you, thank you, thank you.

Now to my readers. My deepest gratitude for buying my books and sharing my stories with me. Knowing you're out there enjoying these characters makes it all worthwhile. When I hear from you through email or a positive review, it's so inspiring. Writing is a solitary endeavor, and knowing that there are readers waiting for my next book and excited about my last, makes all the difference in the world. Thank you for taking this journey with me. Always, always, always feel free to drop me a note or stay current on what's coming next through my website at JeannieLevig.com

Dedicated to

Victoria and Stella

And to all the children and adults with special needs
who face and overcome the challenges of being different
and to their parents who love, nurture,
and fight for them every day.

You bring so much light to the world.

CHAPTER ONE

Leslie Raymond squatted in front of the broken sprinkler head in the backyard of her childhood home. It wasn't a big job to fix it, but she'd have to get a replacement head. She always kept spares, but anything like that had been sold or given away, along with everything else, when she'd decided to move across the country for a fresh start.

"Are you going to water that dry grass?"

Leslie startled at the closeness of the voice. She lost her balance and toppled backward. "Holy sh—cow." She caught her expletive when she realized it was a little girl standing beside her. She looked about seven, Elijah's age. Leslie winced. She tried not to think of him, but he was always right there.

"Cows don't have holes." The little girl's face was expressionless, her gaze fixed on the dry patch. "If they did, their intestines and internal organs would fall out."

Leslie blinked. "Uh, yeah." She rolled onto her side, then rose to her knees. "It's just a saying. Kind of like…" She thought for a second. "Kind of like, oh my gosh."

"My dad says holy shit sometimes. I'm not supposed to say it. Is it like that?"

There was something about the girl's voice, or her tone, or her delivery…something…that drew Leslie's attention. It seemed flat, her words tumbling slightly, almost on top of one another. "Yeah, like that."

"Shit is poop and poop can't have holes either because it's gooey and smooshes, so that doesn't make sense either."

Leslie chuckled. "No, I don't suppose it does."

"My mom doesn't like it when I talk about poop. Or wee-wee. Or vomit. Especially at dinner, but that's when there's the most to say about it because it's all food. I think she doesn't like to talk about vomit because she hates it when she throws up. She doesn't like diarrhea either, but she *really* hates throwing up."

Leslie glanced over her shoulder. Where'd this child come from? She noticed the open gate between her backyard and the neighbor's. She remembered her parents putting it in years ago when they'd gotten close to the family living next door at the time and had invited them to use the pool whenever they wanted.

"Are you?" the girl asked.

Leslie tensed. *What did I miss?* These kinds of conversations with Elijah could go anywhere without notice. The combined joy and anguish the memory brought twisted into an ache in her heart. She hardened against it. "Am I what?"

"Are you going to put water on the dry grass?"

Leslie followed the girl's still riveted gaze, then looked down at the sprinkler head in her hand. "Yes," she said, relieved to be back in the present. She got to her feet. "As soon as I fix the sprinkler."

"I like the smell of water on very dry grass," the girl said matter-of-factly.

Leslie studied her profile. Her blond hair brushed the tops of her shoulders, and the tip of her small nose turned up ever so slightly, like a tiny ski slope. Leslie waited for her to say something else, but she didn't. "I'll tell you what," she said lightly. "When I get everything working, you can come over the first time I turn it on. Would you like that?"

The girl pursed her lips, as though thinking, then shook her head. "I don't like sprinklers. They all go different ways at the same time. I don't like things that go different ways at the same time. They make me have an episode."

An episode? Ah, Leslie was starting to get it. *Maybe some form of autism?* She'd met a woman in Elijah's playgroup when he was two, who had an older son "on the spectrum" as she'd called it. Leslie had learned a little about it from her. The boy went into hysterics one day when the fluorescent lighting was flickering. "Oh, well, I can understand that," Leslie said, considering other options. "How about if we just water it with the hose? Then the water would only be coming out one way."

For the first time, the girl turned and looked at Leslie, but her gaze skittered away again in an instant and landed somewhere past her. Her eyes widened. "You have a dog!"

Leslie turned to the dirty, skinny, scraggly dog sitting perfectly still at the edge of the redwood deck that stretched from the French doors of the family room. She'd picked him up at a rest stop a few days earlier and planned to take him to the animal shelter on Monday.

His amber eyes were intelligent and inquisitive as he watched them, his one huge ear standing straight up, reminding Leslie of a satellite dish. The other looked as though something had bitten it off halfway down its length. He'd been so quiet throughout her exchange with the little girl, Leslie had forgotten about him. Odd, since last she remembered, he'd been racing around the yard with a sock he'd stolen from her duffel bag, dodging her attempts to get it back. It now sat beside him, apparently having lost its appeal. "He's not mine. I just found—"

The little girl moved toward him.

"Hey, you'd better not...I don't know if he..." Leslie let her words and concern trail off as the dog lay down and rested his head on his paws at the girl's approach. He rolled his eyes upward to look at her, his damaged ear twitching.

"He's dirty," she said, her tone entirely without judgment, merely an observation. "You have to wash him so I can pet him. I don't like touching dirty things. Dirt by itself is okay because dirt is supposed to be dirty. It can't help it. But things that are supposed to be clean can't be dirty. I want a dog, but my mom says we don't have time to take care of one." She scrunched her face into a serious expression that made Leslie smile, presumably mimicking her mother's gravity on the subject. "And she doesn't want dog poop in the backyard, since I'm out there a lot. I told her at least she wouldn't have to worry about vomit, because dogs eat their own vomit—they're kinda gross that way, but I still want one. My mom still said no. What's his name?"

Leslie was amazed at how much information could spill out of her in one burst. "Uh…I don't know. I found him. I guess he'll need a new name when he gets a new home."

"I want his name to be Gus," the girl said.

"Siena?" A woman's voice drifted over the fence from the yard next door. "Siena, where are you?"

"Siena?" Leslie asked. "Is that your name?"

The girl didn't answer, seemingly mesmerized by the dog.

"There you are," a woman said breathlessly as she hurried through the gate. Her mid-length, silver-gray hair shone in the afternoon sunlight in sharp contrast to the dark tint of the sunglasses that hid her eyes. She wore a blue and green flowered sundress that tied at one shoulder, leaving the other bare, and strappy, tan sandals snaked their way around her slender feet and pink painted toes.

Leslie tried to make herself speak, but her attention kept returning to the blue topaz and white gold teardrop earring that dangled just above the milky white skin where the woman's neck curved into her shoulder. There was something ethereal about her.

"Oh!" the woman said in evident surprise when she saw Leslie. She came to an abrupt halt. "May I help you?" She edged her way toward the deck, positioning herself between Leslie and Siena.

Leslie gave her head a quick shake to focus. "I…uh…I just…" She heard the question again in her mind. "Help me what?"

"What are you doing back here?" The woman's words were clipped. "This is private property. You'll need to leave."

Private? Leave? Suddenly, Leslie understood. "Oh, no. I live here." She wiped her right hand on her cut-off jeans, leaving a smear of dirt and grass, then extended it to the woman. "I'm Leslie Raymond. I own the house."

"Since when?" The woman glanced behind her at Siena, who remained fixated on the dog.

"Well..." Leslie felt like a doof, standing there with her hand sticking out to some woman she didn't know but abruptly realized she knew way too much about—her feelings on poop and vomit and diarrhea, about dogs and dog poop—all things one usually didn't know about someone at a first meeting. Sometimes never. "I've owned the house since my mother passed, nine years ago, and I've lived here since about two thirty this morning, when I pulled my car into the garage."

"Oh." The woman relaxed a little. "I thought the owner was selling."

Leslie let her hand drop to her side. "She was," she said with mild annoyance. "Now she's not."

The woman laughed softly. "I'm sorry. I can get overly vigilant about strangers. My daughter can be extremely friendly to people she's never even seen before."

Leslie nodded. "No problem. I can understand that." She smiled. "She *is* quite a talker."

At the moment, though, Siena sat stoically beside the dog, her hands folded in her lap.

"Siena?" the woman said, turning her attention to her daughter. "Since you've been visiting with our new neighbor, did you introduce yourself like you've been working on in your class?"

A tiny frown tugged the corners of Siena's mouth downward. She rose and walked stiffly to where her mother and Leslie stood.

Leslie fought back a smile in the name of parental solidarity.

"Hello," Siena said, making eye contact fleetingly. "My name is Siena Cooper. It's nice to meet you." She held her hand out to Leslie.

Leslie took it gently, its smallness and fragility bringing a rush of emotion. It'd been a long time since she'd held a child's hand. She'd missed it so much. "Hello, Siena," she said, managing to keep her voice steady. "I'm Leslie Raymond. It's nice to meet you, too."

Siena turned immediately and went back to sit beside the dog.

Leslie chuckled. "And what about you?" she asked the woman in front of her. "Were you absent that day in class?" She smiled to soften the question to a tease.

The woman's attention was still on Siena, or maybe the dog. With a start, she looked at Leslie. "I'm so sorry." She held out her hand. "I'm Erica Cooper. We've lived next door for the past four years." Her fingers were soft and slender in Leslie's stronger grip, her skin seeming to put off a light glow in contrast to Leslie's darker olive complexion.

Leslie felt a twinge of loss when Erica released her hand, as though something she'd wanted for a long time had just slipped through her fingers. It was the strangest thing. Was it merely attraction? *No.* Erica wasn't her type—or at least if she had a type, Erica wouldn't be it. *Do I still have a type?* What had it been? *Nine years since I've been on an actual date?* Who knew what her type would be these days? But it wouldn't be this woman. Despite her gray hair—probably prematurely gray—Erica was most likely a lot younger than Leslie's fifty-three years, since she had such a young child, *and* there was *that*—she had a child. First and foremost on Leslie's list for potential dates, she'd sworn off women with kids. And younger women. "Leslie Raymond," she heard herself repeating.

Erica smiled. "I'm sure we'll be seeing you again, Leslie, but right now…" She looked at Siena. "We were going to take a walk. Remember, Siena?"

"I don't want to anymore," Siena said, her tone unequivocal. "I want to stay with Gus, even if he's dirty."

Erica paused. She slid her sunglasses down her nose with her fingertip and peered over the top. "He's filthy." She shifted her gaze to Leslie.

Leslie stared, transfixed, at the light blue eyes that were clearly sizing her up—not simply light blue, a pale blue with specks of sapphire. At the judgment in them, though, she flushed with embarrassment. Her defenses flared. "No, no. He's not my dog. I found him like that. I'd take much better care of him if he were mine." *Hmmm, that didn't sound a lot better.*

"Erica!" A man's voice broke the early afternoon quiet.

Erica slipped her sunglasses back into place, the slightest hint of annoyance flashing in her eyes before they vanished behind the tinting once more. "Next door," she called in response.

And there he was at the gate. The dad. The husband. The man. The all-important element of what it took to create *a normal and healthy family environment*, according to some people.

And that cinched Leslie's earlier question of whether Erica could be her type. Younger. Straight. Married. And with a kid. Leslie's stomach clenched with a wave of nausea. *Ain't no flippin' way.* She wanted to turn away from this guy, didn't want to deal with him and everything he represented, but nothing that had happened was his fault.

"Trent," Erica said, "this is Leslie Raymond, our new neighbor."

"Hey." Trent stepped up beside her and shook Leslie's hand, but his attention was on Erica.

"Leslie, this is—"

"Have you seen my cell?" he asked Erica. "I would've sworn it was on the nightstand."

"I put it on the charger in the kitchen," Erica said, evidently letting go of the introductions. "You only had one bar."

He smiled. "Thanks, hon." He kissed her cheek. "You're the best."

"Don't forget we're going to walk down to the park with Siena." Erica's tone held a hint of resignation.

"Yeah, yeah," Trent said, backing away. "I just have to make one call."

Leslie watched the exchange with curiosity. She definitely saw Siena in him—the blond hair and brown eyes, the slight slant of his mouth when he pressed his lips together. She felt Erica's scrutiny of her as well, even though she could no longer see those eyes.

Trent turned and strode back through the arbored gateway and across his own patio, then disappeared into the house.

Leslie could only stare after him, stunned at how summarily she'd been discounted.

"Don't take it personally." Erica's smooth voice cut through Leslie's astonishment. "He's preoccupied." With her own abruptness, she turned to Siena. "Come on, sweetie. Let's let Leslie start getting settled." She held out her hand.

"I want to stay with Gus." Siena scooted closer to the dog but still didn't touch him. "I want to pet him when he's clean."

"Sweetie, I'm sure Leslie has things to do, and so do we." Erica sounded patient, practiced, as though this tableau wasn't uncommon. She glanced at Leslie.

Leslie couldn't tell if she was seeking help or confirmation. "I'll tell you what, Siena," she said, moving toward the deck. "I have to go buy some dog shampoo before I can give..." She faltered. Her grandfather had always said once you name something, it's yours, and she didn't intend to keep...Gus. *Damn it.* "Before I can give Gus a bath," she continued. "How about you go for your walk with your folks, and I'll bring...Gus...over later so you can pet him."

Siena and Gus looked at each other. "Okay," Siena said, standing abruptly. She took a step, then halted, her gaze on the dry spot in the lawn again. "What about the grass? I want to smell it."

Leslie chuckled at Siena's determination and focus on her two goals. "That'll just take a few minutes. We could do that now." She caught herself. "If it's okay with your mom." She looked up to find Erica smiling at her.

"She's been watching that spot for several weeks," Erica said.

Leslie took that as a go-ahead and clapped her hands. "All right. Let's take care of it." She ushered Siena to the rolled up hose by the faucet, careful not to touch her. She knew some people with autism didn't like to be touched, and though she also knew that wasn't true of all from a documentary on Netflix—not to mention the fact that she wasn't even sure Siena had autism—she didn't want to take any chances of violating some kind of boundary with her. She gave Siena the end of the hose and waited while she selected the perfect position beside the dry spot. "Ready?" she called out.

Siena nodded excitedly.

Leslie turned on the water and watched as Siena's face took on an expression of pure concentration.

After a moment, Siena closed her eyes and inhaled deeply. Her lips parted and a huge smile spread across her face.

Leslie looked at Erica, who'd sat down in the precise spot Siena had vacated, her arms looped around her knees, and saw the exact same smile of pure joy shaping Erica's lips as she gazed at her daughter.

So there was one thing Siena had gotten from her mother—*that smile*. And it was infectious. Leslie couldn't help but grin. She waited, simply watching, remembering her own moments of joy with Elijah. She crossed to the deck and sat beside Erica.

"Thank you for doing this," Erica said, her voice soft and tender.

"Sure, it's no problem." Leslie rested her forearms on her knees and clasped her hands. From the corner of her eye, she saw Erica turn to her, but Erica didn't speak.

She seemed to be studying Leslie.

Leslie fidgeted under the scrutiny.

"Most people wouldn't have realized the importance of such a seemingly silly thing," she said finally. "Or even if they did, wouldn't have taken the time."

Leslie considered the circumstances of her life. No schedule. No conventional job to report to. No one to speak of to account to for her whereabouts. No family obligations, except for dinner with her cousin Nell the following Wednesday. Some people would view such a brand new, clean slate exciting, and maybe it would be once she got settled. For now, it felt lonely. She let herself live vicariously through Siena's excitement about the smell of water on dry grass. She turned to Erica and smiled. "Time is something I have plenty to give."

Erica kept watching her.

Leslie wished she could see her eyes for at least a hint of what she might be thinking.

"So where are you from?" Erica glanced back to Siena.

The relief of no longer being under Erica's concentrated focus swept through Leslie like a gentle summer rain. How odd that she could feel the intensity of her stare without being able to see it. She relaxed. "Technically, I'm from here." She tilted her head toward the house. "But I've been in Florida for the past twenty years."

"And now you decided to come home?" Erica seemed at ease. She was obviously comfortable with people, even new ones.

"Yep." Leslie couldn't think of anything else to say that didn't open up the subject to more than she wanted to share, but Erica saved her from the awkwardness.

"And you drove all the way home?" she asked. "That's a long way to drive."

"Yeah, well, you know…" Leslie shrugged. "There's never a pair of ruby slippers around when you need them." She offered a grin.

Erica returned a slow smile.

"I'm done," Siena called.

Leslie and Erica looked to her in tandem.

She dropped the hose and headed toward the gate.

"I guess we're ready for our walk." Erica laughed as she rose. "Thank you for letting her do that."

"My pleasure." Leslie chuckled. "If only everyone's needs were so easily met."

Erica moved across the yard, following Siena. As though in afterthought, she turned around. "Welcome to the neighborhood," she said, walking backward. "Maybe we'll see you again after you've washed your dog?" The sentence trailed up at the end in question.

"He's not my dog," Leslie said as he trotted up to the deck and jumped up beside her.

"So you've said." Erica laughed, then turned with a wave over her shoulder.

Leslie watched the dog…Gus…as he stared after Erica until she disappeared around the corner of the gate. Then he looked up at Leslie. "You're not my dog," she said to him.

He cocked his head.

After turning off the water, Leslie began to recoil the hose. When she bent to free it from where it looped around a tree root near the dry patch, she inhaled deeply. She'd never noticed the smell of water on dry grass, but now that she did, she found it strangely pleasant—simultaneously earthy and lightly refreshing.

She glanced toward the Coopers' backyard. It never ceased to amaze her what she learned from children.

Later, as she sipped from a bottle of orange juice, she stared out the living room window and took in the street she'd grown up on. The trees were bigger, the hedges higher, and some of the houses had additions or had been remodeled completely, but she remembered racing down the same sidewalk on her bike, Nell on the handlebars, on their way to an adventure. She tried to imagine Elijah learning to ride a bike on that same sidewalk, then swallowed hard against the sudden ache in her heart. She looked down at the dog—that wasn't her dog—at her feet, his front paws on the low windowsill and his wet nose smearing the glass.

He tilted his head back and gazed up at her.

"What the heck am I doing here?" she asked, half expecting a response. She got one.

He wagged his stub of a tail.

She sighed. "If only I understood what that meant." She knew what she was doing there, though. She didn't have to ask. *I'm here to get as far away from Miami as I can. To make a fresh start.* And it'd been practical to return to California. She owned a house here outright and could live in it for free. She needed furniture, of course, but that was remedied easily enough. She scanned the living room. Even empty, it held her memories.

She'd first moved into this house with her parents when she was eight and lived there until she'd left for college at eighteen. They'd been a family there—a small one, with Leslie being the only child, but a family, nonetheless. She'd come home for frequent visits over the many years since, until her father's fatal heart attack ten years earlier and her mother's quiet and serene passing in her sleep a year later. Leslie hadn't been home again since her mother's funeral, but she'd been unable to let go of the house and had leased it out. She'd even thought briefly at one point about maybe bringing Cassie and Elijah here to live, but that family was gone, too. What the hell did she need with a family home?

Movement outside drew her attention. The Coopers strolled past—Erica holding Siena's hand, Trent on the other side, his cell phone pressed to his ear. They seemed an odd unit, or maybe it was only Erica. She seemed older than most women with seven-year-olds, which wasn't impossible, of course. Leslie glanced at Trent and saw the shimmer of some gray at his temples she hadn't noticed before. She looked back to Erica, remembered her eyes— that pale blue that had captured Leslie's attention so fully—then in those few seconds she'd tipped her glasses down, the crinkled corners. And now that she thought about it, faint laugh lines around her mouth. Maybe she was closer to Leslie's age.

Did that change anything, though, make her Leslie's new type, make Leslie remotely interested in anything other than being neighbors? *No. She's still straight, still has a husband, and still has a kid.* Three strikes. *And you're out.*

Leslie would have to be an idiot to end up there again.

And she was no idiot.

CHAPTER TWO

Erica poured herself another glass of iced herbal sun tea, then lifted the carafe to her best friend.

Becky shook her head. "I should go soon. I think we've pushed our luck with the amount of time Rosi and Siena have been in the same room together without one of them having a meltdown."

Erica smiled. "They do seem to be getting along better than usual today."

"Should we check to make sure one didn't fall asleep and the other one quietly smothered her?" Becky asked conspiratorially.

Erica squinted past her through the sliding screen door and into the family room. The girls sat next to each other on the sofa just inside the door working on a jigsaw puzzle. "Nope," Erica whispered, never sure when Siena was aware of her surroundings and when she was completely absorbed in her own world. "I can see them. They're both still upright and breathing."

Erica had met Becky in the support group for parents of children with autism when she'd moved to California four years earlier. They'd become fast friends, but their daughters were an entirely different story. Siena and Rosi had nothing in common aside from their age and the fact that they were both on the spectrum. Even *where* they fell on the spectrum differed, Siena being high functioning, Rosi moderate to low. Erica and Becky had decided to push them, though, so they themselves could enjoy a supportive friendship. The first few play dates had been rough, but after a while the girls seemed to get used to one another enough to coexist when they were together.

"Yowza! Who's that?" Becky asked.

Erica returned her attention to Becky to find she'd lifted her sunglasses and was blatantly staring into the yard next door. She glanced over her shoulder. She knew exactly what she'd see, but she looked anyway, just to enjoy the view. From her raised patio, she could easily take in the back end of the adjacent property that held the fenced pool. "That's my new neighbor," she said appreciatively before returning her gaze to Becky.

"Wow!"

Erica shook her head. "I know you love Jack, and you told me when we first met that you're straight, but sometimes I wonder." Erica enjoyed teasing Becky, knowing that she looked at women for Erica, not for herself. She was always on alert to find someone for her to settle down with. She even tried to fix her up on blind dates from time to time, until Erica would put her foot down. Then they'd have another serious talk about why she was done with relationships, and things would go back to normal. Erica did hook up with someone occasionally, only for the physical release, though, nothing more.

"What can I say? You've taught me to appreciate a beautiful woman." Becky dropped her glasses back into place. "Besides, look at those legs. I'd do anything to have legs like that. Except, you know…eat right and exercise. Even then, I don't think mine would look that good." She lifted her shades again for a second perusal.

In the quick peek Erica had taken, it wasn't Leslie's legs she'd noticed. Leslie had been bent over the pool pump, those short little cut-off jeans hugging her hips and a very fine ass. Now that Becky mentioned it, yes, the legs were pretty fine, too. What really stuck in her mind, though, was from earlier—the outline of plump nipples tipping small breasts, just the perfect handful, beneath the faded orange tank top that draped loosely over her torso. It'd been all Erica could do to remain focused on Siena, introductions, and small talk while Siena watered the grass.

"Hello?" Becky's slightly raised voice halted Erica's meandering thoughts.

"Yes, her legs are nice," Erica said, taking a drink of tea.

"Stop gawking. She can see us, too, if she turns around."

Becky smirked. "I asked if you'd met her yet. If she's single. Do you know if she likes women?"

"Oh." Erica's ears went hot. *Busted.* "Yes, I met her this morning for about five minutes. Amazingly, though," she said with mock astonishment, "we didn't discuss our sexual orientations or marital status." *Although, she did say I a lot.*

Becky eyed Erica. "So with this nonchalant act you have going, do you really expect me to believe you don't think she's hot?"

"Of course I think she's hot." Erica rolled her eyes to keep from stealing another glance over her shoulder. "Because...she's hot. But what do you expect me to do? I just met her this morning."

"So in a week or two, you'll hit on her?" Becky grinned.

"Of course not. She's my next-door neighbor. I can't sleep with my next-door neighbor."

"Right, because it would be awkward. And you can't date your next-door neighbor, because what if it all went wrong?" Becky did her best impression of Erica's arguments. "Just like you can't date someone you work with, or the manager of your bank, or the guy on the maintenance crew at the girls' school."

"Becky, please. Don't start." Erica averted her gaze and tucked a lock of hair behind her ear. "You know why I don't date. It's too hard."

Becky sighed. "Okay. You're right. I'm sorry. It's just that when we first met and you told me about yourself, I thought, wow bi *and* single! I was sure I'd get to hear twice as many hot sex stories. I'm supposed to be able to live vicariously through you, but you're utterly boring."

"I know. I'm a disappointment." Erica hung her head, feigning shame. "I do tell you about the sex I have when I have it, though. Doesn't that count?" She smiled at Becky.

"Of course it counts. But, woman, *I* have sex more than you do, and *I've* been married for fifteen years." Becky tilted her head, obviously looking past Erica again.

"Is she still there?" Erica asked, lowering her voice as though Leslie might be able to hear her from a hundred feet away.

"Oh yeah," Becky said. "She's strutting around like the pool guy in a porno movie, only, in this case, a pool girl."

Erica chuckled at the reference. She wanted to look so badly but consoled herself with an image in her mind from earlier. This time, though, what struck her was the smile Leslie had flashed when Siena had introduced herself, the spark of warmth in her lush brown eyes when she'd watched Siena water the grass. And her hair…that thick brown hair, only slightly darker than her eyes, that fell just past her shoulders. It looked like it'd be so soft to the touch. The white strands that wove through it shimmered in the sunlight.

"You're going to at least look, though, right? Enjoy the eye candy?"

Erica blew out the breath she'd been holding. "How could I not?"

"Okay, good." Becky leaned back into her chair. "And if you ever do—"

Erica cut her off sharply with a warning look.

Becky held up her hands. "Okay, I won't go there again. Maybe we should focus on men for you," she added, humor sparking in her eyes. "And speaking of men, where's Trent?"

"He had to leave," Erica said without emotion. "He had to get back to Chicago for some emergency meeting tomorrow."

"Really? A meeting on a Sunday?" Becky frowned. "Did he reach his breaking point with Siena already?"

Erica didn't bother defending Trent's excuse for leaving. "It seemed to come sooner this time for some reason." She ran her fingertip through the condensation on her glass. "He only made it three days. I'm not sure what was going on with him."

"Kudos to you for even caring." Becky pushed her sunglasses to the top of her head and met Erica's eyes. "If Jack bailed on me and left me to raise Rosi on my own, I'd never let him into the same room with me—for his own safety."

"Trent does the best he can, just like we all do," Erica said softly. "You know how hard it is dealing with autism. Some people just can't do it. Besides, Trent and I never had the marriage you and Jack do, even before Siena. I'm just glad he's come around to the degree he wants to visit at all. I think, in the long run, it will be good for both him and Siena."

"As I said, girlfriend." Becky raised her glass to Erica. "Kudos to you."

Erica smiled.

"Would you ever take him back?" Becky asked. "I mean, if he really stepped up with Siena?"

"No." Erica didn't have to think about it. "The divorce was the best thing that could have happened to us. We would have ended up hating each other if we'd stayed together. This way, we both have the chance to be happy."

"Are you?" Becky asked. "Happy, I mean?"

This time Erica did think. She looked at Siena through the screen, then glanced around her patio. She thought of the quiet routine of her job teaching journalism at the junior college and her evenings and weekends at home with Siena. She smiled. "I'm content. And at peace. And I think that's enough. I like that it's only me and Siena, that there isn't someone else whose needs I have to worry about. That was one of the hardest things with Trent, after Siena was born. Then when her behavior started to escalate and she was diagnosed, it became impossible. Everything's better this way."

Becky's expression was reflective. She clearly wanted to say something but didn't.

Erica was grateful. She needed to relax. It'd been such a relief when Trent had left. There'd been so much tension in the air during this visit, but he hadn't said what was bothering him, and she wasn't in the mood to ask. His interaction with Siena, or lack thereof, had been typical—he still hadn't found a way to be comfortable with her, but at least he was trying. And he was preoccupied with work, but that was nothing new. He'd been that way since the day he and Erica met. In fact, that was one of the things that had attracted her to him, since she'd been focused on building her career as a television newscaster at the time and needed to be available to travel at a moment's notice. On this visit, though, Trent had been on edge. There had been a moment, late Friday night after Siena was in bed and he and Erica were sitting outside, when he'd looked at her and she thought he might have something he'd wanted to discuss. But then he'd simply said good night and gone inside.

Becky sighed. "Well, I need to grab my kid and head home," she said, clearly deciding to keep her remaining thoughts to herself. "See you Monday at the meeting?" She downed the rest of her tea.

"Wouldn't miss it," Erica said.

Erica scattered the crispy onions on top of the macaroni and cheese she'd made for dinner, then set the casserole dish back in the oven. "Did you have a good time with Rosi this afternoon?" she asked Siena.

Seated at the kitchen table, Siena swapped the blue crayon she'd been using to color in the sky in her picture for a red one. "No," she said without looking up. "I don't like Rosi."

"You seemed to be sharing your puzzle with her nicely." Erica closed the oven door.

"That's because you said I had to. I don't like it when Rosi touches my puzzle pieces."

"I see." Erica still sometimes mistook Siena's compliance for the possibility that she was enjoying something. Wishful thinking, most likely. When Siena truly enjoyed something, though, there was never any doubt. Erica thought of the pure happiness on Siena's face when she'd been watering the grass earlier that morning. She smiled. "Well, I appreciate you letting Rosi spend time with you so Becky and I could talk for a while. Thank you." She stroked Siena's hair. It was one of the displays of physical affection Siena had grown to accept from her.

"You're welcome."

Siena's reply was rote, but it was better than what it would have been two months earlier. Erica was grateful for the social skills class Siena was enrolled in for the summer. It was making a difference in how she interacted with people in general. While Erica knew Siena wasn't being rude in her responses, the rest of the world wouldn't, and Siena needed to be able to function out in the world. "Dinner's almost ready," she said, cupping the back of Siena's head. "Finish up your drawing, okay?"

A clang from outside on the patio and a scratching sound on the screen interrupted their exchange.

"Hey, get back here. We weren't invited in."

Erica recognized Leslie Raymond's voice. Then a loud rattle and scraping sound carried inside, and a tan and white flurry launched itself into the kitchen, heading straight toward Siena.

Erica's heart leapt into her throat as her protective instincts flared. She grabbed for Siena.

"Gus!" Siena's squeal was filled with joy.

The dog skidded to a stop in front of her, and his whole body became a wriggling mass as he twisted and squirmed, flopping onto the floor, then leaping into the air. He never jumped on Siena, though.

Siena slipped from her chair and knelt before him. He immediately stilled, and she threw her arms around him. "You're clean!"

And there it was—unadulterated, unequivocal enjoyment. Erica laughed, even as she patted her chest to calm her heartbeat.

"Jeez. I'm so sorry," Leslie said from the kitchen doorway. "He took off the second we came through the gate."

Siena ran her hands all over the dog's head, behind his ears, and down his back. She buried her face in his fur.

He stood on his hind legs, his front paws in her lap, his back end and stubby tail shaking like a paint mixing machine.

"Really, I'm sorry," Leslie said again. "Gus—or whatever your name is—get down." She grabbed the dog and started to pull him away.

"Nooo," Siena cried. "I want him."

"It's okay," Erica said, grasping Leslie's wrist, while still trying to get control of herself. "He's okay. Siena's fine."

Leslie stepped back and ran her fingers through her disheveled hair. Its disarray and her distressed expression made her look adorable. "I'm so sorry."

Erica started laughing again.

Siena giggled, her arms tightly around Gus as he wildly licked her ear.

"It's fine," Erica said, finally gaining some composure. She met Leslie's gaze. "Would the two of you like to come in?" She broke into laughter again.

This time, Leslie joined her. "Thank you. I think we will."

"You gave him a bath," Siena said excitedly still running her hands through his fur.

"Actually, I couldn't stand the thought of it, so I took him to a groomer," Leslie said. She looked between Siena and Erica. "And you'll be happy to know that the groomer gave him an 'A' for his behavior—except for when she tried to file his toenails. He doesn't like his feet messed with. And he got a doggie treat. And…" She held up a PetSmart bag. "I got a few toys for you and him to play with," she said to Siena.

Siena scrambled to her feet. "Can I see?"

"Of course." Leslie handed her the bag, then knelt and scratched behind Gus's ear.

Gus tilted his head into her hand and let out a loud groan.

"Look, Mommy, a ball. And a rope with a tire," Siena said, her pitch high.

Erica loved it when Siena called her Mommy. It only happened when she was excited.

"Can we go outside and play?"

"Sure." Another chuckle slipped from Erica's throat. "But keep in mind dinner's almost ready."

"Okay," Siena said. "C'mon, Gus." She raced out of the kitchen, the dog at her heels.

When they were alone, Erica smiled at Leslie. "You just made one little girl very happy. Again."

"Not me," Leslie said, putting her palm to her chest. "That crazy dog. And don't worry. I'll take care of your screen before I leave."

"What?" Erica asked, alarmed. "What happened to my screen?"

Leslie laughed. "He just knocked it off the track in his desperation to get to Siena. It's an easy fix." She slid her hands into the back pockets of those little cut-offs she still wore, drawing Erica's attention to the long, shapely legs Becky had gone on about—and they *were* long.

For the first time, Erica noticed that Leslie stood a few inches taller than her, at least five nine or five ten. At five foot eight, Erica was used to being the one to lower her gaze with another woman, not raise it. It was a novel feeling, and she liked it. She cleared her throat, then stepped around Leslie and moved to the counter to finish the salad she'd been making. "Would you like to join us for dinner as a thank you for making Siena so happy?"

"That's all right." Leslie faltered. "I don't want—"

"Are you sure? There's plenty."

Leslie glanced around, indecision in her eyes. "It does smell good."

"Homemade macaroni and cheese," Erica said tauntingly. "Salad. And peanut butter chocolate brownies for dessert."

Leslie groaned. "That sounds way better than the Twinkies and Funyuns we got from the gas station last night."

"We?" Erica arched an eyebrow. "You fed your dog Twinkies and Funyuns?"

"He had some kibble I picked up, too, but yes, he did have a bite or two of Twinkie. He looked sad." Leslie shrugged. "And he's not my dog. Remember? I found him?"

"That's right." Erica smiled and nodded. "I forgot. So what did you decide about dinner? Should I make you a salad?"

Leslie hesitated. She looked down at herself. "I don't know. I'm really dirty. I've been working in the yard and on the pool all day."

Erica kept herself from following Leslie's gaze over the soiled and sweaty tank top and dirty cut-off jeans, because she knew it wasn't the dirt she'd see. She didn't need to be ogling her new neighbor. "It'll be another twenty minutes before the mac and cheese is done, if you want to run home and get cleaned up." She kept her attention on the tomato she was slicing.

Another pause. "Really?" Leslie sounded more tempted. "You wouldn't mind me barging in on your dinner?"

"You're not barging in. I'm inviting you."

"All right, I'll be quick."

The eagerness in Leslie's voice made Erica smile. She wondered how long Leslie had been on the road, making meals out of the offerings of gas station vending machines and convenience stores. "No rush. We can wait for you."

As Leslie made her way from the kitchen, Erica put together a third place setting, added it to hers and Siena's, and headed out to set the patio table. When she rounded the corner, she halted, a sharp gasp escaping her lips.

Leslie stood on the other side of the screen door, her legs spread wide, her arms outstretched as she gripped both ends of the door, her head tipped back as she stared up at the slot it fit into. In that position, her hips were thrust forward and her breasts strained against the well-worn fabric of the tank top. The slender column of her neck stretched backward, making Erica wonder what those taut muscles would feel like beneath her mouth. Heat flooded her body, and she felt herself flush.

"There we go," Leslie said, fitting the bottom of the door into the track at the threshold. She slid it open and gestured Erica through. "All fixed."

Erica inhaled a steadying breath, then walked outside. The movement took her closer to Leslie than she was comfortable with, but it was only for a split second.

"I'll be back in a few," Leslie said. She jogged across the patio, then hopped off the one step onto the walkway that led to the gate.

Erica took a moment to breathe. Surely, her reaction to this woman who'd simply shown up this morning almost in Erica's backyard would wear off. *Or maybe I just need to get laid.* She'd learned to maintain a somewhat crass terminology around that particular subject in order to keep the romantic that was her natural inner voice under wraps. *How long has it been?* When no answer came, she turned her attention to Siena while her body finished its cooling process. The sight brought a smile to her lips.

Siena threw the ball for Gus, who chased after it, scooped it up, then raced in circles and figure eights around the yard with it clutched in his mouth, while Siena shrieked and clapped her hands. Then he came to a screeching halt in front of her, dropped the ball at her feet, and sat, clearly waiting for the next round.

Erica cast a glance into the yard next door and wondered who Leslie Raymond was. Who was this new neighbor, this stranger, who'd manage to delight Siena twice in one day? It wasn't that Siena was a sullen child. She laughed. She played. She had favorite books and movies and toys that entertained and amused her. But this level of happiness and fun didn't usually come twice in a day. It rarely came twice in a week. An uneasiness rustled through her.

She didn't know anything about Leslie, only that she owned the house next door, she was moving from Florida, and she'd found the dog on her way here. And she somehow knew just what to do to make Siena smile. That was a good thing, of course. How could making someone smile not be good? So why did it make Erica uneasy?

A playful yip from Gus pulled her back to the moment. *And what about the dog?* Leslie kept saying he wasn't hers. Did that mean she wasn't keeping him?

Erica could tell Siena had already claimed him in that way she assumed ownership of anything she liked—it was her form of attachment—and if he suddenly disappeared, Siena would be triggered. It was one of the areas in which they had yet to find any successful replacement behaviors. Siena would ultimately be okay, but it hurt Erica's heart to see her go through such trauma. Leslie knew his name, though, or had given him one, and Gus seemed comfortable with her. Somehow, Erica doubted he was going anywhere, even if Leslie might not know it yet. She hoped she was right.

Erica went back inside to start bringing out the food and drinks. When she stepped outside on her final trip with the macaroni and cheese in hand, Leslie had returned and was sitting on the lawn with Siena, Gus on his haunches between them. Leslie pointed up into the twilight sky and was saying something to Siena that Erica couldn't hear.

Siena listened, then seemed to be repeating Leslie's words.

Leslie grinned. "That's great," she said, her voice rising in evident enthusiasm.

Erica watched as Siena smiled brightly yet one more time. "Dinner's ready," she called across the yard. "Siena, please get washed up before you sit down."

As Siena raced past Erica and into the house, Gus at her heels, Leslie sauntered up to the table. Her hair looked damp, her face scrubbed clean, and she'd changed into tan jeans, a dark orange, button-up shirt tucked in at the waist with the sleeves rolled to just below her elbows, and brown flip-flops.

Erica was glad she had more clothes on, but she still felt the tug of arousal from earlier when she looked at Leslie. She'd have to get a grip on that. She'd meant what she'd said to Becky. She couldn't get involved with someone who lived next door. The situation held too many inherent complications, and they'd only met that morning. Leslie might make a good friend, for both her and Siena, though.

"This looks great," Leslie said, scanning the table. "And by candlelight, no less." Her tone was playful.

Erica laughed. "It's citronella. It keeps the bugs away."

Leslie smiled knowingly. "Isn't your husband joining us?" she asked, taking in the three place settings.

Erica pulled out a chair and sat before answering. She didn't want to talk about Trent for some reason, not with Leslie. Normally, she had no problem with that. But she didn't really like discussing him in front of Siena, and Siena would be back shortly. "No," she said finally. "Something came up at work."

Leslie's expression softened as she lowered herself into her own chair. "I hope everything's okay."

The screen door slid open, and Siena and Gus were back.

"Your dog seems to have made a new friend," Erica said, watching the two. "Excuse me." She glanced at Leslie. "*Not* your dog seems to have made a new friend."

Leslie chuckled. "Yeah, I noticed that."

"He's so good with her. It's like he knows exactly what to do, and what not to do." Erica scooped a large spoonful of the macaroni dish onto Siena's plate as Siena got settled in her seat. She held out her hand for Leslie's plate. "This is hot. May I serve you?"

Leslie gave it to her. "He's a good dog." She reached down and scratched his ear as he settled once again directly between Siena and her. "He was good company the last couple of days of my trip...except for the smell," she added in a gruffer tone.

"He cleans up nicely, though," Erica said, dishing up her own food. "Who knew such a pretty dog was underneath all that dirt?"

"And now he smells good," Siena said, gazing down at him adoringly. "He smells like coconuts."

"Speaking of smelling good, this smells delicious." Leslie waited until Erica was finished plating her own food, then took a bite. She moaned while she chewed. "This is sooooo good. Thank you for the invitation. I can't remember the last time I had homemade mac and cheese."

"Did you know that cheese can make you constipated?" Siena asked in between bites. "That means you can't poop."

"Siena," Erica said, hoping her warning tone was enough to stave off the ensuing discourse she knew Siena was capable of on all the things that could keep one from pooping. Just to make sure, she added, "Not at the table."

Siena frowned.

Leslie cleared her throat. Was there a chuckle underneath?

"Why don't you tell me what Leslie was showing you in the sky earlier," Erica said, offering a new subject. "That looked interesting."

Siena stabbed at several pieces of macaroni with her fork. "We were looking for the first star." She swirled the pasta around in the melted cheese. "You can make a wish on the first star you see, if you say…" She paused, then glanced at Leslie.

"Do you remember?" Leslie asked.

Siena squinted in thought. "Star light, star bright…First star I see tonight…" She pursed her lips, then shot a quick look to Leslie again.

Leslie waited a few beats, then said slowly, "Wish…I…"

Siena sat up straight, a smile lifting the corners of her mouth. "Wish I may. Wish I might. Have the wish I wish tonight." She ate the forkful of macaroni and cheese with a satisfied nod.

Siena's triumphant expression warmed Erica's heart. She was impressed that Leslie had waited until Siena looked to her for help, and then simply gave her a prompt rather than finishing the rhyme for her. Erica had noticed that so many adults who didn't have kids had a tendency to take over when a child hesitated. *Maybe she does have kids. Or had them, and now they're grown?* Despite the fact that her body looked as though it could belong to a much younger woman, Erica sensed Leslie was old enough for the latter. There were the white strands in her hair, although that didn't necessarily mean anything. Erica had gone fully gray in her thirties. Leslie's patience with Siena, though, the cast of wisdom to her eyes, her assured manner, all spoke of a maturity that drew Erica in.

Having a seven-year-old at fifty-one put Erica around much younger people in the parents' club at Siena's school and in the support group where she'd met Becky. Becky was only thirty-four. And in Erica's job, she taught young college students every day. She liked the idea of getting to know someone closer to her age. "And did you make a wish?" she asked Siena.

"Yes." Siena kept her gaze riveted on her dinner, an indication that she was done with the topic. Conversations with Siena went that way sometimes. "I don't want to tell you any more."

Erica caught the slight quirk of Leslie's lips and allowed her own smile, along with a soft laugh, to let Leslie know she didn't take Siena's response as rudeness or back talk. It usually took people a while to understand children, and adults, on the spectrum. "That's okay. We all have our private thoughts," she said, more for Leslie's benefit than Siena's. She turned her attention to Leslie. "How did you end up owning a home here when you lived in Florida?"

As Leslie talked about her parents and growing up in the neighborhood, piquing Siena's interest with the story of Matt, the little boy who lived across the street and pretended he was a kangaroo, and amusing Erica with a recounting of her father's handyman projects around the house, Erica found she was enjoying herself more than she had in a long time. When Siena finally asked to go inside and work on her puzzle, Erica realized she was looking forward to some time to herself with Leslie. "Of course, sweetie. Go ahead." She watched Gus follow Siena inside with unexpected contentment. "It seems you and Gus have won her over," she said to Leslie once they were alone.

"I'm sure it's Gus," Leslie said, a tinge of pink touching her cheeks. "Dogs have that irresistible charm."

Erica wasn't sure of that at all. Leslie had her own way of charming, so much so Erica would need to be careful if Leslie were to be around much. "Yes, but dogs—"

"No, no, no. No, no, no!" Siena's voice rose higher and louder, until all that could be heard was a long shriek.

Erica bolted to her feet, knocking her chair over and hearing a dish shatter on the cement floor of the patio, and dashed inside. She found Siena in the family room, running in tight circles pulling at her hair. Her high-pitched wail rang shrilly in the confines of the room.

Gus stood on his hind legs several feet away, looking frantic and whining.

Erica raced to Siena, covered her hands with her own, and tried to disentangle her fingers from her hair. She was vaguely aware of Leslie calling Gus to her in the doorway.

When Erica had released Siena's grip and had hold of her wrists, she pressed Siena's arms to her sides and wrapped her in a hard, tight hug. Her breath came fast, and her heart pounded. Even though she'd been handling these situations for years, they could still unnerve her. When her hold was secure, she lowered them both to the couch and eased the full weight of her body onto Siena.

Siena continued screaming and struggling beneath Erica. Whatever had triggered this episode was a biggie. What on earth happened? Had the dog done something?

When Siena began to calm, Erica lifted her into her arms and carried her upstairs. In Siena's room, she pulled her special sweatshirt from the closet, the green one that fit her snugly and comforted her following one of these spells. She helped her into it and pulled and tied the drawstrings of the hood, tightening the soft fabric around Siena's head, then lay her on the bed and snuggled close around her. It was the routine.

Later, as Siena's breathing evened and deepened in sleep, Erica felt the length of the day and the constant emotional weight carried by all parents of children on the spectrum overtake her and let herself drift off as well.

When she woke later in the soft illumination of Siena's Winnie the Pooh nightlight, exhaustion still shrouded her like a heavy cloak. She knew she should get up and go downstairs to clean up the kitchen and whatever mess awaited her on the patio from the dish that had broken, but she couldn't make herself move. As she started to close her eyes again, a movement in the doorway drew her attention.

Gus lay across the threshold on his stomach, his head held high, his ears perked, even the one that was half gone, and his alert eyes were trained directly on Erica. If she didn't know better, she would have sworn the obvious question shone in them. *Is she okay?*

Erica watched him, remembering her earlier wondering if he'd done something to upset Siena. Looking at him now, she knew whatever had happened, it couldn't have been him.

He inched forward on the carpet, as though asking permission to fully enter the room.

Erica reached across Siena's sleeping form and dangled her hand over the side of the bed. She wiggled her fingers, beckoning him.

He sprang up on his short little legs and hurried to her, his stubby tail wagging his whole backend. He gently licked her fingers, then once again, looked directly into her eyes, the same question lingering in his.

She stroked his head. "She's fine," Erica whispered. "Everything's okay."

He rose onto his hind legs, his front paws on the edge of the bed, and gazed at Siena. Even more tenderly than he'd licked Erica's hand, he touched his nose to Siena's cheek and gave her the lightest of doggie kisses.

Tears sprang to Erica's eyes as the comfort of someone else sharing her concern for Siena flooded her. It was silly. Gus was a dog. She couldn't quell her emotion, though. She patted the spot in the curve of Siena's tummy, inviting Gus to join them.

And he did. He jumped onto the bed, turned one circle, and curled up closely against Siena.

Erica let her eyes close again and drifted back to sleep, her arm protectively draped over Siena, her fingers gratefully entwined in the warmth of Gus's fur.

The next time she woke, Gus was gone, Siena was sleeping soundly, and the dinner dishes were calling to Erica all the way from downstairs. She hated walking into a dirty kitchen first thing in the morning. It'd be better to tackle the mess now.

She eased herself up from the bed, draped a plush Winnie the Pooh blanket over Siena, and headed to the stairs. In the family room, she stopped at the card table that held Siena's jigsaw puzzle and studied it for a moment. It was coming along nicely. Siena loved puzzles and had already worked her way up to the thousand piece ones that intimidated Erica, but they didn't faze Siena in the least. Erica glanced at the TV tray they'd set up for Rosi and saw the cause of Siena's meltdown. A pile of shredded cardboard that used to be puzzle pieces sat in the corner of the tray. A handful of other pieces remained in the middle, presumably waiting to be destroyed as well.

Erica squeezed her eyes shut and massaged her temples in an attempt to ward off the burgeoning headache.

There were many things that could set Siena off—any situation that felt chaotic, repeated irritations like a fly landing on her over and over, the intermittent beep of a smoke alarm when the battery was dying, the color pink if it got too close, having her things in her room touched or moved. But one of the things hardest for her to recover from was being prevented from finishing something she'd started. And there was no way the shredded puzzle pieces could ever be repaired and fit into the puzzle. There might be a couple more meltdowns over this. She considered clearing the entire puzzle away and throwing it in the trash, but finding it missing completely might actually be worse. There was never any way of knowing.

Erica sighed, wishing she could go to bed and wake up in the morning with it all worked out. But that never happened. Each day brought new things to deal with. She at least needed to get today's dishes done before tomorrow's started piling up on top of them. When she stepped into the kitchen, though, she froze in shock. She blinked, just in case she wasn't seeing clearly. But she was.

The kitchen was spotless. Even in the dim illumination from the light above the stove, the refrigerator door handle and the white tile countertops gleamed. The sink was empty. The light on the front of the dishwasher was on, indicating it'd been run, and the dishtowels were hung precisely over the handle of the oven. She moved out onto the patio to find the table cleared and wiped clean and the chairs pushed into their spots in perfect alignment. The tiny white lights that adorned the latticework around the patio roof and the lower branches of the nearby elm tree reflected cheerfully in the rippled glass of the tabletop.

Emotion threatened to overtake Erica again. Was this what Leslie was doing while her dog was sharing the worry Erica felt whenever she was reminded of what Siena had to deal with on a daily basis? Erica had heard of situations like this, like Jack handling life while Becky soothed and comforted Rosi, or vice versa. Other parents in the support group shared how grateful they were for their spouses or family members that helped them cope and picked up the slack when they needed rest.

Erica, though, handled it all. Her experience was when things got tough, people left, so she'd learned not to count on anyone. She'd learned how to make it on her own with Siena. But this was what having someone take up the slack must feel like, to be able to be upstairs comforting Siena and when she came down, everything was different—better—than how she'd left it. This wasn't her life, though. It was a nice surprise, one she would definitely thank Leslie for, but then do her best not to think about again. This—this feeling of being helped, being taken care of, while she was taking care of Siena—was dangerous. Thinking about it was dangerous. Leslie Raymond and her little dog were dangerous.

But Erica wouldn't get sucked in. She listened to Becky all the time and managed to keep her perspective. *This is no different.*

With a sigh of resolve, she went inside, locked the sliding glass door, and headed upstairs to the luxury of her bed and a few hours of blissful sleep.

Soon enough, it would be tomorrow.

CHAPTER THREE

Leslie woke gradually, first becoming aware that her hand had gone numb, being crushed between her body and the floor, then realizing something was off. She wasn't alone. She could feel it. *Where am I?* She forced her eyes open just a slit, enough to see a wall right in front of her. Something shuffled behind her. She gasped and flipped over to face whoever or whatever it was.

Siena stood not five feet away, stock-still, staring at her like a scientist studying an alien life-form. Gus sat beside her, doing the same, his only movement the twitching of his jagged ear.

Leslie clutched her chest as recognition fully set in. "Oh, good God," she said, her heart beating violently against her rib cage. "Siena. You have to stop sneaking up on me."

"I didn't sneak. I walked. Why don't you have a bed?" Siena asked.

While she calmed, Leslie rubbed her wrist and groaned at the pain of stabbing needles as the blood flowed back into her hand. "What are you doing here? How'd you get in?" She glanced at the front door, then in the direction of the back. The first night she'd arrived, she'd rolled out her sleeping bag along the wall, four steps into the living room. She'd been so exhausted, that's as far as she'd gotten. The previous night, when she'd finished cleaning up at Erica's, she'd come home, slipped into a camisole and silk boxers, and dropped into the same spot. She still wasn't caught up from the long trip.

"I came to play with Gus," Siena said impassively. "And I used the key under the big yellow frog next to the back door. That's how my mom got in when we watered Mrs. Mumford's plants and fed her cat when she and Mr. Mumford went on vacation."

Leslie blinked. *Big yellow frog? Mumford? Cat?*

"Why don't you have a bed?" Siena asked again.

Leslie studied her for any residual signs of the emotional outbreak of the night before. There were none.

Siena seemed rested, refreshed, bright-eyed and bushy-tailed, as Leslie's dad used to say.

Leslie wondered if Erica had recovered as fully. She'd looked so anxious as she'd carried Siena upstairs. "I…" She scanned her surroundings, then ran her fingers through her hair. "I have to buy one." She exhaled and slumped against the wall.

Siena turned in a circle and took in the large, vacant living room. "Is your whole house empty?"

"Yup." Leslie nodded, following Siena's gaze. "Except for the refrigerator and the stove in the kitchen. I have to buy everything else."

"A couch?" Siena cocked her head.

"Mm-hm. Two couches. One for in here and one for the family room." Leslie glanced through the arched doorway. "And some chairs, maybe. And a few tables and a dinette set for the dining room…And a bedroom set…a desk…bookshelves…" The thought of filling an entire house all at once felt daunting as she heard the words leave her mouth.

"I want a blue couch," Siena said in that tone that made it seem as though whatever the topic was had been settled.

"You do?" Leslie was grateful for Siena's ability to bring everything back to that one statement. *A blue couch. One decision made.*

"Yes." Siena sat cross-legged in front of Leslie. "I wanted blue when my mom bought a new couch for our house, but she got a brown one. And I want to put it in there." She pointed toward the family room. "I don't like this room. This is where the people sit who aren't supposed to be here. My grandma—she has wrinkles—she sits in this room at our house when she comes to see us."

Leslie understood completely. She'd felt the same way when she was a kid. This was a formal living room, used for things that weren't for kids, like cocktail parties or wedding showers, or adult discussions with people who came over to see her mother. The family room was just that, for family, the ones you lived with, where you watched TV while you ate frozen dinners on trays for a special treat, or in Siena's case, worked on puzzles. "Maybe we could change that," Leslie said thoughtfully. "If you could put anything you want in here, what would it be?"

Siena hesitated, then her gaze skittered over the floor, up the walls, then across the ceiling. "A jungle," she said finally.

"A jungle?" Leslie laughed and scratched her head. "I'll have to think about that."

"Knock knock?" Erica's voice drifted into the house from the back. "Siena? Are you in there?"

"We're in the living room," Leslie called before she remembered she was still sitting in the tangle of a sleeping bag in a red camisole and a pair of black silk boxers. Her hair had to be a mess. She smoothed her hand over it.

Erica peeked around the corner from the family room. "There you are," she said to Siena. "What happened to coming right back?"

"I'm getting Gus," Siena said.

"I know, but you were supposed to come right home and not bother Leslie." She glanced at Leslie on the floor. "And you weren't supposed to wake her. Remember, you were going to knock softly?"

"I did, but she didn't hear me, so I had to knock louder." Siena stroked Gus's head. "And she didn't hear that, so I had to come in."

Leslie smiled.

Erica shot her an apologetic look. "We're still working on some things."

Leslie laughed. "No problem whatsoever. I should be up anyway. I have a lot to do."

"Can me and Gus go outside and play?" Siena asked, scrambling to her feet.

"Sure, sweetie," Erica said as she made room in the doorway for the pair to race past her.

"His ball's on the counter," Leslie called after them.

The room was awkwardly silent with them gone.

"I'm sorry she woke you," Erica said after a moment. "We're working on boundaries."

"Really, it's no big deal." Leslie started to rise, but her hips and lower back protested. She groaned and slowed. "Sleeping on the floor isn't as easy as it used to be." She chuckled.

"I can't even imagine." Erica looked away, but not before sneaking a peek at Leslie's chest.

Leslie's nipples tightened. *Damn it.* She shifted sideways and grabbed the jeans she'd tossed aside the night before. While she reminded herself that Erica was straight and neither of them had any interest in the other, she slipped them on. *She just likes the camisole.*

Erica took a quick survey of the room. "It looks like your property management company did a good job with the cleaning and painting."

"Yeah, they did." Leslie made a quick check to make sure all her parts were covered while Erica's attention was elsewhere. "I was pleased."

Erica brought her gaze back to Leslie and smiled. "If your kitchen is as bare as this room, would you like me to bring you a cup of coffee or tea?"

"Dinner last night *and* coffee this morning?" Leslie looked skyward. "A next-door neighbor sent by the gods."

"I could say the same thing," Erica said quietly, her tone tempering their interaction.

Leslie turned to her questioningly.

"I want to thank you for cleaning up last night." An emotion Leslie couldn't quite identify shone in Erica's eyes. "I don't know if I could ever explain how much that meant to me. No one's ever done that for me before."

"No one's ever done your dishes?" Leslie asked, surprised.

"No one's ever taken care of routine things while I was handling Siena's needs." Erica gave her a soft smile. "Thank you. It was nice."

Leslie should have simply said, "You're welcome," and moved on, but she was too stunned. "Not even your husband? Trent's never done anything like that?"

Erica's expression turned sad. "No." She tucked her hair behind her ear and averted her gaze. "So it's coffee you'd like?"

Leslie took the hint. She hadn't done her morning meditation or yoga yet but decided she could do it later in the day. "Coffee would be great." She grinned and drew up her shoulders, then rubbed her hands together in an attempt to lighten the mood again. Her efforts were rewarded by the return of a smile to Erica's face.

"I'll be right back," Erica said.

When she was alone, Leslie snatched up the shirt she'd left in a heap the night before and shook it out, but the wrinkles were persistent. She took the stairs two at a time and followed the hall to the master bedroom where she'd deposited her hanging clothes in the closet. It would take some adjustment in her thinking for her to be able to claim this room as hers. It'd always been her parents' private space, and if she thought about it too much, it gave her the eeewies. It seemed that was something a child never out grew, even when the child was over fifty. Maybe once she got new furniture, though, and all of her own things, she'd be able to shake it. After all, it hadn't been her parents' room for a decade.

She pulled a red blouse from its hanger and slipped it over her camisole, then straightened the cuffs of the three-quarter-length sleeves. She felt the need to be more covered after having Erica come in on her earlier. It was silly. She'd actually been wearing more this morning than yesterday when she'd met Erica in her raggedy cut-off shorts and a tank top with nothing underneath, but there was something more intimate about someone seeing her, and having a conversation with her, when she was wearing her sleep clothes. She buttoned the shirt halfway up, then headed downstairs.

When her foot hit the bottom step, she was met with an excited bark and Gus staring up at her from the center of the room.

He barked again.

"What?" Leslie said, actually expecting an answer.

Gus barked a third time, then made a dash toward the back of the house. He turned in the doorway to look at Leslie.

"You want me to follow you?" she asked blankly.

He ran to the back door.

She thought of the old—very old—Lassie series with the collie that was always running to get help to save his little boy who was constantly getting into trouble. "Okay, Lassie," she said with a sigh. "Let's go find Timmy." As soon as she stepped out onto the deck, though, she saw why he was so anxious.

Leslie's heart leapt.

Siena was trying to squeeze her way between the bars of the wrought iron fencing around the pool. There was no way she could fit through the narrow slots, but she might get stuck.

"Hey," Leslie said, hurrying toward her. "What are you doing?"

"The ball went in the water," Siena said with no interruption of her quest. "I have to get it so we can play more."

"Hold on," Leslie said. "I'll get it. Move away from the fence, please." She waited to make sure Siena was complying, then jogged back into the house and retrieved the key to the gate from a kitchen drawer. When she returned, Siena was sitting on the cement beside the fence and petting Gus.

"Siena," she said, manipulating the lock on the gate.

Siena didn't look up.

"Are you listening?" Leslie wasn't sure if forcing eye contact the way she would have with Elijah was the right thing to do, so she just waited for an acknowledgement. She watched her.

Siena nodded.

"I don't want you to ever go into the pool area unless you're with me or your mom. Not through the bars. Not over the fence. Not even if you have the key for some reason. Okay? Do you understand?" Leslie slipped the padlock free and opened the gate, but she blocked the entrance as Siena stood. "Do you understand?" she asked again. "It isn't because it's a bad thing to do. It's not safe, and you could get hurt."

Another nod.

Leslie relented and stepped aside. As Siena and Gus moved past her, Leslie glanced at the dog quizzically. "Good, Lassie," she muttered.

Siena waited while Leslie took the net from its hooks and walked to the other side of the pool to fish the ball out of the water. Gus ran around the deck, barking at the drifting toy.

"Quiet," Leslie said, not certain of the time or whether her other neighbors might still be trying to sleep.

Fortunately, he stopped barking.

"Are you strutting?" Siena asked randomly.

"Am I what?" Leslie pulled back the long pole, then reached into the net for the ball.

"Strutting." Siena tilted her head to one side.

Leslie wasn't sure she'd heard correctly, even the second time.

Siena kept her from having to ask again. "My mom's friend Becky said you were strutting around the pool like the pool guy in a porno movie," she said.

Leslie struggled to keep her eyebrows from shooting upward. "She did, huh?"

"Uh-huh." Siena looked at the ball in Leslie's hand. "Only you're a girl, so you're a pool girl."

Gus barked and jumped for the ball.

Leslie threw it over the fence and watched him race around to the gate and out into the yard after it, while she tried to think of something to say.

"What's a porno movie?" Siena asked.

Leslie's face went hot. "Uhhh…"

"Here we are," Erica called as she came from next door with a tray. "Two cups of coffee and some bagels and cream cheese. And, Siena, I brought you some juice if you want to join us."

"Me and Gus are playing ball," Siena yelled as she chased Gus next door.

Leslie exhaled a deep sigh of relief. She'd never been so grateful to escape a question. She returned the net to its place, relocked the gate, and joined Erica at the picnic table on her deck. She glanced at her. *Strutting like a pool girl in a porno movie?* Is that what she and that woman had been talking about on Erica's patio yesterday? She supposed it was a compliment. "This is great," she said, eyeing the offerings Erica had brought. "Thank you."

"I figured if you didn't have coffee, you might not have anything to go with it either," Erica said brightly. "Except for Funyuns, but I don't think they'd go very well."

Leslie chuckled. "No, probably not. Besides, Gus ate them all." She poured cream into her coffee from the small pitcher and took a swallow. She couldn't hold back the moan of pleasure that bubbled up all the way from her toes. "That's so good." It'd only been two days since she'd had any, but it felt like weeks. And this coffee was something different. "What is this?"

"I grind the beans myself and make a special blend," Erica said, taking a sip of her own. "It's a Columbian roast with some vanilla and cinnamon mixed in."

"It's delicious," Leslie said, taking in the soft curve of Erica's neck and the way the morning breeze gently blew a few tendrils of hair over the creamy skin of her shoulder. What was it about that particular spot on Erica's body that drew Leslie's attention and made her all tingly? She forced her gaze across the lawn.

Erica laughed as Siena and Gus ran back into view. "She sure loves that dog," she said, the same joy shaping her features as yesterday. "And he's so good with her. I've never seen anything like it. Last night, when he came upstairs…" She looked into her cup. "I guess I owe you an explanation for last night."

"No, you don't. Not unless it's something you want to share." Leslie took a pre-cut bagel from the bag and began spreading cream cheese onto it. "Are you a thin layer girl, or the-more-the-better kind when it comes to your bagels and cream cheese?" she asked, allowing Erica a change in subject if she wanted one.

She smiled. "Definitely the-more-the-better."

Leslie slathered on another healthy dollop, then passed the bagel to her.

Erica looked surprised but accepted it. "Thank you." She took a small bite.

Erica had put on her sunglasses when she'd returned to her house for the coffee, and Leslie found herself wishing she could see her eyes, not necessarily to see into her soul or anything profound like that, but simply because they were so beautiful. *What are you doing, Raymond? You're going to screw up what might turn into a nice friendship if you keep this up.* Did she want even a friendship, though? Becoming friends with Erica meant also opening her heart to Siena—she could tell they came as a package deal in any kind of interaction—and that was where the real danger lay. She could fend off an attraction to a woman who had no interest in her. But a child…a little girl who, without even trying, could melt her heart? Who was she kidding? Siena had already melted her heart with that first declaration that cows don't have holes, just like Elijah had with his very first cry the day he was born.

"Siena has ASD," Erica said, rescuing Leslie from the dead-end road her thoughts were leading her down. "Autism Spectrum Disorder. She's high functioning, but there are a lot of things that make her life more difficult than if she weren't on the spectrum." Erica's voice was taut.

"Like having her puzzle pieces torn up?" Leslie asked softly. She'd seen the damage after Erica had taken Siena upstairs. "And sprinklers that go all different ways at once?"

"Yes, like that. And so much more." The muscles in Erica's jaw and throat visibly relaxed. "I'm always hesitant to say much when we meet new people because I don't want her to be defined by the things that cause her problems. It would be like introducing myself by saying, 'Hi, I'm Erica, and I'm set in my ways and lose stuff,' instead of, 'Hi, I'm Erica, a strong, self-sufficient woman who teaches journalism and dreams of writing a novel someday.'"

Leslie could tell how important this conversation was to Erica by the deepening of the vertical crease that ran down the center of her forehead. All she wanted in that moment was to put Erica's mind at ease. "It's a good thing I met Siena before I met you then," she said with a hint of humor. "Because all she showed me was how smart and amazing and enchanting she is. You probably would have messed it all up." She grinned.

Erica relaxed into a smile. "You're probably right." Her forehead went smooth.

Mission accomplished. "You don't need to worry about me and how I might react or what I think," Leslie said, preparing a bagel for herself. "I'll take my cues from you and Siena. And if there's something I want to ask, is that okay?"

"Absolutely," Erica said. "I want you to. You seem to have a natural understanding to some degree, though. Do you have experience with ASD from somewhere?"

"Not really." Leslie thought of the woman from Elijah's playgroup but didn't want to address where she knew her from. "I spent some time with a woman who had a son on the spectrum, and she told me a little. I wasn't around him much, though."

"Do you have kids of your own?" Erica asked casually.

Leslie's chest tightened. Her throat went dry. "No," she said with a little too much emphasis. "Just been around other people's."

"That's a shame." Erica leaned forward and rested her forearms on the table. "You're good with them."

Leslie looked down at her bagel, then took a bite. "Thanks," she muttered as she chewed. She had to get off this topic. "So," she said after a swig of coffee. "Set in your ways?"

Erica laughed without missing a beat. "So I'm told. That was merely an example."

"Mm-hm," Leslie said. And the air around them lightened again.

They kept the conversation easy, steering away from anything serious. They watched Siena teach Gus to dance and chatted about their plans for the rest of the day.

"I need to spend most of it shopping for furniture," Leslie said, rubbing the small of her back where she was still stiff. "And some towels and sheets." She held up the knife that had been stuck in the cream cheese. "And some dishes. I need to put those on my list. I forgot about them."

"You just left everything behind and headed west?" Erica asked, finishing off sounding like a cowboy.

"I thought it'd be easier than packing and moving it all, but now that I'm here, it feels overwhelming." Leslie twisted the tie around the bag holding the bagels to seal it. "I never realized how many things I've always taken for granted. Like the dishes. I mean, of course I have to buy dishes because I didn't bring any, but it didn't occur to me until you mentioned it."

"You can keep these cups and the knife for now, and I'll bring you at least a place setting and a bowl and some necessities you can use until you pick up what you need. That way you can focus on the furniture today." Erica smirked at her. "I saw you drink out of the hose yesterday. Everyone should at least have a cup."

"Are you a nosy neighbor?" Leslie asked teasingly. "What was that woman's name in that old TV show, *Bewitched*? Mrs. Krantz?"

Erica laughed. "Mrs. Kravitz. And I am not her."

"That's right. Gladys Kravitz." Leslie nodded, remembering how much she loved the show—but not because of Gladys Kravitz. It was that sexy witch cousin she always waited to see.

"You were in the middle of your front yard. Anybody could see you." Erica was still talking.

"Okay, Gladys." Leslie stood, chuckling. "Whatever you say." She was struck by how natural the banter felt between them. A warning bell rang in the back of her mind. *No, this isn't like Cassie. My eyes are wide open.*

Erica rose with a huff and started collecting the cups. "Keep the bagels and cream cheese, too, in case you don't get to the grocery store today either. At least you'll have something for breakfast tomorrow."

Leslie had no intention of arguing. "Thank you. That's very nice, especially after I just called you nosy."

In the kitchen, Leslie rinsed off the dishes while Erica set the food in the refrigerator, then made her way around the bar toward the back door. "If you need anything else, you know you can just come over and ask, right?"

"Thanks, I appreciate that. Do me a favor?" Leslie nodded to a notebook on the bar. "Add dishes to that long list."

"Sure." Erica picked up the pen beside the tablet and wrote on the top of the page. She studied the list. "Animal shelter?" She looked up at Leslie.

Leslie drew in a breath. "Oh. Yeah. That's for tomorrow when they open."

Erica frowned. "For Gus?"

"It was, but I'm having second thoughts." Leslie set the cups in the sink to dry. "I don't really need a dog, but he's so…I don't know." She thought of how good he was with Siena, how concerned he'd been the night before when Siena had her problem, how she couldn't keep him downstairs after Erica had taken Siena up to her room, presumably. But then, when he'd finally come down, he didn't hesitate to follow Leslie home and had curled up right beside her on the sleeping bag, rested his head on her arm, and hadn't moved until this morning. Even in the car, when he'd been so dirty and smelly, his presence had given her so much comfort. He was good company. "I'm thinking about keeping him."

The biggest smile Leslie had seen from Erica so far bloomed on her lips and in her eyes. "I knew you would."

"You did, did you? Well, I haven't fully decided yet, so don't blow it." Leslie tried to sound gruff, but she'd never been able to pull that off.

"We'll be home today, if you'd like to leave *your* dog with us while you're out shopping." Erica's tone was playful, but her offer was clearly sincere. "Siena would love it."

"Thanks, I'll do that." Leslie grinned. "Gus will love it, too."

"See you later." Erica started to turn but stopped as her gaze landed on something on the bar.

Shit! Leslie had forgotten about Nell's business card. She'd found it yesterday morning when she'd gotten up, and the note Nell had left on the back that…*Shit*…Erica was now reading.

"There's a nice *piece* next door?" Erica read it as a question, but Leslie knew it wasn't written that way. "I'm thinking happy hour and a couple drinks? You should *tap* that? It'd be good for you." She looked at Leslie and arched an eyebrow.

"I am so sorry." Leslie held up her hands. "That's not me. It's my cousin, Nell. She was working with the management company on the painting and carpeting, so she's been in and out," Leslie added, as though that mattered.

"That's a very disrespectful way to talk about Mr. Billings," Erica said, referring to Leslie's neighbor on the other side.

He'd lived there since before Leslie and her parents had moved in when Leslie was eight. He was now seventy-five.

"And I doubt the new Mrs. Billings would appreciate her husband being *tapped*."

Leslie couldn't even imagine. "I'm sure not," she said, contrite but playing along.

Erica shot her a humor-filled glare, then flipped Nell's business card over between her fingers and read from the other side. "Nell Raymond. Director of the Raymond Children's Center?" She looked at Leslie. "You're *that* Raymond?"

"Well...no. My mother was *that* Raymond." Leslie scanned the kitchen for a dishtowel, then remembered she didn't have one. She shook her hands over the sink. "She was a family court judge here years ago and saw a real need for a place for kids who were taken from their parents due to abuse and neglect until they could be placed with a relative or in a stable foster home. So she raised the funding and opened the center."

"I've heard the stories." Erica sounded awestruck. "She was quite a woman."

The love and admiration Leslie held for her mom swelled in her heart. "Yes, she was."

"And she lived here?" Erica surveyed the surroundings as though she were on a tour of Susan B. Anthony's home. "One of the women in my support group is affiliated with the center and has told me quite a bit about it." Her focus landed on Leslie again. "I'm impressed."

Leslie smiled. "Be impressed with my mom, not with me."

Something passed through Erica's eyes that Leslie couldn't name. "Actually, I'm impressed with both." She laid the card on the bar and started to leave but turned in the doorway. "Oh, and please tell Cousin Nell it would take a lot more than a couple of happy hour drinks to tap *this*." She glided her fingertips down her sides and cocked her hip.

What might it take? Leslie cleared her throat. "I'll be sure to let her know."

Erica turned and sauntered out.

Leslie followed her to the doorway and let Erica get to the edge of the deck. "Oh, and, Erica?"

Erica stopped and faced her.

"Please tell your friend…Becky, is it? I don't *strut.*"

Erica's eyes went wide, and her cheeks flamed. She opened her mouth, but no sound came out.

"And I'm *not* a pool girl." Leslie ran one hand up the doorjamb in a sultry motion and stroked her thigh with the other. "I prefer to be called a cabana goddess."

Erica burst out laughing and buried her face in her hands. "I'm so embarrassed."

Leslie laughed as she returned to her customary stance.

When Erica finally regained her composure, she lifted her head and looked directly at Leslie. "I'll pass that on." She turned and walked down the steps.

"One more thing?" Leslie made an effort to sound innocent.

Erica looked over her shoulder.

"Your daughter wants to know what a porno movie is," Leslie said in a loud whisper.

Erica squeezed her eyes shut. "Thanks," she said, drawing out the word.

Leslie tried to ignore the sway of Erica's hips as she made her way to the gate, and tried not to smile at the image lingering in her mind of Erica's raging blush. She tried not to panic over having a child once again in her life and heart, one that could be taken away as suddenly as she'd appeared, just like Elijah. And she couldn't fathom how she'd ended up with a dog she never knew she wanted. For the moment, though, it all felt good. She'd spent the past year alone, missing her previous life, and this was a nice change.

She'd need to be more careful this time around, but she already knew, short of selling this house and moving somewhere else, she wasn't going to have a choice but to care about this little group she'd found.

She already did.

Chapter Four

E rica yanked the trashcan out from under the sink and pulled it over to the spice cabinet. She could kick herself. *I was blatantly flirting with her.* What is wrong with me? What had her words to Becky been? *I can't get involved with someone who lives next door. I can't sleep with her.* And wasn't at least one of those things the whole point of flirting?

She opened the cupboard and pulled out the bottles of seasonings and herbs she'd bought recently and began digging out ones from the back that needed to be tossed.

Ever since she'd begun a teaching schedule in which she had a month off between the summer session and the beginning of fall semester, she'd committed to using this time for a spring house cleaning as well as for some much appreciated relaxation at home. Siena spent the weekdays during the summer in a day program, so Erica enjoyed the time to herself. If she could get her kitchen cabinets cleaned out today while Siena was home, she'd have several long, luxurious days of reading and napping in the backyard hammock, soaks in the tub, and some catch-up time with her Netflix list. She'd already been off for two weeks and had thoroughly cleaned the house, but there were still some cupboards and closets to get through. And taking out her frustration with herself, by literally throwing old containers into the trashcan, seemed like the perfect way to get another job done.

She chucked an old jar of oregano with an extra umph, then reached for the next one. *It'll take more than a couple of happy hour drinks to tap this.* Had she really said that? How ridiculous could she sound? *I'm not in my twenties anymore. Or even my thirties.* But wait. A woman could still flirt in her fifties, just not with someone she couldn't possibly be more than friends with—especially when she was truly attracted to her. The shattering of glass as one bottle crashed into another in the trashcan broke the rhythm of her mental rant.

"Why are you breaking things?" Siena asked from the doorway.

Erica stilled and took a deep breath to calm herself. "I'm sorry, sweetie. It was an accident." It was, at least the breaking part. "I just got a little mad over something I was thinking about." She was always as honest as she could be about her emotions with Siena in hopes it would help Siena learn to identify and communicate her own.

"Sometimes, I want to break things, too," Siena said, her gaze drifting slightly. "Like when kids make fun of me at school. But Mrs. Archer says breaking things doesn't solve anything and will just get me in trouble." Mrs. Archer had been her first grade teacher the previous year and had been wonderful.

"Mrs. Archer is absolutely right. It doesn't solve anything," Erica said. *Nor does it erase that moment when I made a fool of myself.* She allowed Siena's words to distract her from her own frustrations. It pained her that, in addition to everything else Siena faced every day, she also had to deal with the ignorance and cruelty of other kids. She softened. "Want to help me reorganize the cupboards?" Siena loved lining things up in an orderly sequence that made perfect sense to her.

"No, thank you. I want to…" Siena shifted her stance uneasily and glanced behind her into the family room. "I want to watch *Tangled*, but…" She pressed her lips together in a firm line, a signal that she was thinking hard about something.

"Your puzzle?" Erica had been waiting throughout the morning to see what Siena might want to do with her ruined project.

Siena gave a tight nod. "I want it to go away."

Erica wished, as she frequently did in moments like these, she could scoop her little girl into her arms and give her a hug, but those kinds of gestures needed to be Siena's idea. To have physical contact forced on her increased her distress and sometimes sent her over the edge. The best way to comfort her was simply to do what she'd asked. Erica smiled. "I can make that happen. Do you want me to put it back in the box? Or do you want me to throw it away?" She knew either one would be hard for Siena. Having a project around that she couldn't finish was like...Erica didn't know. She'd tried so many times to imagine what it must be like for Siena to live life with all of her anxieties and stresses, but she knew she never came close to fully understanding. All she could do was listen when Siena was able to tell her what she was feeling and do what she said would help her.

Siena hesitated, her little body tightening in on itself. "Throw it away," she said finally.

Erica pulled a new trash bag from the box under the sink and crossed to where Siena stood. She squatted in front of her, putting herself directly in Siena's line of sight. "I'll take care of it, sweetie. Why don't you and Gus play outside another few minutes, and I'll call you when I'm finished." She glanced at the dog where he'd been sitting right beside Siena throughout the conversation, then scratched him under his chin. She hoped Leslie would decide to keep him.

Once all remnants of the ruined puzzle had been disposed of so Siena could forget all about it—if, in fact, she truly forgot these things—and she was settled in with her movie, Erica went back to work in the kitchen. With her own frustrations left behind and her renewed commitment to behave appropriately with her neighbor, she made short work of emptying and scrubbing out the rest of the cupboards, then neatly replacing all their contents. When she checked the time, she was shocked to find the afternoon gone. She needed to start thinking about dinner. Before she could form a thought, though, a knock sounded at the back door.

"Hello?" Leslie called through the screen.

In the several steps it took Erica to make her way from the kitchen, Gus was already at the door, dancing around on his hind legs.

Leslie stood on the patio, a large white plastic bag and a red and white Kentucky Fried Chicken bag suspended from the finger of one hand and a fast food sack in the other. "Hey," she said with a smile. "Was he a good boy today?" She made a kissy face at Gus through the screen.

"The perfect houseguest," Erica said, sliding open the door. "What's all this?"

Leslie lifted the bags. "You've fed me twice. I figured it was my turn. I brought dinner."

Erica stared, then laughed. "For how many?"

"I didn't know what either of you like, so I got several choices." Leslie cocked her head. "Have you eaten?"

"No. In fact, I was just starting to think about it. This is a nice surprise. Thank you." Erica motioned to the patio table. "Why don't you set everything there, and I'll get some plates and silverware." When she returned with a tray holding the dishes and utensils, along with some drinks and condiments, she found Siena perched in one of the chairs eyeing the bags curiously.

"What's in there?" Siena asked Leslie, pointing at the large white one.

"*That's* Chinese food from my absolute favorite restaurant from my childhood," Leslie said, lifting a takeout box from within and setting it on the table. "Pot stickers, egg rolls, vegetable *and* plain fried rice—in case you don't like the veggies—walnut shrimp, and orange chicken." She placed the last container on the table with a flourish.

"Orange is my favorite color," Siena said excitedly.

Erica watched, intrigued. Siena normally ate many of the same foods, day in and day out, and usually acted suspicious on the rare occasion Erica introduced something new. Maybe the difference tonight was all the choices. Or maybe it was Leslie.

"Then you'll definitely want to try the orange chicken." Leslie reached for the KFC bag.

Leslie was fun, and she'd come with fun things—a dog and toys. She'd let Siena water that dry spot she'd been obsessed with. And now, a surprise dinner. Even her presentation was fun.

"And here we have fried chicken, potato wedges, mac and cheese...I know you like that." Leslie waggled her eyebrows, then continued unpacking the second bag. "And mashed potatoes and gravy and corn on the cob."

Siena scrambled onto her knees in the chair, as though she couldn't stay seated a second longer. "I love corn on the cob." Her pitch was high.

Erica couldn't help but laugh. She set the tray on the table. "Or rather, she loves anything she can slather butter all over."

Leslie met Erica's gaze with a soft smile.

"What's that?" Siena asked, ignoring Erica's comment.

"Here we have your basic burgers and fries," Leslie said, turning the third bag around.

Siena went pale. "Noooo," she said, shaking her head. She began to rock, her eyes wide.

Erica followed her stare and saw the Wendy's logo. "Siena," she said calmly but firmly. "It's okay. You don't have to eat it."

Siena stilled slightly.

Gus lifted his front paws to her thigh and licked the back of her hand that tightly gripped the armrest of the chair.

She pulled her gaze from the bag and looked at him.

Erica waited. She wanted to give Siena the chance to handle herself, and Gus was helping.

Siena watched as Gus's tongue flicked out over her skin several more times.

He looked up at her.

Siena took a deep breath and closed her eyes. "Winnie the Pooh. Piglet. Eeyore, Tigger," she whispered. "Kanga and Roo..." She slipped from the chair and walked out to the corner of the yard where she went sometimes to think.

Gus, of course, trotted alongside her.

Erica relaxed some but stayed vigilant.

"I'm sorry. What did I do?" Leslie's voice was shaky.

"It's all right," Erica said, still watching Siena. "I think she managed to catch herself. She did so great." Pride and admiration at Siena's accomplishment brought a thin veneer of moisture to her eyes. She returned her attention to Leslie and found her almost as white as Siena. "It's okay. Really."

"But what happened?" Leslie asked.

Erica shook her head. "It's the Wendy's hamburgers. She doesn't like it that the patties are square but the bun is round." Erica flashed back to when Siena was four and had lost it in the restaurant because of the pointy things poking out. "She's afraid of the corners that stick out from the bun."

Leslie pressed the heel of her hand to her forehead and dropped into a chair. "Oh God, I'm so sorry."

"It's really okay," Erica said, touching Leslie's shoulder to reassure her. "You had no way of knowing. Besides, it gave Siena the opportunity to use one of her replacement behaviors and gave her a success. I'm impressed."

Leslie sighed and looked up at her. "Is that what the Winnie the Pooh characters were? A replacement behavior?"

"Yes. It gives her something else to focus on. Plus, she likes them. They calm her," Erica said.

"How do you remember the things that upset her?" Leslie asked, genuine interest in her eyes. "I mean, they can be such small things. And it seems like they could be anything."

Erica considered the question as she glanced at Siena again to make sure she was still in control of herself. "I suppose it isn't any different than with anyone you love. You just learn and remember the little things about them that are important because you care about them."

Leslie bit her lower lip and nodded. "Should I get rid of the burgers?"

"Would you mind?" Erica gave her an apologetic look. "She's not going to want to sit near them."

"No problem." Leslie rose and grabbed the bag, then headed back to her house.

"Siena," Erica called, "whenever you're ready, come eat some dinner. The hamburgers are gone."

Siena didn't answer, but Erica knew she'd heard because she rose to her feet from her squatting position.

By the time Leslie returned, Siena was in her seat with a drumstick, some orange chicken, an ear of corn sitting in a pool of melted butter, and a lone pot sticker she'd conceded to trying on her plate. Leslie seemed a bit subdued, and Erica noticed Siena scanning the tabletop every few minutes as though checking to ensure the offending burgers hadn't somehow found their way back, but all in all, everything appeared to be mostly back to normal. Erica smiled to herself, categorizing the incident as a success. "Did you get some things checked off your list today?" she asked Leslie, keeping her manner casual.

Leslie glanced at Siena, then took a deep breath. "I did," she said, scooping some vegetable fried rice onto her plate. "I have furniture coming on Thursday. Just the basics. I'll have to go out again when I figure out what I want to do with the extra bedrooms. I even ordered an outdoor set, a patio swing, and some lounge chairs to go by the pool, in case, you know…" She winked at Erica. "I have a pool party or something."

Erica blushed. It would be a while before she heard the end of this one.

"Did you get a blue couch?" Siena asked eagerly.

"Oh, Siena," Erica said, "not the blue couch again."

"As a matter of fact, I did." Leslie grinned at Siena. "And it's the best blue couch I've ever seen. Wait till it comes. You're going to love it."

Siena let out a loud squeal and bounced in her chair. "See, Mommy. Blue couches are fun!"

Erica laughed. "All right, I stand corrected. I'm outnumbered." She looked at Leslie questioningly. Had she and Siena really talked about her getting a blue couch?

While they ate, Siena gave Leslie a recount of her and Gus's day, which included the slaying of a dragon right in Erica's backyard. Erica hadn't had a clue. Gus, apparently, had been very brave. When only the lone pot sticker still sat, untried, on Siena's plate, Erica said, "What happened to just a taste?"

Siena frowned. "I don't know what's inside."

"That's easy," Leslie said. "I'll show you." She cut one of her own in half, then flipped it around with her fork to display the contents. "It's a mixture of…" She peered into the dumpling. "Well, I'm not sure either. But it's really good." She stabbed half of it, swirled it around in a puddle of soy sauce, and stuck it in her mouth.

Siena watched closely, then looked at her own. She picked it up with her fingers and took a miniscule bite. She chewed much longer than the small amount could possibly require.

Erica rolled her eyes.

"Well?" Leslie asked.

Siena took another bite, this one bigger. "It *is* good," she said, sounding surprised.

"I told you." Leslie popped the rest of her own into her mouth. "You can trust me. I won't steer you wrong." She exchanged an amused glance with Erica.

Siena ate two more, then asked if she could be excused.

"You may, but it's time for your bath, and then bed," Erica said, geared for the usual argument. "It's a school night for you."

"Why do I have school tomorrow but you don't?" Siena asked.

"Because my school has a vacation before the next semester starts." Erica began closing the takeout containers. "Your summer program goes right up until your regular school starts."

"That's not fair." Siena slipped off her chair.

"I know." This was a standard exchange between them that took place any time Siena felt the injustice of the world.

"Can Gus take a bath with me?"

"Gus just had one yesterday. Remember?" Leslie said before Erica could answer. "I think he's clean, but maybe he can sit in the bathroom with you to keep you company, if it's all right with your mom."

"That's fine," Erica said as she stood and picked up two of the plates. "Run and get your pajamas, and I'll be right up to fill the tub."

"I can get this," Leslie said, rising to Erica's side. She took the dishes from her.

Erica looked up at her in surprise. She remembered how shocked she'd been the previous night to come downstairs and find that Leslie had cleaned up everything. She was sweet, but it made Erica uncomfortable. "That's okay. You brought dinner. I'll deal with it after Siena's in bed." She might as well agree, though. Leslie would most likely take care of it while Erica was upstairs, like the night before.

"I don't mind," Leslie said. "You go."

Erica smiled and nodded. "Thank you." She turned to leave, then hesitated. "There's some wine in the fridge, if you'd like to stay for a while. I'd love some adult conversation."

"Sure. That sounds good."

With Siena tucked into bed, Erica came downstairs to find the kitchen spotless again and Leslie seated at the cleaned-off patio table with a glass of white zin in hand and another beside her. The bottle sat in the center. Leslie's long legs were stretched out, and her head was tilted back, her attention on the night sky. Erica remembered Siena's recitation of "Star Light, Star Bright." She wondered if Leslie was making a wish and, if so, what it might be. "Siena would like you to come up and say good night," she said from the doorway.

Leslie twisted around in her chair, then stood, looking surprised. "Okay, sure." She picked up the second glass and held it out to Erica. "Why don't you relax. I'll be right back."

Erica was touched by the simple gesture and Leslie's willingness to take the time to say good night to Siena. A lot about Leslie touched her. "I think I will." She took a seat and set the baby monitor she carried on the table.

Leslie glanced at it.

"I still use it at night for peace of mind, so I can hear if she gets up or has a bad dream." Erica was a little embarrassed to admit this overprotective characteristic of her nature to someone who wasn't the parent of a child on the spectrum. In her support group, she wasn't an oddity, but most parents of neuro-typical children had put away the baby monitor well before their child was seven. Then she realized Leslie might not even know what it was, since she didn't have kids. "It's a nursery monitor."

Leslie gave her a look of understanding. "I know. And I get it."

Erica held Leslie's gaze a little too long, as a sense of truly being seen and accepted stirred deep within her. She brushed her hair back and glanced out into the yard. "Her room's upstairs, second door on the left." She took a sip of wine.

After almost ten minutes, she realized she'd failed to turn on the monitor, as she customarily did when leaving Siena's room. It was as though she'd known somehow Sienna would be safe with Leslie. Even so, they were at such an early stage of whatever this was between them. She quickly flipped it on to hear Leslie reading the familiar lines from *The House at Pooh Corner*, one of Sienna's favorite books, and smiled. She settled back into her chair and listened. Leslie's voice was soothing as it drifted through the speaker.

When the story ended, there was a silence, then the creak of the rocking chair Erica knew so well. She pictured Leslie rising.

"Come on, Gus," Leslie whispered.

"I want him to stay until I go to sleep," Siena said drowsily.

"I thought you *were* asleep."

Another silence and Erica could see Siena shaking her head, her eyelids drooping.

"All right, but you need to go to sleep. No playing," Leslie said. "And, Gus, don't you start reading another book and keep her awake."

Siena giggled softly.

The sound filled Erica's heart.

"Good night, Siena," Leslie said with a chuckle.

"Good night."

Erica waited to see if Siena remembered to say thank you for the story.

She didn't.

As Leslie sat down across from her once more, Erica watched her. "You do a great Winnie the Pooh voice," she said teasingly. "And your Piglet..." She lifted her wine in a toast.

Leslie glanced at the monitor. Her cheeks pinkened under the mini white lights that softly illuminated the patio. "Thank you." She touched her glass to Erica's.

Erica laughed quietly. "Don't be embarrassed. That was the sweetest thing I've heard in a long time. And the melody you put with Pooh's outdoor hum...Well, that was pure—"

"All right." Leslie chuckled. "You realize you weren't supposed to hear any of that, right? I mean, clearly, I forgot about the monitor."

"I'm serious," Erica said. And she was. "Yes, I'm having fun with it, but that's just to get even for your earlier remark about having a pool party. It really was charming. And thank you for reading Siena a bedtime story." *Never mind that I already read her one and she was stalling.* Siena did love *The House at Pooh Corner*, though, and would listen to it over and over again.

Leslie ducked her head with a sheepish grin. "Well, thanks."

A flutter of arousal tickled Erica's more sensitive parts. Her nipples tightened. There was so much about Leslie that turned her on—her looks, her kindness, her genuine interest in Siena, and now, this adorable shyness. She was enjoying this budding friendship too much to go there, though. She wasn't going to jeopardize it, or the one blooming between Leslie and Siena, for a tumble between the sheets. "Would you like some more wine?" she asked, noticing Leslie's glass.

"That'd be nice," Leslie said, clearly grateful for the change in subject.

Erica poured Leslie a refill, then added to her own. She felt nervous for some reason, then realized this was the first time they'd been alone together, where they could have an actual grownup conversation. There were so many things she wanted to ask, not the least of which was to revisit the question of whether Leslie had, or had ever had, kids. Especially after hearing her read to Siena, not to mention how naturally she interacted with her. She couldn't believe she didn't have more experience than simply being around other people's children. But Leslie had seemed uncomfortable with the subject, so Erica moved on. "Do you have a job waiting for you once you're settled?"

Leslie sipped her wine, then leaned back and sighed. "I have *work* waiting for me—a ton of it—as soon as I can get Wi-Fi hooked up in the house. It's first on my list tomorrow." She visibly relaxed into the subject. "I'm a website designer. Self-employed. So I didn't have to quit a job to move out here, then find another one. I just had to time the move between some big projects and take off a couple weeks from a few others."

Erica raised an eyebrow, impressed. "A website designer. That sounds interesting."

"It can be," Leslie said, looking thoughtful. "Or it can be incredibly boring, depending on the site. I've learned a lot about different subjects. What I like best, though, is the creativity involved and the freedom from a nine to five schedule. I can work whenever I want, even in the middle of the night, as long as I get the job done."

"That sounds heavenly," Erica said, trying to imagine, but it was the routine of the life she'd built here with Siena that they'd needed.

"Speaking of schedules," Leslie continued. "You said you're off right now?"

"I did?" Erica had no recollection of that.

"Well, okay, you told Siena the reason she has school tomorrow and you don't is that yours has a break before the next semester. Are you a student or a teacher?"

"Ah, yes, I do remember that," Erica said. It was refreshing to have someone around to witness the conversations that seemed so repetitive sometimes. "I teach journalism at Pasadena City College."

Leslie looked intrigued. "Why journalism?"

"It made the most sense," Erica said with a small shrug. "I used to work in television news, I have a master's degree, and colleges are always eager to hire instructors that have field experience. Hearing from someone who's actually lived the life makes it more interesting to students, not to mention the contacts and connections we have."

Leslie nodded. "Did you work around here?"

"No. I was in Chicago."

"Chicago? How'd you end up in California—and Burbank, of all places?"

Erica laughed. "It was for Siena. She needed someplace quieter. Being in such a busy big city, the tall buildings, the trains, the noise in general—all made it hard for her to be out in the world. Years ago, we had friends who lived in Burbank, and I always liked the older, quieter neighborhoods, while still being so close to the conveniences and activity of a larger city like Los Angeles, so I looked for a job in this area."

"That's quite a change, going from something so fast paced as broadcast news in Chicago to college professor in Burbank."

Erica ran her fingertips up and down the stem of her wine glass, remembering all the decisions she'd had to make during that time. "It wasn't as abrupt of a shift as it sounds. I'd already taken a leave of absence when Siena was born. Then shortly after she turned a year old and we realized something wasn't quite right with her development, we started taking her to specialists. When she was actually diagnosed with ASD, I decided not to go back to work and stay home with her. A year and a half later, we moved here."

"Those are all big decisions," Leslie said softly.

Erica considered each one. "I guess they are, but they didn't seem so at the time. As each came up, all I had to do was listen to my heart, and my heart said to do what Siena needed. So I did. And I'm glad." She took in the peace and comfort of her backyard. "Because each one led us here, and Siena is doing much better." When her gaze met Leslie's once again, she realized she hadn't allowed herself to think about that major life change from an emotional perspective in a long time—and she'd never talked about it. Usually, she avoided the topic altogether, keeping any explanations factual. She couldn't help but wonder, once again, about this new next-door neighbor.

"What?" Leslie asked into the silence.

Erica smiled slightly, a little embarrassed. "You're easy to talk to."

Leslie hesitated. "Thanks," she said, looking into the tree as though there was something of interest there.

Erica knew there wasn't.

"It's great that you and your husband were on the same page with all that," Leslie said.

"What?" Erica asked, confused at what seemed like a drastic change in subject. *Trent?*

"I'd think some couples would have difficulty agreeing on those kinds of priorities," Leslie said. "Trent was obviously willing to relocate as well. I think that's great."

Erica blinked. "Oh," she said, realizing the misunderstanding. She'd let Leslie assume they were still married. "Actually, Trent and I fall into the first category—the couples who don't agree on priorities. He isn't my husband. He's my ex husband."

Leslie looked confused. "Ex? But I thought…"

"He was just visiting." Erica stifled her irritation at Trent's early departure and focused on coming clean. If she sidestepped the topic one more time, it could be perceived as a deception, and there was no reason for that. "We split up at about the halfway point between Siena's diagnosis and the move out here. Siena and I came alone."

"Oh," Leslie said, straightening almost imperceptibly.

Had she lost a little color? "Trent's always had difficulty accepting Siena's autism," Erica said, adopting her more matter-of-fact delivery.

Leslie's forehead crinkled. "So he just left?" She seemed to have recovered from whatever her initial reaction had been, unless it'd simply been replaced by disbelief.

"Again, not as abruptly as it sounds. It happened over time." Erica never liked people thinking badly of Trent. He was a decent guy. He just had his limitations. *Don't we all?*

Leslie stared at her, evidently waiting for more.

Erica found she didn't mind explaining. "He never wanted a traditional life with a stay-at-home wife, kids, and a steady, predictable job to go to every day. Neither of us did. When we met and fell in love, it was that element in our relationship that made it exciting. He loved being with a woman who was up-and-coming in the fast-paced world of broadcasting, who traveled all over at a moment's notice, and I loved being with a band manager in the wild world of rock and roll. Neither of us wanted kids, and there was no room or time for them in our lives."

"So what happened?"

Erica laughed. "Siena happened. I got pregnant. Against *all* odds. I was on the pill. I was forty-three. I was already in perimenopause, according to my gynecologist. Hell, Trent and I were barely having sex every couple of months by that time."

Leslie made a face.

"Okay, TMI. But you get the picture," Erica said with a chuckle. "And then, out of nowhere, there was this little baby fighting her way into the world."

Leslie laughed. "She does know how to get her way." A whine came from the other side of the screen door, and Leslie got up to let Gus out.

"Definitely." Erica took in Leslie's easy gait as she walked, enjoying the movement of her backside in her snug jeans. Then she lifted her wine to her lips as Leslie made her way back to her seat. "And she's been doing it ever since." She refocused. "The point is, Trent never wanted to have a family, and he'd been clear about that from the beginning. When I found out I was pregnant, he tried to go with it, but when Siena started showing signs of..." Erica sighed. "He certainly didn't know what to do with a special needs child."

"And that's when he left?" Leslie scoffed. "That isn't any better."

"Not so much left," Erica said. "More that he just didn't come home as much. He travels a lot, too, so there's a lot of room for ambiguity. I was actually the one that brought up the divorce, largely to cut the tension when he did come home, but it was time."

Leslie's expression softened. "Being the single parent of a child with autism has to be tough."

"Sometimes." Erica felt a wave of that sense from earlier, of being understood. "But I'll take any part of it over co-parenting with someone who doesn't want to be here with us."

Something that looked like anger flashed ever so briefly in Leslie's eyes, then vanished. "How often does he visit?"

"Not very, but more than he used to." Erica tried to sound satisfied with Trent's efforts. "For the first couple of years after we split, he didn't ask to see Siena at all, but he's seen her three times in the last year or so. It's an improvement."

Leslie looked as though she had something more to say about that but simply nodded. "So do you miss Chicago?"

Erica hadn't realized she'd grown tense talking about Trent until she felt herself relax. She smiled. "I *don't* miss the winters," she said, remembering the icy winds off Lake Michigan. "I love walking outside here, in the middle of January, needing nothing but a light jacket. But I *do* miss Giordano's pizza." She feigned a swoon.

Leslie grinned. "That good, huh?"

"Oh, my God! It's so good." Erica's mouth started watering just thinking about it. "Their meat lover's pizza is to die for."

"That's high praise." Leslie chuckled. "And how long has it been since you had it?"

"Four years." Erica drew the words out to emphasize just how really long it'd been. She leaned forward and folded her arms on the table. "I dated a woman a couple years ago who went to Chicago on a business trip, and she ate there and agreed on how delicious it is, but that's the closest I've come since the move." She started to laugh, but it died on her lips at Leslie's expression. "Is something wrong?"

"You dated a woman?" Leslie asked in the same tone of astonishment one would use to ask, *You grew up on Mars?*

Ah, another uncovered topic. "I'm sorry. I'm so comfortable with you, I forget we don't really know each other very well," Erica said lightly. "I'm bisexual." This time, there was no doubt in her mind that something shifted in Leslie. "Is that a problem?"

"Uh, no. Not at all." Leslie's voice regained its normal pitch, but her body held tension. "I apologize. I didn't mean to sound like it was."

Erica's defenses inched up. "I assumed it wouldn't be an issue, since you're obviously either bi or gay."

Leslie arched an eyebrow.

"Your cousin left you a note about tapping the hot piece next door, who, by the way, happens to be a woman," Erica said, answering the unspoken question.

Leslie took in a breath and gave a single nod. "You're right. I'm gay, and I do apologize." She met Erica's gaze with sincerity. "Please, forgive me. I just...I had it in my head that you were straight and married. That's all."

"Why would that matter?" Erica was genuinely perplexed. Unless...*Is she attracted to me?* But if that were the case, wouldn't Leslie be happy to find out she was single and a possibility?

"It doesn't. I..." Leslie faltered. "Look, I'm sorry. I should go." She rose, and Gus leapt up from where he'd nestled alongside her foot, his chin resting on the toe of her shoe.

Erica could only stare at her, bewildered. *What just happened?*

Leslie pushed her chair beneath the table. "Thank you for the wine and the conversation." The last word trailed off.

Erica wanted to say something, to stop her and get her to talk about whatever was going on, but she didn't know Leslie, and wasn't sure what might push her away rather than convince her to stay. It wasn't as though she could go far. *Maybe I can catch her tomorrow, after she's had some time to...* Think? Process? "Okay," Erica said, studying her. "I'm sorry for whatever—"

"No, you don't need to be sorry. It's..." Pain flashed in Leslie's eyes. "It's my stuff. I just need to go."

And suddenly, Erica understood. She nodded. "Thank you for dinner and the evening," she said quietly.

The corners of Leslie's mouth lifted in a sad smile. Without another word, she walked away, Gus close behind. At the gate, he turned and looked at Erica before they both disappeared around the corner.

"Take care of her, Gus," she whispered and wondered who could have hurt such a special woman so badly.

Chapter Five

L eslie took a bite of strawberry pie and let the buttery crust melt in her mouth while she savored the sweetness of the fresh berries. The evening had been wonderful—delicious food, great company, and a lot of laughter, but this moment held combined elements of some of her favorite childhood memories— fresh fruit pie and her cousin Nell. It was nice to be home.

"Molly wants you to take a seat on the board," Nell said from across the large table. Her wife, Paula, had made partner at the firm she'd worked for since her days as an associate right out of law school, and between that and Nell's position at the Raymond Center, they did a lot of entertaining. The size and elegance of the formal dining room epitomized their home and life, even if sometimes, like tonight, Nell looked and acted like she was twelve again. Short, blond tufts stuck out from beneath her Angels baseball cap, and a swipe of whipped cream smeared her upper lip.

Paula, in customary contrast, sat between them at the head of the table, every strand of her salt-and-pepper hair still in place after a long workday and her black business suit somehow as crisp as if she'd just put it on. Paula could be wearing a nightshirt and she'd still manage to come off as the embodiment of decorum.

Leslie listened, enjoying the familiarity and comfort of the voice of her cousin, who was also her lifelong best friend, rather than considering what she was actually saying. She had no intention of becoming a board member of the Raymond Children's Center, no matter how much she believed in its mission and admired her mother for starting it. "I'd rather just be a volunteer."

"Board positions are volunteer," Nell said, then licked some glaze off the bottom of a huge berry. She was a fascinating dichotomy. She was the responsible, dedicated, and professional director of the center that moved seamlessly through daily administrative duties, promotional and fundraising events, and the rocky terrain of child protective services and the family court system. And yet, somehow she was still such a child at heart. Just that afternoon, she'd gone directly from fighting for, and winning, additional funding from regional services to a staff versus kids softball game at the center. She and Leslie had played on the kids' team.

"You know what I mean." Leslie didn't understand why they were having this conversation. Nell knew how she felt about meetings and budgets and all the things boards spent their time living and breathing. "I'd rather be with the kids."

"Molly thinks it'd be great for PR and fundraising, given who you are and all," Nell said without regard for Leslie's comment.

"What do I care what Molly thinks?" Leslie asked, stabbing her last strawberry with a little too much fervor. Molly was the president of the board of directors for the center, but she wasn't anything to Leslie. "I've only met her once." And that had been at her mother's memorial service. In fact, she had difficulty taking the woman seriously. Every time Leslie heard the name, all she could think of was her dad breaking into his Little Richard imitation and singing "Good Golly Miss Molly" any time Molly came up in conversation. It'd made Leslie's mother smile.

"That's because you haven't been home in nine years," Nell said.

And here we are, back to where we always end up. But not anymore. "I'm home now," Leslie said with a smile. "I guess you'll have to find something else to bitch at me about."

Paula chuckled softly.

"I know." Nell emphasized the words by increasing their length and volume. Her green eyes flashed with excitement, and she grinned. "I'm so glad you're home." She rocked her chair backward onto its hind legs.

In an obviously practiced move, Paula reached over and pressed down on the armrest, returning all four legs to the floor.

Leslie laughed, wondering if either of them noticed how in sync they were.

"How are you doing with all that?" Nell asked more seriously, waving a strawberry on the end of her fork.

"I'm fine," Leslie said, knowing what Nell was hinting at and not really wanting to go there.

"Have you heard from Cassie?" Nell asked. "At all?"

"No." Leslie pushed her plate aside, her interest in her dessert suddenly gone. "Not since we met to close out the joint checking account." She shrugged, trying to appear nonchalant even though the memory of that day could still tear her apart if she let her guard down. It'd been her last chance to try to convince Cassie to allow her a place in Elijah's life, or at least to see him one last time. She'd failed on both counts.

Nell searched Leslie's face, clearly seeking more information. She'd always had questions, ones that Leslie couldn't bring herself to answer at the time. Nell had been patient with her and her healing process. "I know the basics. You know, she left you for a man. She took Elijah and wouldn't let you see him. Can you talk about it yet?"

She could. She still didn't want to, but Nell deserved to know the whole story. She'd been there for Leslie every step of the way, from clear across the country. She'd checked on her by phone and text every single day, usually a couple of times. She'd taken two weeks off from work and flown to Florida when Cassie had first moved out, without a word, leaving Leslie to come home from a conference to an empty house. Then she'd taken off another three weeks when Leslie had finally had to face the truth that she might very well never see Elijah again. She hadn't answered Nell's calls for several days in her despondency, and Nell had shown up on her doorstep and stayed until she'd gotten back on her feet enough to function. And when Leslie had decided to come home, Nell had taken care of all the details of preparing the house for her. She deserved to have her questions answered. "What do you want to know?"

Nell's eyebrows shot up. She was so used to the topic being avoided. "Are they still in Miami?"

Leslie shook her head. "No idea. I don't know if they're even still in Florida. That's why I had to get out of there—because of the not knowing. I realized I was sitting around waiting, jumping every time the doorbell rang, looking for them in movie crowds or shopping malls. It was making me crazy. I couldn't move on." The last words caught in her throat.

Paula took her hand. "What she did to you was horrible. You're smart to make a fresh start."

Leslie squeezed Paula's fingers in gratitude. "I know. And it isn't her I was waiting for, other than she'd have to be the one to have a change of heart. He's only seven." His bright eyes and freckled face flashed in her mind, his smile pulling her in as it always did. Tears welled in her eyes, the effort to hold them back constricting her throat. It destroyed her to think he might believe she was the one who'd left, that she didn't want to see him. She had no idea what Cassie had told him. She swallowed hard. "My cell's the same, or she can reach me through my website, if she ever wants to."

"What a bitch." Nell's voice was sharp. "And after everything you did, everything you gave them, she really said it would be better for Elijah to be raised in a house with a mother and a father?"

"She really did," Leslie said, the anger she'd stuffed way down deep beginning to rise.

"And that guy isn't even his father. *You've* been with Elijah, a parent to him, since he was born. That should count for something." Nell looked at Paula as she always did when she needed her world set right again.

"There's no explanation that's going to make sense of what Cassie did, honey." Paula took Nell's hand with her free one. "And she holds all the power. She's the biological parent."

"Why didn't you get a lawyer?" Nell asked, returning her attention to Leslie. "I don't mean it critically. I just...Why didn't you fight it?"

"You don't think I tried?" Leslie clenched her jaw, reliving all those calls, all the appointments, all the denials. "There wasn't a lawyer that would take the case. They all said it was a lost cause. We weren't married. There was no second parent adoption. I didn't have anything to stand on." She remembered the day she'd known it was over, that short of Cassie changing her mind, Leslie would most likely never again see the beautiful little boy she loved as a son. Her tears. Her rage. Her heartbreak. She couldn't relive it. "I have to trust that he's fine. That he's happy. For all her faults, I know Cassie will take care of him. Even with her lies to me about being in love with me and wanting the three of us to be a family, that's all she was ever trying to do."

"Bitch," Nell said, the word almost a growl.

It warmed Leslie's heart. She'd always been able to count on Nell to champion her causes, whatever they were. She let out a small, humorless laugh. "Thank you."

Paula patted Leslie's hand. "Nell mentioned you bought some furniture," she said in a clear change of subject.

"I did," Leslie said with an effort to brighten her tone. "At least, I ordered it. Most of it gets delivered tomorrow."

"You've gotten everything you need already?" Paula asked as she watched Nell scoop up the remaining strawberry glaze and whipped cream from her plate with her fingertips, then lick them clean.

"What?" Nell asked defensively. "It's just Leslie here."

Paula laughed and shook her head, her love evident in her soft expression. She leaned close and kissed her, and when she eased away, the whipped cream on Nell's upper lip was gone.

Leslie smiled. She'd always enjoyed being around Nell and Paula. It kept her belief in love intact, regardless of whatever train wreck had just occurred in her own love life. "I got the basics," Leslie said in response to Paula's question. "I found this enormous furniture store that was having a huge sale, and when I saw they had this really great blue couch, I just looked for everything else there, too. I'll get the rest over time."

Nell tilted her head quizzically. "You're centering your décor around a blue couch?"

"I'm not *centering my décor* around anything," Leslie said, feeling Gus shift against her foot. "I'm just buying furniture. And I promised Siena a blue couch." At the thought of Siena, she pictured her snuggled up with Gus in her bed, listening to *The House at Pooh Corner*. Then she remembered Erica's revelations about Trent being her ex, not her husband, and about being bi. She shifted uneasily in her chair.

"Who's Siena?" Paula asked.

"Is that the hot...uh, I mean..." Nell glanced at Paula. "Is she the woman next door?"

Paula shot Nell a glare.

"I only pointed her out to Les in case she might be interested," Nell said in her defense. "Right, Les?"

"That's true," Leslie said, coming to Nell's rescue. "Nell left me a very descriptive note about my new next-door neighbor..." She leveled her own glare on Nell. "Which she saw, by the way."

"How'd she see it? I left it on your bar." Nell's eyes widened. "She was in your house? Wow, you move fast."

Leslie rolled her eyes. "She was helping me clean up after breakfast. She loaned me some dishes, until..." She knew she wasn't making any sense. She hadn't made sense to herself since Sunday night and her last conversation with Erica.

"Breakfast?" Paula's interest was piqued now.

"No. Not like that," Leslie said, running her hand through her hair. "She's been nice. She invited me for dinner Saturday night, then brought some bagels and fruit over on Sunday morning, since I didn't have anything in the house to eat."

"That *is* nice," Paula said with a smile.

"And she's really great to look at." Nell grinned at Paula.

"You hush," Paula said, then turned back to Leslie. "And her name's Siena? That's a pretty name."

"No. Her name's Erica. Siena's her daughter. Siena's seven." Leslie wondered how Siena's week was going. She'd made herself scarce the past few days to avoid Erica, but in the process, she'd missed Siena. If she were completely honest, she'd missed Erica, too. "She's a sweetheart. She loves Gus. They're adorable together. And she's fun to talk to. She has autism, and Erica is amazing in how she deals with her. I kind of blew it when I took dinner over there Sunday night. I got Wendy's hamburgers, not knowing they freak her out…" Leslie trailed off at Nell's and Paula's stares. "What?"

"How much time have you spent with them?" Nell asked.

Leslie shrugged. "I ate with them a couple times over the weekend." That wasn't all she'd done, though. She left out cleaning up the kitchen twice, all the thought she'd put into her selections for the dinner she'd provided, and reading Siena a bedtime story, because she knew what that would sound like. She knew what those things were. They weren't things someone did with new neighbors. They were intimate things, things that said someone belonged somewhere. That's why they'd felt so good. She hadn't *belonged* anywhere since Cassie had left with Elijah.

"You sound kind of taken with them," Paula said softly.

Leslie avoided her gaze.

"What about her husband? The mom's, I mean," Nell said, far less gently. "I saw a guy over there last week who looked pretty comfortable."

"He's Erica's ex. He was only visiting." Leslie couldn't bring herself to look at Nell. *I'm an idiot, and I'll see it written all over her face.* She relinquished any thought of defense. These two knew her too dammed well. "Look, I know. Yes, I'm *taken* with them," she said to Paula. "Yes, I know how stupid it is," she said, addressing Nell's yet unspoken admonishment. "I just…fell for Siena so instantly. And, like you, I thought Erica was straight, and I *know* I'll never do *that* again. I thought it might help the healing to spend some time with them." In truth, she hadn't thought at all. She'd simply been pulled into the dynamic.

"You *thought* she was straight?" Nell asked in obvious disbelief. "She isn't?"

Leslie felt sick, and the same wave of nausea from when Erica had told her rolled through her stomach. "She's bi."

"I don't understand," Paula said. "If you like her, isn't that better?"

Leslie grimaced. "Under any other circumstances, I would've been thrilled. If we didn't live next door to one another and could just have a fun fling…if we'd met years ago, before Cassie tromped over my heart…if Siena weren't in the picture as a reminder of how much more it hurts to lose a child…" There was no denying her attraction to Erica. Erica was beautiful, intelligent, tender, and nurturing. Her smile lit Leslie deep inside. She was fun. "As long as I thought she was straight there was no way I'd go there again, not after Cassie. And even if she were bi and still married, she'd be off limits. But to find out she's single and bi, that she's available…" And possibly interested, if a couple of looks Leslie had caught were indications. "But she has Siena. And Siena's already twisted my heart around her little finger. Siena makes it…Erica could snatch her away from me without a word, or a warning—without even letting me say good-bye." Leslie fought back tears. "All it would take is for her to meet some guy who wouldn't require any explanation to friends or family, who she might someday deem *better* for Siena than me, or even her ex suddenly deciding he wants his wife and kid back."

"Wait a minute," Paula said.

"Uh-oh." Nell shifted her gaze between Paula and Leslie. "Now you've done it."

"Tell me you're not suggesting that a bisexual woman can't be faithful and monogamous with a woman," Paula said stonily. "Have you forgotten I've been with your cousin for over twenty years? And without a single temptation toward a man?"

"Of course not." Leslie sighed. "I'm not talking about you."

"You could be, if you didn't know me, like you don't know this woman." Paula straightened in her chair and folded her hands on the table, assuming her lawyer posture. "You haven't even given her a chance to show you who she is. And her being bi, doesn't have anything to do with what happened with Cassie. Cassie was straight. There's no actual correlation."

Leslie was so confused. Paula was right. Paula was always right. Leslie didn't know how Nell stood it. "I know," she said weakly. "It's just…"

"It's just that, in your mind, it leaves that door open for the possibility of another man swooping in and taking everything that matters to you," Paula said, softening. "I understand that. If you're scared, if you're not ready, then okay. But don't make it about something it isn't. If you like this woman and are attracted to her, maybe you're more ready than you think. Don't slam the door on it. Let yourself get to know her, as a friend. Then as you finish healing, maybe see what happens."

It sounded so easy when Paula said it. Leslie returned to Sunday night, stepping onto Erica's patio after reading to Siena the way she used to read to Elijah. It was different, though. Erica had greeted her so warmly with her teasing and her appreciation. By the time Elijah had been old enough for bedtime stories, Cassie wasn't waiting for Leslie. She was on the phone or already in bed, asleep. They'd been friends in the beginning of it all, but they'd never fallen in love. And Cassie had never looked at Leslie the way Erica did even now. Leslie knew she could fall hard for Erica, if she let herself. And then what? Then she'd be even more vulnerable than she'd been with Cassie. "No," she said, jerking back from an invisible edge. "I won't ever get involved with someone with a kid again. Bi, straight, or gay. Not going to happen."

"I don't think that's what Paula was going for," Nell said.

"I know it wasn't," Leslie said, meeting Paula's gaze. "And I'm sorry. I know you love me and mean well, but I can't. I'm so not there. And even when I am ready to start seeing someone, it'll have to be someone without kids. I've been left by women. I can handle that. But kids? They're a game changer. Losing a kid rips your heart right out of your chest. So…no kids." Leslie let out a short laugh. "You wouldn't think that would be hard at our age. How many fifty-year-olds have seven-year-olds, for cripe's sake?"

"All right, then," Paula said, clearly conceding the point. "But think about a friendship. It's nice to know people in your own neighborhood to spend time with."

Leslie simply nodded. She wasn't going to argue, but she didn't think she could do that with her attraction to Erica. No, even friends might be too much. Siena and Gus could remain friends, certainly, and she'd, of course, always be a good neighbor. Her parents had taught her that.

Yes. That's enough. Good neighbors.

Erica switched off the mini lights around her patio and crossed to the porch swing along the far side. She settled into the softness of the thick cushion, grasping a cup of chamomile tea in one hand and the nursery monitor in the other. She liked winding down this way, the darkness all around her, the cool night air caressing her skin, the gentle motion of the swing smoothing any rough edges left from the day.

Her yard wasn't as dark as it usually was. The past few evenings, since Leslie had moved in, the pool area next door was lit into the night. It wasn't bright, just a gentle illumination from the old-fashioned lamps and a soft magenta glow rising from beneath the surface of the water. It was pretty.

Erica leaned her head back and wondered where Leslie had been. She'd only caught brief glimpses of her. Once doing something in one of the flowerbeds in the backyard—Leslie had waved and called out a hello—another time backing out of her driveway and heading off somewhere, Gus's wet nose smearing the passenger's side window. She knew Leslie was busy. She'd said she had work to catch up on, and then there was getting settled into a new life. And Erica had been finishing the deep cleaning of her house, reveling in some much-needed down time, and had been taking care of her and Siena's routine commitments. Monday evening they'd been at the autism support group, Erica with the other parents and Siena with the playgroup, and tonight they'd gone to the quarterly joint gathering of several groups in the Los Angeles area. They'd all met for dinner, then gone miniature golfing. They'd been home Tuesday evening, and Gus had come over to play with Siena, but Leslie had stayed away.

What happened Sunday night? Erica pondered the question for probably the fiftieth time. She'd thought back through, over and over again, the topics they'd covered. The teasing. Their respective work. Erica's move from Chicago. Trent, both of their orientations. Something had triggered Leslie and brought up whatever had hurt her. Erica just couldn't figure out what it could have been.

She took a drink of her tea, then toed the swing into motion once more. A ripple of queasiness wriggled through her stomach, and she slipped her hand under her T-shirt and stroked her belly. She closed her eyes, enjoying her own touch. The queasiness ebbed, then returned. She set her tea and the monitor on the side table and stretched out along the length of the cushion, continuing the gentle caress.

She woke to a quiet yip and a hushed, "Shhh." When she blinked, she saw Leslie crossing from the back door of her house to the pool. Gus trotted behind her. Erica watched sleepily. Had they just gotten home? The house had been dark earlier.

Leslie wore faded jeans and some kind of baseball jersey. Her feet were bare. She moved with languid grace. She unlocked the gate to the pool and stepped through it. Then, before Erica could anticipate her plan, she stripped off her shirt and dropped it to the ground. Next went the sports bra.

Erica drew in a sharp breath. She remembered imagining Leslie's breasts, filling in the details from the outline of the small mounds and plump nipples through the thin fabric of her tank top, but here they were before her. No imagination needed. They were perfectly shaped, her nipples erect in the cool night air. Erica's clit stirred in its own waking. How long had it been since she'd held a woman's breasts in her hands, stroked them, sucked a taut nipple between her lips? She squeezed her thighs together, increasing her arousal. The motion of Leslie's hands to the button of her jeans drew Erica to a sitting position.

The swing creaked.

Gus looked in her direction.

Erica froze. Could she be seen in the darkness?

Leslie didn't seem to have heard the noise or noticed Gus's reaction.

Erica remained still. *I shouldn't be watching. I should go inside.* How could she, though, without drawing Leslie's attention and embarrassing them both? Besides, who was she kidding? She couldn't tear her gaze away.

Leslie slid her jeans down her legs and stepped out of them, then straightened and stretched her arms high above her head, her torso tight, the triangle of dark hair at the apex of her thighs enticing. She dove into the water and disappeared beneath the surface.

Erica went limp, as though she were a puppet on a string that had just been cut. She blew out a breath. Now was her chance. She grabbed the speaker from the table and started to rise.

Leslie surfaced at the other end of the pool and shook the water from her face and hair.

Erica waited. A soft jingle drew her attention to Gus, who sat at her feet, gazing up at her. Panic seized her. She looked from him to Leslie, then back, praying he wouldn't make any noise that would draw Leslie's attention.

Leslie pushed off the wall and began a slow back stroke down the length of the pool.

Gus jumped onto the swing and snuggled up against Erica's leg.

"No, Gus," Erica whispered, keeping an eye on Leslie's movement. "I have to get inside." She eased him off the swing.

He jumped back up, planted his front paws on her thigh, and started licking her ear.

It tickled. She couldn't help but giggle, but kept it quiet. "You're an evil dog," she whispered, conscious of the splash of Leslie's strokes. She ran her hand over Gus's head, then caressed the jagged edge of his damaged ear.

He leaned into her touch and closed his eyes.

Erica glanced toward the pool.

Leslie was still swimming, but stopped and lifted her head from the water every once in a while. Was she trying to find Gus? Checking to make sure none of her neighbors were up and around, possibly watching her?

Erica heated with embarrassment. She could no longer see Leslie's nudity. Not really. Just a pinkish swirl through the water that flowed over her as she swam. She checked the distance to her back door. Could she make it? It wasn't open, so there'd be the noise of it sliding. She was concealed by darkness where she sat in the corner of the patio, but as soon as she stepped out toward the house, there was more light, more shadow, more possibility of being seen. She could say she'd been asleep and Gus woke her. Pretend she hadn't seen Leslie strip. Still petting Gus, Erica felt a collar around his neck and heard the light jingle of tags. Apparently, Leslie had decided to keep him. "I guess you found a new home," she said softly.

He nestled down beside her and sighed.

She smiled. *Maybe two.*

As abruptly as Leslie had vanished into the water, she was out, walking up the steps, her nakedness front and center once more.

This time, it had a slow burn effect. Erica took in the water sluicing off all that smooth skin, the lines of Leslie's lithe body, the subtle curve of her boyish hips. She imagined pressing up against her, feeling Leslie slip her thigh between Erica's parted legs. She remembered Leslie posed playfully in the doorway, her sultry look and tone. *Cabana goddess, indeed.* She'd blown her chance, slim as it was, to get into the house undetected. She waited to see what would happen next.

Leslie picked up her shirt and pulled it over her head. As she smoothed it down her torso, she scanned the yard. "Gus," she called softly, her voice low. "Gus. Where are you?"

Gus lifted his head from Erica's lap and looked up at her.

"If you go quickly and get me out of this, I'll buy you a special treat," Erica whispered hopefully.

As though understanding every word, Gus jumped from the swing and scurried across the patio toward the gate.

Erica held her breath until he was safely back in Leslie's yard.

"There you are," Leslie said to the dog. "What are you doing over there? Siena's asleep." She murmured something else as she leaned down to pet him, then they headed toward the house.

Erica sighed with relief when she heard the soft closing of Leslie's French doors. She retrieved her tea. The cup was cold. She took a sip, and her stomach turned. *That was so close.* After the way their last conversation had ended, Erica knew it was important to ease into their next encounter. It should be light and friendly, not her being discovered spying on Leslie in private. Although, Leslie had some culpability in the matter as well. Who strutted around naked in their backyard? *A cabana goddess.* Erica chuckled.

Suddenly, she felt chilled and exhausted. She needed some sleep, but tomorrow, she'd drop in and offer some help with Leslie's new furniture. *Yes. Light and friendly.*

Chapter Six

Leslie stepped out into the bright morning and stretched. She'd waited to let Gus out until it was late enough to be sure Erica had left to take Siena to school but not so long that she'd be back yet. She'd watched all week to get their schedule down. *What a chicken.* She needed some distance, though.

Gus did his business, then ran through the gate leading next door.

"Come on, Gus," Leslie called. "She's not home." She felt guilty keeping him and Siena apart because of her fears and insecurities but didn't see a way around it. Maybe Gus could still go over to play with her whenever she was home. Leslie just wouldn't go with him. When Gus didn't return, Leslie started after him. He'd done the same thing the previous night while she was doing a few laps in the pool to relax. Maybe he'd found something gross to get into. He was a dog after all. A good dog, but a dog nonetheless. When she got to the gate, she came up short.

Siena sat on the edge of the raised patio, wearing her Wonder Woman pajamas, and stroking Gus's head.

Leslie glanced at the house. The sliding glass door and screen were open, but there was no sound or movement from inside. "Siena?" Leslie said as she approached. "Is everything okay?"

"Yes." Siena continued petting Gus.

Leslie squinted and looked deeper into the house. "Where's your mom?"

"In her bathroom." There was nothing unusual about Siena's tone.

Leslie nodded and sat beside her. "Everybody runs late sometimes," she said, drawing her own conclusion. *But damn. So much for keeping a distance.* She didn't want to leave Siena out here, though, until she saw Erica.

"How come you haven't come over to see us?" Siena looked across the yard at a bird hopping around on the grass.

Leslie tensed. "I've just been busy. And you've been at school," she added, trying not to sound defensive.

"School doesn't start till next week," Siena said in her matter-of-fact tone.

"Right. I mean your day program." Leslie glanced over her shoulder. Still no sign of Erica. "Did your mom say she'd be down soon?"

Siena fidgeted. "She said to go downstairs and wait for her, but I came out here because I don't like being inside alone."

Something in Siena's answer set off an alarm in Leslie's head. "Siena, what's your mom doing?"

"She's throwing up." Siena shifted her gaze to Leslie ever so briefly, then quickly looked away. "She's not in a good mood. She hates throwing up."

Leslie looked again into the house, uncertain. *Should I check on her?* They didn't know each other well enough for that, under normal circumstances, but with Siena sitting outside in her pajamas, waiting presumably forever for her mother to come down and take care of everything, these weren't normal circumstances. "You stay right here with Gus, okay? I'll be right back."

She knew where the master bedroom was, the floor plan being identical to hers. She knocked lightly on the partially open door.

No answer.

Then she heard it—the unmistakable sound of retching coming from the en suite. The bedroom reeked of vomit, and as she crossed to the bathroom door, she noticed a towel thrown over one side of the unmade bed with a wet outline creeping out from beneath the edges. She peeked into the bathroom.

Erica knelt in front of the toilet, her arms around the porcelain bowl, a pale blue T-shirt hiked up around her hips. She wore nothing else.

Leslie froze. How could she do this without embarrassing Erica, or both of them, for that matter? The question became moot as Erica reached for the flush handle, missed, and started to fall into the gap between the toilet and the wall. Leslie rushed forward and caught her around the waist before she hit her head.

"Oh, fuck!" Erica gasped. "Becky! Thank you for coming. I'm so sorry." She slumped against Leslie's legs. "Can you get Siena's breakfast ready and take her to school?"

Leslie winced. *This is going to kill her.* "It's not Becky," she said gently. "It's Leslie from next door."

Erica went rigid. "Oh, my God." She groaned. Then her middle clenched in Leslie's grasp and she threw up again.

Leslie shifted her so the contents of her stomach went into the toilet, then flushed it down. "I'm sorry," she whispered.

"Oh, my God," Erica said again in almost a whimper.

"It's okay." Leslie knew the words would have no effect, but she didn't know what else to say.

Erica folded her arms across the toilet seat and buried her head in them. "Oh, my God."

There was no way to console her. Not now. Not when she was half naked and bent over the toilet. Maybe refocusing the conversation would help. "What do you need me to do?" Leslie asked, taking charge.

It seemed to work. Erica lifted her head slightly. "Siena," she said weakly. "Where's Siena?"

"She's out back with Gus. She's fine."

"She needs breakfast." Erica upchucked again, as though the mere thought of food was too much. She wiped her mouth with the back of her hand and gulped for air. "I texted Becky. I'm sure she'll be here soon."

Leslie moved to the sink and soaked a hand towel in cool water, then squeezed it out. "I'll get her fed and ready to go." She dabbed Erica's forehead, then released the towel into her grasping hand. "Is there anything you need while…"

Erica wiped her lips. "There's a bucket under…" She pointed behind her at the counter. "I think I might—"

"Got it." Leslie leapt to retrieve it and set it beside Erica.

"Thank you," Erica said feebly.

Leslie stood in the bathroom awkwardly, not wanting to leave her alone but knowing it would be best. Besides, Siena needed to be ready when Becky came. "Okay," she said finally, more to herself than Erica.

Outside once more, she sat beside Siena with a plan in place. "All right. As you know, your mom's sick, so we're going to have to help her out."

Siena turned to her expectantly.

Leslie studied her. She didn't know what Siena could or couldn't do on her own, what might cause her to melt down, so the best approach would be simply to ask. *Right?* "Can you get dressed by yourself?"

Siena brightened. "Yes."

"Great!" Leslie said. *Good start.* "So you go get dressed, and I'll make you some breakfast. Is there anything you want in particular?"

"Chocolate brownies," Siena said eagerly.

Leslie laughed. *Should've seen that coming.* "Nice try. Let me ask a different question. Is there anything you absolutely don't like for breakfast?"

"Eggs," Siena said, scrunching her nose. "There's pancake batter in the refrigerator. Do you know how to make pancakes?"

"I do." Of course Erica would have an efficient morning routine.

"I want pancakes," Siena said.

"You got it. I'll make them while you get dressed." Leslie rose and held her hand out to Siena. "Come right back when you're finished. Okay?"

Siena nodded and led the way into the house.

As Leslie flipped the last pancake onto a plate, she heard a sound behind her. "All dressed?" she asked without a glance.

"Yes," Siena said, happiness in her voice. "I wore all my favorite things."

Leslie turned. The sight stopped her in her tracks.

Siena wore purple camouflage shorts, a wrinkled, bright red shirt with big blue and yellow flowers, Winnie the Pooh socks, and lime green sneakers. "Look, my shoes have lights." She stomped her foot, then grinned at Leslie after a red flash lit up the side.

"I see that. Those are cool shoes," Leslie said, stalling for something else to say. The outfit was nothing like the color-coordinated, well-kempt clothing she'd seen Siena in before, even on the weekend. Clearly, she wasn't usually in charge of dressing herself. *Oh well. Desperate times and all...* "You look beautiful."

Siena beamed.

"Your breakfast is ready," Leslie said, setting the plate on the table beside the butter, blueberries, and syrup she'd found in her search of the fridge and cupboards. Erica's cabinets were the most organized she'd ever seen.

The doorbell rang.

Ah, Becky. If the outfit was unacceptable, she'd know how to deal with it. She knew Erica and Siena far better. When Leslie opened the front door, though, she found a man with bags under his eyes, stubble covering his cheeks, and his reddish hair looking as though it'd never met a comb.

They blinked at one another.

"May I help you?" Leslie asked.

"Who are you?" the man asked.

"My name's Leslie. I live next door."

"Oh," he said, a spark of recognition in his tired eyes. "I've heard of you. I'm Jack. My wife Becky and I are friends of Erica's."

"Oh. Yes," Leslie said. "I was expecting Becky. You threw me." She stepped back to let him, and the little girl she'd just noticed hiding behind his leg, inside.

"Becky's at home, puking her guts out, just like Erica, I assume." Jack lifted an eyebrow.

Leslie nodded.

"We had a support group dinner last night. Seems everyone who ate the chicken is in the same boat this morning." He looked around the living room. "I've always liked this room," he said, as though there was nothing out of the ordinary about the two of them being there together.

Leslie followed suit and took in her surroundings, realizing she'd never been in that part of Erica's house. She always came in the back. She remembered what Siena had said about it being for people who don't belong there and her grandma with wrinkles. She almost laughed. She wondered whose mother that grandma was.

"Is Siena ready?" Jack asked, returning to the problem at hand. "Do you need help with anything?"

"She's eating breakfast," Leslie said, leading the way toward the kitchen. "And I'm not sure about what she's wearing."

"Hey, on a day like today, if she's wearing anything at all, it's good," Jack said. "Rosi's already had two meltdowns because things aren't going the way they usually do."

Leslie glanced at the little girl. She seemed perfectly fine now.

"Routine's important with a lot of kids on the spectrum." Jack smiled at Siena as he stopped in the kitchen doorway. "Hey, kiddo. Ready to go to school with me and Rosi?"

"School doesn't start till next week," Siena said, her focus on her plate. "And my mom takes me."

Leslie moved to her and squatted beside her chair. "Your mom's sick, remember? She's upstairs...you know..." She watched Siena carefully for any signs that she was upset. The problem was, she wasn't sure what she was looking for. "So do you want to ride with Jack and Rosi? Just for today?"

"No, thank you." Siena took a bite.

Leslie shifted and tried again. "Siena, your mom called Jack to help her this morning. Remember, we talked about your mom needing help because she isn't feeling well? This is how we can help her."

Siena stiffened, and her eyes widened slightly. "I don't want to go with Rosi. I don't like Rosi." She began to rock. "My mom takes me."

Gus jumped up from the other side of the chair where he'd been watching and landed his front paws on her leg, like he'd done Sunday evening.

Leslie waited for Jack to step in, but he didn't. She remembered Erica's approach. "It's okay," she said softly, "but I think you have to go to school…or…to your day program, I mean."

"No. No, no." She rocked faster. "My mom takes me." Her voice rose.

"All right." Leslie stroked her arm to calm her. "It's all right."

Siena pulled away and shrieked.

Leslie jerked back, her hands in the air. "I'm sorry. I won't touch you."

Siena froze, still in the chair, and stared down at Gus.

But now what? Leslie thought fast. *Winnie the Pooh. The characters.* "Do you remember Winnie the Pooh and Piglet? And Eeyore and Tigger?"

Gus whined and licked Siena's thigh.

Siena began to rock again, but she picked up the chant. "Winnie the Pooh. Piglet. Eeyore…"

Leslie moved back to Jack and maneuvered them into the dining room. "Is it a big deal if she misses a day at her program?"

Jack shrugged. "Not to me. She seems better with that diversion from routine than with anyone but Erica taking her there. But is Erica doing well enough to watch her? If she's anything close to as sick as Becky, she's not going to be handling anything."

"No. From what I saw, she's out of commission for the day, at least." Leslie thought about her furniture being delivered, all the setup and unpacking she needed to do, and the upcoming launch of the new Trinfinite Photography website, one of her biggest clients. She sighed, then decided. "Siena can stay with me. We'll just need to be back and forth between the two houses. I can make sure Erica's doing okay, too."

"Great," Jack said. "I owe you one. Becky told me to keep an eye on them in addition to getting Rosi and the boys where they needed to be. Plus, like I said, Becky's feeling pretty lousy herself. We try to keep tabs on Erica, since she's on her own with Siena, but today's a mess."

"Don't worry about anything here." Leslie patted him on the shoulder as they walked through the house to the front door.

"And tell Becky this family's fine. I mean, Erica and Siena…That family," she said, catching her wording.

Jack seemed oblivious as he herded Rosi out. "If you need anything, let me know."

They quickly exchanged numbers.

She watched him buckle Rosi into the back seat of his car, then returned to find Siena.

She was in the backyard again, sitting where Leslie had found her earlier, still repeating the characters of the Hundred Acre Wood to herself. She was calmer, though.

Leslie sat beside her again and waited.

"Are they gone?" Siena asked after a few minutes.

"Yes. You're going to stay with me and Gus for the day. Is that okay?" Leslie held her breath, hoping the answer was yes. She didn't have a clue what to do if it wasn't. That was the only option she could see at the moment.

"Yes," Siena said. She ran her hand down Gus's back and pulled him close.

Leslie felt a wave of relief. "I'm going to need your help, though."

"With what?"

"There's a lot going on today," Leslie said, glad to see more curiosity in Siena's expression than anxiety. She thought of what Erica had said the night of the Wendy's incident, that Siena had managed to handle herself. She'd done well today, too—and Leslie was even a little proud of herself. "My furniture is coming between noon and two, and—"

Siena gasped. "The blue couch?"

Leslie laughed. "Yes, and a lot of other stuff. So we have to tell the delivery people where to put everything. Then we have to unpack the things I brought with me and put them all away. Plus, we need to take care of your mom and make lunch and dinner. Can you help me with all that?"

Siena nodded with enthusiasm.

"And there's something else," Leslie said cautiously. "And this is really important." She leveled her gaze on Siena.

Siena grew serious.

"I don't know many of the things that upset you, so I need you to tell me if something makes you feel anxious or scared or anything at all that isn't happy. Will you do that?"

Siena set her jaw and nodded. "I will."

Leslie smiled, her heart warming at Siena's sincerity. "All right, then. That's our day." She slapped her thighs and stood. "I'm going to go check on your mom. Why don't you and Gus play some ball. I got him a whole bunch of new ones, so if any go in the pool, you can grab another one. They're in the box right outside my back door."

Siena and Gus had both scrambled to their feet at the word *ball* and were on their way.

Leslie stared after them, saying good-bye to her plan to keep her distance.

Erica woke, conscious of her cheek against a soft pillow and her body cushioned by the mattress beneath her. She tried to open her eyes, to lift her head, but she couldn't move. Was she dead? *No. I feel too horrible to be dead.* Every muscle in her body ached, and despite the thick blanket covering her, she shivered. She forced herself onto her back, then moaned at the pain. Where was she? She let her eyelids flutter open. She was in her bedroom, in her own bed. That was good.

But how'd I get here? The last thing she remembered was throwing up in a bucket at the same time her bowels were expelling brown water into the toilet. *Lovely.* And there was more. Lying on the cold tile of the bathroom floor. Heaving. *So much heaving.* Someone there. A shriek. She bolted upright. "Siena?"

"Take it easy. Siena's fine." A familiar voice.

A wave of nausea overtook her. She clamped her arms over her stomach and curled onto her side. She clenched her eyes shut and swallowed a mouthful of saliva.

Someone stroked her back. "Breathe. Deep breaths."

Becky. Erica followed the instruction, and her stomach began to settle.

"That's it. If you do need to throw up, there's a bowl right here."

No. Not Becky. A flash from earlier in the bathroom. *Noooooo. Please, not Leslie.* But she knew it was.

Leslie pressed her hand to Erica's forehead. "You're running a fever."

"I'm so cold." Erica couldn't stop shaking.

Leslie pulled the blanket up over her and tucked it in around her.

"Siena. I heard her scream."

"That was a couple of hours ago," Leslie said. "She didn't want to go with Jack when he came to take her to her day program, but she worked it out."

"She went with him?"

"Not at all. She's downstairs." Leslie's voice was tender. She brushed back Erica's hair with her fingertips. "We were playing Crazy Eights when I heard you moan through the monitor. I came up to check on you."

"She's with you." It wasn't a question, rather a relieved acknowledgment. She didn't need to worry about Siena if she was with Leslie. She knew that deep in her soul. "Thank you."

"Not a problem," Leslie said. "We're having fun. You can relax."

Leslie's words swirled around in Erica's head, bringing images into focus like a kaleidoscope. Siena. Gus. Crazy Eights cards. Jack. *Jack? Why Jack, not Becky?* "Where's Becky?" she asked, her throat starting to burn from talking.

"She's sick, too." Leslie adjusted the blanket again. "Apparently, the chicken wasn't the thing to order last night. You've got food poisoning."

With the thought of her meal the previous evening, Erica felt her stomach lurch. She pushed up. She had to get to the bathroom.

Then Leslie's strong arm was around her, holding her in place. "Here you go," Leslie said, supporting her as she held something in front of Erica. "Here's the bowl. Just sit for a minute. It might pass."

It didn't. Erica heaved once. Twice. On the third one, clear bile spilled from her mouth.

"At least there's nothing left in your stomach," Leslie said, as she shifted around, still holding Erica tightly. "Do you want some ice chips?"

Erica shook her head, then let Leslie ease her down onto the pillow. She couldn't think of anything to say. She couldn't think. She felt Leslie's touch across her temple again, then along her cheek and neck as she tucked Erica's hair away from her face. It wasn't like a lover, or even the affection of a friend. It was like a mother's touch, maternal and soothing. Erica sighed and closed her eyes. How long had it been since she'd been nurtured in any way?

"That's it," Leslie whispered. "Go back to sleep. It's the best thing for you, according to Google. If you need anything, I'll have the nursery monitor with me. Just say my name, and I'll be right here."

Erica smiled weakly. She could rest. Siena was with Leslie. Erica could sleep. A comfortable darkness enveloped her.

When she woke again, her body still ached, and she was still exhausted, but her head was clearer. She could actually remember some things—sitting on the swing the night before; feeling queasy; Leslie, naked in the dim poolside lights. *That was nice.* And almost getting caught. *I owe Gus one of those great big cow bones.*

She struggled to a sitting position and tried to comb her fingers through her hair, but it was matted with sweat and...*Eww.* She winced at the memory of waking in the early morning, her stomach clenching, and vomiting in her bed. She startled and looked to the empty side. There was nothing there, only the rumpled, but clean, blanket she'd thrown off when her chills turned to heat. It wasn't her comforter, though, nor were the sheets the same as when she'd gone to bed. Someone had changed the bedding, cleaned up the mess.

Leslie. She groaned. Was there no end to this string of utter humiliations? Then, of course, there was what she'd already recalled in vivid detail—Leslie coming into the bathroom while she was bent over the toilet, puking like a frat boy, wearing only a T-shirt. It all had to be universal payback for hiding in the dark and ogling Leslie's oh-so-tempting body.

"You're awake," Leslie said, strolling into the room. "How are you feeling?"

Erica shoved aside her thoughts of the night before and attempted to straighten. "A little better." She tried not to think about what she must look like, or worse, smell like, as she met Leslie's concerned brown eyes.

"That's great," Leslie said with a smile. "We should probably see if we can get some water into you, so you don't get dehydrated."

"I'm still so tired." Erica closed her eyes briefly.

"You're going to need a lot of rest in the next few days." Leslie squatted beside the bed. "Don't rush yourself on that."

"What I need is a shower," Erica said, self-conscious in Leslie's close proximity.

"Really? You look pretty pale." She studied Erica. "Are you sure you're up to it?"

Erica turned away. She was so embarrassed. "I'll be fine. I'll take it slowly. I have to get clean." She shifted her legs over the edge of the mattress.

Leslie rose and backed away, giving her space. "Do you want some help?"

"No." The word came out sharp. Erica winced inwardly. Leslie didn't deserve that. Hell, she deserved a medal for everything she'd already done. Erica softened. "I'll be fine. Thank you." She steadied herself with her hand on the nightstand before attempting an actual step, then made her way on wobbly legs to the bathroom. She felt Leslie's eyes on her the whole time.

When she got there, she had to sit for a few minutes on the toilet lid to rest before starting the water, then again before adjusting the temperature. And yet again between wrestling her way out of her T-shirt and climbing over the edge of the tub to get beneath the hot stream of cleansing water. She'd never felt anything so decadently luxurious as that steady caress of warm liquid sluicing over her skin. She moaned with pleasure as she turned in a slow circle and the ache in her muscles began to ease.

She managed the body wash over her torso with no trouble. Lifting one foot, then the other, to the small ledge in the corner to run her soapy hands the full length of each leg and over her buttocks caused more difficulty. When it was time to lift her arms and shampoo her hair, though, she had no energy left. Her legs began to tremble, and she crumpled to the ground. She felt useless. She began to cry.

"Do you need some help?" Leslie asked from somewhere in the bathroom.

Erica couldn't muster the indignation to question how long she'd been there, nor could she answer at first. All she could do was suck in air between small sobs and draw up her knees to hug them tightly against her bare breasts. "Yes," she said finally, relinquishing all pretense that she could manage anything on her own right now. "Please."

Leslie inched the shower curtain aside and waited.

Erica kept her gaze riveted to the floor of the tub, but she knew Leslie was looking down at her. What else would she be doing? She could imagine, though, what she was seeing and thinking— Erica at her weakest. Embarrassment turned to anger in a flash, but she lacked the strength to express it. *Just as well.* She heard the rustle of the curtain and Leslie moved to the end of the shower where Erica sat.

"Let me wash your hair," Leslie said quietly.

Erica cried harder. She didn't know which was worse—the embarrassment and humiliation at Leslie seeing her so vulnerable and needy, or Leslie's kindness that made Erica so tempted to lean into her, the lure of her mere presence at a moment such as this. Erica didn't do this. She was strong. She was independent. She handled things—*all* things—on her own. This was the very kind of situation that drove people away. But in this case, hadn't it been what had brought Leslie back? She'd been absent ever since their conversation Sunday, and yet here she was.

"Is it okay if I wash your hair?" Leslie asked.

Erica hesitated. Wasn't the grossness of her hair the very reason she'd been so desperate to take a shower, though? Still crying softly, she nodded.

Leslie took the nozzle from its holder and let it hang loosely while she worked shampoo into Erica's hair. Her hands felt so good, washing and rinsing her hair clean. Then she added conditioner, combing through the tangles with her fingers and gently massaging Erica's scalp. She didn't speak. Finally, she let the warm stream flow over Erica's head, shoulders, and back for a few minutes before turning off the water. Leslie draped a towel over Erica's hair and squeezed out the excess water. Her ministrations were so gentle, so careful. When she finished, she ran the towel over Erica's shoulders, down her back and sides, over her arms.

Gradually, Erica calmed. "There's a robe on the back of the door," she said between sniffles. "Will you please get it for me?"

"Of course." In seconds, Leslie was wrapping it around Erica and guiding Erica's hands into the sleeves. Then to Erica's astonishment, she stepped into the tub and leaned down. "Put your arms around my neck," she said.

Erica looked up into Leslie's eyes. She searched her face, unsure what was happening.

"I'm going to help you up. That's all." Leslie's tone was reassuring.

Erica did as she was told, and before she knew it, Leslie's arms were around her and she was being half coaxed, half lifted to her feet. She pressed into Leslie for balance.

Leslie took a moment to steady her, then with one arm tightly around Erica's waist, she pulled the robe closed with her free hand. "Ready?"

Erica's legs were still wobbly. They shook under her weight. She knew she wouldn't make it to her bed on her own.

Leslie moved back, stepping over the side of the tub, then helped Erica after her. She kept a snug hold on her as they made their way into the bedroom.

At the sight of the bed—her comforter and sheets, obviously laundered and returned, the covers turned down as though in a hotel—Erica balked.

"I figured, once you were clean, you'd want clean bedding," Leslie said, answering without actually being asked. "I ran down and grabbed them out of the dryer."

Tears, this time of pure gratitude, burned Erica's eyes again. A smidge of embarrassment still lingered as well, but at least the second set of sheets hadn't been as disgusting as the first. All she could do was nod.

Leslie settled her into bed, leaning her against the stack of pillows.

Erica sighed with relief to be able to rest again.

"I brought you some ice chips." Leslie handed her a cup and a spoon. "You need to get some liquids into you."

Erica took them gratefully and put a small scoop into her mouth. The ice melted quickly on her hot tongue, and she realized she was still running a fever. It felt and tasted so good. She moaned softly, as though it was filet mignon. "Thank you," she whispered.

"No problem," Leslie said, her tone truly convincing.

Erica ate a few more small bites, letting the cool liquid soothe her parched throat as she swallowed. She waited to see how her stomach reacted, but so far, so good. "You know," she said, unable to meet Leslie's gaze, "when this is over, one of us is going to have to move. I'll be way too mortified to face you after all this." It was a weak attempt at a joke, maybe because there was actual truth to the statement.

Leslie chuckled, the sound low in her throat. "It's too bad I didn't know that before I had all that furniture delivered."

The comment piqued Erica's interest. She glanced at Leslie. "Did it come?"

Leslie nodded. "It did."

"How did you manage that, since you've been here all day?" Erica asked.

"We were back and forth," Leslie said, kneeling beside the bed. "But I was listening for you. You were never alone."

Erica remembered what Leslie had said earlier about keeping the nursery monitor with her and all Erica had to do was say her name. That thought and Leslie's words, *You were never alone,* brought a heated blush to Erica's face. They were words Erica had longed to hear, dreamed of hearing, first from Trent after Siena was born, later mostly in the fantasy life she sometimes allowed herself to indulge in, but now, they struck fear in her heart. She couldn't let herself get sucked in. *It's ridiculous. Leslie didn't mean them in any kind of real way.* Besides, she didn't need anyone like that. This situation was an anomaly. At the first twinge of her stomach, she handed the cup of ice back to Leslie. "I think that's enough for now." She scooched down the pillows and started to curl into a fetal position.

"Hold on," Leslie said. "We should get you out of that damp robe. Do you have pajamas, or another nightshirt, or something?"

Erica flinched. *Oh, what the hell. She's seen everything anyway.* "The top drawer," she said, waving toward the dresser.

Leslie returned with one of the oversized T-shirts Erica slept in when she wasn't trying to impress anyone, which was almost always, and—for one more humiliation—a pair of Erica's panties. She slipped her arm beneath Erica's shoulders and eased her up, then helped her out of the robe. "Don't worry, I won't look," Leslie said, a hint of humor in her voice.

Erica laughed. The irony of the situation wasn't lost on her. "This is Karma for last night."

"What happened last night?" Leslie asked as she pulled the shirt over Erica's head.

Oh, God. Had she really said that? She pushed her arms into the sleeves, then pulled the shirt down around her body.

Leslie was staring at her, realization shaping her features. "That's why Gus was in your yard. Why he took so long coming when I called him. You were there?"

Erica sighed. "I'm sorry. I was on the patio when you came out. I never expected you to strip. Then when you did, it was too late for me to get back into the house unnoticed."

Leslie waited a beat. "Well, then," she said thoughtfully. "Maybe *I* should have looked more." The teasing in her voice was evident. "You owe me."

Erica reclined onto the pillows and offered her a small smile. "So what have you and Siena and Gus been doing all day today?" she asked, changing the subject. Even if she'd had the energy to flirt, she'd promised herself she wouldn't.

"Let's see..." Leslie repositioned herself on the floor beside the bed. "We made pancakes for breakfast. Thank you for the batter in the fridge, by the way." She winked at Erica. "We played some games. We met the furniture delivery people and showed them where to put everything."

"I'll bet Siena loved that," Erica said, enjoying the glint in Leslie's eyes. "She makes a good supervisor."

Leslie laughed. "She was an excellent supervisor, until the blue couch got unloaded. Then she abdicated her supervisory role in order to bounce on it. I could barely get her off of it to come over here and check on you."

"You're going to have to tell me what's so amazing about this blue couch." Erica let her eyelids droop closed, then opened them again, as she spoke. She was fading.

"Siena wanted to see you," Leslie said, pulling the covers over Erica's bare legs. "Why don't I go get her, and she can tell you all about it."

Erica nodded. "I'd like that."

Leslie grinned and left.

A wave of exhaustion moved through Erica. The clean bedding and clothing, the comfort of someone being there with her, for her, handling things, taking care of both her and Siena. ...It all lulled her into a false sense of safety and support. It wouldn't last. She knew that. But for now, just this once, she let herself go there.

Just for now.

CHAPTER SEVEN

Leslie dumped a scoop of laundry detergent into her brand new washing machine, then poured fabric softener into its designated compartment. She turned to Siena. "How are you coming with that?"

Siena looked up from the package of sheets she was struggling with. "It's hard," she said.

"Want me to do it?" The answer would be no. Leslie had learned Siena liked doing things for herself, like her mother. Leslie waited, giving her the opportunity.

Siena had turned out to be quite the little helper in all that was going on. She obviously enjoyed being in the middle of everything, taking part in all the happenings of the day. It was different from what Leslie was used to with Elijah. He had a tendency to hang back and want someone else to handle everything. Leslie had to encourage—sometimes manipulate, bribe, and even trick—him into helping with a project. She wondered how Cassie's husband dealt with that. She hoped he was patient. The pain of that no longer being her role was slowly diminishing, but it still hurt.

Finally, the plastic packaging tore and the sheets fell out. Leslie and Siena shook them from their tightly folded constraints.

As Leslie stuffed the sheets into the washer, it wasn't lost on her that this was the third set of bedding she'd laundered that day, but at least this set was clean, and she was only doing it to get the stiffness out of them before putting them on the brand new bed waiting for her upstairs. Not that she'd get to sleep in it tonight. She'd already determined she'd be spending the night on Erica's couch—but it was nice to know she had a bed and her stint of sleeping on her living room floor was over.

"What do we do now?" Siena asked as she ran through the kitchen ahead of Leslie and into the family room. Without the slightest pause, she leapt onto the couch and flopped into its overstuffed padding. She wriggled into the corner where the two pieces of the sectional met, a huge grin on her face.

Leslie smiled. "Something tells me you'd be happy sitting there for the rest of the evening." She dropped onto the other end and laid her head against the armrest. She could do with a breather. It'd been a long day what with finding Erica so sick first thing, then the delivery of the furniture. Nell had stopped by with some Jell-O, Gatorade, and broth Leslie had asked her to pick up for when Erica started feeling better and had won Siena over with a couple of magic tricks. Other than that, Leslie had been Siena's entire entertainment for the day, and she'd forgotten how much energy that took. She didn't mind, though. She was tired, but it was a good kind of tired. She stretched.

The couch was comfortable—and fun. She'd liked it the second she'd seen it, and she might have bought it even without Siena's request for a blue couch. It was upholstered in faded denim fabric and had compartments sewn into it in strategic places that looked like the back pockets of old blue jeans, presumably to hold things like remotes, or reading glasses, or anything else one might want to keep track of while lounging around. It was perfect for the casual atmosphere of a family room.

A soft rustling sound came from the speaker on the coffee table.

Was it Erica or Gus? While Siena had brought Erica up to speed on all she'd missed while she'd been puking and snoring, as Siena had so delicately put it, Gus had snuggled into the lush comforter and sprawled out along Erica's side. When she'd fallen asleep before the end of Siena's discourse and Leslie had tried to coax both girl and dog quietly from the room, Gus had refused to budge, only staring back at Leslie, a clear message in his eyes. He'd been with her ever since. Leslie had heard a surprised, "Hi, Gus," at one point, followed by the crunch of some ice in the cup and a murmured, "You're a good boy," as Erica settled back into sleep, but other than that, the monitor had been quiet into the early evening.

"Are you getting hungry?" Leslie asked Siena. "Think you could help me with one more job before we make dinner? It's an important one."

"What is it?" Siena straightened with her question. She seemed to enjoy helping with *important* things.

"Come on, I'll show you." Leslie led the way into the living room and pulled the hard plastic shipping box from where she'd placed it on the lower shelf of a marble topped credenza near the front door. She sat beside it and opened it.

Siena peered inside. "What's in there?"

"Let's see," Leslie said with a grin. She loved Siena's curiosity. *Face it. I love pretty much everything about her.* She shouldn't go there, though. Regardless of her growing affection, once Erica was on her feet again, Leslie's plan of keeping a distance had to go back into place. The whole day had felt so much like family, what with caring for Erica while she was sick, then keeping Siena occupied and fed all day, and she'd let herself enjoy it. A family was what she'd always wanted. Wasn't that what had drawn her to Cassie, once Elijah was born? She had to remember, though, Siena and Erica weren't *her* family. Looking back, that's where she'd gone wrong with Cassie and Elijah.

Leslie withdrew a heavy bundle from the box and unwound the towel around it, then peeled away the tape that held several layers of bubble wrap in place. She held up the statue for Siena to see.

Siena gasped. "What's that?" she asked, wonder in her tone.

"It's a Buddha statue carved from a stone called blue lapis lazuli," Leslie said, turning the art piece in her hands and checking for damage from the trip. She doubted she'd find any. She'd packed it carefully, and the box had been nestled behind the driver's seat, with her unrolled sleeping bag and several pillows stuffed around it the whole way. "I thought you'd like the color, since you have such a fondness for blue couches."

Siena's eyes shone with excitement. "I do. It's so pretty. What's a Buddha?"

"A Buddha," Leslie said, setting the statue on one end of the credenza, "is someone who's gotten rid of all their mean and scary thoughts about themselves and others and the world and realized that who and what they really are is love. It's called achieving enlightenment." There was a lot lost in the translation, but it would give Siena the basic idea.

Siena was listening intently. "Can anyone be a Buddha?"

"Yes, as a matter of fact." Leslie loved talking with children. They could always grasp the concept of love more easily than most adults. "We're all actually, in a way, already Buddhas. We just have to uncover that part of ourselves by getting rid of all the negative things we've learned from being in the world, like hate, and meanness, and jealousy, and greed, and a lot more. So really, there have been a lot of Buddhas, and there can be even more."

"Is that why he looks so happy?" Siena pointed at the statue. "And how come he's so fat?"

Leslie laughed. "This is Hotei. He's the Chinese Buddha of contentment and happiness and the guardian of children. He's also called the fat Buddha or the laughing Buddha. This sack he's carrying?" She stroked a bag draped over his back. "It's said to be filled with an unending supply of treasures and food and drink so he can feed the poor. And it's said to be good luck if you rub his fat belly whenever you pass him." She demonstrated.

Siena tentatively followed her lead, then grinned. "What else is in there?" she asked returning her attention to the box.

Leslie took out another bundle and unwrapped it. "This is another Buddha," she said, holding up a jade sculpture. "This is the very first Buddha, Siddhartha. He was the first one to achieve enlightenment and taught others how to do it."

"Why are his eyes closed?" Siena asked, tracing the statue's lids.

"He's meditating," Leslie said, already opening the third bundle. "That's when you sit quietly and concentrate on a particular thing until you can really feel it, and then answers to your questions come. At least, that's one way to meditate."

"I like him, too." Siena moved close to Leslie and put her hand on Leslie's shoulder.

It was the first time Siena had touched her. It was an important moment between them. A rush of emotion stole Leslie's breath.

"Who's that?" Siena whispered, staring at the third figure in Leslie's hands. She ran her fingertips over the smooth marble folds of the gown covering the figure's form.

Leslie cleared her throat, regaining her composure. "Her name is Quan Yin." Leslie set the statue in its place on the table.

"Is she a Buddha, too?" Siena's gaze remained fixed on her.

"Some people call her a Buddha; others say she's what's known as a bodhisattva, which is someone who's learning and following the teachings of Buddha and is *almost* one. Either way, she's known for her compassion."

"What's compash..." Siena glided her fingertips over the statue's serene expression.

"Compassion?" Leslie thought for a moment on how to explain such a concept to a seven-year-old. She was impressed as hell that Siena was following the conversation as well as she was. Despite her issues, she seemed more advanced in some ways. "It's like taking love and concern and being able to feel what someone else is feeling and putting them all together. And in Quan Yin's case, it's like a really strong and protective love, like the way a mother loves her child."

"Like my mom," Siena said, clearly coming to a conclusion.

Leslie smiled, thinking of the way Erica looked at Siena, her vigilance where she was concerned, the choices she'd made. "Exactly like your mom."

"But can Buddhas live in jungles?" Siena asked.

"What?" Leslie wasn't following the shift.

"You said we can make this room a jungle. But what if they can't live in a jungle?" Siena looked from one statue to the next.

Oh. I did say I'd give the jungle motif some thought. But now that things had changed… "Actually, they can," she heard herself saying. "They've found Buddha statues—great big ones, twenty feet tall—in jungles all over the world. In Vietnam. In Thailand. In Peru, I think."

Siena's forehead scrunched, and she pursed her lips in thought, then nodded.

Leslie adjusted all three statues on the table, positioning them the way she liked. They'd been with her everywhere she'd lived for a long time. Now that they were unpacked and displayed, she was truly home again.

"Who are these people?" Siena asked. She'd pulled something else from the box.

Leslie glanced at the picture her parents had taken on their fortieth wedding anniversary. "That's my mom," she said, pointing, "and that's my dad."

Siena studied the photo. "Where do they live?"

"Well," Leslie said considering how to proceed with this one. "They don't live anywhere here on Earth anymore. Do you know what it means when somebody dies?"

"Yes." Siena's answer was decisive. "Grandma Millie died. And my goldfish, Hazel, died. I didn't see Grandma Millie after she died, but when Hazel died, she didn't swim anymore and she didn't eat fish food anymore and she didn't poop anymore. So she was done being a fish." She tilted her head with a thoughtful expression. "I bet Grandma Millie didn't poop after she died either." She turned to Leslie. "We buried Hazel in a matchbox in the garden. She makes the flowers on the camellia bush pretty with her bright colors."

Leslie blinked, amazed at Siena's level of understanding and her ability to put it into words. "Okay. That's very good. So my mom and dad died about ten years ago, but they used to live right here in this house. And so did I, when I was growing up. That's why I came back here."

Siena squinted one eye and studied her. "I thought you came here to be with me and my mom. And to bring us Gus."

Leslie opened her mouth to speak, but nothing came out. What did one say to a statement like that? It did fit with Leslie's beliefs about life, that each of us had contracts, so to speak, with others, to come into one another's lives for specific reasons. She hadn't considered that aspect of her current life. "Uh...well, maybe. Maybe that, too."

Siena was digging around in the box again. She pulled out another framed photograph.

Leslie knew what it was. She hadn't thought of it before opening the box. She braced herself.

"Is this your little boy?" Siena asked after a beat.

Leslie swallowed. He wasn't, technically, and yet, she couldn't deny him. He was her little boy, no matter what anyone else said or did. He'd been her son in her heart from day one. "Yes," she said in defiance of everything that had happened. "That's Elijah. He's about your age now." In the picture, he was younger. It was his school photo from kindergarten, and the most recent one she had. It might very well be the last one she'd ever have.

"Where does *he* live?"

Siena's questions suddenly seemed endless. "He lives with his other mom," Leslie said. It felt good to claim him and her position with him again, even if it was only with a child.

Siena cocked her head and shot Leslie a sideways glance. "He has two moms?"

He did, but not anymore. Leslie only nodded.

"My friend Jerry in my day program has two moms," Siena said brightly. "My mom says a lot of kids do."

But Siena didn't. She had a mom and a dad, even though the dad had left. It'd infuriated Leslie to hear that Trent hadn't wanted to stay once Siena was born, hadn't wanted Siena at all. She knew it was her own resentment she was feeling from having Elijah taken from her, but it still angered her if she thought about Trent. He'd thrown away the very thing Leslie had wanted desperately and had been denied. And yet, if he and Erica were still married, if the three of them were a traditional family, Erica and Siena wouldn't have been living here when she returned and she never would have met them. Even in the short time she'd known them, she had to admit they'd already touched her. *Had* she come home to be with them? If so, in what capacity?

She wondered if Erica had ever been with a woman for any length of time. She'd said she'd dated one since she'd been here, but Leslie hadn't let her elaborate or asked her any questions. Siena clearly had no experience of her own with having two moms, though.

Leslie couldn't let herself wonder about such things, or care. She had to keep her emotions about Erica and Siena, about Elijah, under control, and this whole conversation with Siena was threatening to unhinge her. "Hey, can you do me a favor?" she asked Siena. "Can you take both of those pictures upstairs and put them on my dresser?"

Siena scrambled to her feet and ran up the stairs without answering.

Leslie blew out a breath. *Erica will be feeling better soon. Then I can go back to getting my own life here established and let them get back to theirs. Distance.*

When Siena returned, Leslie was putting the new sheets into the dryer. "Are you ready for dinner?" she asked, setting the heat dial.

"Can we watch the stars come out first and say 'Star Light, Star Bright?' I want to make a wish."

"Sure," Leslie said with a chuckle. Maybe a wish would do her good as well, get her mind off Elijah and what she'd lost. Then it was time to get back to business. She needed to check in with Erica to see if she wanted to get Siena to her program the following morning or let her stay home again. She doubted Erica would be up to eating anything yet, but she should touch base with her on that, too. It could all wait a little while longer, though. A little girl wanted to make a wish, and what was more important than that?

❖

Erica heard voices. She couldn't decipher what they were saying—they were too far away—but she recognized the lilt of

Siena's that always made her smile, then the timbre of Leslie's. She opened her eyes and took stock of herself and her surroundings.

Gus was gone. The French doors leading onto her balcony were ajar, letting in a gentle breeze. She remembered opening them for fresh air on her way back from the bathroom earlier. After successfully keeping down a spoonful of ice chips every so often, she'd gotten delusions of grandeur and tried to drink an entire glass of water, only to have it come right back up a mere fifteen minutes later. The bright side was that she'd managed to make it to the bathroom on her own *and* she hadn't thrown it up in her bed. An improvement, albeit a marginal one. Then it'd been back to bed, as that little journey had wiped her out once more.

God, I feel so useless. She couldn't remember anything like this ever happening to her before. Sure, maybe as a kid, but not since becoming an adult, and certainly not since Siena had been born. She never would have been able to imagine turning Siena over to someone else because she was too weak, or too predisposed in the bathroom, to even get up and make breakfast. And to a virtual stranger no less. But thank God for that virtual stranger.

With a sigh, Erica kicked off her covers. She needed to use the restroom, although for the life of her, she couldn't figure out why. There couldn't be anything in her system. And she *had* to brush her teeth.

On her way back, she heard Siena's laughter and slowly covered the distance to the open French doors. When she stepped outside, the cool evening air felt so good on her bare legs. It brightened her mood and had a rejuvenating effect as it whispered across her face. She was met by the grayish blue of dusk. She'd slept the entire day away. She looked down into the backyard and saw Leslie, Siena, and Gus all lying on the grass, side by side, Siena and Leslie staring up at the sky.

"Look, there's one," Siena said, pointing into the encroaching darkness. "Star light, star bright..."

Erica smiled and wondered what Siena was wishing for. She lifted her face to the heavens to make her own. *Why not? Star light, star bright. First star I see tonight. Wish I may, wish I might, have the wish I wish tonight.* And that was it. That was all she could manage. She struggled to concoct an actual wish. She lowered herself onto the lounge chair. *I wish I could stand for more than three minutes at a time.* A simple one—a waste under normal circumstances—but right now, she'd give almost anything for it.

After a few minutes, the trio below rose and turned toward the house.

Leslie glanced up and met Erica's gaze. A broad grin lit her face.

Erica could only manage a two-finger wave, then she leaned back and closed her eyes. This was pathetic. It had to pass soon. How long could bad chicken maintain so much power? She wondered if Becky still felt as lousy as she did. She'd have to try to call her tomorrow.

A cold, wet nose poked into her palm.

She smiled. "Hey there, bed buddy," she said. "Where have you been?"

"You're up," Leslie said softly. "How're you feeling?"

Erica opened her eyes to find her standing in the doorway and Siena beside the chair. She grinned at the sight of Siena's outfit, recalling how proud Siena had been earlier when she'd announced to Erica that she'd dressed herself. *Indeed.* She'd made a mental note that she should suck up her parental ego and let Siena do that once in a while. "There isn't much different on this front. What have you guys been up to?"

"We unpacked," Siena said. "I helped."

"You did?" Erica chuckled as she ran her fingers through Gus's fur. "What did you unpack?"

"A bunch of movies that Leslie said we could watch. Some clothes. That was boring. And Buddhas." Siena's eyes flashed with the last word. "And they can live in jungles, so they'll be fine in the living room."

"Buddhas?" Erica wasn't sure she was following. The jungle threw her.

"Uh-huh. There's a fat one that's blue. What's his name again?" she asked Leslie.

"Hotei." Leslie stood leaning against the doorjamb, as patient as ever.

"Yeah, Hotei." Siena turned back to Erica. "And a green one with his eyes closed. And a lady, that some people think is a soft bow tie, but I want her to be a Buddha, like you."

"A soft bow tie?" Erica looked to Leslie for help.

"I think she means a bodhisattva. It's a statue of Quan Yin," Leslie said, a twinkle of amusement in her eyes. "How about if we let your mom come see them for herself when she's feeling better?" she asked Siena.

"That's a great idea," Erica said gratefully. She wasn't tracking much of this conversation. "Then you can tell me all about them."

"Okay." Siena sat cross-legged next to Gus and started petting his other side.

"We just came in to say hi and see if you were up to trying anything for dinner." Leslie's manner was relaxed, though she seemed a little tired. No wonder, with everything she'd handled today. "We have lime Jell-O on the menu for you. There's also broth and soda crackers, but those might be too much."

Erica's stomach flipped over on itself and saliva collected in her mouth. She swallowed. "I don't think I'm up to anything yet. I'll stick to ice chips. Did you two go to the store?" Of the items mentioned, she had only the crackers in her kitchen. She felt uneasy at the thought of Leslie taking Siena somewhere without her knowing.

"No," Leslie said quickly. She seemed to pick up on Erica's apprehension. "I called Nell. She brought some things by."

"She found a quarter in my ear," Siena said, a puzzled look on her face.

Erica laughed. "Maybe we should do a better job of cleaning your ears."

Siena wrinkled her nose. She hated having her ears cleaned. She said the Q-tips made her head squeak.

"Okay," Leslie said, humor in her voice. "Siena, will you run downstairs and fill a pot with water for me? Don't do anything else. I'll be right there."

"All right." Siena and Gus were on their way in a flash.

Leslie watched Erica. "You look exhausted still. Do you need some help getting back to bed?"

Erica looked out over her backyard, taking in the tiny lights in the trees and the pink glow of Leslie's pool light next door. It was so pretty. "I think I'll stay out here a while. It's nice." She looked at Leslie. "Will you all come back up after you eat?" She was getting a little lonely. "Maybe we could play some Go Fish? I think I can concentrate enough for that." She let her eyelids close, then opened them again.

"Sure," Leslie said. "Do you know what you want to do about tomorrow? If you want Siena to go to school or if it'd be better for her to stay home again?"

Erica drew in a deep breath. She hadn't considered tomorrow. "How bad was it this morning?" she asked. "All I remember hearing was one shriek, but that usually means there's more."

Leslie looked thoughtful, then lifted one shoulder. "I'd say it was somewhat worse than Sunday night with the Wendy's burgers but not nearly as bad as the night with the puzzle."

Erica nodded. She couldn't imagine she'd be able to drive by morning, but she couldn't monitor Siena all day either. Maybe she could get one of the sitters from the service who worked regularly with families in the support groups, although they might already be booked, depending on how many people ended up with food poisoning from the night before. Once again, she envied Becky having Jack.

"She can stay with me again," Leslie said, evidently utilizing her mind reading skills. "I don't mind."

Erica raised her gaze to Leslie's. Guilt mingled with gratitude. How could she take up another of Leslie's days when Leslie had so much to do? And yet... "I'm sorry. I don't really know what else to do. The caretakers we normally use—"

"I don't mind," Leslie said again, this time more firmly. "I enjoy Siena, and she's good free labor."

Erica laughed weakly. "I don't know how I'm ever going to thank you enough for this."

"Isn't this what neighbors do?" Leslie's dark eyes were warm in the glow of light spilling from the bedroom. She must have turned on the bedside lamp on her way through.

Erica curled her hair behind her ear and looked away. "What you've done, and what you're doing, far surpasses any good neighbor policy."

"I know that little hair-tuck, look-somewhere-else move you do means you don't want to talk about whatever the subject is, so I'll just say, don't worry about it." Without saying more, Leslie left the balcony. "I'm sure there will come a time when I need to borrow an egg or something," she called from inside. She returned with a blanket, then leaned down and covered Erica's legs.

Erica was stunned into silence, both by the gesture and by Leslie's acute observation. She'd known people for years who'd never picked up on that tell of hers—Trent at the top of the list. How could Leslie have even noticed it, let alone deciphered its meaning, in such a short period of time?

Leslie's fingers brushed the bare skin of the back of Erica's thigh as she tucked the blanket around her.

The touch sizzled, heating Erica's blood. The intensity almost burned her flesh. Then it was gone, leaving a crackle of energy like a flash of lightning.

"You could get chilled out here," Leslie said, her face close to Erica's.

Not with you here, in more ways than one. "Thank you," Erica whispered. Were those tears pricking her eyes?

"You're welcome." Leslie's cheeks looked flushed, but it was hard to tell in the dim light. She straightened, then cleared her throat. "Is it all right if we forgo Siena's bath tonight? She didn't do much to get dirty today, and I don't know how comfortable she'd be with me doing it."

"Of course," Erica said. She wanted to say thank you again, and again. And again. Thank you for the hugeness of everything Leslie was doing, for the thoughtfulness of considering Siena's feelings about the bath, for the blanket, for the making of Siena's meals, the call to her cousin to bring Jell-O and broth for Erica.

Her gratitude swelled into a tidal wave that threatened to bring on the tears full force. And then there was that touch—a single connection of flesh that set Erica on fire. Leslie hadn't seemed to notice. *Thank God.*

"We'll be back then, so get your Go Fish game on, Cooper," Leslie said with a teasing lilt. She turned at the door to the bedroom. "I have to warn you, though. *I am* the all-time reigning champion of Go Fish. And I won't take pity on you because you're sick."

Erica smiled, her competitive spirit igniting. "Thanks for the heads-up, *Raymond.*" She played along. "But even sick, I think I'm up for it. It will be a pleasure taking down the reigning champion."

Leslie chuckled. "Be back soon."

Erica watched her move through the bedroom and disappear into the darkened hallway. In some moments, she felt so close to her, and yet, there was so much she didn't know about Leslie. She had to keep in mind they'd simply been thrown into this incredibly intimate circumstance, and once it was over, it wouldn't mean a thing. If anything, it would speed up Leslie's retreat. Who would stick around after this kind of a beginning, even as a friend? This was the kind of situation you had to build up to. At least this time, the person running wouldn't be running because of Siena's needs and demands, or not completely anyway. For some reason, that made Erica feel better.

At a bare minimum, though, Erica owed Leslie an extremely nice thank you gift, then they could put all this behind them and settle into being much more traditional neighbors. She sighed and snuggled into the blanket. For now, she could rest and be thankful for Leslie Raymond, whoever she was.

Chapter Eight

Leslie lay on Erica's couch, staring at the ceiling of the family room. She couldn't assuage her awareness that Erica's bedroom was directly above her—that *Erica* was directly above her. *Yeah, and she's sick.* Even sick, though, something about her kept drawing Leslie closer. Not the previous morning when she was *sick* sick—no one was alluring when they were throwing up—but last night.

When Leslie had looked to the balcony and seen Erica was up and moving under her own strength, Leslie had been immensely relieved, illogically so, as though she'd come back from the brink of death. Then there was that inadvertent touch, that moment when Leslie's fingertips skated over the bare skin of Erica's thigh. It'd sent a jolt of...well, there was no denying it...of arousal, straight to Leslie's core. She'd known she was attracted to Erica...*But Christ.* Even now, at only the memory, she felt the unmistakable stirring in the pit of her stomach. And when Erica had risen to Leslie's playful challenge about the card game. As it turned out, their short bout of competitive posturing had been irrelevant because Siena had cleaned both their clocks, but still, the glimpse of that side of Erica had charmed Leslie.

Finally, there was the moment that was nearly Leslie's undoing, when she realized just how much trouble she could be in if she didn't start doing something differently, and quick. She'd just closed the book after the story Siena had requested and looked up to find Siena cuddled against Erica, Erica's cheek pressed to Siena's hair, and Gus stretched out across both their laps. All three appeared sound asleep. Leslie basked in the image, then startled when she realized Erica had opened her eyes at some point and was staring back at her. Something like contentment—or no, genuine happiness—shone in them.

Leslie flinched, then scrambled for something to say. "Do you want me to put her to bed?" she whispered.

"In a minute," Erica said, letting her eyelids close again. "I don't get many moments like this. I want to savor it."

When Leslie returned from tucking Siena in, she found Erica curled on her side, hugging a pillow, deep in sleep. A tiny smile shaped her lips. Leslie had wanted so badly to brush a lock of that silvery hair from Erica's cheek, but she hadn't dared touch her. She'd been afraid if she did, she wouldn't want to stop.

Leslie groaned and flipped onto her side.

Gus grunted and shifted his position at her feet.

It'd surprised her when he'd followed her downstairs the previous night and nestled into her blanket with her. He always seemed to know, though, who needed him most, and he must have sensed what a mess Leslie was following the day of playing house with Erica and Siena. Her emotions had snuck up on her. That was all. Today would be better. She'd be on guard. Then in a couple more days, Erica would be back on her feet, and Leslie would be able to focus on starting her brand new life instead of letting herself get sucked into this fantasy one.

Leslie heard the shuffling of footsteps on the stairs and glanced up.

Siena descended the steps, her hair tousled and her expression grumpy.

"How's the Go Fish champion this morning?" Leslie asked as she sat up and patted the cushion beside her.

Siena didn't answer, just crossed to the couch and flopped onto it. "I want breakfast."

Leslie scratched her head and yawned. She'd forgotten how instantaneous parent mode needed to be first thing in the morning.

She used to make a point of getting up a couple of hours before Elijah to ensure she had time to get fully awake as well as to get in a meditation, some yoga, and a shower. She might have thought to do that this morning had Erica wanted her to try getting Siena to her day program, but she'd gone to bed knowing today would be another casual one. "Do you want pancakes and blueberries again?"

"No. I want cookies." Siena stole a sidelong glance at Leslie.

Leslie smiled. "How about pancakes for breakfast, then we'll make cookies later."

"My mom let's me have cookies for breakfast," Siena said, folding her arms across her chest.

"I doubt that," Leslie said. She almost laughed at the idea.

"She does." Siena jumped up and spun around to face Leslie.

Surprised, Leslie held up her hands. "Easy, I didn't mean anything by it." She scooted to the edge of the sofa cushion. "Let's go make some pancakes. Then we can get some more stuff put away at my house, and that leaves the afternoon free for cookie baking."

"No!" Siena's voice rose shrilly. She stomped her foot. "I don't want pancakes!"

Leslie balked. She stared at Siena, tension tightening her muscles. Had she done it again—ignited one of Siena's meltdowns? This seemed different somehow. She watched Siena closely.

"I don't want pancakes! I don't want pancakes! I don't want pancakes!" Siena yelled.

Leslie searched her brain. *What to do.* She tried to remember. She knew not to touch her but couldn't come up with what *to* do. "Siena," she said calmly.

Siena glared at her. "I don't want them! You can't make me—"

"Siena Amelia Cooper, knock that off!" Erica's voice rang through the room. It held a hard edge Leslie hadn't heard in it before.

Siena froze.

Leslie looked up with a jerk to find Erica teetering at the top of the stairs.

Erica clung to the handrail.

Without thinking, Leslie raced up to her. She slid an arm around Erica's waist just as Erica sank to the floor. She sat down with her.

Erica leaned into her. "Whoa, I think I got up too fast. I'm dizzy." Leslie held her tightly. "Take a minute and breathe. Deep breaths."

Erica took in a gulp of air, then looked down the stairs. "Siena, you go back to bed, and set your alarm for a five-minute time-out. And when you come back, you'd better be ready to apologize to Leslie."

Siena's face crumpled, and she burst into tears as she ran past them.

Shaken by the entire scene, Leslie jumped at the slam of the bedroom door behind them. "I'm so sorry. I don't seem to be very good at this."

"At what?" Erica propped her elbows on her knees and held her head in her hands. "Telling a child that cookies aren't an appropriate breakfast food? I think you did fine."

"Yeah, but it caused a meltdown." Leslie listened but didn't hear any crying or yelling from Siena's room. In fact, she heard no sound at all.

Erica drew in another deep breath, then straightened. "That wasn't a meltdown. That was a good, old-fashioned temper tantrum aimed at manipulating you to give her what she wanted."

"Really?" Leslie blinked at her. Was that the difference she'd noticed? "How do you know?"

"There's a deliberateness to a tantrum," Erica said. "She's in control, even though it might not appear so at first glance. She'll look at you to check to see if she has your attention, whereas in a meltdown she's completely unaware of you. Her focus is inward. And during a tantrum, there's a specific goal. In this case, cookies for breakfast." She smiled at Leslie. "You did great."

Leslie frowned. "Only because you stepped in. I was about to try to handle it the other way. That was the first I've seen of that side of her." She chuckled, thinking back to Elijah's occasional tantrums. She knew it wasn't unusual behavior for any kid, or even adults at times, for that matter. "How did you know from all the way in your room?"

Erica laughed. "It's not *my* first time. And I was already out here. I got up because, as you now know, she doesn't always wake up in the best of moods. "

"Still, that's pretty impressive."

"Her voice has an entirely different sound to it," Erica said, returning to the question. "You'll learn it, if you stick around."

Leslie stilled. *If I stick around?* Did Erica know what she'd been thinking? How could she? Leslie wasn't sure what to say. She couldn't offer her any assurances.

Erica did her hair-tuck, look-away move and broke eye contact.

Leslie cleared her throat. "Can I help you back to bed?"

"No," Erica said with some force. "I'm sick of my room. I'd like to go downstairs."

"Sure." Leslie rose and held out her hand.

"I think I can make it," Erica said, gripping the handrail again and pulling herself to her feet.

Leslie nodded but stayed close all the way to the couch. "Can I get you anything?" she asked, once Erica was settled.

Erica looked up at her, her face pale. "I'd kill for a cup of coffee."

Leslie gave her a sympathetic smile. "It might be a little too soon for that, but there's still the delicious lime Jell-O from last night, if that sounds doable."

Erica paused, looking thoughtful. "Well," she said slowly, "my stomach didn't turn at the mention, so I guess I'll try it."

When Leslie returned from the kitchen, she handed Erica the gelatin, then casually dropped onto the love seat across from where Erica sat. She wanted to avoid any more accidental touches of bare skin. She'd noticed that Erica had slipped on a pair of lounge shorts beneath her T-shirt, but there was still a lot of leg showing. As challenging as it was not to look, it would be more difficult to be sitting right next to her.

Erica took a bite of Jell-O. "Mmmm. This actually tastes really good."

"How's it feel on your stomach?" Leslie watched Erica's lips close around a second spoonful, then the movement beneath the smooth skin of her throat as she swallowed. Her pulse quickened. She averted her gaze.

Erica waited. "It seems okay."

Leslie shifted in her seat, acutely aware that she and Erica were alone together. They usually had Siena as a buffer. Was that all that kept sparks from flying between them? Not them. Her. *I'm the only one acting like an idiot. She's just eating Jell-O.* It was Leslie that was having trouble controlling her attraction. Erica didn't even have one. *And what the hell am I doing looking at her like this? She's the last woman I should be thinking of that way.*

"My alarm went off. Can I come out?"

Siena's voice drew Leslie from her inappropriate thoughts to the top of the stairs where Siena stood.

"Are you ready to tell Leslie you're sorry for throwing a fit when all she was trying to do was make you breakfast?" Erica's tone indicated she was still in full-on Mom mode where Siena was concerned.

"Yes." Siena's manner was a bit sulky.

"All right then. You may come down." Erica leaned closer to Leslie. "Don't expect anything heartfelt," she whispered. "Apologies are pretty rote at this point, but we take what we can get."

Leslie nodded.

Siena plodded up to them and looked at Erica.

Erica lifted her eyebrow.

Siena turned to Leslie. "I'm sorry. I thought about it in my room, and I want pancakes now."

Leslie stifled a smile. "Apology accepted," she said with a dip of her head.

Gus whined from where he sat by the sliding glass door.

"Can I go outside and play?" Siena asked.

"Until breakfast is ready." Erica went back to her Jell-O, and the entire incident seemed to be over. "Thank you for letting us practice on you," she said to Leslie when they were alone again. Her demeanor was nonchalant. Clearly, the scenario wasn't anything new to her.

But how does she stay so calm? Leslie was growing increasingly in awe. She laughed quietly. "Happy to be of service." Before she had a chance to start feeling awkward being alone with Erica again, she stood. "Let me get those pancakes going before she changes her mind."

Breakfast, for the most part, went without incident, although the smell of the cooking made Erica queasy. Leslie helped her out to the patio and into the fresh air, but all the activity had drained Erica. She decided on a morning nap on the swing. The rest of the day had all the appearance of things reverting to normalcy. There were no further tantrums, no meltdowns, and no more vomiting. Things were looking up.

Leslie and Siena spent the morning as they'd planned, continuing to put things away in Leslie's house, then after lunch, they made the promised cookies, while Erica remained outside, texting with Becky. By dinner, Erica was ready to try some broth and even managed a few bites of a peanut butter cookie for dessert. As they settled in to watch *The Wizard of Oz*, one of Siena's favorite movies, Leslie found herself feeling far too at home once again. She'd kept her guard up throughout the day, but there was something about the evening that lulled her into complacency. She caught herself glancing at Erica occasionally, amused by how riveted to the movie she was, as though it was her first time seeing it. She was curled up on the opposite end of the couch snuggled into the pillow Leslie would be using again later that night, the blanket covering her legs. Siena sat between them with Gus's head on her lap.

What was this world Leslie had stumbled into, where this ready-made family seemed to have been waiting for her? She remembered Siena's words about how she thought Leslie had come there to be with them. She'd said it so matter-of-factly. For all intents and purposes, at least so far, that seemed to be the case. When Leslie glanced at Erica again, she found Erica watching her.

As their eyes met, Erica smiled, then returned her attention to the TV.

An unwanted tenderness moved through Leslie. How had she let this happen? And what did she do about it now that she had? One voice in her head screamed, *Get the hell out of here as fast as you can, and stay as far away as possible.* Another one, a softer and somehow more certain one, said, *This is where you belong.* That couldn't be right, though. *This* was where she'd been. Not here exactly, but close enough to be a parallel universe—and look what that had gotten her. That softer voice persisted, luring her in. It felt so good here. But she also heard the stir of echoes from the past loud and clear, as though each and every fragment of her heart that had been so broken at the loss of Elijah was keening a resounding *no*.

But Leslie, Siena, and Erica didn't have to be a family. Couldn't they all be friends, next-door neighbors that spent time together as her parents had with several of the families that had lived in this very house over the years? How could she deal with that, though, with as strongly as she was beginning to feel in such a short period of time? Wasn't it only going to get worse?

She sneaked another peek at Erica. Maybe if she simply talked to her, explained her past with Elijah and Cassie, her fear of it happening again, how much she adored spending time with Siena. Maybe she could even tell Erica about her attraction to her. That, in and of itself, would no doubt put an end to it. She'd tell Erica. Erica would let her down gently. Then Leslie could get over it. And everything else would be out on the table and maybe they could work something out that would allow all of them to be friends without the risk seeming so high. *Or is that a crazy amount of pressure to put on someone I've just met?*

But Erica seemed to want to be friends, too. This wouldn't be a one-sided thing. Erica had implied that she missed adult company. Her life seemed somewhat isolated, which was probably not too uncommon for single parents of autistic children. It was clearly important to keep a certain routine in Siena's life, to keep it quiet. Weren't those the very reasons Erica had given for her move from Chicago? In doing so, though, how much did that limit Erica? Having a close friend right next door might be the very thing that could help her as well. Maybe Leslie could talk to her about it later.

By the time the movie ended, Erica had drifted off to sleep. Leslie got Siena into bed, then read a book Siena picked out about how friends say they're sorry when they're unkind to one another. She wondered if this was her real apology. The thought brought her an inner smile. When she'd finished, she switched off the light and left Gus to keep an eye on her. Downstairs again, she leaned over Erica. "Hey," she whispered, not wanting to startle her.

Erica didn't make a sound or even flutter an eyelid.

"Erica." Leslie tried again.

Still no response.

Tentatively, she touched Erica's shoulder, feeling the warmth of her body through the fabric of her shirt. She gave her a gentle shake.

"Hmmm." Erica shifted onto her back.

Leslie's fingertips grazed the soft skin of her throat. The same jolt of desire from the previous night, shot through her. This time, she let herself feel it. It'd been a long time since she'd reacted this way to a woman. She brushed a few strands of hair from Erica's forehead. They were silky.

Erica slowly opened her eyes. She blinked, confusion in her expression. "Did I fall asleep *again*?"

Leslie smiled. "You need rest."

Erica sat up and scanned the room. "Where's Siena?"

"In bed asleep, like you should be." Leslie straightened. She'd like to have the conversation she was considering earlier— get it over with—but there wasn't much point in trying it tonight. "Come on," she said. "Let's get you there, too."

When she came back down, she dropped onto the couch and stuffed the pillow behind her head. Frustrated, she stared up at the ceiling, ending her day exactly as she'd begun it. To punctuate this realization, Gus jumped onto the sofa and snuggled down beside her.

She couldn't do this, and no amount of conversation with Erica would change that. In truth, Erica was the last person she should talk to about everything she was feeling. She turned over and punched the pillow to fluff it up. A faint puff of vanilla drifted up from it. Erica's shampoo.

Great! That's just what I need. She smooshed the pillow into a wad and hurled it across the room. *This will be over soon. Erica's getting her strength back. It has to be over soon.*

Chapter Nine

E rica waited for her garage door to open, then pulled inside. She'd noticed Leslie's car in its driveway—she always noticed if it was there—which meant by the time they got inside, Gus would be waiting for Siena on the patio.

As soon as they came to a stop, Siena wrestled out of her seat belt and yanked on the door handle. She'd noticed Leslie's car, as *she* always did, as well.

"Change out of your school clothes before you and Gus get playing," Erica called as Siena raced into the house, then she gathered her purse and briefcase and followed.

It was the third day of school for her with her new courses at the city college and for Siena in her second grade class. Both of them were adjusting, Erica to being back to a full-time work schedule, since her summer session was lighter, and Siena to a new teacher, classroom, and group of kids to navigate. She knew it wouldn't take long, though, for them to establish a routine and settle in.

As Erica passed Siena's bedroom doorway, Gus barked at her from the foot of the bed, his stump wagging frantically.

Erica laughed. "Yes, I see you." She crossed to him and leaned down to pet him. She even let him bury his nose in her hair and lick her ear wildly. She wasn't fond of the greeting—she thought it more something for him and Siena, or even him and Leslie to share—but it made him so happy, she allowed it occasionally.

"All right, I'm glad to see you, too," she said after a moment. She pressed her hands around his trembling body and calmed him. "That's enough." She kissed the top of his head. At least they still got to see him.

Leslie, on the other hand, had been MIA for the past week and a half. She'd only waved a few times from her car when they'd seen her leaving and the several attempts Siena had made to see her were met with a nice but definite, "I'm sorry, honey, but I have a lot of work to do." Erica supposed that could be true, but even her invitations to dinner, something she thought might be welcomed by someone too swamped to make something to eat, had been politely rebuffed. And it'd all been since the Sunday morning Erica had gotten her strength back following her bout of food poisoning. Erica had hoped she could find a way to talk with Leslie about it, but so far, there hadn't been an opening.

Erica turned in the opposite direction from the thundering of Siena's and Gus's footsteps on the stairs and headed to her room to change clothes. As she pulled a V-neck shell over her head, her phone rang.

"Hey, girlfriend," Becky said in her customary upbeat tone. "Just called to see how your first week's going."

"Pretty good, actually. I have a few hotshot students in my classes this semester, which always makes things more interesting, and Siena hasn't had too many complaints about her new class, which is usually a sign that everything's going okay. She's still working with Mrs. Dixon for reading comprehension and, of course, social skills with Jeff. I think that consistency with last year helps a lot." Erica lay across her bed and drew up her knee. "How about you?"

"Brandon made it all the way to his second day of kindergarten before losing his morning recess for the rest of the week, Rosi is still on her paper shredding kick and shredded her school lunch card, and Jack wants to buy a ski boat, for some reason I can't comprehend. He can't even swim."

Erica laughed at Becky's ability to roll with the complexities of her life. Erica had enough difficulty dealing with only herself and Siena. She didn't think she could handle a partner and two additional children. Becky hadn't mentioned her older son's antics, but he was always up to something.

"Have you heard from cabana goddess yet?" Becky asked, abruptly changing the subject. She'd referred to Leslie as cabana goddess ever since Erica had told her about the exchange they'd had.

Erica suspected this was the real reason she'd called. "No, and I may not. She seems to be done with us. Three days of taking care of a sick woman and a child with autism would be a lot for most people."

"That doesn't make any sense. Jack said she seemed perfectly fine with it all," Becky said.

"He saw her at the very beginning of day one." Erica had thought a lot about this. What else could it be? "It's not particularly unexpected."

"Maybe if you stopped *expecting* your life to be too much for people, it wouldn't be."

Erica could tell the words came out of Becky's mouth without her giving a thought to them. "What's that supposed to mean?"

"Just because Siena's ASD was too much for Trent, doesn't mean it will be for everyone. That's all." Becky's tone had softened, as though she'd realized her statement might sting.

Erica rolled onto her side and gazed out the window. "I've dated three people since Trent and I split up, and none of them stuck around once they witnessed a true-blue meltdown."

Becky scoffed. "Okay, but you didn't really like the two you dated here. Kathleen notwithstanding, since you didn't actually *date* her. You and she just—"

"I liked them," Erica said defensively, sidestepping the entire topic of Kathleen Duvall. "I wouldn't have gone out with them if I hadn't."

"But you didn't like them the way you'd need to like someone in order to want them to stick around. You weren't even all that upset when they broke things off, other than the meaning you assigned to it." Becky was slightly breathless, obviously doing something else while they talked. She rarely sat still. "And I didn't know the guy in Chicago, but from what you've said, he sounded like he was a transitional thing. And good sex."

Becky's memory and bluntness irritated Erica sometimes, but she couldn't deny anything Becky was saying.

"You like this woman," Becky said after a pause. "And she did keep coming around after she'd seen a meltdown and even paid attention to how to handle one. If you like her, which I know you do, don't let her just slip away without trying to find out what might really be going on."

Erica sighed. "Maybe." It was the best she could offer.

"Okay, good. That's better than nothing," Becky said lightly. "So have you heard from Dickwad?" Another sharp turn in the conversation.

Erica burst out laughing. Dickwad was Becky's endearment for Trent—not to his face, of course. "He called a few days ago," Erica said, thankful to be off the topic of Leslie. "He said he wants to come for another visit in a few weeks."

"So soon?" Becky's surprise was evident. "That's strange."

"Hmm." Erica recalled his previous stay. "There was something bothering him last time he was here, like he wanted to talk about something but never did. He sounded a little like that on the phone, too. Maybe he's coming back for that."

"What do you think it is?" Becky asked.

"I have no idea. My aptitude for reading his mind vanished years ago." Erica had never been all that in tune with Trent, but she'd never needed to be. They'd always had their separate lives in many ways. She envied Becky's and Jack's ability to finish each other's sentences, to know exactly what the other was thinking—ski boats aside. Maybe she just romanticized it, but still, it would be nice.

Becky gasped. "Maybe he wants you back." The words came out as a croon.

Erica rolled her eyes. "Please." She sat up. "I'm hanging up now. I have to make dinner."

Becky giggled. "Hey, want to do lunch or a movie this weekend? Maybe Sunday?"

"Let me see if there's a sitter available that Siena likes," Erica said. "I'll get back to you."

Over fried chicken and mashed potatoes, Erica listened as Siena chattered for more than twenty minutes about the special game of ball she and Gus had made up in the backyard. She was always so happy playing with him. It was as though he was endowed with some kind of super power to brighten anyone's mood.

"What about school?" Erica asked, when Siena came to the end of her story. "How was your day there?"

"It was okay," Siena said, the light in her eyes dimming. She looked down at her plate. "I wish Kiley was still there."

Kiley was a little girl who'd been in Siena's class the previous year and had been a good friend to Siena. She'd sat by her at lunch, played with her at recess, and helped her with class work if Siena needed it. For her contribution to the friendship, Siena had helped Kiley with math. She was a whiz with numbers. Kiley had even stood up for Siena against a boy that made fun of Siena, a student that Erica had difficulty not thinking of as a horrid little child. Erica had thought more than once that Kiley was a chivalrous butch in the making. She'd been almost as sad as Siena when they'd learned Kiley's family was moving to Oregon over the summer. "I know, sweetie. I'm sorry."

"Tim Davis calls me weird," Siena said. Her shoulders slumped ever so slightly.

Erica tightened her jaw. *And speaking of the little devil.* "Tim Davis is a bully." She had trouble holding her temper when this subject came up, but it was more important to try to help Siena understand that people's reactions to her were about them, not her. "He's one of those people who can only feel good about himself by making someone else feel bad."

Siena frowned. "Is that why Leslie doesn't come over anymore?" Her tone was more curious than anything else, as though she'd been pondering the question for a while. "Because I'm weird?"

Erica was stunned. Of all the directions this conversation might have taken, she hadn't seen this one coming. "What?"

"She doesn't want to play, or have dinner with us, or spend the night anymore. Is it because of me?"

Erica was speechless.

Siena stared at her food. "Because I'm not like her little boy? Because I'm weird?"

Little boy? Erica struggled to find her voice. She had to clear her throat. "Leslie has a little boy?"

"Uh-huh." Siena didn't look up. "His name is Elijah. He lives with his other mom."

A little boy. Why had Leslie lied about not having children? And where was he? Back in Florida? Erica remembered Leslie's judgment of Trent the night she'd learned of Erica and Siena's move to California. Had her reaction been out of guilt? Questions flooded her mind, but now wasn't the time to ask anything more. This conversation was about Siena. "You're not weird, sweetie. That was a mean thing for him to say. And Leslie certainly doesn't think you're weird."

"But I'm different than other kids." Siena poked at her food, her head bowed slightly.

"Yes, sweetie. You are different in some ways than other kids," Erica said, not wanting to diminish Siena's observation while also attempting to point out some additional truths. "But you're also very much like a lot of other kids."

"How?" Siena asked, twirling her fork.

"You like to color," Erica said thoughtfully. "Don't most of the kids in your class like to color?"

Siena tilted her head. "Yes," she said finally.

"And don't a lot of the kids at school like and talk about some of the same movies you like?" Erica watched Siena closely, seeing the small changes in her expression and posture as they spoke.

Siena nodded.

"And what about pizza day in the cafeteria? I'll bet you're not the only one who loves that." Erica let a note of teasing into her voice and was rewarded with the tiniest quirk of the corners of Siena's mouth.

Siena lifted her gaze to Erica's. "But what if Leslie's little boy doesn't like those things, so she thinks I'm weird, and that's why she doesn't want to be my friend anymore?"

A spark of anger flickered to life in Erica's chest. How dare Leslie do this—waltz into their life with her smile and her easy manner and her kindness and her dog and make Siena so happy, then vanish on her, leaving her thinking it was *her* fault. In reality, it was probably Erica's. She was the one who'd gotten sick and asked too much of Leslie. She wouldn't try to explain that to Siena, though. Siena needed something different. "Leslie certainly doesn't think you're weird. In fact, she told me what she does think of you."

"She did? What?" Siena asked eagerly.

Erica smiled, keeping her anger to herself. "She told me she thinks you're smart and amazing and enchanting."

Siena sat up taller, her eyes widening. "And that morning when you were throwing up and I got dressed all by myself...she said I was beautiful."

"Well, there you are." Erica stroked Sienna's hair. "It isn't likely that someone who thinks you're beautiful, smart, amazing, and enchanting is going to think you're weird and not want to be your friend."

Siena cocked her head. "What's enchanting?"

"Why don't you ask Leslie the next time you see her," Erica said. *And there will be a next time.* She'd make sure of that. She wasn't putting up with this. It was bad enough Siena had to deal with being teased and ostracized sometimes at school and that her own father wanted little or nothing to do with her, but now someone she'd actually been forming a connection with? *No, this isn't going to happen.* If Leslie had a problem with Erica, fine. Erica wouldn't need to be a part of it. *And I certainly won't ask anything of her for myself.* But Siena *wasn't* going to be hurt by all of this.

They finished with dinner, then played a game of Aggravation, fitting for Erica's mood. The more she thought about Leslie's disappearing act and what it'd caused Siena to think, the angrier she got. By the time she closed the book after a bedtime story and adjusted the covers around Siena's sleeping form, she was ready for battle. She glanced at Gus. "Are you coming?" she whispered.

He buried his face in Siena's pillow.

"Smart boy." She felt better leaving him with Siena anyway. She snatched the nursery monitor from the shelf by the door and switched it on as she stalked toward the stairs.

She banged on Leslie's back door—once, then again.

Before she could raise her fist for a third, harder pounding, Leslie appeared in the arched doorway between the family and living rooms. She looked confused, then quickened her pace when she saw Erica. She yanked open the French doors. "What's the matter? Is Siena okay?"

"I want to talk to you," Erica said, pushing past her.

"All right," Leslie said slowly. "But is Siena—"

"Siena's fine." Erica whirled around to face her. "I mean, yes, she's okay, but she's…"

Leslie closed the door, clearly waiting for Erica to finish.

"She doesn't understand why you stopped coming over or letting her come see you," Erica said, trying to keep calm, but she kept hearing Siena's question. *Is that why Leslie doesn't come over anymore, because I'm weird?* "She's sad, and she's hurt."

Leslie sighed and ran her hands over her face.

For the first time, Erica noticed her tousled hair and the dark circles under her eyes. Her white cargo shorts and tank were rumpled. Had she been asleep? It was only eight fifteen. Erica wanted to ask if she was okay, but she couldn't let herself get distracted. This was about Siena.

Without a word, Leslie walked past her and into the kitchen.

Erica followed. "Where have you been? I mean, I know you've been home because we see your car. And Gus comes over."

Leslie turned on the faucet at the sink and cupped her hands beneath the flow. She splashed water onto her face.

"Look," Erica said, wanting to get all the words out before she lost her momentum, "if I did something to make you mad or upset or if I took advantage when you offered to help when I was sick…Maybe being in our life the way you were those first couple of weeks was too much for you. If so, that's fine. Things can be, and will be, different. I really never get sick, and if I do again, I won't ask—"

"You think I stopped coming around because you needed some help?" Leslie's tone was brittle. She turned off the water and grabbed a towel.

Her sudden response startled Erica. "I don't know. It could be."

Leslie scoffed as she dried her face. "You obviously don't think much of me."

Erica hesitated. "Well, what happened then?" She searched her mind. "If there's something about me being bi, or single, or hell, just being next door, you don't have to have anything to do with me." Her temper rose. "But I'll be dammed if I'll let you hurt Siena like this. You're the one that started it all with that dry spot and your adorable little dog and your blue couch. *You* won Siena's heart with your wishes on stars and your Winnie the Pooh voice. You can damn well step up now and follow through on the friendship you started, at least with Siena."

Leslie planted her hands on the edge of the counter and stared out the window, shaking her head.

"Whatever it is," Erica went on, "please, don't bail on Siena. She formed an attachment with you, a connection. Do you know how rare—?" Her voice broke. "No, of course you don't. But she hardly ever does that with anyone."

Leslie said nothing, still only staring out into her backyard.

Erica's temper flared hotter at Leslie's silence. *What's wrong with her?* "Do you know what she asked me?" She waited for an answer, or even the smallest spark of interest. When none came, she tightened her jaw. "She asked me if the reason you don't come over anymore is that you think she's weird, like the kids at school do."

Leslie squeezed her eyes shut.

At least it was something. "She wanted to know if you don't want to have dinner with us or come over and play games anymore because she's weird, because she's not like your little boy."

Leslie went rigid, as though an electrical current shot through her.

"The little boy you don't even admit—"

"Stop!" Leslie spun to face her. "Stop, right there." She looked stricken. "You've made your point." Her voice was icy. "Are you finished?"

Erica stilled. She'd gone too far—but even if she hadn't been finished, the anguish in Leslie's eyes would have silenced her as effectively as an off switch. "Yes," she said softly. "I'm sorry if I crossed—"

"Okay, then." Leslie clamped her arms around her middle. "I'd like you to go."

Erica studied her, regret swelling in her. She shouldn't have brought up Elijah. Why had she? She knew how vulnerable children made their parents. She knew the answer, though. *She* was there to protect *her* child. She'd lost sight of everything else, and in doing so, she'd hurt Leslie deeply. "Leslie, I'm—"

"Please go," Leslie said, her voice trembling. Tears shone in her beautiful brown eyes.

Erica had noticed at some point that they were almost the same shade as Siena's. The pain in them now hit her almost as hard as when Siena's hurt showed in hers. Yet this was worse in some ways, because Erica knew she'd been the one to cause this pain. She had to fix it, but not now. Leslie obviously needed some time. Erica simply nodded, then turned and left.

On her way back across the yards, she wondered if she could have possibly screwed that up any worse. She never should have violated Leslie's boundaries by bringing up Elijah. It wasn't her business. Whatever Leslie had shared about him with Siena was between the two of them. And now, Erica would have to start all over again with a brand new conversation about Leslie remaining in Siena's life again.

If she'll ever talk to me.

Chapter Ten

Leslie sat at her computer desk where she'd positioned it in front of her living room window and watched Erica's car pass by her house. It'd been two days since Erica's visit Wednesday evening. When Erica had left, Leslie had spent the rest of the night feeling sorry for herself, then finally cried herself to sleep at about four in the morning. When she awakened Thursday, it hit her what an ass she'd been. She'd been so thoughtless and selfish when she'd made her decision to pull back, to create the distance she thought her heart needed from everything she'd found next door. She hadn't been thinking at all. She'd just been running.

Her plan hadn't worked, though. For the entire week and a half she'd forced herself to stay away from Siena and Erica, she'd been a wreck. She'd had difficulty sleeping and eating. When they weren't home, she'd spent most of her time wondering where they were or what they were doing, and when they were, she'd had to force herself to stay in her own house, and sometimes even leave, to keep from throwing her whole plan out the window. And all of it hurt like hell. When she'd first seen Erica through the French doors on her deck, Leslie's breath had caught. It seemed like so long since she'd seen her up close. She'd wanted so badly to take her in her arms and kiss her. It'd surprised her. But then the look on Erica's face had registered, and the only thought in Leslie's head had been, *is Siena okay?* Everything combined, she'd been in no shape to face Erica's wrath, but she'd had no choice.

And *wrath* it'd been. Erica had come at her like a lioness protecting her cub, and Leslie knew from the moment Erica pushed past her that she deserved whatever was coming. She'd barely had time to steel herself before it hit. She'd been about to try to apologize when Erica had brought up Elijah and Leslie lost her ability to speak. Then it felt as though Erica had thrown him in her face when she'd said, *A little boy you won't even admit...* Leslie had cut her off, but she knew the next words—won't even admit to having. And Erica was right. Leslie had denied him, denied ever having him, ever loving him. And now she was trying to do the same thing—albeit differently, but still—with Siena. She deserved Erica's anger, but more than that, she understood it. When someone hurt your child, all bets were off.

On top of that, it'd broken Leslie's heart to hear Siena thought Leslie was staying away because she thought Siena was weird. What had she been thinking? Kids internalized everything. She couldn't simply vanish from Siena's daily life after the way they'd connected without there being a price to pay—for both of them, but Siena's would be higher because she didn't understand. If Leslie truly hadn't wanted another child in her life and in her heart, she should have walked away that first day. She had to make all this up to Siena, and to Erica.

She'd spent all day Thursday pondering what she'd done, beating herself up, and working on a surprise for Siena. She'd planned to make her apologies that evening and try to set things right, but Erica and Siena hadn't come home until well after Siena's bedtime. Leslie hadn't wanted to try to fit her apologies into the rushed routine before they left for school this morning, so she'd made herself wait. Ultimately, it'd given her the extra time she'd needed to finish the surprise, to make everything perfect. Now, here they were, pulling into their garage, and it was time.

Gus leapt off the new couch from where he'd been watching out the front window as well and ran to the French doors.

Leslie followed and let him out. The first few days of her self-imposed exile, he'd waited, even come back for her a couple of times before leaving her behind. By now, though, he only gave her a glance, then raced outside and through the gate. Today, Leslie would hang back long enough to give Erica and Siena time to get settled into being home. She also wanted to get over there quickly enough, though, so Erica didn't start making dinner. She went into her kitchen and stirred the pot of spaghetti sauce simmering on the stove. She had a lot of making up to do.

When she stepped up to Erica's open patio door, she saw Erica standing inside next to the entertainment center going through the mail. Leslie froze. Her body responded as strongly as it had that first day to Erica's beauty, her stature, her demeanor.

Erica was turned away, an ash colored pencil skirt hugging the curve of her hips, the tasteful slit at the hem revealing just enough thigh to catch the eye. She wore a burgundy silk blouse with loose cut, cuffed sleeves, the silvery gray of the French braid that fell between her shoulder blades elegant against the rich color of the fabric.

Leslie swallowed hard. There was also that—confessing everything about Elijah and Cassie as well as her attraction to Erica. She should have done it two weeks earlier. That way, Erica would at least understand why she went all wonky. Now, though, Siena came first. Leslie knocked on the doorframe.

Erica's back and shoulders stiffened slightly. Of course she knew who it was. No one but Leslie came to the back door.

She turned and met Leslie's eyes. Wariness and hope warred in her expression.

"Hi," Leslie said through the screen, her voice cracking. She cleared her throat. "Can I come in?"

Erica glanced up the stairs, then back at Leslie. "It depends on why you're here," she said quietly. Her tone wasn't angry, or harsh, or even judgmental. It was neutral. "If you're just here for Gus, I'll send him home. I don't want Siena seeing you, unless you're going to come back into her life. I don't want to get her hopes up."

Leslie lowered her gaze, ashamed. She hated being someone Erica needed to protect Siena from. "Actually, I came to see Siena, if that's okay." She looked at Erica again, searching her face. "I'd like to apologize and see if we can start over."

Erica's manner softened, and her expression went tender. "Thank you." Before Leslie could answer, Erica turned toward the stairs. "Siena," she called, "will you come down, please? You have company."

"I don't want to see Rosi." Siena's voice drifted down.

Erica gave Leslie an amused look. "Please, come in." She walked to the bottom of the steps and set the mail on the newel post. "It isn't Rosi," she called to Siena again. "I promise." There was a smile in her voice.

In seconds, Siena and Gus were halfway down the stairs. Gus started barking and yipping and ran to Leslie, as though he were the one who hadn't seen her in over a week, but Siena slowed to almost a glacial pace. She stared at Leslie.

"Hi, Siena," Leslie said. "I was wondering if I could talk to you for a few minutes."

Siena said nothing. She watched Gus run back and forth between them.

"Would that be okay with you, Siena?" Erica asked.

Siena cast her a glance, then nodded. She continued down into the family room and stopped in front of Leslie. She gazed at her expectantly.

Leslie took a deep breath and knelt. "Siena," she said carefully. She bit her lower lip. She was aware of Erica watching them and Siena's reticence, so different from her usual talkative nature. Even Gus seemed to be waiting to see what Leslie had to say for herself as he planted himself on his haunches beside Siena. "Siena," she said again. "I…I owe you an apology. I haven't been a very good friend to you by not coming over anymore and not spending time with you. I'm sorry."

Siena's focus shifted to Gus, then out the window, then to the picture on the wall—anywhere but on Leslie. "Did you go away because I'm—"

"No," Leslie said quickly, unable to bear hearing the word come from Siena. "It wasn't because of you in any way. I promise."

"Why did you then?"

The innocence in Siena's tone tore at Leslie's heart. She hadn't considered she'd have to go into the details. She squeezed her eyes shut.

"Siena." Erica's voice snapped Leslie back. "I don't think—"

"It's okay," Leslie said, holding up her hand. "Friends deserve an explanation."

Siena finally met her gaze. She waited.

Leslie took a moment to gather her thoughts. *How does one explain heartbreak to a child?* But Siena wasn't just any child. "Remember we talked about my little boy, Elijah?" Leslie began. "And how he lives with his other mom?"

Siena nodded solemnly.

"Well, that..." Was she really going to do this? "Him going somewhere to live with his other mom...wasn't my idea." Leslie's throat threatened to close, but she pushed on. "His other mom didn't ask me, or him, what we wanted. And I don't get to see him, or even know where he is. And it hurt me..." Tears welled in Leslie's eyes. She fought them back. "It hurts me very much in here." She pressed her fist to her chest. "In my heart. And when I met you and realized how much I like you and enjoy spending time with you, and started feeling you in my heart, I got scared. I was afraid if someone took you away, I'd feel all that hurt again, if I couldn't see you anymore. I thought it would hurt less if I stayed away from you on my own. I was wrong. And it was wrong of me to make you think it was your fault. I'm sorry." A tear started to roll down her cheek, and she quickly wiped it away.

Siena tilted her head curiously. She went around the coffee table and opened a drawer. She took out a card and studied it, then looked back at Leslie. She showed it to Erica. "Is Leslie sad?"

Erica's eyes glistened as well. "Yes, sweetie."

Siena returned to Leslie and held out the card. It was a picture of a girl, crying, with the word *sad* printed at the bottom. "When I see someone who looks like this, I'm supposed to do this." She patted Leslie's shoulder. "Jeff says it'll make you feel better."

Fresh tears filled Leslie's eyes, but these were of love. "Thank you, Siena. It does make me feel better. Very much."

Siena stepped away. "Will you eat dinner with us, like you did before?"

And all seemed forgiven. Leslie swallowed the lump in her throat at the same instant she heard Erica choke back the combination of a small sob and a soft chuckle. She swiped away the moisture on her cheeks. "I was hoping you and your mom would join me for dinner at my house for a change. I made spaghetti, and I got Wonder Woman Golden Lasso ice cream for dessert."

Siena's lips rounded into an o.

"*And* I have a special surprise for you." Leslie knew she'd gone a little overboard, but she had a lot to make up for.

"What kind of surprise?" Siena bounced on her toes.

Leslie grinned. "One you're going to like a lot."

Excitement sparked in Siena's eyes. She turned to Erica. "Can we? Can we go over to Leslie's?"

Erica gave Leslie a tender smile. "Yes, we can." She returned her attention to Siena. "Let me get changed."

Ten minutes later, as they approached Leslie's back door, she stopped them. "Okay, you both have to close your eyes before we go inside."

Siena immediately complied.

Erica arched an eyebrow. "Really? Me, too? I thought this was a surprise for Siena."

"I want you to see it all at once," Leslie said, moving in front of them to block their view. "Trust me. It will be better that way." She could barely contain her own anticipation.

Erica sent her a teasing smirk, then obeyed.

Leslie reached for both of them, then caught herself. "Siena, I need to touch you in order to guide you. Is that okay?"

Siena nodded eagerly. "Hurry. My eyes don't want to stay shut."

Leslie chuckled and took each of them by the hand and led them through the doorway of her living room. She positioned herself where she could see both of their faces. "All right. Open."

They did and gasped in unison. Identical wide smiles spread across their lips, and amazement shone in both brown and blue eyes as they took in numerous vines strung across the ceiling and down the walls; the artificial tree, the leaves of which created a canopy over Leslie's workspace in the corner; and the large, fuzzy green snake that twisted around the lowest branch, its head dangling just above the desk chair.

Siena squealed. "It's a jungle!" She jumped up and down. "You made the jungle!"

Erica was laughing.

"Look, Mommy!" Siena ran across the room and up the steps of the front staircase. "It's Bagheera." She hugged the stuffed black panther from *The Jungle Book* that Leslie had attached to the banister at the landing. "And Baloo!" She pointed at the bear in the far corner, then broke into song with "The Bare Necessities." She twirled back to where Erica still stood just inside the doorway. She grabbed her hands, and they began to dance.

Leslie watched, pure joy filling her heart. The two moved in sync. It was obviously something they'd done many times.

At the end of the second verse, Siena spun away and turned circles in the center of the room, her arms outstretched. "I love our jungle!"

"What do you say to Leslie?" Erica asked, still laughing.

"Thank you, thank you, thank you!" Siena ran to Leslie.

Without thinking, Leslie bent to scoop her up. It wasn't until Siena had already launched herself into Leslie's arms and was hugging her tightly around the neck that Leslie remembered Siena's aversion to being touched. Apprehension seized her, but then she understood. If Siena initiated it, it must be okay. She squeezed Siena in a gentle embrace, then straightened, lifting her off the floor.

Siena wrapped her legs around Leslie's waist.

It felt so good to hold her, Leslie almost cried again.

"I want to touch Kaa," Siena said, reaching toward the snake.

Leslie moved to the corner and smiled as Siena petted his head. "Hello, Sssssiena," she said in her Kaa voice.

Siena giggled. "Is that Shere Khan?" she asked, looking at the tiger print couch.

"Yes," Leslie said, standing her beside Gus on the cushion, where he'd been watching the entire show. "I wasn't sure we wanted a mean tiger in our jungle, so I thought he'd be better as furniture."

Siena dropped onto her butt and bounced a few times. "I like him as a couch. He's not so scary."

"That was exactly my thought," Leslie said with a laugh. She glanced at Erica.

Warmth shone in Erica's eyes, and something else, something Leslie couldn't quite name. "This is going to take some explaining when you bring a date home," Erica said in a teasing tone.

Leslie couldn't hold back a short burst of a laugh. "All my numerous dates will just have to understand."

Erica chuckled.

"And, Mommy, look at the Buddhas." Siena rushed to the credenza near the front door. "See, the Buddhas *can* live in a jungle."

Erica followed to where Siena was rubbing Hotei's big, round belly. "And if you do this when you come in, you'll get good luck."

Erica ran her fingertips over the blue stone, then studied the other two statues. "These are beautiful."

"Thank you." Leslie walked up behind her. "I've had them a long time. They go wherever I go." The fact that this was the first time Erica had seen them reminded her of the number of days she'd stayed away, which reminded her of what a shmuck she'd been, which in turn threatened to make her feel guilty all over again.

Erica was watching Leslie over her shoulder. That unidentifiable look remained in her eyes. She'd changed into a royal blue, sleeveless shell and a pair of faded jeans, but her hair was still woven into its intricate braid. She smelled of something light and floral.

Leslie wanted to breathe her in, to release her hair and run her fingers through it, to caress the creamy white skin of her upper arms. And all of *that* reminded her of the talk she still needed to have with Erica. And it needed to be soon. For now, though, she only wanted to enjoy the evening. "Who's hungry?"

Chapter Eleven

Erica marveled at how delicious and fun dinner was. Siena hadn't wanted to leave her new jungle, so they'd eaten mouth-watering spaghetti, a beautiful salad, yummy garlic bread, and Wonder Woman ice cream at a folding table in the living room. Was Leslie truly a fabulous cook, or was it simply so wonderful to have someone else make dinner on a Friday following a hectic week? Or maybe it was eating in the middle of *The Jungle Book* that made it feel so special.

Siena was back to her usual chatty self—with the added delight she tended to express around Leslie—and Erica was relieved. She hoped things were back to normal. Something still wasn't quite right with Leslie, though. Erica could sense it in the occasional furtive glance Leslie shot her way.

Maybe she'd been right. It was possible Leslie's withdrawal could have something to do with Erica as well, even though her explanation to Siena hadn't included that. Leslie had extended the dinner invitation to her, too, but that might have been only to keep things from being awkward. That was okay. If Leslie had an issue with her, she didn't mind stepping back. She trusted Leslie with Siena. It would be fine for the two of them to be friends without much involvement from her. In the short term, it might actually be better. That would give Erica a chance to get over her attraction to Leslie.

Siena scooped a spoonful of ice cream into her mouth. "How do they make the golden lasso part?" she asked, staring into her bowl.

"The gold chunks are caramel chips, and the lasso is swirls of graham cracker," Leslie said, studying her own dessert. "I think that's what was on the carton."

Siena looked thoughtful. "That's a really good way to make a golden lasso. I wonder whose idea it was."

Leslie smiled. "I don't know, but it was someone very smart."

Siena tilted her head and looked at Leslie. "My mom said that you think *I'm* smart."

"I do," Leslie said. "And you are. You understood everything I told you about Buddha, and you told me things I needed to know to help you and your mom when she was sick. And you helped me figure out the right way to put my new sheets on my bed."

Siena grinned.

Erica suspected Leslie could have managed getting her sheets on without help, but she appreciated Leslie's way of pumping Siena up.

"And my mom said you think I'm amazing," Siena went on.

"You *are*." Leslie rested her arm on the table and leaned forward. "The way you made sure those delivery people got all my furniture in the right rooms...*that* was amazing."

Siena sat up taller in her chair. Then she squinted quizzically at Leslie. "What's enchanting?"

"Enchanting?" Leslie asked. She glanced at Erica and sent her the tiniest of smiles, obviously remembering their conversation that first weekend they'd all met.

Did Leslie have any idea how at ease she'd made Erica about Siena meeting someone new with just that one little teasing sentence?

"Uh-huh," Siena said. "My mom said to ask you what it means, because you think I am."

"I see," Leslie said, returning her full attention to Siena. "Enchanting means there's something special inside you that wins people over and makes them want to be around you."

"Something? Like magic?" Siena asked, her eyes twinkling.

"Yeah," Leslie said with some consideration. "Kind of like magic."

Siena turned to Erica, her whole being smiling. "Mommy, I'm magic."

Erica laughed, the sound bubbling up from the swell of pure pleasure. "Yes, you are, sweetie." She couldn't help a quick look at Leslie. *And so are you.*

As they all pitched in to do the dishes, Erica let most of the interaction be between Leslie and Siena. She enjoyed the game of Yahtzee they all played, listening as Siena told Leslie about her first few days of school. She'd even learned a little more about Siena's teacher and a couple more kids in her class. Erica quietly played, petted Gus, and watched.

As the hour approached Siena's bedtime, Siena's eyelids drooped. She balked at the idea of leaving, but Leslie assured her the jungle would be there the next day, and the following, and every day after that. It surprised Erica. She'd have thought it was more of a temporary thing. Siena wanted her nightly story and, of course, wanted Leslie to read it, but she wanted Leslie to read it to both her and Erica as they'd done when Erica was sick. So she and Siena and Gus had all piled onto the bed, while Leslie sat in the rocker and read the first of the Mowgli stories from the copy of Kipling's *The Jungle Book* she said she'd picked up for Siena when she'd been shopping for all things jungle related.

As she lay beside Siena with Gus tucked between them, Erica had a feeling of contentment, of settling into something new. She let herself explore it for a brief moment. She watched Leslie's lips move as she read the words and did the voices of the story. She smiled at the faces she made that brought giggles from Siena. She studied her hands as she turned the pages. And she felt something else. Not contentment. Not even something particularly new. That same stirring of attraction, of arousal, that same longing for something she'd never known. She closed her eyes to block the image, to stop such thoughts and feelings. Leslie was Siena's friend, and Erica couldn't and wouldn't do anything to make that difficult. When the story was over, she opened her eyes to find Leslie staring at her. Siena was asleep.

Leslie closed the book and smiled over the top of it.

In unspoken communication, they rose, Leslie from the chair and Erica slipping off the bed, and left the room together. As they stood at the bottom of the stairs, an awkward pause hung between them as each seemed to be waiting for the other to speak.

"Thank you again," Erica said finally. "For coming back and making things right...for Siena, I mean." Her cheeks heated. *Don't ruin it.* She grazed her fingertips across her temple to brush her hair back. She'd forgotten it was still in a braid.

Leslie caught her wrist. "Don't do that," she said. "Please? Don't try to avoid...I was hoping we could talk, if you're not too tired."

Erica laughed softly. "I kind of hate that you've figured that out about me."

Leslie lifted the corners of her mouth. She released her hold. "Sorry."

"I kind of like it too, though. No one's ever paid attention like that before." Erica wished Leslie hadn't let go of her. She missed her touch.

"That's one of the things I want to talk to you about," Leslie said a bit shyly. "That...and I want to explain some things."

"You don't have to explain anything," Erica said. "I mean, you can if you want to, but you don't have to."

Leslie held Erica's gaze, hers sincere. "I want to."

Erica nodded. "Okay." She took Leslie's hand long enough to give it a reassuring squeeze. "Would you like some tea? This sounds serious, and my mother always said that any serious talk should take place over tea."

Leslie smiled, but it seemed strained. "That would be nice."

They chatted in the kitchen while waiting for the kettle to boil, the small talk dangling in the air between them like a snared rabbit until it simply died. It wasn't that there was anything wrong with talking about Erica's first few days of the semester or the new website Leslie was building. There was something else, though, waiting to be said, and until it was, there wasn't any point to anything else.

When they were seated on the couch in the family room, steaming mugs in hand, Leslie leaned back and stared at some invisible point or moment in front of her. "I want to start with an apology to you, too," she said. She held up her hand, stopping Erica's objection. "Just hear me out. I'm sorry I pulled away. That isn't the kind of friend I usually am, and I want to explain. This might be a bit of a long story, but I want you to hear it so you'll understand if I act strange from time to time." She ran the pad of her thumb along the edge of her cup. "I want to tell you about Elijah."

Erica waited.

Leslie didn't go on. Finally, she shook her head. "I don't really know how to start. I've never told anyone the whole story at once."

Erica was touched. She could tell how hard this was for Leslie. "Would it help if I asked some questions?"

Still not looking at Erica, Leslie gave a slight nod. "Maybe."

Erica thought for a moment. Whatever this story entailed, it was going to be painful for Leslie. Maybe she could ease her into it. "Siena said Elijah lives with his other mom. Tell me about her. How long were you with her? How did you meet?"

Leslie didn't move, but her expression shifted from one of anxiety to recollection. She seemed to have found a starting point. "We met through work. She was a graphic designer in the PR department of a company I was hired to do a website for."

"How long ago was that?" Erica asked.

"About eleven years." Leslie sighed, her shoulders visibly relaxing.

"What's her name?" As a journalist, interviewing people, Erica had learned to begin with simple questions, ones that didn't take much thought but that put the person she was interviewing at ease. Then at some point, a switch would be flipped, and the person would just start talking.

"Cassie," Leslie said.

"How long were you together?"

Leslie hesitated, as though pondering the question. "I don't…" she started, then faltered. She looked into her tea. "We weren't ever together. Not as a couple. Not the way you mean."

"But you had a child together," Erica said, genuinely curious. "Doesn't that make you somewhat of a couple?"

Another pause, then Leslie lifted one shoulder. "We were friends. When we met, we really clicked…in a friend way. We liked a lot of the same things. Movies, concerts, restaurants. Our work overlapped. We had similar senses of humor. We just started doing things together, hanging out. She was straight and a lot younger than me, and I was more of a big sister figure to her. She was cute and funny, and I had a little bit of a crush on her, but it wasn't anything I would have acted on under normal circumstances."

"So what happened?"

Leslie glanced at Erica, then sighed and leaned her head against the back of the couch. This was it—her turning point. "We'd been friends, really close friends, for about three years. Confidants. Workout partners. There for each other after bad dates and breakups. Then one afternoon, she showed up at my front door in tears, told me she was pregnant by the guy she'd been seeing for the past several months, and she didn't know what she was going to do. I told her whatever she decided, I'd be there for her."

Naturally. Erica smiled to herself.

"The guy ended up being an asshole, not wanting anything to do with the baby." Leslie stopped abruptly, realization moving across her face, then gave Erica an apologetic look. "Sorry. I didn't mean…"

Erica chuckled. "It's all right. I've thought of Trent that way myself at times. Go on."

"Anyway, he didn't want the baby, or Cassie at that point, and Cassie couldn't bring herself to have an abortion, so she decided to go through with the pregnancy, thinking she'd go the adoption route. I meant what I said about being there for her, so we planned on doing the birthing classes together and me being in the delivery room with her. And I did all the midnight craving runs and took her onion rings and Frosties at two in the morning. Then at seven months, there were complications, and she was ordered to bed rest for the remainder of the pregnancy. Since she lived alone, her doctor was going to admit her to the hospital for the last two months, so I said I'd stay with her and take care of the things she needed." Leslie frowned. "That made us even closer. She was so grateful, and we really were very compatible."

Leslie had slipped into the memory, a pleasant one, Erica could tell from her tone and the faraway look in her eyes. She waited, silent, letting Leslie enjoy that slice of her past.

"Then when he was born and I held him..." Leslie broke into a brilliant smile. She shook her head, obviously reliving her disbelief in that long ago moment.

Erica could relate. That instant with Siena when the nurse nestled her into Erica's arms and Erica had looked into that tiny face for the first time resided firmly in its own special place in her mind and heart. To this day, it brought tears of wonder, awe, and overwhelming love to her eyes.

"He was so amazing, so perfect," Leslie said, astonishment in her voice. "And he looked straight at me." She turned to Erica for the first time since they'd sat down. "It felt like he was seeing right into my soul. And that was it. I was in love. I thought I'd been in love before, but I'd never felt *anything* like *that*." She searched Erica's face, as though seeking confirmation, or maybe understanding.

Emotion filled Erica's chest like the swell of a huge wave. It rose into her throat, drowning any words. She nodded. *I know.*

Leslie drew in a deep breath, then released it, as though gathering herself. "Cassie had a C-section, so I planned to stay with her and Elijah for a while longer. Until she got back on her feet and got used to taking care of him on her own. We figured maybe a couple more months, but then it stretched out to another. And we'd gotten settled into a routine. And it all started feeling like we were a family." She was staring straight ahead again, her expression pensive. "Finally, when Elijah was six months old, I thought it was time. It wasn't that I wanted to move back to my own place. It was that I knew I was probably in the way of Cassie making her own life with Elijah. I knew I'd still see them. When I told her, at first she said okay, she understood. But a couple of nights later, she met me at the door when I got home from the gym. She'd put Elijah to bed and made a nice dinner that she had all set up with candles and music. She told me she'd fallen in love with me and she wanted me to stay. She wanted the three of us to be a family. And she kissed me."

The story held Erica in thrall, even though she had to wonder if Cassie had been telling the truth, or if she'd woven a web of manipulation.

Leslie glanced at her. "I know. I'm an idiot."

Erica hadn't been aware she'd let her doubt show. "I don't think that," she said softly.

Leslie grimaced. Clearly, reliving everything brought up the old pain. "It's just that I didn't want to go." She shrugged. "Not because of Cassie. I knew deep down that she wasn't in love with me, that she was pretending. I think because she was scared of doing it all on her own. And my feelings for her were friendship, a deep one, but still…friendship. But we were comfortable with each other. We knew one another better than anyone else did. It was easy. And I was so in love with Elijah. I couldn't imagine not being there with him in the morning when he woke up, or getting to witness all his firsts, or being the one that gave him a bottle in the middle of the night. That was our special time—just him and me." A sheen of moisture shone in her eyes.

Erica gently took her hand. She ignored the tingle that ran through her, the heat that ignited in their touch, the subtle yet definite throb between her thighs. This was about comforting Leslie, nothing else.

Leslie squeezed Erica's fingers, then slipped from her grasp. "So I pretended, too." She sighed. "We had sex that night and pretended we were making love. Got up the next morning and pretended everything was new. Went on from there, pretending we were a couple. The weird thing is that we didn't have to pretend the three of us were a family. That part came so naturally. So we did that. For five years."

Erica waited, watching the past move through Leslie's eyes, travel over her face, tighten the muscles in her neck and shoulders. When Leslie didn't go on, Erica asked, "What happened at five years?"

Leslie cut her a glance. She seemed startled, as though she'd forgotten Erica was there. She gave her a closed-lip smile, and a short and humorless laugh sounded in the back of her throat. "You can only pretend for so long before everything comes crashing down." She leaned forward and set the mug that held her untasted tea on the coffee table. "Cassie came home from work one day and announced she'd been secretly seeing someone, and he'd asked her to marry him. And she'd said yes."

Astonishment overtook Erica. She felt her jaw drop and her eyes widen. "That's it? There was no discussion of what that meant?"

Leslie rose and crossed the room. "I don't think what followed would be called discussion. There was some disbelief, some yelling, a lot of begging on my part, apologies and crying on hers. Nothing that mattered. The decision had been made and plans were already in the works. Russell—that's his name—wanted to meet Elijah right away, and he'd made it clear he wanted me out of the picture entirely, because he wouldn't know how to explain my role in Elijah's life to his friends and family. He didn't want anyone to know about Cassie having been with a woman."

"And she went along with that?" Erica was outraged. With what she knew of Leslie—how Leslie was with Siena, how thoughtful she was, willing to do anything for anyone—she couldn't fathom someone treating her that way. "She just used you because she was afraid of raising her child on her own, then threw you out of their lives when something more acceptable came along?"

Leslie looked surprised at Erica's outburst. A small smile touched her lips. "Pretty much. Although, in all fairness, I used her, too. If I'd been honest and told her I understood she was scared and I still intended to be there for her and Elijah—if I'd made her admit she wasn't in love with me—things might have ended much differently. I've come to terms with all that. It took me a while, but

I did. What I still have a hard time bearing is Elijah's absence in my life and mine in his. I don't know what they told him or what he thinks happened. It kills me that he might believe that I left him without a word."

Erica stared at her. "You didn't get to say good-bye?"

Leslie shook her head. "I thought there was still time. I had to go out of town to a conference, and when I got back, they were gone. All their clothes, Elijah's toys, anything that was strictly Cassie's—all gone." Her voice broke. "And I never saw him again."

Erica sprang from the couch and rushed to her. She reached her just as Leslie began to cry and took her in her arms.

Leslie resisted at first, then relented. She leaned into Erica and gripped her in a hard hug.

Erica brought Leslie's head to her shoulder, tenderly stroking her hair. "I'm so sorry," she whispered.

Leslie let Erica hold her, let her comfort her as she cried, for longer than Erica would have thought, but then she stepped back and turned away. She wiped her eyes with the back of her hand. "I'm sorry," she said, sounding stuffy. "It's been a long time...I'm sorry."

Erica pulled a couple of tissues from a box on one of the shelves in the entertainment center and handed them to Leslie. "No need to be. You've been through a lot."

Leslie swiped them over her face, then blew her nose. "You know, I think I'm past it, and then all of a sudden..."

"I don't know that I'd ever get past something like that." Erica watched Leslie. She was looking at something on one of the shelves. "If someone took Siena from me..." She realized Leslie was studying a picture of her, Siena, and Trent. She took in a sharp breath of realization. "That's why you pulled back, why we haven't seen you. Because of how close you were getting to Siena. And because Siena and I and Trent look like them, as a family."

Leslie clenched her jaw, as though fighting back more tears.

"Leslie," Erica said quietly. She pressed her fingertips to Leslie's cheek and coaxed her to face her. "I'd never do that. I'd never interfere with your friendship with Siena. I can see how important you've become to her, how deeply she's connected with you, and that seldom happens for her. I can see how much you care about her. I promise, I wouldn't—"

"I know," Leslie said. "I don't realistically think you would. It's just…Ever since I moved in next door and started getting to know you and Siena, I have these moments when it feels like Elijah and Cassie all over again, and I don't want that pain." She choked on the words. "But here it is anyway, even when I tried to get away." She shook her head.

With a gentle sweep of her thumb, Erica brushed some moisture Leslie had missed from her cheek. "How about if you feel that way again, you tell me, and I can assure you that Siena isn't going anywhere. Can you do that?"

Gratitude filled Leslie's eyes, and she nodded. "I can do that. Thank you." She hesitated, then shifted her gaze to some abstract point over Erica's shoulder. "Before we get all caught up in a Kumbaya moment, there's something else I need to tell you. So everything's out on the table."

"Okay," Erica said slowly. "That sounds ominous."

"Not really. It's just something I think you should know before we make any decisions about how things are going to be." Leslie looked around the room, as though seeking an escape. "Can we go outside? I need some air."

"Sure," Erica said, curious. "Would you like me to warm up your tea?"

"No, thank you. That's okay." Leslie rubbed her stomach. "I'm still full from dinner, and…you know…nerves."

There's still something to be nervous about? "Okay." Erica picked up the monitor from the coffee table but left her own cup as well. On the patio, she led the way to the swing. It was more comfortable than the chairs around the table, and the lighting in the corner was dimmer, though still enough to see one another. It might make it easier for Leslie to say whatever else she had to say.

When they were settled, Leslie sat silently for a long moment. She stared across the yard, her focus on her pool, so prettily lit and inviting in the warm evening air.

Erica remembered sitting in that very spot and watching Leslie undress, then dive gracefully into the water. She wondered if that was what Leslie was thinking about, too. A hot blush crept up her neck from her chest and into her face. She was grateful for the shadows where they sat.

"I could ease into this, but I think I'm just going to say it." Leslie turned to look at her. "Rip the Band-Aid off, so to speak."

"Oh! Is it going to be painful?" Erica was turned toward Leslie, her legs crossed at the knees. She noticed Leslie glance down at her partially bare thighs.

Leslie shook her head slightly. "I don't think so." She kept her gaze lowered. "Maybe a little for me, but not for you."

What on earth can this be about? And if it was going to hurt her at all, why would she do it at the same time as telling Erica everything else she'd shared tonight? "Should I get the Neosporin?" Erica asked, trying to lighten the mood. It worked.

Leslie laughed. "That won't be necessary." She looked directly into Erica's eyes, her expression soft, maybe a bit sad. She studied Erica's face, as though memorizing it. She lingered on Erica's mouth.

Involuntarily, Erica found herself looking at Leslie's. It seemed only fair. She couldn't help but wonder what that plump lower lip would feel like caught gently between her teeth. Her blood went hot at the thought. She jerked her attention back to Leslie's eyes to find her staring questioningly at her.

Leslie looked out across the yard again. "Okay, I need to do this." She took in a gulp of air. "Erica, I'm really attracted to you. You're so beautiful and smart and interesting. And I feel like there could be something between us…maybe." She tipped her head back and clenched her eyes shut. "Christ, I can't believe I'm going to tell you this. When you came over the other night all fired up and Mama Bear after I hadn't seen you in so long, all I wanted to do was kiss you. And tonight, when I first saw you in that skirt and blouse…I could have taken you right there on the floor. But I know that can't happen. We can't be that…*I* can't be that. It would feel too much, seem too much, like Cassie and Elijah. Even though I never had those kind of feelings for Cassie, it's how we lived. And even if you were attracted to me, which I don't think you are, I feel like we're becoming friends—good friends—and I don't want to risk that. Plus, I can't put myself in a position where I freak out at the slightest hint of feeling that pain again. That's not fair to anyone, least of all, Siena."

The words came at Erica in a rush. She was stuck, though, on the beginning. *Attracted to you…so beautiful…wanted to kiss you…could have taken you.* She had to listen to the rest, though, had to *hear* the rest. *Can't do it…freak out…friends.*

Leslie was still talking. "I don't want to blow this. I enjoy doing things with you and Siena so much. I don't want to risk that. I'll handle my feelings, and they'll pass. I promise. You don't have to do anything, or change anything. I just wanted you to know, like with the stuff about Elijah and Cassie, in case I need a little space sometimes." She lifted her face to the night sky, then swallowed. "But if I ever go too far again, if I'm hurting Siena, I want you to promise you'll come get me, like you did the other night."

Erica's throat closed with emotion. She was moved by Leslie's honesty, her willingness to lay out her feelings and fears so naked and exposed, to be so vulnerable. She examined Leslie's profile. "I will. I promise." She wanted to reach out and touch her, slip her fingers into her hair. But that wouldn't offer Leslie any comfort right now. Leslie looked, and probably felt, so raw and open after everything she'd shared about Elijah, and now this. Erica had to respond in kind, had to share something equally as significant. *She* had to be as vulnerable.

It wasn't as though she had to dig very deep for what to share. She had her own feelings for Leslie, her own baggage that would make things difficult if they tried to explore anything, her own fears—for herself *and* Siena—of being left behind. She wasn't used to that level of openness, but she owed it to Leslie, to the friendship they, apparently, were going to try to have. "Well," she said slowly. She stretched her arm across the back of the swing seat and tilted her head to take in the stars. "If it helps, you're not alone in all this."

Leslie turned to face her. "I'm not?"

Erica met her gaze and shook her head. She gave herself a brief pause to take in Leslie's features one more time, then sighed. "I'm very attracted to you, too. I have been since the day we met. I even considered a fling, or a quick one-nighter with you, but with you living right next door…Besides, now I know that would never have been enough. I would have needed more of you once I got a taste. It'd be too tempting with you so close."

Leslie arched an eyebrow. "Really? You never let on."

"Neither did you," Erica said, surprised at how easy this conversation felt. "Besides, I was sure if there'd been even a flicker of interest on your part, it would have been completely extinguished after cleaning up after me so many times when I was sick."

Leslie chuckled. "That wasn't that bad. It needed to be done. The only thing it did do was make me feel…I don't know…like I had a place with you and Siena. Like a family, which then kicked up all my other stuff I told you about. It was the feeling and the fear that made me run, not the act of taking care of the two of you."

"And you running and cutting yourself off from us kicked up my stuff about no one sticking around because life with Siena—then compounded with anything additional like me getting sick—is too much." She thought it all through briefly. "Wow, we'd be a train wreck as a couple."

"You really believe that?" Leslie sat up and shifted around in her seat. "That you and Siena are too hard?"

Erica shrugged. "Yes." She had to admit it. "Becky says it's because I believe it that I push any possibility of an intimate relationship away. That's why I'm glad I didn't act on my attraction to you when we first met. Had we slept together, I would have cut you off afterward—if Becky is right—and Siena and I wouldn't be able to be friends with you now."

Leslie smirked. "I don't know how much stock you can put in Becky." There was an obvious teasing lilt to her tone. "She thinks I could be a porn star at fifty-three."

"She didn't say *star*," Erica said in Becky's defense. "Although...from what I saw..." She quirked an eyebrow. *Oh my God!* She was flirting again. Hadn't they just decided they'd be friends, nothing more? Could friends flirt?

"That's right." Leslie glanced at her pool area, then back to Erica. "I'd forgotten. You still owe me."

Apparently, friends could. They laughed.

"Seriously, though," Leslie said gently. "Yes, Siena's different, and someone would have to make an effort to learn how to interact with her, but you really can't think there's no one who would."

Erica's cheeks heated with embarrassment. She hoped Leslie couldn't see her that well in the darkness. "It's been hard not to, since Trent's reaction to Siena's ASD—and even now her behavior sometimes. And most of our friends vanished, and even though I do know that can happen when you have a baby and your friends don't, I still wonder if that's the real reason. Even my relationship with my mother changed after Siena's diagnosis. She didn't disappear, but we do see her less, and she stopped making much of an effort."

"Is she Grandma Millie who died and probably doesn't poop anymore?" Leslie asked thoughtfully. "Or is she the grandma with wrinkles who sits in the front living room when she comes, where only people who don't belong here sit?"

Erica buried her face in her hands. "Oh my God. I don't want to imagine the things you've heard from talking with Siena."

"Let's see," Leslie said, laughter in her voice. "I know you don't like Siena talking about poop, or wee-wee, or vomit at the dinner table. I heard that you hate throwing up, though I did get my own firsthand experience of that one. Oh, and I heard it didn't matter to you that dogs eat their own vomit; you still didn't want one, because you didn't want to clean up after it. You're lucky Gus forgave you for that one."

Erica couldn't help but chuckle.

"I heard the colors of your camellias are so pretty because Hazel the goldfish is buried underneath the bush, and that Trent's poop is the stinkiest of everyone's."

This one drew out a full laugh. "It really is," Erica said conspiratorially. "I don't know what the man eats."

A warm smile lit Leslie's face. "You don't need to worry about anything Siena tells me, especially about you. I like hearing about you. I particularly like it from Siena. She's so certain of you. It's evident she knows you're always there for her."

"That's nice to know," Erica said, ignoring the flutter that Leslie's interest in her caused. *We are friends.* "Things like that aren't always clear when she's mad at me for making her do something on her own."

"I think that's a hard call with any child, knowing when to step in and when to let them learn from their own experience." There was a wistfulness in Leslie's voice. It was clear she was thinking of Elijah.

"You seem very good at that. I've seen it with Siena." Erica wasn't sure whether to press the topic of Elijah. The earlier discussion had obviously taken a toll on Leslie. Now that things were settled between them, there'd be time for more talking later.

"Thank you," Leslie said with a note of closure. "So what are your plans for the weekend? Any chance you and Siena might want to join me and Gus for a barbecue?"

"That sounds nice. I try to keep the weekends focused around home," Erica said, going with the shift. "As busy as the weekdays get, it's good for Siena to have some down time. It doesn't hurt me any either."

"I'd like to invite Nell and her wife, Paula, too. Would that still work?"

And just like that, they were back on neutral ground, the deeper discussions and confessions tucked away.

Erica smirked, remembering the note Nell left Leslie about her. "I'd love to meet Nell, director of the Raymond Children's Center, matchmaker, and mysterious magician." She chuckled. "Siena's still trying to figure out how a quarter got in her ear."

"Nell could keep her entertained for hours," Leslie said. "She's great with kids."

"Do you know which day you want the barbecue? Becky and I were going to do lunch or a movie on Sunday." Erica realized that would be moot if she didn't remember to make some calls to backup sitters the next day. Rachel, Siena's favorite, wasn't available. "That is, if I can find someone Siena likes to watch her. I used to be able to leave her with Jack and the kids, but ever since the puzzle incident, Siena doesn't want to be around Rosi at all."

"She can stay with me," Leslie said without hesitation. "We haven't had any time together since you were sick. We can catch up. Maybe give Gus a bath. He's due for one."

"You don't have to do that," Erica said, grateful for the offer but not wanting to take advantage. "You have to be back to some kind of work schedule by now, I'm sure."

Leslie shrugged. "I work mostly at night. My creative juices flow better when it's dark and quiet."

"How will you get any work done with that snake hanging above your head?" Erica asked teasingly. She pictured the jungle that was now Leslie's living room. She couldn't believe she'd done that for Siena.

"Kaa? He's my buddy." Leslie's tone was childlike. "He proofread over my shoulder last night while I finished the layout of the text. It really sped things along."

Erica laughed. She'd been so irritated with Leslie the past week, she'd almost forgotten how much she enjoyed her. She'd missed her.

"I'm serious about Siena staying with me on Sunday. We can do the barbecue tomorrow," Leslie went on.

"Are you sure?" Erica asked hesitantly.

"Positive. You and Siena take care of Gus for me," Leslie said with a hint of humor. "Let me repay you."

Erica considered the comparison. "Actually, I think Gus takes care of us."

"Well, yes. That could be. I think Gus takes care of all of us." Leslie was watching her, clearly waiting for an answer to her offer.

"If you're sure," Erica said.

"I am," Leslie said definitively. "It's what friends do, right? You and Becky go have fun for a while."

Erica paused, meeting Leslie's gaze, then dipped her head in ascent. An agreement had been forged—they were friends. But she couldn't deny a twinge of sadness at the loss of the possibility of anything more.

Chapter Twelve

Leslie tossed her keys onto the bar and headed out her back door to see how close Erica and Siena were to being ready to go. She'd spent the past five hours at the Raymond Children's Center, helping with the setup for the annual Halloween carnival, while Erica and Siena stayed home to decorate the pumpkin-shaped sugar cookies for the bake sale and make a marble fudge cake for the cakewalk.

The carnival was one of the regular fundraisers for the center. More importantly, it was a lot of fun for all the kids being housed there and the foster families connected with the center. It'd always been Leslie's favorite event. She'd scheduled her visits home to coincide with it from time to time for the sake of all the fond memories it held. Although she'd been home for three months now, spending the afternoon with Nell, Paula, and some of the board members and staff she'd known for years anchored her in that sense of home. All that was missing were her parents.

"*Hola, amigas,*" she called as she opened Erica's sliding glass door.

Gus wriggled between her feet and made a mad dash for the kitchen.

"Gus!" Siena squealed.

"In here," Erica called.

The scent of baked goods, butter, and sugar tickled Leslie's nose. "Something smells great." She came to an abrupt halt at the scene in the kitchen.

Siena stood on a chair, her arms wrapped around Gus, who'd jumped up beside her and was licking what looked like chocolate frosting off her cheek. Erica, in a pair of ratty blue jeans and a threadbare, faded black T-shirt, was hunched over a cake pan on the counter, squirting icing from a pastry bag. Six plates of cookies covered in plastic wrap, each topped with a grinning jack-o'-lantern, peppered the second countertop.

The tableau was so perfect, Leslie couldn't help herself. She pulled her phone from her pocket. "Hey," she said sharply.

All three turned to look at her.

She snapped the picture.

Erica gasped. "That's just mean. If that shows up anywhere online, you're going to pay." She pointed the bag of icing at her like a gun.

Leslie laughed. She'd never do that. The picture was only for her. She moved behind them and watched over Erica's shoulder as Erica returned her focus to her task.

"I'm almost finished," Erica said. She drew a white B in the speech bubble coming from the ghost on the chocolate frosted cake. A smear of icing, similar to the one Gus had licked from Siena's face, adorned her cheek.

Leslie was so close…All she'd have to do is turn her head to lick it from Erica's creamy skin. She wanted to so badly, considered it briefly, but of course, she wouldn't. They were friends.

How many times since their talk two months earlier had she had to remind herself of that? *Too many to count.* She'd truly believed her attraction to Erica would wear off, that once they'd agreed anything other than friendship was off the table, it wouldn't be a struggle. And it wasn't always. Much of the time, when they were all watching a movie, or having dinner, or she and Erica were helping each other work something through, she felt genuine affection and caring, but she wasn't fighting her attraction to her or lusting after her. Every once in a while, though—okay, maybe more than once in a while—a moment like this would spark something and tempt her to try something outside the boundary of friendship. But most of the time…

Erica finished the word *Boo* and straightened. She bumped into Leslie. "I'm sorry," she said, her face flushing. "I didn't know you were—"

"Taste the frosting," Siena said. "It's really good." She grabbed Erica's hand and pulled it to Leslie's mouth.

Erica's fingertips were coated in chocolate. "No, Siena, it's—"

"She'll like it." Siena pressed Erica's fingers to Leslie's lips.

Without thinking, Leslie opened, then sucked gently. Her pulse quickened and throbbed softly between her legs. She fought to keep from squeezing her thighs together, to hold back a quiet moan, at the feel of Erica's fingers in her mouth. It only lasted a split second, but for that split second, she had no choice but to admit she wasn't thinking of Erica as a friend.

Their eyes met, and Erica pulled her fingers free.

"Isn't that the best frosting you've ever had?" Siena asked with excitement.

Leslie cleared her throat. "It most definitely is," she said, turning to Siena.

In the same instant, Erica reached around, scooped up the bowl, and put it in the sink. "Okay, we need to get cleaned up and into our costumes, if we're going to get to the carnival in time to man our booth. You're sticky," she said to Siena. "And you..." She ran her gaze over Leslie. "Are dirty and sweaty."

Was there a matching hint of Leslie's arousal in Erica's eyes? "That's right. Clean up," Leslie said. "I'm going to go get a shower. I'll be back to help carry all this to the car." She drew in a deep breath, still savoring the taste of chocolate and the feel of Erica on her tongue. She needed a shower. A cold one.

Four hours later, Leslie, Erica, and Siena were stationed in the beanbag toss booth and had a line of waiting customers. The carnival grounds, also known as the playground of the children's center, was filled with people of all ages there to have a good time. The smell of popcorn, cotton candy, and hotdogs wafted in the air, and "Monster Mash" and other favorite Halloween tunes from the cakewalk added to the atmosphere.

Siena positioned herself beside the wooden cut out of the witch with the large hole for the mouth and two smaller ones for eyes, so she could retrieve the beanbags and return them to Leslie for the next player. She'd wanted to help, but hadn't wanted to have to interact with all of the strangers. She was doing a great job. Erica collected the tickets, while Leslie monitored the actual tosses and cajoled and chatted with everyone. She flashed back to earlier years, particularly the first few when both the center and the carnival were new. Both were much bigger now, having grown substantially over the years, and Leslie felt a sense of pride and a deep rush of love for her mother and the compassion and vision she'd had.

As she surveyed her surroundings, she found Erica watching her. When she tipped her head in question, Erica only smiled.

The Kanga costume Siena had picked out for Erica, to go with Siena's Roo, was twisted a little to one side, allowing Erica to sit comfortably on the low bench of the booth, rather than on the big lump of her kangaroo tail. She looked perfectly content.

Leslie's Winnie the Pooh costume was bulky and heavy, but she was happy to wear it for the smile it'd brought to Siena. Siena even had Nell dressed as Tigger and Paula walking around somewhere as Piglet. Both seemed to have fallen just as hard for Siena as Leslie had. How could they not? Leslie glanced at Siena, watching her collect the beanbags the current contestant had thrown, with Gus's help, then took them from her as she approached. "You want to give our winner his prize?" she asked her.

"No," Siena said. "I'm hungry. Can I have a hotdog, please?"

"Sure," Leslie said. She turned to the teenage boy who'd just made a perfect throw into the witch's mouth. "Would you like a prize, or would you like to buy three more chances? If you do it again, you can upgrade your prize. And if you make it into one of her eyes, you get two upgrades."

The boy grinned and nodded. "I'll take three more." He walked away a few minutes later with a giant Mr. Goodbar and a huge smile.

"I'm still hungry," Siena called from behind the cutout.

The line to their booth had dwindled, and there seemed to be a lull. "Okay. Want to go with me?"

"No. Thank you." The second part seemed to be an afterthought. "I'll stay with Gus. Nell says he has to stay in our booth."

"I'll go get it," Erica said, stepping up beside Leslie. She'd been unusually quiet all evening.

"That's okay." Leslie smiled. "I think I'll have an easier time maneuvering through the crowd." She took hold of the end of Erica's tail and wiggled it to make her point. "You want something to eat or drink?"

"I've seen nachos going by all evening. Can you hunt those down?" Erica gave her a playful look.

"I can, and I will." Leslie sat on the table at the front of the booth and swung her legs over it. "I'll be back," she said in her best Terminator voice.

"Hey, where you going?" Nell called as she approached the booth.

"To hunt the mighty nacho," Leslie called back. "Help Erica and Siena."

As she made her way back through the crowd from the refreshment area, she noticed Molly talking with a couple of the other board members and Stacey, the after-school program coordinator. She tried to avert her gaze before she was spotted, but was a nanosecond too slow.

They all waved.

Leslie could only send them a return nod while balancing a nacho boat on top of two hotdogs in one hand and two stacked canned sodas in the other.

Molly hurried over. "Would you like some help?"

"Oh, I think I've got it," Leslie said, knowing it wasn't going to work.

Molly took the nachos and one soda. "There. That should make it easier." She smiled.

"Thanks." Leslie wasn't sure what Molly could want, other than her usual badgering of trying to get Leslie on the board for the next term. She'd already tried twice since Leslie had moved home. She waited.

Molly simply looked around as they walked. "This is a great turnout," she said. "I think that new website you made for us is making a difference. I'd like to put ticket sales for the annual dinner fundraiser on it. Would that be difficult?"

"Not at all," Leslie said, surprised. "Just send me the info and let me know when you want sales to start, and I'll get it done."

Molly gave her a bright smile. "I'll do that right away. Thank you."

At the booth, Erica was in a conversation with Nell and Paula as a family moved away with their prizes.

"Are you running off all our business?" Leslie asked Nell jokingly as she climbed back into the booth.

"I'll have you know we've been busy the whole time you were gone," Nell said. "It's only now that you're back we don't have any customers."

Erica and Paula laughed.

"Enough, you two." Paula turned to Molly. "Hi, Molly. How are you?"

"I'm well, thank you. Thank you for all your help today. I've heard you've been here since this morning."

Paula gave a nonchalant wave of her hand. "For better, for worse. For richer, for poorer. At carnivals and at home."

Everyone chuckled.

"And I don't think we've met," Molly said to Erica. "I'm Molly Snowe, the president of the board for the center." She held out her hand.

"Oh, my God, I'm so sorry," Leslie said with a sputter. "Erica, this is Molly, as she said. And Molly, this is my friend, Erica Cooper. She volunteered to donate a bunch of baked goods and to work the booth with me all night."

Erica shook Molly's hand. "It's nice to meet you. This has been so much fun. It seems like a pretty successful fundraiser."

"Yes, it does very well, especially since we own all our own booths and equipment and don't have to rent a space. Most of what we make is profit. And I was just telling Leslie how much of a difference I think the new website she put up for us made." She ran her hand up Leslie's arm.

"That's wonderful," Erica said with a smile.

"Our big moneymaker, however, is our annual dinner and dance coming up next month. A lot of our more affluent supporters attend and are very generous. It's always a nice evening, with a gourmet meal and dancing afterward. We try to make it as elegant as we can."

"It sounds lovely," Erica said. "I can't remember the last time I went dancing."

"You should come," Nell said, her Tigger tail bouncing behind her. "You can be Leslie's date. Can't she?"

Leslie's heart leapt. "Sure." She tried to remain casual, but the thought of dancing with Erica in her arms made it difficult. "If you want, I mean. It's kind of a stuffy affair."

"Only if you're comfortable with it," Erica said, adorably shy for some reason. "I don't want to horn in or anything."

"No, not at all," Leslie said, trying to figure out what was happening. "You know I wouldn't feel that way."

"Well, whatever you decide," Molly said, interrupting, "know that Leslie will also be with me part of the evening, schmoozing with some of our donors who are very anxious to meet the daughter of our founder." She was touching Leslie's arm again, this time slipping her hand down to Leslie's and squeezing it. She was always so touchy.

Normally, Leslie didn't think much of it. Tonight, though, it irritated her. She didn't want Erica to get the wrong—*Friends. We're just friends.*

"Remember?" Molly turned to Leslie. "You promised." Then in evident surprise, she shifted her gaze past her. "Who's this?" she asked with a smile.

Siena stepped up to Leslie and pressed against her.

Leslie pulled her hand from Molly's. "This is Siena, Erica's daughter."

"Well, hello there, Siena. I'm Molly. Are you having fun tonight?"

Siena considered her briefly, then moved forward. "Hello," she said. "My name is Siena Cooper. It's nice to meet you." She held out her hand.

Leslie could feel Molly's glance flicker over her, but she was too proud of Siena to acknowledge anything else. She gave Siena a smile and a wink.

Molly shook Siena's hand. "It's nice to meet you, too, honey." She turned back to the adults. "Well, I should start bringing this evening to a close. If you'll excuse me. Erica, it was wonderful meeting you and your daughter."

Erica clearly wasn't listening. She was beaming at Siena.

After a chorus of good nights from the rest, Molly drifted away.

"And I should go oversee the counting out of the money," Nell said. "We've been doing it periodically throughout the night, but we'll need to do a final tally."

"I'll be over soon," Paula said to Nell. "I'm going to stay and help here for a while, so these three can eat their dinners." She moved to take the tickets of a young couple that had just stepped up to play.

"Thanks, Paula." Leslie slid Siena's hotdog and a 7 Up down the table to her where she'd settled on the bench Erica had been sitting on. "Ketchup only," she said with a proud grin. "You did great with that introduction." Then she unwrapped her own dog and took a bite. From the corner of her eye, she saw Erica take her phone from the pouch of her Kanga costume, look at it, then frown. "Something wrong?"

Erica licked some cheese off her fingers, then started a series of taps on the screen. She shook her head. "It's Trent. He's at the airport."

The flutter of arousal in Leslie's abdomen at the memory of the feel of Erica's fingers in her mouth was dowsed at the mention of Trent's arrival. "Did you know he was coming?"

Erica sighed. "He's been saying he was coming for weeks, but he kept canceling. Now, when he hasn't mentioned it at all, he's here."

"Oh." Leslie stifled the flare of what she had to admit was jealousy and tried for a more mature reaction. "Do you need to go get him? I can finish up here." They'd brought both of their cars to the carnival in case the crowd, or noise, or anything else, set Siena off and Erica needed to take her home.

"No." Erica returned her phone to her pouch and picked up another cheese-drenched chip. "He can take an Uber to the house. I told him we were busy and we'd be home in a while. There's no rush."

Erica's indifference to Trent's arrival soothed Leslie's emotions. It was ridiculous for her to be jealous, even if there were still something between Erica and Trent, which Erica had said there wasn't. She had no right, no claim on Erica, no place in her life that warranted such a response. If anything, if Erica wanted to start something with Trent again—or with anyone else—as Erica's friend, she should support her in whatever would make her happy. *Yeah, right.* Like she could actually do that. She was grateful this situation didn't call for that from her. But what about when that day came?

"So Molly's interesting," Erica said, blessedly breaking into Leslie's thoughts.

"Molly?" Leslie glanced across the grounds in the direction Molly had departed. "I guess. I don't know her that well." She took a bite of her hotdog and chewed.

"It's pretty clear she'd like to get to know *you* better," Erica said, something sparking in her eyes.

"What do you mean?"

"She's obviously interested—all that touching and her flirtatious tone," Erica said with a shrug.

"No," Leslie said, trying to sound dismissive. This was exactly what she hadn't wanted to happen. "She's just like that. She's one of those people that touches everyone a lot." Even if she and Erica were just friends, she didn't want her thinking there was anything between her and Molly. *Damn it!* If she didn't get a handle on her feelings, this friend thing was going to be hard.

Paula scoffed from behind Leslie. "I've known her for years, and she doesn't touch me."

Leslie turned to her and lifted one eyebrow. "She doesn't?"

"No, sweetheart, she doesn't." Paula laughed. "You'll have to forgive Leslie," she said to Erica. "She can be obtuse when it comes to realizing someone is interested in her." She returned her gaze to Leslie and tipped her head slightly in Erica's direction.

Leslie stared at her. *What is she doing?*

"All right," Paula said, sounding deflated. "I'll leave you two then. I need to make sure Nell didn't get talking and wander off from what she's supposed to be doing. Otherwise, we'll be here all night. Erica, it was very nice seeing you. We'll all have to get together again soon."

Erica smiled. "That would be great. I think it's my turn to host dinner. Check your calendar and text me a few dates you and Nell are free."

A little girl and her mother stopped in front of the booth, and Leslie bailed on the rest of the conversation to take their tickets.

On the drive home, as she followed Erica's taillights, she considered the evening. It'd been fun, but why had Erica been so quiet? Was she upset about what had happened with the frosting? Leslie never should have done what she did. Erica hadn't seemed upset at the time, though. In fact, from the look in her eyes, just the opposite. Maybe that was the problem. Maybe Erica had been affected the same way and as strongly as Leslie had been; maybe Erica's attraction to Leslie wasn't fading either; maybe after the fact, Erica was mad at Leslie for crossing their agreed upon boundary.

Leslie wished they could talk when they got home, after Siena was in bed, but Trent was there. Surely, he and Erica would have things to discuss. Even if they didn't, it'd be rude for her and Erica to have a private conversation with him there. Any talk they might be having would have to wait, but at the very least, Leslie owed Erica an apology.

Chapter Thirteen

Erica stepped into her laundry room from the garage and heard voices. *Voices? The TV?* No, one of them was Trent's. The other, a woman's. The smell of coffee filled the air.

Caffeine never keeps Trent awake. What an odd thought to have. A more fitting one for this situation might have been: Surely, Trent knows better than to bring a total stranger into the house without allowing for Siena to be prepared. But no, Trent didn't know better, because he'd either never paid attention to the things that could trigger Siena, or he simply remained in denial about anything to do with Siena's autism. The truth was probably both, depending on the moment.

Siena stiffened in the doorway.

"It's all right, sweetie," Erica said softly. "It's only your dad. Remember? And it seems he brought a friend." She tried to lighten her voice on the latter part.

"You didn't say he had a friend," Siena said sulkily. She was tired. It was late, way past her bedtime, and it'd been a long day. And she didn't do well with surprises like strange people in the house.

"I didn't know," Erica said, more to herself than to Siena. She sighed. She was exhausted, too. "Let's just get through this, okay?" She started to slip her keys into the front pocket of her purse, then realized she didn't have her purse. *Great.* She'd left it in the car. She set the keys on the counter as she walked into the kitchen just as Trent entered through the other doorway.

A broad smile shaped his mouth and lit his eyes.

Erica would always remember the first time she'd seen that smile. She'd been at a little dive of a diner where she liked to have breakfast in the wee hours of the morning, either having just landed on a return flight from an assignment or after finishing a particularly difficult article and being too wound up to sleep. She'd been alone in a corner booth, buttering an English muffin, when he'd appeared beside her table. She hadn't noticed him come in, and there were only three other people there, the waitress and a couple at the counter. To this day, she didn't know where he'd come from. His smile had captivated her, that smile that, in this moment, irritated her.

"Hey, you're home," he said in place of a greeting. Something about his demeanor was entirely different. "I made some coffee." He waved one of the cups he held toward the carafe on the hot plate of the machine. "I didn't think you'd mind. You want some?"

Erica stared at him, trying to process. Yes, he'd made coffee. She could see that. Of course she didn't mind, because seriously, who would? And no, she didn't want any, because caffeine *did* keep her awake if she had it past two in the afternoon—something one might think he'd be aware of, having known her for seventeen years. None of this explained why he was here without any advanced notice or who he'd brought with him. "No, thank you," she said.

"And there's my girl," he said to Siena, more loudly than necessary. He'd never called her that in her life. "Did you have fun at the carnival?"

Siena eyed him curiously, as though trying to figure out who he was.

Erica was attempting the same thing.

Siena turned to her. "I want to go say good night to Gus," she said without acknowledgement of his question.

"You already did, sweetie," Erica said. "Before we left the center. It's time for you to get to bed."

"I have a surprise for her first," Trent said, his attention back on Erica. "I want her to meet someone. And you, too."

"I don't want a surprise. I want Gus." Siena's gaze flitted around the kitchen.

"It'll only take a minute, and then your mother says it's time for bed. Whoever this Gus is can wait until tomorrow." Trent's voice grew a little louder again.

Suddenly, Erica understood. This show wasn't for her or Siena. It was for whoever was in the next room. Her temper flamed hot. Who the hell did he think he was, coming in here, acting like a parent when he'd never had the slightest interest in that role before? *And* with no clue as to *how* to do that with Siena's special needs. Before she could let loose on him, though, the sprightly face of a young thirty-something woman appeared around the edge of the doorjamb.

Her green eyes flashed luminously above high cheekbones, and her russet colored skin set off perfect white teeth. She smiled apologetically. "Am I interrupting?"

"No, honey," Trent said, leaving Erica speechless.

Honey? But of course. Why else would Trent bring a woman with him? Why had he never mentioned her, though? Is this what he'd been so uncomfortable about the last time he visited and why he'd been so weird on the phone?

"Erica," Trent said, slipping his arm around the woman's waist. "This is Cynthia…my fiancé."

Fiancé? First honey, and now fiancé? Erica blinked in astonishment. In the four and a half years since their divorce, Trent had never spoken a single woman's name. He'd never mentioned a date. He'd never uttered a sound about any kind of social life. And here he was out of the blue with a fiancé. Erica had nothing, but that didn't matter, because he was on a roll.

"Cynthia, this is Siena's mother, Erica."

Siena's mother. As though he'd picked out her file at a surrogate agency, because he'd always dreamed of being a single dad. Erica's blood was pounding in her ears.

"It's so nice to finally meet you, Erica," Cynthia said. "I've heard so much about you both."

And yet, we've heard nothing about you. Erica managed a smile. "It's nice to meet you, too," she said. None of this was Cynthia's fault. She shot a glare at Trent, then felt a movement beside her.

Siena had begun to rock, her arms clamped around her torso.

"And this is Siena," Trent said to Cynthia. Amazingly, he was still talking. His words indicated he hadn't noticed Siena's behavior, but at least there was a hint of uncertainty in his eyes. "Siena, say hello to my friend Cynthia." He reached for her in an obvious attempt to stop her motion.

Erica made a grab for his wrist but missed.

Siena let out a high-pitched keen and spun away.

Erica dropped to her knees in front of her. "Sweetie…Siena… it's all right." She watched for the signs of full meltdown, the walking in circles, the pulling of her hair. "Can you think about Winnie the Pooh? And Piglet? And—"

"What's happening?" Cynthia asked, her voice shrill. "Is she okay? Is something wrong with her?"

"She's fine," Trent said. "She just gets upset sometimes. She'll be fine."

"Shut up, both of you," Erica said, keeping her tone low. She needed to focus on Siena. She couldn't deal with all three of them at once.

A loud rap sounded at the patio door.

Leslie! Erica squeezed her eyes shut. *Thank you.* "Come in," she called over Siena's whimpering and Trent's and Cynthia's murmurings to each other.

In an instant, Gus was there.

Siena immediately squatted and clutched him. She buried her face in his fur. "Winnie the Pooh. Piglet…"

Gus looked at Erica over Siena's shoulder. He appeared a little frantic, maybe at the tightness of Siena's hold, but he didn't struggle or squirm. He simply let her hold on for dear life.

You sweet, amazing dog. Gratitude overtook Erica. She drew in a breath and scanned the room.

Leslie stood in the doorway. She took in the scene in one long sweep, her eyes coming to rest on Siena, then Erica. "What do you need me to do?"

Erica bit her lower lip. She had to deal with Trent and Cynthia—at least to put an end to this night, since they could hash things out in the morning—and she knew Leslie and Gus could handle Siena. If Siena did go into a full meltdown, Erica would hear her. "Could you and Gus take Siena upstairs and help her get calm and ready for bed?"

"No problem." Leslie pushed between Cynthia and Trent and made her way to Siena. She leaned down and spoke softly in Siena's ear.

Erica rose and faced Trent and Cynthia. "Let's go in the other room." She followed them out of the kitchen and all the way to the living room, Trent in the lead, as though he were trying to get as far away from the scene as possible. She thought of Siena's opinion of the room, the one where people who didn't belong sat. She'd tried her best to ensure that Trent had a way to belong there, for Siena, if he chose. He had, for the most part, his own bedroom—very few other people had ever used the guest room. He had a key to the house. He even kept a few things there—some toiletries, a few changes of clothes, an extra charger and a pair of reading glasses. And yet, here they were, in the room for people who don't belong, on furniture far less comfortable than that for the people who do belong. She flashed on getting a cushy blue couch for in here, then sighed and pressed her forehead into her hand, trying to settle on an emotion. "I'm not sure what to say."

"Don't feel you need to apologize, Erica," Trent said, sounding oh-so-soothing. "We understand."

His comment brought forth a dominant feeling—anger. "You understand? No, Trent, you don't understand. You've never understood because you've never taken the time or made the effort to. You've never had the slightest inclination to. You've never been around enough to." She pushed up from the couch and began to pace. "If you understood you would have done *everything* differently tonight. First, you would have called several days ago to let me know you were coming; you would have remembered what I've said—oh, I don't know—a thousand times about Siena being susceptible to changes in her routine environment. Hell, last week when we had an unseasonable rainy day and she had to close her window, she ran circles around the house for three hours, repeating the line from *The Wizard of Oz* about things beginning to twitch and pitch." She was rambling, and Trent and Cynthia were staring. She stopped in front of them. "If you understood," she said to Trent, "when you called from the airport, you would have told me you had someone new with you, so I could have prepared her. If you understood, you would have known to back the hell off when her eyes went unfocused or when she started rocking." Her voice rose on the last sentence and tears of rage stung her eyes. *Why does her father not know these things?*

"Erica, we're so sorry," Cynthia said softly.

Erica ran her hand over her face, catching the moisture that threatened to wet her cheeks. "You don't have anything to be sorry about, Cynthia. I'm sure you're a perfectly lovely person, and I'm equally certain Trent hasn't told you that his daughter has autism."

Cynthia's eyes widened slightly, and she looked at Trent questioningly.

He appeared adequately ashamed as he stared at the floor.

Erica blew out an exasperated breath. "Trent, what were you thinking?"

He shrugged like a child. "I thought it would be okay. She was fine the last two times I was here. There wasn't any of *that*." He waved his hand in the direction of the kitchen.

"No, there wasn't, because the last two times you were here were close enough together that you weren't almost a brand new person to her again, and because it didn't disrupt her routine." *Because even when you're here, you're not really.* She wondered how long he and Cynthia had been together and if she was the reason he'd been coming more often, but now wasn't the time to ask. "We knew you were coming, so it wasn't a surprise. She had time to adjust to the idea. "

"You didn't tell Erica we were coming?" Cynthia asked, watching Trent closely.

He looked sick.

Erica almost felt sorry for him. *Almost.* She dropped back into her seat, exhausted. "I'm so mad at you tonight, Trent, I can't be sure I can even remain civil. I'm tired. I need to see to Siena. Just go to bed, and we'll talk in the morning. We can start over."

"Maybe it would be better if Trent and I found a hotel," Cynthia said hesitantly.

"There's no need for that," Erica said, feeling a bit chagrinned. "I mean, unless you'd be more comfortable after my outburst." She smiled apologetically. "I'll talk to Siena in the morning before she comes downstairs and make sure she's prepared. She'll be fine."

"Are you sure?" Cynthia asked. "Because we wouldn't mind, if it would make things easier." She took Trent's hand.

"I'm sure." Erica glanced at Trent. "You're both welcome here. Trent's Siena's father, and it's good for her to see him. And with the two of you getting married, she'll need to get to know you. I promise, it isn't usually like this, although it would be good for both of you to learn how to deal with her ASD. Please, feel free to stay, and we'll start fresh in the morning."

In Siena's room, Erica found almost exactly what she expected—Siena in her bed asleep, her elfin face scrubbed clean, with hands to match no doubt; Gus snuggled in beside her, on guard with slitted eyelids; and Leslie in the rocker with a book. The only thing out of the ordinary was that Leslie was also sound asleep, her head tipped back, and the book she'd been reading, *But No Elephants*, draped open over her chest.

Gus rolled onto his back for a tummy rub when he saw Erica.

She was happy to oblige. "You're such a good boy," she whispered as she leaned over and scratched his belly. "I think I owe you another big soup bone." She'd gotten him one from the butcher's counter for their secret deal the night she'd watched Leslie in the pool, and he'd loved it. He chewed on it for days. Then it'd vanished, reappearing occasionally, covered in dirt, for another round.

Gus made a soft growly noise in his throat and pawed the air.

Erica laughed. She pulled Siena's covers up and tucked them in around her, then kissed her on the cheek. "Sweet dreams, sweet baby."

When she turned back to Leslie, she expected to find her awake and watching her, like she did sometimes, but Leslie's eyelids remained gently closed, her breathing soft and even. She studied the lines of her face, smooth and relaxed in sleep, and she lingered on Leslie's lips. What would it be like if they were together—a couple—if she could kiss Leslie awake? *Yeah, yeah,* she said to that naggy little voice in her head. *I know. We're friends.* What had that been in the kitchen that afternoon, though, with the frosting? A wave of fatigue hit her at the mere idea of having to figure it out. She eased a lock of hair that had fallen across Leslie's forehead to the side, then ever so lightly, trailed her fingertips through the layers.

Leslie's eyelids fluttered.

Erica withdrew her hand. "Hey," she whispered.

Leslie opened her eyes and gazed up at her. She blinked, then cleared her throat. "Is everything okay?"

"Well," Erica said contemplatively. "Everyone's still alive. That's a good thing, I guess."

Leslie laughed quietly. "I'm glad to hear it. I'd hate to have to bail you out of jail."

"Awww." Erica tilted her head to one side. "But you would?"

"It depends on how much blood you left for me to clean up." Leslie chuckled, then sat up. "What was going on?"

Erica nodded toward the door. "Come on. I'll fill you in." She grabbed the monitor on the way out.

In the hall, she turned toward her bedroom rather than the stairs. "I need to change clothes," she said as explanation. Leslie had already exchanged the jeans and T-shirt she'd worn beneath her Pooh costume for a pair of swirly purple lounge pants and a soft lavender tank. She looked cuter than cute, but Erica tried not to dwell. "If you don't mind." It wasn't as though Leslie hadn't ever seen her bedroom.

"So what was that all about," Leslie asked as Erica stepped from her bathroom in an oversized T-shirt and a pair of athletic shorts.

"I'm still not actually sure." Erica cleared a few things from the bed, then sat on the side she slept on. She propped a pillow against the headboard and leaned back on it. "Cynthia, the woman, is Trent's fiancé, whom he's never said a word about."

Leslie's eyebrows shot up.

"I know," Erica said, still perplexed. "She said she'd heard all about me and Siena, but Trent's never mentioned a word about her. I'm wondering if she wasn't pushing him to see Siena more often, or maybe to introduce her to us...or something...and if that isn't what's behind his increased visits. But he hadn't told her that Siena has ASD."

Leslie lowered herself to the foot of the bed as she listened.

"And you should have seen him," Erica went on. "I mean, I know you haven't seen much of what he's usually like."

"I've seen enough, if that first day was any indication." Leslie's mouth quirked in a less-than-impressed smirk.

"It is. But tonight...He was acting like his involvement as Siena's father was crucial to her future success as the heir to his throne. And since he's never paid any attention to how to interact with her or understand any of her triggers, or that she even has some...Well, you saw what happened. It didn't even occur to him it was his doing, didn't remember Siena needs to know when someone brand new is going to be in the house."

"She didn't have trouble the first time I came over," Leslie said. "At least, not because I was here."

"No, but she'd already met you in your yard and had a positive experience with you." Erica tilted her head back and stared at the ceiling. "And when you did come over later, you brought a clean dog and toys. You were more like a visit from Santa. Cynthia's a complete stranger whose name Siena has never heard before, and she was introduced by Trent, who wasn't acting at all like the father Siena's used to. Granted, she was really tired and had already probably pushed her limits being at the carnival for so long..."

"She did great there, didn't she?" Leslie sounded so proud, it touched Erica's heart.

She smiled. It felt so good to be able to share that pride in Siena's success with someone. "She really did." She looked at Leslie again. "And see, you know that, because you're around her and have cared enough to get to know her with all her idiosyncrasies. Trent, on the other hand, doesn't have a clue how to interact with her." She kept her voice low, since she wasn't sure if Trent and Cynthia had come upstairs. Wherever they were, she was sure he was getting an earful from Cynthia.

"Siena's amazing, Erica," Leslie said, drawing up her knee and leaning back on one elbow. "It's his loss."

Erica considered Leslie's words—and Leslie, with her strong shoulders and toned arms set off by the lines of the tank top. Something scratchy and distracting at the back of her mind kept her from fully appreciating what she was seeing, though. "What are they doing here now, after all this time? What does he want?" She focused on Leslie as if she might have the answer.

Uncertainty…or doubt…or maybe even fear passed through Leslie's eyes. She looked away. "Did you talk about that?"

"No, I mostly just yelled at him. I was too angry to make any sense of things tonight." Erica ran her fingers through her hair, then rested her head in her hands. "It's been a long day, and Siena's episodes always drain me. We can all sit down in the morning and talk about it."

Leslie nodded. "I should let you get some sleep then," she said after a pause. "The morning's on its way." She rose and moved toward the door.

Erica followed. "Leslie?" She didn't want her to go yet, but how could she say that? It was late. The day *had* been long for both of them. They needed rest.

Leslie turned, her expression inquiring.

Erica wavered. She was stalling. "I just wanted to say thank you…for today, for the carnival. It was so much fun. Siena and I both had a wonderful time, and it was really good for Siena to be a part of something like that."

Leslie smiled. "It *was* fun. I had a great time, too."

"And thank you for tonight." Erica stepped close and slipped her arms around Leslie's shoulders in what she hoped felt like a friendly hug.

Leslie stiffened almost imperceptibly, then slid her arms around Erica's waist. "You're welcome."

"I don't know how I would have handled Siena along with everything else, if you hadn't shown up." Erica knew she should let go, but she couldn't make herself. "I don't know what made you come over, but I'm so grateful."

"Oh, that reminds me," Leslie said, still holding Erica. "Your purse is on the couch in the family room. It got bundled up with the costumes and ended up in my car."

Erica tightened her embrace. "I wondered where it was. I thought it was in *my* car." Erica marveled at the inanity of her words, and yet, inane or otherwise, she couldn't think of anything else to say. Nor, it seemed, could she release Leslie. She breathed in Leslie's scent, absorbed her warmth, felt comforted in the cradle of her arms. The hug went too long, the silence too deep.

"Are you okay, Erica?" Leslie whispered.

Tears sprang to Erica's eyes and she buried her face in Leslie's hair. *Damn it!* She shook her head. "I'm sorry. I don't know what's wrong with me." She tried to ease away.

Leslie adjusted her hold and pulled Erica into her. "It's okay. Let it out." She backed Erica to the bed and lowered her onto the edge, then knelt in front of her. She held her until Erica regained her control.

"I'm sorry," Erica said again.

Leslie touched a fingertip to the underside of Erica's chin and lifted her face to hers. "Talk to me. What's going on?"

The sincerity and concern in Leslie's eyes threatened Erica's fragile composure. She felt her mouth quiver. "I don't want you to go," she said shakily. She hurried on before Leslie could answer. "I know there's all this stuff between us and we agreed to just be friends. And that's okay. I'm not asking that we do anything. I just want to be with you. You're the only one who's ever understood what I feel...what I need...after a scene with Siena...and I just want to be with you. Everything can go back to normal tomorrow. I promise. I only need this one night."

Leslie's expression went soft. Without a word, she took Erica in her arms again and tucked Erica's head beneath her chin. She held her like that for a tender moment, then rose and went around to the other side of the bed.

Erica watched her as they both slipped beneath the covers.

As she eased down after switching off the bedside lamp, she felt Leslie's arm slide beneath the crook of her neck and her body spoon into Erica's backside. Leslie closed the circle by draping her other arm over Erica's middle and pulling her snugly against her. It was like being enveloped in a warm, protective cocoon. She'd never felt so safe, so cared for, so understood by another human being.

And for only that moment, she let herself pretend it wasn't just for one night.

Chapter Fourteen

Leslie lay on her mat in Savasana pose, bringing a close to her morning yoga practice. She took a few extra minutes to contemplate just how stupid she'd been the previous night. Usually, yoga and meditation cleared her head and centered her for the day, but her mind wasn't any quieter now than when she'd started over an hour earlier.

She felt better physically, the stretching and movement of the poses having worked out the kinks in her muscles from being so tense all night, holding Erica in her arms while trying to control her arousal. *Holy crap! What a long night.*

Mentally and emotionally, though, she was a mess. Even now, at the end of her practice, when she normally felt peaceful and serene, a voice in her head kept screaming: *What were you thinking? How could you have stayed with her? Are you a masochist or just a moron?* And when she could manage to quiet that, flashes of specifics—like the scent and silky caress of Erica's hair against Leslie's face; the innocent way her soft, bare foot had slipped between Leslie's feet in the middle of the night; the torment of her ass pressed into Leslie's groin and Leslie's inability, or unwillingness, to move away—rushed in on her.

She'd known better than to stay. She should have said no, but there was no way she could, not in the face of Erica's pleading expression and tear-filled eyes. Erica had told her how alone she felt sometimes following one of Siena's reactions, and this had clearly been one of those times. Erica had needed someone. So she'd stayed, and there was nothing to be done about that. The only thing left to do this morning was figure out how to forget the night, handle the feelings and desire that had come raging to the surface, and tuck it all away again so they could go back to the agreement they'd made. Erica had said it was only for one night, and that night was over.

Leslie rose and took one last languid stretch, reaching high above her head, then bending all the way over to touch the floor. She needed to get some work done. She would have been up and at it by three had she not been in Erica's bed and hadn't wanted to risk waking her. She gave an inner scoff. Didn't that sound noble and considerate?

She'd known what would happen had Erica turned to her in her arms, her hair tousled, her eyes sleepy. Leslie would have kissed her. With the deep ache between her thighs and the sensitivity of her stiff nipples from pressing against the soft fabric of her tank and Erica's back, she wouldn't have been able not to. She would have pressed her lips to Erica's, and when she'd felt their softness, she wouldn't have been able to stop there. She would have slid her tongue between them, moistening them, parting them. Then she would have—*Christ! I wouldn't have been able to stop at any point.* So she'd stayed another few hours, until Erica had eased from bed and gone into the bathroom. Leslie feigned sleep until she heard the shower turn on, then she too had gotten up and slipped out.

Work. That's what she needed. *And maybe the distraction of conversation about someone else's life.* Erica would most likely be occupied for the day—perhaps the next, depending on how long her company stayed—so Leslie could do a quick check on her and Siena, then head over to Nell's for a while. That sounded like a plan. She took the stairs two at a time, thinking a nice, long shower might help clear her head as well.

Refreshed and dressed—she'd also given herself some much-needed release under the shower massage—she sank into one of the deck chairs to put on her shoes. She set her cup of coffee on the small table beside her and pulled on a sock.

"Morning." A man's voice cut off the sound of the birds in the surrounding trees.

Startled, Leslie looked up.

Trent stood at the gate, a mug in hand, in the exact spot she'd first seen him several months earlier.

He hadn't been there when she'd come out. She was certain. It'd become habit for her to glance in that direction anytime she stepped out her back door. "Good morning."

He scanned her yard. "That's a nice pool."

"Thank you." Leslie slipped her foot into her Nike. She had no interest in a conversation about her pool.

"I guess that's a great thing about living in California. Lots of swimming pools," Trent said, as though she'd asked his opinion on the topic.

To Leslie's surprise, he moved through the gate and walked toward her. "It's so cold in Chicago. I'm not home enough to use one much anyway." He stopped a few feet in front of the deck, his gaze taking in the cup beside her, the shoes, and her. "Mind if I join you?"

Leslie couldn't have been more stunned if he'd asked if he could strip naked. *Why* would he want to join *her*? She had no inclination to spend time with him, but there was something in his eyes—those brown eyes, so much like Siena's—that gave her pause. "I don't suppose so." She waved in invitation to the chair beside her.

He climbed the two steps and perched on the edge of the seat, propping his elbows on his splayed knees. "Erica said you grew up in this house. That you've only been back here a few months."

Did he not remember their introduction? Erica had said he was...what? Preoccupied? Rude was the descriptor Leslie would use. She had no use for this guy. "That's right."

He hesitated, as though searching for something else to say. "It seems like a good neighborhood to grow up in," he said finally.

Leslie eyed him, taking in his profile as he stared out across the lawn. What did he want? He seemed to be making an effort, but to what end? Russell, Cassie's husband, sprang to mind. *Russell doesn't want you in Elijah's life.* A wave of wariness moved through her, the same she'd felt the previous night when Erica had pondered what Trent and Cynthia were doing there. She tried to curb it. *Erica said she'd never do that.* "It is," Leslie said. "I mean, it was. I assume it still is, since there are families living here." She pulled on her other sock, then reached for her shoe.

An awkward silence stretched between them.

Leslie grew irritated. She wanted to enjoy the pleasant morning with her cup of coffee, sitting out here by herself, and throwing the ball for Gus. Where *was* Gus? She assumed still at Erica's. He'd stayed the whole night with Siena. Leslie saw him stretched out along Siena's side when she'd stolen past Siena's room earlier. He'd lifted his head and looked at her, but that was all. Everyone had to be up by now, though, and normally Siena or Erica, or both, would be sitting with her on a Sunday morning. Where were they now? And Cynthia? Out of the number of possible scenarios, why was she sitting here with Trent?

"Erica and Cynthia were both really mad at me last night," Trent said, as though it were a natural segue from talking about the neighborhood. "And they're still mad this morning."

Leslie glanced at him. *Oh, well. At least we won't be discussing where I was last night.* "Is that why you're over here?" She gave a final tug on her shoelace, then straightened in her chair. "You're hiding?"

He turned his head and looked at her. He seemed to be searching for something. "No. Erica told me if I wanted to learn how to get to know Siena and get her to want to know me, I should come over here and talk to you. So I did."

Leslie's heart swelled in her throat at the sentiment. She suspected the suggestion had been thrown at him like a dart rather than offered as a helpful idea, and she could understand why. "After seven years, you want to get to know Siena?" The question was out of her mouth before she could stop it.

His lips twisted into a sheepish quirk.

Leslie tamped down the anger she always felt at Trent for throwing away what she'd been so devastated to lose. Maybe he was trying. "I'm sorry. I don't mean to be—"

He held up his hand. "No. That's a fair question." He returned his gaze to some undefined spot in the yard and pressed his lips together.

Leslie smiled to herself at the sight of Siena's thinking face on this grown man. She softened toward him.

"Did Erica tell you our history, how we didn't want kids for a long time, and how she got pregnant accidentally?" he asked after a pause.

"Yes." Leslie settled back, curious to hear Trent's experience of the same events.

Trent swirled the remains of his coffee in his mug. "When she told me she was pregnant, I...I panicked. It changed everything we'd talked about, everything we'd planned. It changed Erica. Then when Siena was born and I held her that first time..." He swallowed hard. "I was terrified. I looked into her eyes, and I realized, I'm her father. And she's going to look to me for things, for important things...for everything. And what if I fail her?" He faced Leslie, the fear he spoke of evident in his expression.

Leslie remembered that fear with Elijah, not that she was his father, but that she could fail him nonetheless. That he could need something from her that she didn't have or couldn't give. That maybe she wouldn't be good enough. Even now, with Siena, she had flashes of it. Maybe all parents felt that way at times.

"Then I started getting used to it," Trent went on. "I started looking forward to coming home from trips and seeing her, seeing what new things she was doing. I realized a new way of living had evolved, and new plans were being made. And I was seeing a side of Erica I never knew existed, a protective and nurturing side. And she was so beautiful when she looked at Siena. I mean, she's always beautiful, but when she looks at Siena..."

Leslie knew that, too. She loved watching Erica watch Siena.

"Then..." Trent's tone lowered. It was like that moment in a scary movie when the music changes and the shark comes after the hero. "I'd just started thinking maybe it'd be okay to have a kid, and then Erica said something was wrong. The baby wasn't doing things she should be doing, and she wouldn't look at us anymore. Then the tantrums started..."

Not tantrums. Meltdowns. Leslie wanted to correct him, wanted him to understand.

"And then they said it." He shook his head defiantly. "And there were all these new things that had to be done, or couldn't be done. And they said she was autistic, but what the hell does that really mean? I still don't know what it means."

Leslie considered continuing to listen, simply letting him talk until he had nothing left to say. In fact, it's what she should do, since she doubted Erica had actually meant for him to come ask her anything. Besides, what did she know about dealing with Siena as a baby? That had to be so much harder than at seven, when Siena could verbalize some of her anxieties and feelings and could be reasoned with to some degree. She couldn't do it, though. He'd opened up so much, she owed him the truth. She shifted in her seat toward him. "I have to throw the bullshit flag, Trent."

He twisted around, his eyebrows arched. "What?"

"I understand your fears of failing Siena as her father, of not being good enough, and I understand you not knowing how to deal with autism back when she was diagnosed. But it's been…what? Five years? If you wanted to know, you could have learned."

His expression darkened with evident anger.

She thought he was going to get up and storm away.

Instead, he studied her. His glare slowly softened. "You're right."

"So what's really going on?" Leslie asked. "Why haven't you been willing to learn?"

He averted his gaze and remained silent for a long time. "It's not that I don't love my daughter." He bowed his head and rubbed his eyes. His shoulders began to shake. "It's that I'm… embarrassed. I'm embarrassed that she has autism in the first place, that she has all these issues and weird stuff that sets her off, and I'm ashamed that I don't know how to deal with it."

"Don't be ashamed, Trent, just learn how to deal with it. If you want to be Siena's father, you're going to have to learn how to be. If you don't want to, then let that be okay. Quit beating yourself up over it. But decide, one way or the other." She wanted to add that Erica had it handled but thought that might be too much.

"How did you learn?" he asked after regaining his composure. "To interact with her, I mean. And in such a short time? I saw you last night. You knew exactly what to do."

Leslie marveled that he hadn't told her to go screw herself and stalked off to tell Erica what a bitch her neighbor was. She released an inner sigh of relief. She couldn't imagine having to tell Erica that she'd ruined what little willingness Trent had to be around. "A lot of it, I asked Erica, or Siena herself."

"I couldn't ask Erica." Trent sat up straighter, seeming to collect himself more.

"Why not?"

"I can't stand seeing my failure in her eyes. I saw it for too many years."

"I don't think that's what you'd see," Leslie said softly. "I think she'd be happy you're asking."

"No," Trent said. "I can't."

"All right, then read a book. There are tons of titles on all facets of autism. I have three good ones in the house you can borrow." Leslie waved toward her back door. "And there are some good documentaries on Netflix and PBS. And there's a great show on Netflix about a high-functioning teenage boy and his family. I've learned a lot from watching that. And I'm sure you can find some support groups in Chicago where you can ask any questions you want, or just listen and learn. I haven't been to one, but I know the one Erica attends helps her."

"Wow, it sounds like there's a lot."

Leslie smiled. "I'm sure there's way more. The information's out there if you want it. All you have to do is decide if you do. It's work, that's true, but it's worth it."

Trent considered her. "I can see why Erica fell for you."

Leslie blinked, unsure she'd heard correctly. "What?"

"I said I can see why Erica fell for you. You're very kind. And intelligent. And if you don't mind me saying so...and I'm not hitting on you, I swear...beautiful." Trent blushed with the last rush of words.

Leslie felt her own cheeks heat. "No. Erica and I are friends." She sounded flustered. She calmed herself. "We're just friends."

"Oh! I'm sorry," Trent said sincerely, but he didn't look convinced. "It seemed last night…the way she looked at you when she first saw you. She used to look at me that way eons ago. And she trusts you so much with Siena…I just thought." He shrugged.

The way she looked at me? Leslie had been too caught up in trying to determine what was going on to notice. She did remember how Erica had looked at her in the kitchen when she'd sucked the frosting off Erica's fingers—and how *she'd* looked at Erica.

"Maybe what I saw was gratitude for you being there and knowing what to do." Trent seemed to be backpedaling, trying to leave his comments in such a way that Erica wouldn't kill him. "It's too bad, though. I think you'd be really good for her. I know in the past she's felt alone in dealing with Siena—no thanks to me. You obviously help her with that." He suddenly found something fascinating in his coffee cup.

Before Leslie could think of anything else to say, Siena and Gus appeared in the gateway.

"Hey there, what are you two up to?" Leslie called, thankful for anything to get them off the previous subject.

"We can't find a ball," Siena said without a glance at Trent. It was like he wasn't there.

He didn't seem to notice.

"Hold on." Leslie rose and retrieved an orange one from the box of dog toys near the back door. "Here you go." She threw it across the grass and chuckled as Gus ran after it mindlessly.

She and Trent watched as the two began to play.

"You want to start now?" Leslie asked him.

"Start what?"

Leslie tipped her head toward Siena. "Getting to know your daughter?"

Trent's eyes widened. "Now?"

"Come on, I'll help. Start a conversation," Leslie said encouragingly. "Ask her something."

Trent shifted his gaze to Siena, then back to Leslie, then to Siena again. "Hey, Siena, where's your mom and Cynthia?"

Leslie rolled her eyes. "Not that."

"I don't know," Siena said, not turning around.

"Something to do with her," Leslie said quietly. "Say something about her shoes. She loves them."

Trent took a deep breath. "I like your shoes," he called to her.

Siena stopped in mid-throw and turned to him, her expression puzzled. "They light up," she said cautiously.

Gus danced around her, obviously eager for the game to continue.

Leslie ducked her head. "Ask if you can see them," she said into her hand.

"Really?" Trent said, improvising. "Will you show me?"

Siena crossed the grass to where they sat, lifted one foot, then stomped it down on the deck. She smiled at the flash of light. She repeated the motion with her other foot. "See?"

"That's great." Trent sounded entirely out of his element, but he was trying.

"And it looks cooler in the dark," Siena said.

"I'll bet it does. Maybe you can show me tonight." Trent's suggestion seemed genuine. He shifted in his seat.

"Okay. I'll show you my crystal that glows in the dark, too." Siena turned and threw the ball. "My mom and I grew it from a kit I got for my birthday last year. I didn't know you could grow a crystal, especially one that glows in the dark. It was the best birthday I ever had."

Leslie smiled at Siena's enthusiasm. It reminded her of the first day she'd met Siena and the conversation about poop and vomit. She watched Trent.

He seemed to be relaxing a bit more.

Gus returned with the ball and tried to give it to Siena. When she paid no attention, still talking about birthdays and how for her next one she wanted a bigger kit to grow a ginormous crystal, he dropped the ball at Leslie's feet.

She, in turn, slipped it to Trent.

Within seconds, he'd thrown it and had become a part of the play. By the time Erica and Cynthia showed up at the gate, he still appeared a little stiff but was holding his own.

Cynthia laughed and joined in on the game.

Erica stood, her mouth hanging open, watching. After a few minutes, she looked at Leslie. As she approached, her smile grew wider. She stepped up onto the deck. "How the hell did you pull that off?"

"Pull what off?" Leslie asked innocently.

Erica moved beside her and stared out at the game going on in the yard. Her expression was one of wonder. "Trent's never played with Siena before. I mean, yes, when she was six months old, he might have jangled his keys at her to keep her quiet, but never like this."

Siena squealed as Gus raced past her with the ball, making her chase him. Trent made a grab for him but missed.

"Did you talk to him?" Erica cut Leslie a sidelong glance.

"We chatted." Leslie kept her focus on the activity in the yard, but she could see Erica in her peripheral vision. The feel of their bodies spooned together all night rushed back in on her.

"Did he tell you they're thinking about moving to Los Angeles?"

Leslie looked at Erica. "They are?"

Erica nodded. "After the wedding. Trent's been offered a position with a recording studio here." She was smiling, her expression reflective as she continued watching the game. "That could be so good for Siena."

Leslie's wariness from earlier, her fear, the pain of losing Elijah to the change in Cassie's life, hit her hard. She folded her arms, clamping them around her middle. "He's not as bad a guy as I thought he was," she said, hoping it was true. "His desire to get to know Siena and understand her seems genuine."

Erica studied her for a long moment, then found Leslie's hands and unfolded her arms. "And it won't change what you have with Siena. I promise." Her voice was gentle and reassuring.

Reluctantly, Leslie met her gaze. She wanted to believe her. She had to. She couldn't imagine going through that again. But all she could manage was a single nod.

Erica moved close and brushed her lips across Leslie's cheek. "Thank you," she whispered. "For talking to him."

And without warning, Leslie was once again reliving the night before, her body heating, her emotions swirling and churning. She couldn't take it, this fluctuation between all these intense feelings. *I have to get out of here.* She squeezed Erica's fingers, then moved away.

The kiss had been soft, affectionate, sincerely grateful. It was a kiss she'd received from Paula many times, from her mother years ago. She could picture Erica kissing Becky that way, and yet, the kiss set every single cell in Leslie's entire body ablaze with desire. Suddenly, the yoga, the meditation, the shower massage… everything she'd done to calm her body was out the window. She might as well be back in Erica's bed, pressed up against her. She had to go. "I told Nell I'd come over and help her with some stuff today," she managed the lie. "Gus seems to be having a good time. Can he stay with you?"

"Of course." The blue of Erica's eyes was several shades darker with emotion. Questions swam in its depths. No doubt she wanted the details of Leslie and Trent's conversation, wanted to know what Trent had asked her.

But Leslie couldn't do that now. All she could do was grab her laptop, her keys, and get the hell out of there. At Nell and Paula's, she could work, or maybe there was still cleanup to be done from the carnival, or a movie they could go to.

Anything to keep her from imagining everything she wanted to do to *her friend* Erica.

CHAPTER FIFTEEN

Erica sat in her car, in the dark, down the street from her house—from Leslie's house. This hadn't been her plan for the evening, this stalkerish behavior. She wasn't stalking, though. She was thinking, trying to figure out how she'd made such a mess.

Hadn't her reasoning for not acting on her attraction to Leslie from the beginning been to avoid ending up where she sat right now? And she *hadn't* acted on it. She'd behaved herself so as not to make the situation awkward, not to blur the lines and confuse the issues between friendship and something else, not to endanger Siena's connection with Leslie. Yet here she sat, feeling awkward, blurred, and confused—and *without* getting to actually *have* sex with Leslie. She sighed in the darkness. At least Siena and Leslie's relationship was intact.

The week had been frustrating. Erica's emotions had been in chaos, ever since the previous Saturday night when she'd arrived home to find Trent and his new fiancé camped out in her living room. Or maybe it was since Leslie had appeared at the exact right moment, with the exact right thing to do and say, as always. No, it'd started before both. It was in that moment earlier that same day, when Leslie had sucked chocolate icing off Erica's fingers and turned her insides to liquid fire. Erica hadn't been able to hold her focus on anything since, and here it was, the following Friday.

She kept trying to figure out what had actually happened Saturday night. She'd come home. She'd gotten mad at Trent. Leslie had shown up and taken Siena upstairs so Erica could deal with Trent and Cynthia. The next thing she knew, she was crying in Leslie's arms. *How did that happen?* Stranger still, was the moment she'd heard the words, "I don't want you to go...I just want to be with you...I only need this one night," then realized she was the one saying them. And in that moment they'd felt completely right. And when Leslie had rounded the end of the bed and crawled in next to her, when she'd snuggled up behind Erica and taken her in her arms, Erica, for the first time in her life, knew she was exactly where she belonged.

Her mortification and fear hadn't set in until the next morning, when she'd thought back on the evening. She, Erica Cooper, award-winning journalist, competent college professor, independent and self-sufficient single mom of a special needs child, had crumpled like a rag doll low on stuffing in the face of...what? Her ex-husband showing up? *That's not all that earth-shattering.* The fact that he was engaged? *Who cares?* She wished them well. That Trent had upset Siena? *Square hamburger patties upset Siena. Life goes on.* Siena was fine.

Somewhere in the night, though, everything had changed. Like when you go to sleep having wound the cord of your ear buds into a neat, round little circle, but when you wake up, it's a snarled mess, somehow Erica's feelings of all that rightness and belonging had gotten twisted and knotted up with beliefs that she needed to handle everything on her own. That she shouldn't need—or even want—anyone's help. That she couldn't let herself get used to that, because it wouldn't last.

Then there was the sex, or rather, the wanting of it and the lack thereof. Erica couldn't even think anymore when she was around Leslie. Since Trent and Cynthia had left on Tuesday and the distraction they'd provided had gone with them, Erica had found herself daydreaming in the middle of a class about the feel of Leslie wrapped around her and the softness of her lips as she'd sucked Erica's fingers. Erica could still feel the brush of Leslie's hand on the back of her bare thigh that night on the balcony, when Leslie had covered her with a blanket. And once Erica started into those thoughts, one thing led to another, and…Hell! Who was she kidding? She wasn't having daydreams. She'd found herself in the middle of an all-out fantasy the previous afternoon while sitting in the classroom monitoring a test. How could she possibly sort out her feelings and thoughts and beliefs that were all so intertwined with one another and figure out what the hell she was truly feeling when all she could think about was ripping off Leslie's clothes and fucking her?

That's when she'd gotten her idea for tonight. If she could satisfy her sexual needs, she could then focus on the rest. It'd been a long time since she'd slept with anyone. Maybe it wasn't entirely a desire for Leslie. Maybe a good, decadent roll in the hay with someone else would suffice. Enter, Kathleen Duvall.

Erica had met Kathleen through mutual acquaintances shortly after she and Siena had moved to California. Kathleen was like Erica in that she was busy, content with her life as it was, and had reasons for not wanting emotional ties, yet enjoyed the pleasures and conveniences of having a familiar sex partner. They'd slept together periodically, as well as served as dates for one another for professional or community events. Then Kathleen's work had taken her to Europe for two years. She'd called Erica a few times since she'd been back, but getting together hadn't worked out. Until tonight.

They'd decided to meet for dinner to catch up on each other's lives and go from there. It'd taken Erica all of fifteen minutes to realize it wasn't just sex she wanted. It was sex with Leslie. So here she was, sitting alone in the dark after gently but firmly turning Kathleen down. *Shit!* Maybe if she and Leslie talked, reestablished their agreement. It'd made all the difference in the world the last time they'd had a completely honest conversation. Surely, it would again.

Erica steeled herself and started her engine, then reconsidered. If she drove the short distance and pulled into her driveway, Rachel would hear, and Erica didn't want her to leave yet. She wanted someone with Siena so she and Leslie could relax and talk. She turned off the car and climbed out.

It felt strange to go to Leslie's front entrance, so she went around to the back. She knocked softly on the French doors, then waited. A dim light from the living room spilled from the archway into the family room, but there was no shadowy movement and no sound. And no Gus. Maybe Leslie wasn't home. Maybe she'd had a date tonight as well. She thought of Molly the previous weekend and how she'd touched Leslie, her interest so obvious. Jealousy uncoiled in her stomach and reared its ugly head at the image. She stomped it down. *Uncalled for. I don't have any claim.* How much longer could she pretend she didn't want one? She knocked again.

Still nothing.

She turned the knob and opened the door. In the stillness, she heard the tapping of typing on a keyboard from the living room. She moved to the doorway and stopped.

Leslie sat at her computer in the corner of the jungle, Kaa offering his assistance from over head. Full headphones covered her ears, and she was absorbed in the images on her screen.

Erica didn't want to startle her, so she waited, leaning against the jamb, and studied her. She wondered what Leslie was listening to, if it was classic rock Erica knew she liked, or something softer, more conducive to her creative process.

Leslie's long, slender fingers danced over the computer keys, as though she were playing a piano with the skill and artistry of a maestro. The muscles of her face were soft, relaxed rather than contorted, and in her concentration, her eyelids were half closed. She wore a loose-fitting, finely knit sweater—cashmere perhaps— the chocolate shade making her olive skin glow and the sleeves pushed up to her elbows, revealing the delicate ropes of muscle beneath the smooth flesh of her forearms. Jeans covered her lower half, tapering to the exquisitely feminine lines of her bare ankles and feet. *God, she's tempting.*

Without warning, Leslie turned her head, her eyes going wide at the sight of Erica. She gasped and slapped her hand to her chest. She pulled off the headphones. "Jeez. You scared me."

Erica smiled. "I'm sorry. I wasn't sure how not to, since you didn't hear me knock."

Leslie considered her, swiveling her chair to face her. "What are you doing, standing there, looking..." She ran her gaze down Erica's body, then more slowly, back up in evident appreciation. "Like that."

In all of her emotional and mental turmoil, Erica had forgotten how she'd dressed for her...date? Rendezvous? Booty call? Her dress wasn't fancy, a rich dark purple with simple lines, but its halter neckline that dipped low to reveal ample cleavage and its hemline, not slutty but definitely suggestive, made it sexy as hell. "Like what?" She tried for innocence, but couldn't keep one corner of her mouth from lifting, giving herself away.

A blush darkened Leslie's cheeks, but she looked anything but embarrassed. Her eyes held her answer in their heated depths— *like you want to be fucked.*

And oh, sweet mother of God, she did. Now that she was here, it was *all* she wanted.

"I thought you had plans with Kathleen tonight," Leslie said.

Leslie's words snapped Erica back from her narrowly-focused reverie. *Kathleen? How does she...?* The coloring books and box of crayons on the edge of the desk caught her attention. *Of course.* Siena had been over. And of course, she'd told Leslie why Rachel was watching her. Siena told Leslie everything. She might have to be more careful about what she said in front of her. Erica gathered her thoughts. "I did."

"It's kind of early to be home from a date." Leslie sounded casual. There was something in her tone, though, that hinted otherwise.

Is she fishing? "It wasn't a date," Erica said, not wanting to admit the truth but knowing she had to. "Kathleen is more of a..." She couldn't make herself say fuck buddy. That was too crude for anywhere other than in her head. A pillow pal? *That's just sappy.* "A friend with benefits," she said. Not exactly accurate. Erica had never thought of Kathleen as a friend. No, Kathleen had always been pure benefits.

Leslie turned her attention to her computer monitor. "That explains the dress," she said, studying the screen. "Friends with benefits are nice to have sometimes." She moved the mouse, then tapped the keyboard.

Erica watched her.

Leslie seemed uncomfortable all of a sudden, as though she was trying to escape into the world of whatever website she was building.

Erica walked slowly to where she sat. "It used to be," she said, wondering what had changed, but deep down she knew. "It used to work very well, but it seems that's over."

After a beat, Leslie lifted her gaze to Erica. "Why is that?"

Erica met Leslie's eyes. The question was only three simple words—and the answer just as short. *Because of you.* The meaning of the two together, though, opened up a huge cavern of possibilities, some of which, Erica didn't know if she was ready for. What she did know, though, was that she couldn't stay where they were. Her heart began to pound with a blend of anxiety and excitement. "Because when I was sitting across from her in the restaurant, listening to her talk about life in Barcelona, all I could think about was you."

Leslie didn't move, didn't speak. The brown of her eyes had darkened to a smoky shade of black.

Her stillness prompted Erica to continue. "I remembered how good it felt to be in your arms last weekend, pressing up against you. You wrapped around me in my bed all night." As she spoke, she relived each sensation, reexperienced every response. The steady pulse of desire that had throbbed between her legs all week—sometimes beneath the surface, but always there—surged to full need. She shifted closer to Leslie, gazing down at her. "I thought of all the times since I've met you that I wanted to be close to you, to touch you," she whispered. She combed Leslie's hair away from her temple, from her cheek, then leaned down, closer still. "Wanted to do this." She pressed her lips lightly to Leslie's.

Leslie sighed and arched up to meet her.

They held the kiss, suspended in its softness for one, two, three, maybe four seconds, then Erica began to explore. She ran the tip of her tongue over that plump lower lip she'd noticed that very first day. She moistened the slight opening between it and the upper one. She teased Leslie, and herself, with a quick dart inside, then a gentle nip.

Leslie moaned softly, opening against Erica's mouth.

Erica slipped her tongue inside, covering Leslie's lips with hers more firmly, coaxing Leslie back in her chair. She wanted to take more, to take it deeper, to take everything from a kiss that could ever be taken. She wanted it to last.

Leslie's breath came fast and hot. She took Erica in, met her in a delicious swirl of their tongues. She brought her hands up and framed Erica's face, holding her in place.

They kissed long and deep, first Erica exploring Leslie's mouth, then Leslie claiming Erica's. Leslie caressed Erica's cheeks, her neck, her bare shoulders, while Erica drove her fingers into Leslie's thick, soft hair. The kiss went on and on.

Finally, Erica broke free. She gasped for air. Her knees trembled, and she had to straighten to keep from sinking to the floor. "Whew," she said, pulling her hair up off her neck. A deep flush heated her face, throat, and shoulders.

Leslie stood. In her bare feet, with Erica in heels, they were eye to eye.

Erica gripped Leslie's shoulders to steady herself. She opened her mouth to speak, but Leslie silenced her with another searing kiss. She clamped her arms around Leslie's neck and immediately lost herself again in her hunger. A thought tried to claw its way into her mind—something about stopping—but she drove it away. She clung to Leslie and moaned as Leslie moved from her lips, to her neck, kissing her way down Erica's chest and into the plunging neckline of her dress.

She licked between Erica's breasts, sucked the inner curve of one, then the other.

Erica groaned as the fabric caressed her already rigid nipples.

All the while, Leslie stroked the bare flesh of Erica's back.

Shivers ran down Erica's spine, and goose bumps rose on her skin beneath Leslie's palms, only to be warmed again by Leslie's heated touch.

Her mouth again on Erica's, Leslie backed toward the couch, pulling Erica with her. In a fluid motion, she sank onto the cushion, her head on the armrest. She guided Erica over her, never breaking the kiss. Her hands, still traversing Erica's back, found their way to the edges of the bodice of Erica's dress and slipped beneath it. She caressed the sides of Erica's breasts, slowly, teasingly.

Erica remained on her hands and knees, aching to feel Leslie's fingers, her touch, her caress on her nipples. "More," she murmured impatiently.

Leslie didn't hesitate. She cupped Erica's breasts, palming her nipples, then closed her fingertips around them in a tight squeeze.

Erica arched and threw her head back. Her cry of pleasure surprised even her. The sensations arrowed straight to her clit, and she ground against Leslie's thigh.

Leslie rolled Erica's nipples, pinched them gently, then began a torturous rhythm that threatened to drive Erica over the edge.

But Erica wasn't ready. She wanted more pleasure, wanted it to last. She lifted her hips, relieving the pressure on her clit.

"You're so fucking sexy," Leslie whispered. She stared into Erica's face, her arousal and need evident in her eyes, in the hoarseness of her voice, in the low groan she'd released with Erica's movement. With one hand, she reached beneath Erica's hair and loosened the ties holding up the bodice of the dress. When it fell free, she arched her neck and captured her nipple between her soft lips. She sucked greedily.

Erica clenched her eyes shut. She was lost. She wanted to stay in that moment, with Leslie beneath her, doing things to her she'd dreamed of but never believed would happen. She wanted more and more and more. And she got it.

Leslie worked Erica's nipples, tantalizing, teasing, tormenting them, for a long time. Finally, she clutched the skirt of Erica's dress with her free hand and dragged it up Erica's thighs and over her ass. She toyed with the dimple at the base of Erica's spine, fondled and squeezed her cheeks through the satiny panties, ran a fingertip along the edge where the thigh met the buttock. Then she slipped her fingers under the fabric and into Erica's hot, drenched folds.

She sank deep into the wetness, stroking the length of Erica's sex, dipping inside her, then retreating.

Erica groaned, then whimpered, then began to writhe. She pumped her hips.

Leslie pushed inside her and began a rhythmic thrust.

When she found Erica's clit and stroked it simultaneously, Erica lurched and began to shake. She couldn't hold back a second longer. "I have to come," she whispered, her entire focus on the exquisite sensations consuming her. It was all too much.

"Yes," Leslie murmured, before closing her teeth tenderly on Erica's nipple.

Erica cried out as her orgasm ripped through her.

Leslie didn't stop. She stroked and sucked and kissed Erica through the very last spasm, until Erica collapsed on top of her, breathless. As she nestled her cheek into the hollow of Leslie's shoulder, Leslie closed her arms around her and held her in a gentle embrace. They lay in stillness for a long time.

Gradually, Erica realized how comfortable she felt lying in Leslie's arms, no self-consciousness about how vulnerable she'd allowed herself to be, no first-time nerves. It felt as though they'd been intimate for years and tonight was merely a typical evening at home. *Yeah, right.* Her body thrummed. *And what about Leslie's?* She shifted to the side and ran her hand over Leslie's stomach, the softness of the cashmere caressing her palm. "This is a pretty sweater," she said quietly to break the silence.

"Thank you," Leslie said. There was a smile in her voice.

Erica waited for more. Okay, maybe she did feel a little bit awkward. She lifted her head and kissed Leslie's neck, then looked up into her face.

The smile Erica had heard played on Leslie's lips.

"Say something," Erica said.

Leslie's expression sobered. Her gaze went hot. "You're gorgeous when you come. I'd like to see it again. I never want to lose that image."

The intensity in Leslie's voice stole Erica's breath, but she also blushed. "Are you kidding? With the orgasm I just had?"

She ducked to avoid Leslie's gaze. "Besides, there are more new things I'd like to explore." She slipped her fingers beneath Leslie's sweater and traced light circles on her stomach.

Leslie jerked and tightened her hold. She let out a low groan. "That particular new thing won't take very long."

"Really?" It was Erica's turn to smile. She slid down Leslie's body and settled between her legs, her breasts pressed to the crotch of Leslie's jeans. "Let's see about that." She pushed up the sweater to reveal smooth, bare skin, then lay her mouth where her fingers had been.

Leslie's muscles tightened. She leaned her head back and stroked Erica's hair.

Erica let out a sigh of contentment. She picked up where she'd left off with her fingers and began languid circles with the tip of her tongue. Leslie's skin was hot, dampened by a thin sheen of sweat. She tasted of salt and something mildly sweet, and a faint scent of lavender hugged her skin. She kissed the flat of Leslie's stomach, remembering the sight of her naked body that night in the pool. Impossibly, her clit stirred again. It was time for Leslie, though, time to give her as much pleasure as she'd given Erica. She pressed her palms to Leslie's sides, then inched upward.

Leslie squirmed beneath Erica's mouth and hands. She cupped the back of Erica's head and twisted her fingers into her hair. "You're being mean."

Erica smiled against Leslie's skin. "You won't feel that way when we're finished," she whispered. "I promise."

Leslie's throaty chuckle turned to a moan when Erica reached her breasts and massaged them through her bra. She thrust her hips when Erica grazed her engorged, stiff nipples.

Erica looked up Leslie's body. She wanted to see her face, watch her reactions. She rose to her knees and stretched over Leslie. She pushed the sweater farther up, eliciting Leslie's help to shed it completely. When Leslie curled forward and pulled it over her head, Erica captured one hard nipple in her mouth through the thin bra cup, and gently tweaked the other between her fingertips.

Leslie jolted upright and sucked in a breath, then dropped back onto the couch. She gripped Erica's head and held her mouth firmly to her.

Erica settled her hips into the cradle of Leslie's open thighs and feasted on Leslie's breasts.

Leslie moaned and writhed, pushing her mound against Erica's.

Erica pushed back, giving her plenty of purchase. She felt a little like she was back in high school, rolling around on a couch, still fully clothed and Leslie in only jeans and a bra. They were adults. They *could* undress. They could even move to Leslie's room and be in a bed. *Nah. Who needs a bed?* And the clothes... Erica could fix that. She flicked the front clasp of Leslie's bra and shoved the cups aside. Her lips found flesh, and she groaned with pleasure.

Leslie's breathing was ragged, her legs clenching and unclenching around Erica. "Erica. Erica." Her voice was a raspy whisper.

Erica continued her worship of Leslie's breasts—those perfect handfuls she'd wanted to touch and taste since day one—but she knew Leslie needed to come soon. And she wanted to make her come. She wanted to know, as Leslie now knew about her, what she looked and felt like in that pure, unguarded moment. Finally, she relinquished the nipple in her mouth, hoping there would be another time for more, and made the return trek down Leslie's body. She worked the button at Leslie's waistband.

"Oooooh, yes." The words came as a plea.

Their urgency amped up Erica's arousal, and she quickened her pace. In seconds, she had Leslie's jeans in a heap on the floor and was once again between her legs, breathing in her musky scent. She brushed her lips over the patch of soft curls at the apex of Leslie's thighs, then kissed her outer lips.

Leslie let out a loud groan and spread her legs wider. Her need was palpable, her desperation flagrant.

Erica couldn't hold out another second. She plunged her tongue into Leslie's soaked sex, licking the length and savoring the taste. She closed her lips around her clit and sucked it gently, while sliding a finger inside her.

Leslie bucked and grasped Erica's head. She held it tightly but allowed Erica to set the pace.

Erica didn't make her wait much longer. She quickly found the exact spots and techniques that drew the deepest responses. She flicked her tongue back and forth across the very tip of Leslie's clit, while she thrust two fingers rhythmically inside her.

Leslie's legs trembled. Her body shook. Her muscles clamped hard around Erica's hand, and she pumped her hips, giving Erica everything she had.

Erica rode out the orgasm, easing off a little at a time as Leslie came down. She nuzzled Leslie's center with her lips, until she felt Leslie's hands stroking her hair.

"Oh, my God," Leslie said, still catching her breath. "Oh, my God."

Erica smiled. "Still think I'm mean?"

Leslie moaned softly. "Oh, my God, no."

Erica moved up beside her and snuggled against her. "Good, because that might mean you wouldn't want to do it again."

Leslie wrapped her arms around her and pulled her in closer. "Not a chance of that. I was having a hard enough time keeping my hands to myself when I didn't know what this would be like. Now that I know…Oh. My. God."

Erica let her fingers play over Leslie's skin as she wondered. They were both talking like they could be together like this again, but would they be? It was less than five minutes since they'd finished enjoying each other, and already her turmoil and concern from earlier was trying to crowd back in. She didn't want to deal with all those conflicting thoughts and emotions, all those worries and fears. She simply wanted to lie here, cuddled with this woman who'd shown up out of nowhere and made such a difference in her life, who made her laugh and took care of things when Erica needed help—and now, who'd given her the most bone-melting sex she'd ever had.

"You don't have to go right away, do you?" Leslie sounded uncertain.

Erica was curious. She rose onto her elbow and considered her. "Do you want me to stay a while?"

"I do," Leslie said simply. She touched the lines at the corner of Erica's eye, then ever so gently, traced a path to the sensitive spot just below her earlobe.

Erica shivered but smiled. "I suppose one of the good things about having sex with my next-door neighbor is that my walk of shame is short."

Leslie grinned. "And you have a secret passage through the backyards."

Erica laughed, but something stirred deep inside her—a reluctance to talk about what had just happened. What was there to say? She'd tried and tried to figure out what she felt for Leslie, what *the right thing* would be to do, what their relationship should or shouldn't be. She could feel the question hovering above them. *What does this mean?* Why did sex always have to mean something? She merely wanted to lie here, feel Leslie close, touch her freely, and not think.

Leslie ran her hand down Erica's back. "I need to ask you something," she said softly.

Erica squeezed her eyes shut. *Here it comes.* "Okay," she said with resignation.

"This is twice now you've seen me naked, and I've only seen you once—and that was when you were sick and crumpled on your bathtub floor. You owe me big time." A hint of humor tinged Leslie's voice, but underlying it was the lust Erica had heard earlier. "What do you say we go upstairs, and you pay up."

Relief washed through Erica, followed closely by renewed need for more of Leslie. She'd be safe from her thoughts a while longer. "I'd be happy to." Erica leaned down and kissed Leslie fully. "I always pay my debts."

Chapter Sixteen

Leslie heard her back door open, then close. She looked across the bar from the kitchen sink just in time to see Siena run through the family room and into the living room. "Hey there," she called. "How about a good morning."

"Good morning," Siena yelled over her shoulder. She'd taken to making sure she rubbed Hotei's belly every time she came into Leslie's house in hopes that it would make Tim Davis's family move to another city like her friend Kiley had. She'd spent a few star wishes on the subject as well. She returned in seconds and threw herself onto the blue couch. "I want to make cookies."

Gus jumped up beside her, shook himself, then flopped down.

Leslie smiled at the picture. The two had literally become inseparable, unless Erica or Leslie were in some kind of distress. Then Siena had to share. Leslie wondered how she'd ever gotten by without either of them. "Did you already ask your mom and she said no?"

Siena frowned. "Yes. She has to grade papers."

Leslie had texted Erica when she finished her meditation and yoga, their established signal that it was all clear for Siena to come over if she wanted. They'd conversed some during the week, and Leslie knew Erica had given her classes midterms. She might appreciate Siena being occupied so she could work uninterrupted. "Let me check with her and see if she minds you doing it over here with me."

Things had been a little weird between them since the previous weekend. Erica's unexpected visit and everything they'd done during those few hours had been mind-blowing. Leslie couldn't have come up with a more perfect fantasy than the reality they'd shared. She'd thought Erica would be passionate in bed from her emotional responses to other things at times—but damn!

When they'd gotten upstairs, Leslie had no sooner caught her breath from their first round before Erica had given her a striptease—emphasis on *tease*—then had her flat on her back for three more shattering orgasms. Finally, Leslie had to beg for mercy. In concession, Erica had stretched out in Leslie's bed—a sight Leslie knew she could easily get used to—and requested her own repayment. Her exact words: "It seems *you* owe *me* now." Everything between them felt so new. The good night kiss they'd shared later on Leslie's deck seemed like the perfect ending to a perfect beginning.

Something wasn't quite right, though. Throughout the week, they'd seen each other. They'd interacted. They'd gotten along fine. They'd even exchanged a few smoldering looks, and Leslie had needed to make herself come a few nights in order to get to sleep. It wasn't difficult with Erica's energy, her scent, and all the memories still in Leslie's bed. Somehow, though, it seemed they'd lost something between them. Shouldn't they have gained something from a shared experience like that?

They weren't talking about it, which was odd. They'd been able to talk about their pasts, their heartbreaks, their attractions to one another. They'd even been able to work out Erica's anger at Leslie for hurting Siena and Leslie's remorse over it. But now, when they should be even closer, they weren't talking about anything of importance. *Why not?* Finally, this morning, Leslie had figured out what was wrong, at least on her part. It'd hit her from Erica's return text message.

Leslie had texted, *I'm up & at it. How'd you sleep?*

There'd been a longer wait than usual for the reply. When it came, there was a smiley face. *One of those times when a friend with benefits would have been nice.*

Leslie had an immediate reaction from her libido, a stirring between her legs and a flash of Erica climaxing, but a twist of anxiety knotted her stomach as well. She wasn't sure how to interpret the comment. Was Erica thinking of their time together, subtly asking for more, or was she lamenting the loss of Kathleen and reconsidering that decision? Either one bugged Leslie but for different reasons. If the reference was to Kathleen, it was pure jealousy. If Erica was talking about Leslie…She wasn't sure she wanted that role in Erica's life. The realization had surprised her. She'd drafted and erased several responses, then settled on an answering smiley. She'd have to think about it, and maybe they could discuss it tonight. They'd be attending the fundraiser dinner and dance for the children's center, so they'd have some time without Siena. Maybe afterward…There was that flash again. She shook her head to clear it.

"Hey, there's something I want to talk to you about," she said, coming back to Siena. "But it might involve you keeping a secret. Is that okay?"

Siena nodded. "As long as I can tell Gus."

Leslie chuckled and moved to the couch. "Gus is right here. He'll already know it." She got comfortable. "Besides, it's not a secret from him. I was just wondering what you and your mom usually do for her birthday. I'd like to surprise her with something."

"My mom doesn't have a birthday," Siena said flatly. She was petting Gus, her focus on him.

Leslie was shocked. "What do you mean? Of course she does. Everyone has a birthday." Could it be that Erica didn't celebrate hers?

"Why does everyone have one?" Siena seemed intrigued, as though this had never occurred to her.

"Because if you're a person walking around on this planet, it means you were born." Leslie drew her legs up under her and got comfortable. "And that's what a birthday is—the day you were born. So she does have one, and it's next week."

"How do you know?" Siena eyed her.

Leslie's face warmed. She was a little ashamed to admit the answer. "I sort of...sneaked a peek at her driver's license when her purse got put in my car after the carnival."

Siena's expression didn't change. "You're not supposed to open her purse. Her purse is a private space, like your bedroom, or your bathroom drawers. It isn't nice to open someone else's private spaces without asking them if it's okay." Clearly, Erica and Siena had had this conversation. Siena narrowed her eyes. "But she opens my bathroom drawers to get my toothpaste and my hair brush, and she's never asked me if that's okay." She paused thoughtfully. "How come she gets to do that but we can't open her purse?"

How quickly things went off track. "Hmmm, that's a good point. Maybe you should ask her. I'm sure she can explain it to you." Leslie could see that conversation going on for a while, and she wanted to figure out Erica's birthday. "Do you want to know the secret?"

Siena's eyes brightened, and she nodded.

"Okay." Leslie rubbed her hands together. "There's this pizza restaurant in Chicago, where you and your mom used to live, that your mom really, really loves. She told me it's one of the only things she misses about Chicago." She paused for effect.

Siena leaned closer.

"And I looked up the restaurant online and found out that they'll ship their pizzas anywhere," Leslie continued. "So I thought—"

"Why would they put their pizzas on a ship?" Siena looked puzzled.

"No, no," Leslie said. *Damn.* She'd been doing so well. "They don't put them on a ship. If you ship something, it's like when you mail it, like if I mailed you a letter, it would come to your house in the mail."

"I like mail," Siena said with excitement. "Did you mail me a letter?"

"Okay...no." Leslie waved her hands in a *cancel that* gesture. "I didn't mail you a letter."

Siena's face fell.

"But I can, if you'd like." Leslie couldn't stand seeing Siena's sad face. She was blowing this.

Siena smiled. "I'd like that."

"Okay." *Note to self—write and mail letter to Siena. Now...* Leslie took a deep breath and considered her next words carefully.

Siena had drawn herself into a cross-legged position and was watching her expectantly.

"You know how sometimes you get a package delivered to your house?" Leslie asked, hoping this one would be clear.

Siena thought for a minute. "Like a box?"

"Exactly," Leslie said, holding up her hand for a high five.

Siena grinned and slapped it. "Uh-huh," she said in answer to the question.

"All right. Those were shipped to you from the company that sent them." Leslie waited.

"Okay," Siena said after a beat.

Leslie nodded. *Okay.* "So the restaurant will ship the pizzas here from Chicago, and we can all eat your mom's favorite pizza for dinner on her birthday."

"In a box?" Siena asked, double-checking.

"In a box." Leslie added the confirmation, watching as Sienna processed.

"Okay," Siena said lightly. "I don't like stuff on my pizza."

"Then we'll make sure one is only cheese, just for you," Leslie said, hoping to conclude that part of the conversation. "Now, what about a birthday present?"

"You said the pizza was the present."

"That's her present from me." Leslie was glad to see Siena was still fully engaged in the plans. It would mean so much to Erica. "But you should give her something that's from you, too."

"Like what?" Siena asked.

"I don't know." Leslie reached between them and combed her fingers through the fur on Gus's rump. She was enjoying this conversation. "What do you think she'd like?"

Siena was quiet for a moment. "I could draw her a picture," she said finally, but her tone lacked conviction.

Gus flipped onto his back and pawed the air.

Siena rubbed his belly, still thinking. "I could sing her a song," she said much more enthusiastically. "And I could teach it to Gus. We could both sing it."

Leslie laughed. "I *know* she'd like that."

"But she's already heard all the songs I know." Siena's voice dropped, matching the look of discouragement on her face. Then she perked up again. "I could make up a brand new song for her." The wheels were clearly turning. "What should I put in it?"

"Anything you think she'd like. It's your gift to her," Leslie said. "I'd make sure to include I love you, though. Moms always like to hear that."

Siena hesitated. "But I don't know if I do." She flopped back into the thick upholstery of the couch. It all but swallowed her. "I don't know what love feels like."

Leslie didn't recall ever having actually thought about what love felt like. *Does anyone, or do we merely say the words?* She revisited all those times she'd held Elijah and looked into his bright green eyes, or even now as she sat here and looked at Siena. She softened as something moved within her. "Well, I feel kind of warm and tingly inside when I love someone. Do you ever feel that?"

Siena crinkled her forehead. "I don't think I have tingles in me."

"Okay, well, let's see." Leslie shifted in her seat and stretched her legs to rest her feet on the coffee table. "Does it feel good when your mom tucks you in at night and reads you a story?"

"I like it a lot. And it's even okay if she kisses me then. I don't like it when other people kiss me," Siena said. "Is that the same thing?"

"Yeah. I think so." They might be getting somewhere. "Most people don't mind when the people they love kiss them." Who'd have thought she'd be sitting around some Saturday morning trying to explain feelings to someone who didn't have the same feeling process other people did? And what did she know anyway? She couldn't even figure out what *she* felt for Erica. "And how does it feel when she makes you macaroni and cheese?"

"That's my favorite dinner. She makes it for me when I do good at something or when I'm sad. That makes me want to smile."

Leslie nodded and raised her eyebrow. "Again, the people we love make us want to smile. Anything else?"

Siena cocked her head. She didn't speak for several beats. "I like it that she smiles more now that you came to live with us. I think she likes you being here more than when Mr. and Mrs. Mumford lived here."

Leslie had difficulty focusing on the real topic with this new piece of information, but she managed. She slapped her thigh. "People always want the ones they love to be happy. That settles it. With all those things, it seems safe to say that you do love your mom."

Siena broke into a huge grin. "Okay, I'll put it in the song then. But it might have to rhyme with something."

"Of course." Leslie bit back a laugh and let herself enjoy her own moment of love. "So…we have pizza, we have presents, and if you'll tell me what kind of cake you think she'll like, I can arrange that."

"Chocolate with chocolate frosting." Siena showed no hesitation on that item.

"Chocolate it is," Leslie said. "I think we're set."

They got online and ordered the pizzas, then started on the cookies, but Leslie kept drifting back to the criteria they'd established for knowing you loved someone.

She couldn't deny any of it where Erica was concerned. She certainly liked it when Erica kissed her, Erica definitely made her smile, *and* she loved seeing and making Erica happy—hence, the pizza being shipped all the way from Chicago. And yet, did that truly mean anything? Surely, a seven-year-old's love was much different, less complicated, than that between two grown, baggage-laden adults.

But no, it wasn't. Love was love. And if she went any farther down this road, she was going to have to admit she'd fallen in love with Erica.

And what am I supposed to do with that when all she wants is a friend with benefits?

❖

At seven fifteen, Leslie checked her reflection in her bedroom mirror as she fastened the gold and onyx choker around her neck. The strapless tuxedo jumpsuit she'd bought for the fundraiser fit her perfectly, and she was happy with the way it looked. It'd been quite some time since she'd attended any kind of formal affair, and although she didn't usually like dressing up this much, tonight it felt nice. She was looking forward to the evening, not so much the schmoozing and hobnobbing, but certainly the dancing with Erica. The rest she could tolerate for the sake of the center.

As she reached the bottom of the steps, she was greeted by a wolf whistle.

"My, my, Ms. Raymond, but you do clean up nicely." Erica's voice was sultry. She was seated on the Shere Khan tiger couch in the jungle, wearing a classic little black dress with shimmery black stockings and strappy black heels. She smiled alluringly.

"And look at you," Leslie said, her tone revealing the surge of arousal that had hit her, she was sure. "How many of those sexy dresses do you have hidden away?"

Erica rose. "I knocked, but I figured you were getting ready," she said, sidestepping the question.

Leslie wanted to take her into her arms and kiss her senseless, but she knew if she did, the rest of the evening would be lost. She was hoping there'd be the opportunity for such things later, but first, they had to get through cocktails, networking, dinner, and dancing, plus a conversation about Leslie's revelation from that morning concerning being friends with benefits. She'd gotten a little clearer on it as the day had passed, but she remained unsure of exactly what she needed to say. Leslie held out her hand. "Shall we go?"

Erica interlaced her fingers with Leslie's and they headed for the car.

On the drive, that strange silence that had been between them throughout the week settled over them. What *was* that? What happened to their banter and the ease with which they usually moved from one topic to the next? What happened to their friendship? The only thought in Leslie's mind was that damned friends with benefits thing. Why couldn't she come up with anything else? And why didn't Erica?

"Those cookies you and Siena made this afternoon were good," Erica said finally. She sounded as though thinking of the subject had been just as much of a struggle for her as Leslie was having. "I've never had coconut chocolate chip cookies before."

"Siena found the coconut in my pantry and wanted to see what happened if we added it." Leslie shifted as she changed lanes. "I bought it to try making coconut shrimp one night this week."

"That sounds good." Erica stared out the windshield.

How could they be close enough that Erica clearly knew the dinner was for all of them and still only be able to talk about coconut on a date? *Maybe this isn't a date. It didn't start out as one.* It'd only begun as Nell suggesting Erica come with Leslie for the dancing. Maybe that was their problem—there was just too much confusion around them. Silence shrouded them again. *Jeez, does Erica feel as idiotic as I do?*

The second they walked in the door to the benefit, Molly swooped in and dragged Leslie off to meet Jason Reginald Lucas III. For the next hour, it was one Jason Reginald Lucas III after another, with a couple of Alexandria Templetons thrown in. These were the people who paid the bills at Raymond Children's Center, though, so Leslie smiled and was gracious and appreciative. Without the money in this room tonight, there would be a lot of children with no bed to sleep in and no safe roof over their heads.

Leslie kept track of Erica in the crowd. She seemed to be holding her own quite well, sometimes chatting with donors or board members, other times hanging out with Nell and Paula. Always, her eyes met Leslie's, and her smile said, *I'll be right here when you're done.* Apparently, the awkwardness between them was only when they were alone—and *not* in each other's arms. *Good to know.*

When dinner was finally announced, Leslie found Nell. "Where are Erica and Paula?"

"Restroom," Nell said, smiling at a passerby. "What the hell's up with you and Erica?"

"What do you mean?" Leslie played innocent.

"You two can't keep your eyes off each other," Nell said, keeping her voice low. "It's a good thing Molly had you occupied, or the two of you would have been groping in the corner like teenagers at a house party. Give it up, cuz. Did you two do the horizontal tango?"

Leslie knew she might as well fess up. Nell wasn't going to let it go until she did. "What if we did?"

Nell's eyes grew wide and her mouth dropped open. "No way. Really? That's great. Why didn't you tell me?"

"Because I knew you'd do this." Leslie wiggled a finger back and forth between them.

"Do what? I think it's great. I like Erica. It is great, isn't it?" Nell stepped closer. "You didn't get yourself in another situation with someone who doesn't want what you want, did you?"

"I don't know. I don't know what she wants." Leslie sighed. "I'm not even a hundred percent sure what I want."

"What are you two whispering about?" Paula asked as she slipped an arm around each of them. She leaned into Leslie. "Are you all done rubbing elbows with the royalty? Ready to join us peons again?"

Erica laughed from Leslie's other side. She slipped her hand into Leslie's. "Let's go eat. I'm starving."

The four of them were seated at a big, round table with Molly and several donors. Molly kept the conversation focused and moving, so there was no opportunity for Nell to pin Leslie and Erica to the wall about what had happened between them. *Thank God.* It would be hard enough to bring up the topic with Erica in private, never mind trying to navigate it in a group forum. When the cover band took the stage, Leslie was more than ready to hit the dance floor, if only for a moment of peace with Erica.

She leaned close to Erica's ear. "Would you like to dance?" she whispered.

Erica turned and smiled at her. "Very much." The pale blue of her eyes sparkled with what could only be delight.

Erica's movements were graceful and fluid as they moved through the first two songs. The music was a combination of lighter pop and some soft jazz, nothing too fast, so their steps and pace were relaxed. When a true slow dance began, Erica moved naturally into Leslie's arms. Her hands were warm on Leslie's bare skin as she slid them around Leslie's shoulders and laced her fingers together at the back of Leslie's neck. "Mmmm, this is what I've been waiting for all night," she said softly.

Leslie encircled Erica's waist and took the lead. Her body responded to Erica's proximity, to her words, to her breath fanning across Leslie's cheek. She pulled her as close as propriety allowed and began an easy sway. "Me too," she said quietly.

"I'm very proud to be your date tonight." Erica seemed to be back to her usual self, other than the desire evident in her eyes. "Thank you for bringing me. It feels good to be out with adults," she added with a note of humor.

Leslie laughed. "It *is* easy to get caught up in the parenting role. I'm sorry I neglected you for so long earlier. Molly's a taskmaster, but I understand that my name and presence can make a difference."

"At least she wasn't all over you tonight." Erica tightened her hold on Leslie. "I'd like that to be my job later." Her tone was teasing.

Leslie smiled. "She'd never do that at a function like this. She's in professional mode."

"I liked watching you," Erica said thoughtfully.

Leslie felt herself blush. "I could tell."

Erica smiled. "I'm sorry. Did that bother you?"

"Not bother," Leslie said, remembering the clench of arousal in her abdomen every time she looked up to find Erica's gaze on her. "It was a little distracting, but I enjoyed the challenge."

"I've never seen this side of you." Erica's thigh brushed Leslie's as they moved in time with the music.

Leslie's pulse jumped. She tried to put a half inch or so between them. "Which side is that?"

"I've seen you at home as a friend and neighbor and how thoughtful and considerate you are in that role."

Friend and neighbor? Was that all?

"And I've seen the playful as well as the more serious side of you in your relationship with Siena and how connected to her you are," Erica went on. "And last weekend, I got to see—and experience—your passion and what an amazing lover you are." She paused and smiled. "And tonight I've enjoyed watching your professional and socially conscious persona moving through the crowd, shaking hands, and making a difference. It's all quite the package." Affection shone in Erica's eyes.

Was this going where Leslie thought it was, where she was hoping it was? *Was* she hoping for that, for something more? Was that the piece that had been nagging at her all day? "Thank you," she said, wanting more time to sort it out. "Does this mean you're going to take me to some swanky college professor shindig, so I can see you in your professional hat?" she asked teasingly.

Erica laughed.

Leslie loved the sound.

"I'm not sure college professors ever get this swanky." Erica nodded to their surroundings. "But there are times I can use a date by my side. Now that Kathleen's gone…"

Kathleen again. Friends with benefits. Suddenly it hit Leslie full on—that *wasn't* what she wanted to be. She *did* want more. She wanted it all. She wanted Erica in her arms like this every day, in her bed every night. She wanted Erica to come home to her after good days and bad. She wanted her as a friend, a lover, a wife. She wanted Siena and Gus flopped on the blue couch and all of them to be together, to plan birthdays and Christmases and vacations. Friends with benefits could *never* be enough.

"Erica…" She shouldn't say it now, not here. She should wait, at least until they got home, where Erica could leave if it made her uncomfortable, if she didn't feel the same. Did she? Could she? She'd just said Leslie was quite the package. Had that only been flirting, part of the seduction of their friends-with-benefits evening? But the words were coming, fast and frantic, up her throat, like a diver out of air, desperate to break the surface of the water. She couldn't stop them. "I don't want to be your—"

"I'm sorry to interrupt," Paula said from beside them, "but, Erica, your phone keeps vibrating. I thought it might be something important." She held the clutch purse Erica had left at their seats.

Erica pulled from Leslie's arms, her expression alarmed. "Thank you." She snatched the bag and retrieved her phone. "It's Rachel," she said, sweeping the screen. She put the phone to her ear as she left the dance floor, Leslie and Paula in tow. "Rachel, what's wrong?" she said after a moment.

In the pause, Leslie could hear Rachel talking in rapid-fire but couldn't distinguish any words over the noise of the gathering. She waited, anxiety tightening every muscle in her body.

Erica went pale. "What hospital?"

Leslie's stomach plummeted.

"I'm leaving now." Erica ended the call. "I have to go." She looked around her, clearly panicked.

"What happened?" Leslie asked, her own hysteria just below the surface.

"It's Siena. I have to go." Erica's voice rose. "I need your car."

"I'll take you," Leslie said, shifting into emergency mode. Erica wouldn't be in any shape to drive, even if she'd *had* a car.

"No. You have to stay..." Erica waved her hand around the room. "Just give me your keys."

Leslie was stunned. Did Erica really think... "Erica, I'm not staying. I'll drive you. Let's go." She slipped her arm around Erica and ushered her out the door.

What the hell happened?

CHAPTER SEVENTEEN

Erica sat in the passenger's seat, pushing her right foot into the floorboard, willing the car to go faster. How long had they been driving? It seemed an eternity since she'd spoken to Rachel. They'd hit every red light, gotten stuck behind every slow moving vehicle. It was Saturday night; the traffic was heavy. She gritted her teeth as they came to yet another stop. Leslie was saying something. "What?"

"I was wondering if you could tell me what Rachel said." Leslie glanced at her, taking her eyes off the cars in front of them for only a second. "I mean, if you're not too—"

"Of course. I'm sorry." Erica tried to drag her thoughts back to the phone call. It'd been only five minutes—maybe ten at the most—but it felt like so much longer. "Um…she said…" Her voice trembled. "Siena fell down the stairs." Erica drew in a steadying breath. She had to keep herself together. "She was unconscious, and Rachel called 9-1-1. An ambulance took her to the hospital." A sob threatened to break loose on the final word. Absently, she felt Leslie's fingers cover her fist that clenched her cell phone in her lap.

"We're almost there," Leslie said.

The reassurance in her voice did little to calm Erica. Her heart pounded. Her thoughts raced. *Has the ambulance arrived yet? Is Siena there?* She lifted her phone to call and find out.

It vibrated in her hand, and Providence St. Joseph's Medical Center appeared on the screen.

"Hello. This is Erica Cooper," Erica said in a rush. "You have my daughter, Siena, there?"

"Yes, Ms. Cooper. My name's Karen." The woman spoke with equal rapidity. "Your daughter arrived about fifteen minutes ago, and she's regained consciousness. She's become hysterical—"

"She has ASD." Erica sickened at the thought of how scared Siena must be. "She's autistic."

"Yes, the EMTs informed us of that. The doctor needs your consent to sedate her so we can treat her and so she doesn't injure herself more seriously."

"If you hug her tightly or apply—"

"We can't apply deep touch pressure without knowing the extent of her injuries." Karen's tone was patient but firm. "Her arm is broken, and if she has any fractured ribs or internal bleeding, that kind of pressure could do more damage. We need to sedate her to get x-rays and run tests. Do we have your consent, Ms. Cooper?"

The woman obviously knew what she was talking about, but it didn't help. Erica gripped her phone more tightly and clenched her eyes shut. God, how she wished she were there. "Yes." She snapped back to the question. "You have my consent. And I'll be there soon."

"Does your daughter have any allergies to medications?" Karen asked.

"No." Erica bit her lower lip to hold back tears.

"Okay, thank you. Tell one of the intake nurses when you arrive, and they'll bring you to us."

"Thank you," Erica said, but the line was already dead.

"I'm going to drop you off at the ER entrance before I find a parking space," Leslie said as she maneuvered the car into a driveway. "I'll be right in."

Erica could only nod. She climbed out and hurried inside.

"Erica!" Rachel jumped up from her chair across the room and rushed toward her. "Siena's with the doctors. They wouldn't let me ride in the ambulance, so I got here after they did. They wouldn't tell me anything."

Erica scanned the large, crowded waiting area. She spotted three intake windows along the wall. She moved toward the long line feeding all of them, coaxing Rachel along with her, and stepped in behind the last person. "It's okay." She squeezed Rachel's shoulders. "I talked with a nurse on the way here. Siena regained consciousness but then went into a meltdown. They sedated her." Erica's heartbeat quickened as it all became more real.

Rachel covered her mouth with her hand. "Oh, no."

Erica was only half aware of Rachel's reaction. She watched as the woman and two children at the far window walked toward the seating area. *How long is this going to take?* Her anxiety rose, then a gentle touch on the small of her back soothed her. *Leslie.*

"Everything going okay?" Leslie asked.

Erica turned with an exasperated sigh. "I can't just stand here and wait. Siena's already back there. I need to be with her."

Leslie continued a soft caress of Erica's back. She looked past her. "How are you doing, Rachel? Are you okay?"

Rachel frowned. "I'll be better when I know Siena's okay."

Leslie nodded distractedly. "Excuse me a minute. Stay here and hold our place." She moved away and approached a security guard.

Erica instantly felt Leslie's absence. She pressed her palms to her face and sucked in a deep breath. She held it, counting to ten, then blew it out. She had to calm down. She lowered her hands. "Rachel, what happened?"

"I'm not sure," Rachel said.

"What do you mean, you're not sure?" Erica's tone was sharp. "You were there, weren't you?" So much for calming down. "I'm sorry."

Rachel appeared unaffected—no more or less upset than she'd been when Erica had arrived. She seemed to understand. After all, she dealt with this kind of thing all the time. Well, maybe not this exact kind of thing, but with parents of children with ASD, who had cause for being what some might call overprotective.

Erica bowed her head and massaged her temples, trying to ward off a headache. "I didn't mean that."

"I know, dear." Rachel patted Erica's arm. She shook her head. "The evening went fine. We ate dinner. I gave Siena her bath and put her to bed. Then later, I was in the family room reading, and I caught sight of something out of the corner of my eye. I looked up and saw Siena about halfway down the stairs, and before I could even say anything, she was falling. I don't know if she tripped, or if she was sleepwalking...I just don't know. Gus started barking and licking her face, but she was unconscious." Her voice quavered.

The security guard Leslie had been talking to disappeared through the door from which nurses had been calling people, and Leslie returned.

Erica shot her a questioning glance.

"He's going to see what he can do," Leslie said quietly.

Erica sighed with relief, then returned her attention to Rachel. She took Rachel's hand and gripped it between both of hers. "It's okay. She's going to be okay." She managed not to let her fear creep into her voice for Rachel's sake—and for her own. *She has to be okay.*

"Ms. Cooper?" A blond woman wearing maroon scrubs stood in the doorway beside the guard. "Siena Cooper's mother?"

"Right here," Erica called. She started toward her.

"Come with me," the blonde said, holding the door open for her.

Erica froze, realizing she couldn't face this without Leslie. She turned back to her. The awareness made her uneasy—she handled things on her own—but she couldn't stop the words that were already leaving her mouth. "Will you come, too?"

Leslie's expression shifted from complaisant to surprised. "Uh, yeah, sure." She caught up to Erica.

"Rachel, one of us will be out with an update as soon as we can." Erica was familiar enough with Rachel to know she wouldn't go anywhere until she knew Siena's condition.

Rachel gave her a shaky smile. "Thank you."

The second Erica stepped through the doorway, she gasped in anguish, and her gait faltered. The bright lights, the cacophony of clashing noises, all the strangers rushing around, the chaos. Any one of those things could send Siena into a meltdown—but all of them combined? Every cell in her body ached for Siena, for the sensory overload and panic she must have felt when she woke— never mind the pain she must have been in. Erica's heart broke.

"I'm Karen," the nurse said. "I spoke with you on the phone."

"Yes," was all Erica could choke out. She felt Leslie's strong arm slip around her waist and was grateful for the support.

They moved through the bedlam, evading medical personnel and sidestepping gurneys and equipment until they came to a curtain. Karen pulled it aside and ushered them into a small room.

Siena lay still and pale on a bed, a man in navy scrubs beside her, writing in a chart.

"This is Dr. Weston," Karen said. "He's been with Siena since she got here."

He turned and smiled.

Erica extended her hand, but she couldn't tear her gaze from Siena. "Erica Cooper," she said. She felt his grip, then heard Leslie's voice. She moved to Siena's side and stroked her forehead. "I'm here, sweetie." Finally being with her, able to see and touch her, eased some of Erica's anxiety. She turned to the doctor. "What..." She couldn't find the right words.

Weston took charge. "What we know so far is that her left arm has a severe break, possibly two, and she did lose consciousness from her fall. The good news is that she did wake up right after she arrived. She's only out now because of the sedation. Her pupils are reactive. We'll know more after a CT. I've paged our orthopedic surgeon for a consult on her arm. X-ray's backed up tonight, so we're waiting."

"Thank you, Doctor," Leslie said.

"Yes," Erica said through the fog of concern and relief swirling around her. "Thank you."

"I'll be back to check on things, and a technician will be by with a portable machine for x-rays as soon as possible." Dr. Weston pulled back the curtain to leave.

"Can I go with her?" Erica asked quickly.

Weston gave her a soft smile. "Of course."

She nodded her gratitude.

"And if you fill out these forms while we're waiting, I can get them and your insurance card up to intake, so you'll be all set." Karen set a clipboard on the bedside table as she looked from Erica to Leslie.

"We'll take care of it," Leslie said.

When they were alone, Leslie stepped behind Erica and ran her hands up her arms. "How are you doing?" she asked gently.

Erica drew in a deep breath and leaned against her. She tipped her head back and closed her eyes. "I've been better."

Leslie kissed her temple and began an easy massage of her neck and shoulders. "I'm sure."

Erica relaxed under Leslie's tender kneading as she gazed down at Siena. "She always looks so little when she's asleep." She took Siena's hand. It was cold. She pressed it between her palms to warm the skin and became acutely aware of the connection from Siena to her to Leslie. They were linked somehow, cosmically bonded together. But that was ridiculous. There was no such thing, not for her. She did things on her own and was quite capable. Leslie had brought her to the hospital because they'd been together when she'd gotten the call. She'd come in here with her for support, like Becky would. Erica couldn't get sucked into this. She released Siena's hand and straightened. "I should get this paperwork taken care of." She picked up the clipboard.

"Sure," Leslie said, stepping away.

But when Erica gripped the attached pen and tried to write Siena's name on the first line, she trembled.

Leslie closed her hand over Erica's, stilling it. "You want me to do it?"

Erica sighed and nodded. She could let her help like Becky would.

Leslie took the clipboard from her and began filling in the lines she knew—name, address, phone, emergency contact— while Erica returned her attention to Siena. The noise from the ER was loud and constant, but inside their little curtained room, the only sound and movement was the tapping of the pen tip against the metal clipboard. It grated on Erica's nerves.

Finally, Leslie flipped a page. "I need your insurance card, baby."

Baby. The word in Leslie's warm alto tone eased Erica's tension. Had Leslie meant to say it? She didn't seem to be aware she had. Erica opened her purse and pulled out the small packet of cards.

"Oh, I need that, too." Leslie pointed to Erica's driver's license on top.

Erica handed over the requested IDs.

"There are a couple of places you need to sign," Leslie said when she'd finished. "And some medical history I don't know. Do you want to tell me the answers and I'll fill them in?"

Erica studied Leslie, the sincerity in her eyes, the caring in her expression. It tugged at her heart, tempted her to step into Leslie's arms and let her hold her, give her comfort, keep her and Siena safe. She needed some time to herself to regain her equilibrium. "You know what you could do for me that I'd really appreciate?"

"What's that?"

"Run home and bring me back a change of clothes." Erica watched closely for Leslie's reaction. She didn't want to exclude her. Leslie cared too much about Siena to be able to sit at home and wait and wonder. She had to have some space, though, just a little. And she *did* want out of that dress. "This outfit looks great, but it isn't very comfortable."

Leslie looked wary.

"The truth is," Erica said quickly, "I didn't intend to be in it this long tonight."

Leslie gave her a knowing smile. "I can do that," she said, clearly shifting gears. "Anything in particular you want?"

"Something comfortable." Erica entwined her fingers with Leslie's. "Thank you."

Leslie tightened her grip on Erica's hand. "It'll give me a chance to check on Gus. God knows what he's going through at home all alone."

"Rachel said he was barking and licking Siena's face after the fall." Erica pictured how frenzied he'd probably been.

"Did she say where she left him?" Leslie asked. "If she put him outside or locked him in one of the houses?"

Erica shook her head.

"All right," Leslie said, leaning in to kiss Erica's cheek. "I'll be back as soon as I can."

"If they move us, I'll text you." There was so much more Erica wanted to say, so much more she *should* say, but her mind was too jumbled. The conflict between wanting Leslie's arms wrapped around her, holding her tight, and feeling so afraid to let Leslie that close, to make herself that vulnerable was too confusing. All she could do was let her go, for now.

When Leslie returned to the waiting room, she saw Rachel in the chairs with Becky hysterically waving beside her. They both jumped up at Leslie's approach.

Becky and Leslie had met only once at a barbecue she and Jack and their kids had been invited to, along with Nell and Paula. The main purpose was to let everyone who might be running into one another from then on to meet and get to know each other. Leslie had been struck by the true sense of family she'd felt that afternoon.

"How is she?" Becky asked, her eyes wild with worry.

Leslie filled them in on what the doctor had said, which wasn't a whole lot more than what they'd known before, but somehow having been in the same room with Siena and seeing her made a big difference.

"And what about Erica?" Rachel asked. "Is she okay?"

"She's holding up," Leslie said, wishing she were still with her. She understood, though. "She asked me to go pick up a change of clothes for her."

Becky looked at her strangely. "*I* can do that. Why don't you stay—"

"I think she wanted a little time to herself." Leslie hoped that's all it was. She hadn't wanted to leave, afraid Erica might be pushing her away, but then she'd been reassured when Erica said she'd text if she and Siena were moved.

"You're good for her," Rachel said.

Leslie looked at her in surprise. Hadn't Trent said the same thing, or something like it? "I do what I can to help."

"No," Rachel said firmly. "*You* are *good* for her." She leveled her gaze on Leslie. "You calmed her down tonight. That's not always easy to do with mothers of special needs children."

Leslie wasn't sure what to say. She couldn't really take credit. She hadn't done anything but drive Erica to the hospital, talk to the security guard, and fill out some papers. She gave Rachel a small smile. "I know things were hectic and crazy tonight, but do you happen to remember where Gus was when you left? Did you put him in the backyard or leave him in the house?" She hoped he wasn't outside. She wasn't sure the fencing would hold him if he really tried to get out to find Siena. *But what would he do locked inside?* Suddenly, her need to go felt urgent.

"Oh, my goodness," Rachel said. "I don't know. I think he was inside, but he might have gotten out when the ambulance was there. I'm so sorry. It was all so fast, and I was worried about Siena."

"Of course," Leslie said. "I'll just go check on him." And give Erica her time. *At least I'll have the clothes she wants when I come back, so she'll have to let me in. Right?*

When she turned onto their street, her house was dark, but the lights were blazing in Erica's. Leslie cut through her own place and went directly through the yards. No sign of Gus. As she approached Erica's patio, she noticed something all over the lower half of the sliding glass door. She squinted at the red substance illuminated by the light behind it. *Blood?* She quickened her pace and fumbled with the handle.

A high-pitched howl sounded from inside, then something hit the glass—hard.

Leslie jumped back, then realized it'd been Gus.

He leapt at it repeatedly, scratching and yipping and howling.

She yanked open the door, and he flung himself at her. "Hey, it's okay. Shhhh. Shhhh. It's okay, boy."

He shook violently in her arms, whining and crying. His feet were cold and wet with something sticky.

Leslie looked down.

His front paws were covered in blood.

"Oh, Gus," Leslie whispered. "What did you do?"

He continued to cry but slowly became less frantic.

Leslie held him tightly against her and stroked his head.

A pathway of mingled and overlapping bloody footprints ran between the patio door and the front door, obviously from him running back and forth, trying to get out. A lighter stream ran up and down the stairs and through the kitchen. The bottom of the front door was covered in blood and marred with scratches and deep gouges. He'd clearly tried to dig his way out to follow Siena. Several of his toenails lay on the floor. One was imbedded in the wood of the door.

Tears filled Leslie's eyes, and she clutched him to her chest. He rested his head against her and panted heavily.

"I'm so sorry, Gus," she whispered. She sank onto the floor and rocked him.

As time passed, Leslie knew she needed to get back to the hospital, but she couldn't leave Gus again, not in the state he was in. He hadn't moved in the cradle of her arms once he'd calmed, and when she'd lowered him to her lap and continued stroking his head, he'd only stared up at her, his ever-present question in his amber eyes. "She's okay, buddy," Leslie said soothingly. "And you're okay. Everything's going to be all right." Finally, she took out her phone and called Nell.

By the time Leslie got back to the hospital, she'd received a text from Erica giving her a room number and telling her to use the ER entrance again and Karen would give her a sticker to wear so no one would stop her on her way up. When she stepped into the dimly lit room, she found the scene not much different than the one she'd left a couple of hours earlier. Siena lay, resting quietly under sedation in a bed, and Erica stood beside her, holding her hand.

Erica smiled weakly.

"Hey," Leslie said, letting the door close behind her. "What did you find out?"

"The CT came back clear, so there's nothing to worry about from her hitting her head." Erica stroked Siena's hair as she spoke. "But she broke both of the bones in her arm. The orthopedic doctor said they'll have to do a surgery in the morning to set the bones, then a metal rod will be inserted into Siena's forearm to ensure they remain straight and in place during the healing process. In four months, she'll need another surgery to have the rod removed." Erica paled when she got to the second surgery, but overall, she seemed to be doing relatively well.

Leslie reached for her, but Erica discreetly evaded her grasp, taking the bag of clothing instead.

Erica came out of the bathroom ten minutes later, hugging herself, her outfit from the fundraiser stuffed into the grocery bag dangling from one hand. "This feels good. Thank you."

Once Nell and Paula had arrived at Erica's, and Nell had gently taken Gus to get him to the emergency vet while Paula started cleaning up the mess, Leslie had gone to Erica's room and gotten her a change of clothes. She'd picked out a pair of soft blue jeans and a worn-thin Chicago Cubs jersey she'd seen Erica wear frequently since the weather had cooled to LA fall temperatures. She'd also grabbed her sneakers and a warm pair of socks. Hospitals got cold.

"How'd you know this was my favorite comfort shirt?" Erica asked.

Leslie smiled. "A wild guess."

Erica studied her, her throat working as though she might say something, but she remained silent. The laugh lines around her mouth and at her temples were deep with fatigue. The crease between her brows revealed her constant state of worry. Gratitude swam in the pale blue of her eyes but beneath it, a school of fears.

Before Leslie could move to her or even utter any reassurance, a nurse came in and began taking Siena's vitals. She smiled at Erica. "I'm Bridget. I'll be on duty until seven and will be taking care of Siena."

"I'm Erica, Siena's mom." Erica stepped closer to the bed. "And this is...Leslie."

Yes. What else is there to say? Leslie flashed back to moments like these with Cassie and Elijah, only Cassie, at least, introduced her as a close friend. But what did she expect? It wasn't like Erica would introduce her as her friend with benefits.

"My daughter has ASD," Erica said, "So it would be good if we could keep the lights dimmed and the volume of the monitors low, if not off."

"Yes, ma'am. The doctor has that in her chart," Bridget said congenially. "Although it looks like she'll be kept sedated until after her surgery for her own safety and comfort."

Erica nodded.

"If you'll both be staying, I can bring in another chair for you. And a couple of blankets?" Bridget added as she walked toward the door.

"That's very nice," Leslie said. "Thank you."

When Leslie turned back to the bed, Erica was standing beside it. She gazed down at Siena. "She's so little in this big bed. She barely takes up any of it."

Leslie stepped up to the opposite side. "She's strong, Erica. She'll come through this like a champ."

Erica didn't answer; she simply stared at Siena. Then she made a choking sound in her throat and brought her hand to her mouth. "I need a minute," she said and fled the room.

Leslie listened as the door closed behind her. She wanted nothing more than to go after Erica, hold and comfort her, but she honored her need to be alone. She leaned over Siena's bedside and brushed a lock of her blond hair away from her eyes. It felt strange to touch her, since she did it so seldom. She knew Siena would hate it if she were awake, so she pulled her hand back. "You're going to come through all this. You have to. Remember, we have your mom's birthday next weekend," she said softly. Had it only been that morning they'd been planning that? It seemed like so long ago. "And Gus misses you already, so you need to get home to him." *Poor Gus.*

In that moment, Leslie's phone vibrated, and she opened a text from Nell. *At the vet. No major injuries. Cleaning out the wounds on his paws and stitching up where the nails were torn off. Had to remove 2 danglers. He'll be sore for a while, but he'll be fine.* She sent her thanks, then thought of Nell's only response to the middle-of-the-night call being, *we'll be right there*, and Paula's offer to stay at Erica's and clean up all the bloody paw prints. Then she thought about Erica, and what Jack had said the morning he'd come over to take Siena to school. *We try to look out for her because she's doing this alone.* She couldn't imagine being in Erica's shoes on a night like tonight, if she'd had to deal with all this alone. The thought made her realize Erica had been gone over ten minutes, and it drew her out into the hall. She found Erica outside the door, bent over, her arms clenched around her middle.

Erica immediately straightened.

Leslie reached for her.

"No!" Erica jumped back, her hands in the air. "Don't touch me. I have to stay strong. I can't break down. Not here. And if you touch me, I will. I can do this."

"I know you can." Leslie gave her some space. "But you don't have to do it alone. I'm here."

"I do." Erica hugged herself again and drew up her shoulders, shrinking in on herself. "I do have to do it alone. I always have. It's the only way I know how. And that's okay. I can do it. You can go."

"What?"

"You can go," Erica said again. "You can leave. Go home and get some sleep. I'm sure we'll see you when we get home." Her gaze darted around the empty hallway. "After Siena's released."

What's she saying? She doesn't want me here? Fear sucker punched Leslie right in the gut. Her vision dimmed, and all she could see was the living room in her and Cassie's house with Cassie's books and photos missing from the shelves and the bare spot where the stereo had been. She remembered Elijah's vacant closet, his missing toy chest. All she could feel was the emptiness of that day, and so many more after it.

But no. Erica wasn't Cassie. She'd promised she'd never do what Cassie did, never kick Leslie out of Siena's life. It'd been a different Erica that had said those things, though. Who knew what *this* Erica would do? And now there was even more at stake. Now, she'd let herself…What? Fall for Erica? *Christ! Am I going to lose them both?*

Anger at such a cold dismissal surged up in Leslie, but she fought to tamp it down. This wasn't about her, or even about Erica and her. She knew a defense mechanism when she saw one. Erica was right. Handling things by herself was all she knew. Leslie couldn't imagine Trent hanging around hospitals and doctors' offices with Erica, waiting for test results and diagnoses. She also doubted this was the first time Siena had ever been injured and needed medical treatment and could easily believe Erica had faced it alone before. In stressful situations it was human nature to revert to the familiar. Leslie wouldn't make this about herself, but nor was she leaving.

"I'm not going anywhere, Erica." She sounded strong, but her insides trembled. "If you need your space, that's fine, but you aren't kicking me out." She put a bit of a warning in her tone, since she knew Erica actually could do that if she so chose. There was no fucking way she was leaving, no way she'd let Siena wake up the next day and think Leslie had left her. She lost Elijah that way. She was taking a stand for Siena.

Erica either heeded it or hadn't intended to force the issue to begin with, since she merely nodded.

Bridget brought the promised chair, along with a couple of blankets and pillows.

Leslie took her cues from Erica as to where in the room to position themselves for the couple of hours remaining before dawn and found herself on the opposite side of Siena's bed from Erica. The chairs were the kind that at least partially reclined, and she wriggled around until she found a position that resembled comfort.

She stared at the ceiling, thinking of the day and evening, remembering how vibrant Siena had been during the planning of Erica's birthday, how happy Gus had been stretched out between them, that first sight of Erica in her little black dress on the tiger couch. She remembered the moment she almost told Erica she didn't want to be her friend with benefits, that she wanted so much more, and wondered if *this* moment would be different had they had that conversation.

She listened to both Erica and Siena breathe and took solace in the sound. She thought of Gus and hoped Nell and Paula had let him sleep with them. She considered saying good night to Erica but didn't. She knew she wouldn't answer. She was awake, though. Leslie could feel it. And yet, here they sat, not talking, not touching, almost as though they were nothing to each other.

What a far cry from how either of them had imagined this night might end.

Chapter Eighteen

G in," Erica said, laying down her hand.

Becky tossed her cards onto the coffee table. "I don't want to play anymore. You're kicking my butt. It's depressing."

Erica laughed. "You're such a bad sport."

"I'm not a bad sport. I just hate to lose." Becky lay back on the floor and stretched her arms over her head. "Besides, I had expectations. When you asked me to come over this afternoon because you needed some adult time, I assumed you'd at least let me win, since I'm doing you a favor. What's that about anyway? I figured since you've been off the whole week with Siena, you'd be having plenty of adult time with Ms. Hottie next door."

Nope. No time with Ms. Hottie. I've made sure of that. "My reason for staying home was to take care of Siena. She's still on some pain meds, and the cast is making her more volatile." Erica hoped her veer away from the topic of Leslie wasn't obvious. "It's hard and constricting and smelly and rough. You know, all the things that set her off? I wanted to stay close."

"She's sure been quiet this afternoon." Becky said.

Erica started collecting the cards. "She's been taking solid naps all week. The doctor said between the medication and her body still recovering from the shock of such a trauma, it's perfectly normal for her to sleep more. In fact, it's a good thing."

"All the more time for you and Ms. Hottie." Becky grinned. "You didn't think I could be swayed off track so easily, did you?"

Erica rolled her eyes. "I should have known better."

"Seriously," Becky said, sitting up. "What happened with that? You guys seemed to be doing great, having barbecues, mingling your friends. You finally had what you described as fabulous sex—but only once, I'm sad to point out—and the two of you went to that fundraiser together. A real date. I saw how amazing Leslie looked that night, and I know how well you clean up. You two must have been gorgeous together."

Erica noticed Becky had been careful not to say that night at the hospital, drawing attention only to the earlier part of that evening. That night had begun with so much promise and possibility only to end completely in tatters.

A knock sounded on the patio door.

Erica stiffened involuntarily. She hated that she couldn't control her reactions to Leslie's presence.

"Speaking of the cabana goddess," Becky said, looking over Erica's shoulder.

"Come in," Erica called. She heard the door slide open.

"Hi, Becky," Leslie said lightly. "Erica," she added in a slightly heavier tone.

"Hey, Leslie," Becky said. "How's Gus doing?"

"He's hanging in there." Leslie came around the end of the couch into Erica's peripheral vision. "He hates the cone of shame, but his feet don't seem to hurt him quite as much. He goes back to the vet next week to get his stitches out."

Erica winced inwardly at the memory of seeing Gus for the first time the day they'd brought Siena home from the hospital. His front paws were bandaged, and he'd been hobbling in circles, obviously in pain, trying to get to Siena. It'd broken Erica's heart. She'd been so grateful to Paula for her willingness to work so hard at cleaning up his bloody paw prints. It was difficult enough just seeing the smears that hadn't come off the door and a few stains that still marked the carpet in the front room. He hadn't left Siena's side since, except for when she or Leslie literally picked him up and carried him outside to do his business.

"Erica?"

Leslie's voice broke into her thoughts.

She'd always liked the way Leslie said her name. She looked up at her in response.

"I told Siena I'd come get her at three. Is it okay if I go up?" She jabbed her thumb over her shoulder toward the stairs.

"Of course," Erica said. "She might still be asleep, but she's had a long nap. She'll probably wake up for you."

Leslie turned away. "Oh, I scheduled the appointment to have your front door replaced for Monday. That way you don't have to deal with it."

"I told you that you didn't have to do that." In truth, Erica was tired of the argument. It irritated her that Leslie insisted on replacing her front door when the damage wasn't her fault in the slightest.

Leslie stopped at the gate that now barred the first step. Her back went rigid. "And I told you," she said in a clipped tone, "that Gus is my dog, and I'll fix what he did."

Erica sighed.

After a moment, Leslie unlatched the gate and headed upstairs, evidently taking Erica's silence for agreement.

"What the hell?" Becky mouthed when Erica met her eyes.

Erica touched a finger to her own lips. She wasn't about to let Leslie overhear any part of a conversation about her.

In a few minutes, Siena appeared at the top of the stairs, Leslie beside her, and Gus in Leslie's arms. Leslie worked the latch of that second gate and supervised Siena's descent.

Erica was sure there'd come a day when Siena would be able to navigate the stairs again with ease, but for now, she was way too wobbly. There would, of course, also have to be a few serious conversations about the importance of leaving one's dreams in one's sleep, though. Siena had shared that the night of her fall she'd been trying to stay in the dream she was having about her and Gus playing with Elijah by keeping her eyes closed while coming downstairs to get some juice. Erica shuddered at the thought of reliving the ordeal. Maybe she'd just leave the gates in place.

Becky greeted Siena, and Erica smiled at her, then the trio made their way out, closing the door behind them.

"What the hell was that?" Becky raised up slightly to look out the window.

Thankfully, she'd kept her voice low. "Now you know why I wanted *your* company today, instead of Ms. Hottie's."

"What happened between you?"

"She doesn't like it that I prefer to remain independent and self-reliant," Erica said, finishing her collection of the playing cards.

Becky narrowed her eyes. "What did you do?"

"What did *I* do?" Erica stuffed the deck into its box. "What makes you think I did something?"

Becky eyed her suspiciously. "You pushed her away, didn't you?"

Erica glared at her.

"You used this whole thing with Siena's broken arm as an excuse to put the brakes on whatever was happening between the two of you, and you retreated back into your safe, little I-can-only-count-on-myself world." This wasn't a question.

Erica had no response. She couldn't deny it, but she was embarrassed to admit it. Becky was right, though. She'd nailed it. "You know," Erica said, mildly annoyed. "You're supposed to be *my* friend."

Becky softened. "I am your friend, Erica. Which is why I want to slap you right now."

Erica flopped back against the couch cushion.

"You're always saying you want what Jack and I have," Becky continued her lecture. "And from what I've seen and heard, Leslie could very well be your Jack, and yet, right when things are showing promise, you throw it all away. What's going on? What are you scared of?"

Erica stared at the ceiling, blinking back tears. She flashed back to the moment in the hospital corridor with Leslie. "The night Siena broke her arm, Leslie wanted to hold me and comfort me."

"Oh, my God, no." Becky put her hand to her chest, her eyes wide. "Not that."

Erica couldn't help a small laugh. "But if I'd let her, I would have lost it. I would have dissolved into a sobbing mess, and then I wouldn't have been able to be strong for Siena. And I needed to be strong for Siena."

"Oh, Erica. What about letting someone be strong for you?" Becky rose and came around to sit next to her. "Do you have any idea how many times Jack has been strong for me with Rosi, or even our neurotypical, supposedly-easier-to-handle boys? That's part of being partners. Yes, sometimes you'll be the strong one, but sometimes you get to have someone to lean on, to hold you, to be strong when you can't be. And that doesn't make you any less strong for your child. You can have, and be, both."

Erica couldn't hold back the fear any longer. She began to cry. "But what if I learn to count on her being there, and then she isn't?"

Becky cupped Erica's chin and turned her face to hers. "Why wouldn't she be? She was there for you when she barely knew you. Remember the food poisoning? And she was there in the hospital even when you pushed her away. She stayed, didn't she?"

Erica nodded.

"And she's still here now, even when you're being kind of a bitch to her. She's fixing your door and spending time with Siena."

Erica hiccupped. "When Siena came home, I think Leslie was worried I wouldn't let her see her anymore, which is what happened with her ex. But she's come to get Siena every day this week and taken her over to her house, and obviously I'm fine with it. She's really good for Siena."

"Really?" Becky said, sounding surprised. "What are they doing over there?"

"I don't know. Siena says just playing in the jungle." Erica sniffed. "Whatever it is, it makes Gus howl."

Becky laughed. "Oh, well maybe we don't want to know then."

"I know you're right," Erica said, growing serious again. "I know Leslie's amazing and probably could be my Jack. I just don't know how to not be alone."

"No, you're just scared." Becky pulled Erica into her arms and held her. "But in order to prove to yourself that your fears are unfounded, you have to be willing to take a risk and let Leslie prove to you she's your Jack."

Erica's throat started to close, and her tears threatened again. "I don't think she wants to be."

"Why not? She sure seems to me like she does."

"Because she said so." Erica pulled away from Becky and sat up.

Becky watched her expectantly. "She said she didn't want to be your Jack? I find that hard to believe."

"No, she didn't say *that*, because she doesn't know about being someone's Jack."

Becky sighed in evident exasperation. "You're not making any sense. Give me the details, and then tell me what she said exactly."

"It was at the fundraiser. We were dancing." Erica let herself relive the moment. "I was telling her how amazing and wonderful I thought she was, how much I loved watching her interact with all the patrons of the center. I told her I was proud to be her date."

"Wow!" Becky said, interrupting. "You really went all out."

"Do you blame me? You saw her in that outfit." Erica released a soft moan at the image in her mind.

"Yeah, I did." Becky said. "I think I'm a little jealous. I think your Jack is better looking than mine."

Erica laughed. "But yours is proven, tried and true."

"Good point," Becky said. "So go on."

"Anyway…" Erica refocused. "I was telling her all that and told her she was quite the package. And she said, 'Erica I don't want to be your…'"

Becky waited. "Your what?" she asked after a beat.

"She didn't finish."

"She said, 'I don't want to be your,' and then she didn't finish? Why not?"

"Because that's when I got the call from Rachel, and everything went all crazy."

Becky stared at Erica, her expression incredulous. "Erica! You have to let her finish. You can't make up what you think she was going to say. That's just...stupid."

Erica scoffed. "That's ridiculous. How would I get her to finish now?"

"Ask her," Becky said emphatically. "Tell her all those things again, and then ask her what she was going to say. That's your homework." She slapped Erica on the leg. "And I expect a report... soon."

Erica considered her assignment. Could she do it? She doubted it, but she smiled at Becky. "Thank you," she said, grasping her hand. "Whatever I do or don't do, getting all this out feels good. I really needed this."

"Well, don't just brush it all away as a feel good moment. Think about what you might be throwing away. Or better yet, think about what you could have."

Erica nodded. She had to think about what she truly wanted before she made a move of any kind.

"Okay, now, before I leave...what are we going to do for your birthday tomorrow?"

Erica groaned. "Oh, God, not my birthday. Can we just wait until things settle down and go to dinner some night?"

"How did I know that's what you were going to say?" Becky got to her feet. "Oh, I know. Because that's what you say every year."

Erica laughed. "I promise, we'll do it." She rose and gave Becky a hug.

"We'd better," Becky said. "Because you don't get your present until we do."

"I don't need a present," Erica said. "I have you. Thank you."

"Any time." Becky squeezed her tightly.

As Erica waved good-bye from the front steps, she considered Becky's words of wisdom. Should she do it? Should she say all those things again and ask Leslie what *she* was going to say? What if she was going to say, I don't want to be your girlfriend? That would be humiliating—and not just a little heartbreaking. But what if that wasn't what she was going to say at all? She folded her arms across her middle, trying to fend off the warring questions.

I guess I'll never know unless I ask.

❖

At three forty-five the next afternoon, Leslie still hadn't come over to get Siena for their daily play date, and Siena was still asleep. Erica needed to get her up or, recovery or no recovery, she wouldn't get to sleep until midnight. Just as she was about to set her book aside, Siena appeared at the top of the stairs behind the gate.

"I want to go to Leslie's," she said, sounding more excited than she had all week. "And you have to take me. And we have to wait for Gus to poop and wee-wee."

Erica chuckled. "Yes, sweetie, I know the drill." She carried Gus and walked Siena down, then straightened Siena's sling that held the weight of her cast, while Gus did his business. "Everybody set?"

Siena grinned and nodded eagerly.

"Boy, you must have something really special planned today," Erica said as they crossed the backyard to the gate. She remembered with some sadness the last time she'd taken this walk in her black cocktail dress. She'd been as excited that night as Siena was now.

Siena stopped suddenly. "How do you know?"

Erica cocked her head, curious at Siena's reaction. "I don't know anything. I'm just wondering why you seem so excited, but you don't have to tell me, if you don't want to. I trust you and Leslie." *I trust Leslie with my daughter but not my heart? How crazy is that?* She'd thought a lot about her conversation with Becky the previous day, about taking that risk and letting Leslie prove to her there wasn't anything to fear. She'd only thought, though. She hadn't come to any conclusion.

"Okay," Siena said and started moving again.

When they got to Leslie's French doors, Erica noticed that the furniture in the family room had been rearranged. It was an odd arrangement, though. The blue couch actually faced out to the backyard. Was it another indulgence of Siena's?

Erica knocked, but Siena turned the knob and walked right in. The most amazing aroma wafted out and caressed Erica's senses. It was oddly familiar. "Hello?" she called from the doorway. "Leslie? Are you here?"

"Come in, Mommy." Siena bounced on the balls of her feet. "You have to come in."

Erica stepped over the threshold.

In a flurry of motion, a group of people—Nell and Paula, Becky and Jack, Rosi and the boys, Leslie—and Trent and Cynthia—jumped up from behind the couch, waving blue and orange flags with a brightly colored SURPRISE!! on each one. The only sound in the room was the rustling of the fabric.

Siena ran to the couch, picked up her own flag, and began to wave it furiously. "Happy birthday, Mommy," she said, her eyes brighter than Erica had ever seen them.

"Happy birthday," everyone else chimed in, but they were all careful to keep the volume down.

What a wonderful gift. Erica burst out laughing. She pointed at Becky. "You! You knew yesterday when you were giving me a bad time about my birthday."

Becky smiled and dipped her head.

"And you two." Erica crossed to Trent and Cynthia, giving each a warm hug. After Trent's conversation with Leslie, their previous visit had turned in to what Erica hoped would be a fresh start for Siena and her father. "What a nice surprise. How long are you here for?"

"This time, just a quick turnaround," Trent said with a grin. "But I decided to accept the job offer from Sunset Sounds, so when Leslie called about your party, we thought we'd look around at some areas to live while we were here. That's what we've been doing today, but we have a flight back tonight."

Erica raised an eyebrow in surprise. "Congratulations. It'll be great to have you both here. And thank you for coming to the party. That's so sweet." *And speaking of sweet...* Erica met Leslie's gaze.

She knew very well who was behind this celebration. Her eyes brimmed with tears.

Leslie smiled at her, but it was a sad smile. "Okay," she said, breaking eye contact. "Dinner will be served in about ten minutes, so everyone get a drink. There's an ice chest with sodas and juices in the kitchen."

Erica finished greeting everyone, enjoying Jack's bear hug, Paula's arm around her, and Nell's playful antics with a new card trick she was showing the kids. She did a quick check to make sure Siena and Rosi were getting along okay, then slipped onto a stool at the bar. She inhaled deeply. "I know that smell," she said, trying to place it. "What is it?"

"It's your first birthday present." Leslie opened the oven and slid a piece of cardboard under something on the rack.

"Interesting," Erica said teasingly.

With a flourish, Leslie slid a pizza onto the counter in front of Erica.

Everyone gathered around.

"Pizza!" Erica said. "I love pizza."

"Not just any pizza," Leslie said. "I have it on the very best authority that *this* pizza is *to die for*." Now her smile was full.

Erica looked from Leslie to the pizza. She took in the deep crust, the layers of toppings, the extra sauce on top. Her eyes widened, and her mouth began to water. "Nooooooo." She looked back at Leslie. "How did you…"

Leslie grinned. "They'll ship it."

"And, Mommy, it's shaped like a heart," Siena said, bouncing again. "I picked that because Leslie says that hearts usually say I love you on them, even though this one doesn't."

Erica actually squealed. She didn't know if she'd ever done that before. "Oh, my God! Giordono's pizza!" She clapped. "Hurry! Cut it! Cut it! Cut it!"

Leslie was laughing, along with everyone else, as she slid the knife through the thickness. "And the first piece goes to the birthday girl."

Erica ate herself sick.

When everyone had finished, more presents were on the agenda. A booklet of gift coupons for childcare from the service the support group used from Becky and Jack. A beautiful sweater from Paula. A gift certificate for a day at a local spa from Trent and Cynthia. And a magic trick from Nell to present Erica with a bouquet of flowers. Then to Erica's amazement, Siena rose and stood in the middle of the room.

"And now Gus and me have a song we'd like to sing for you," Siena said in an obviously practiced announcer's voice.

That alone could have been Erica's present. She was so filled with love and pride.

Siena raised her unbroken arm over her head, and Gus lifted up onto his hind legs, holding his bandaged paws in front of him. Siena turned in a circle, as did Gus, and she began to sing. "I'm Siena. My mom is Erica."

Gus began to howl along.

"And she is pretty and nice and reads me stories." Siena swayed from side to side. "And for her birthday, I have this song, so she can sing it whenever she worries."

Erica couldn't contain her emotion. She wiped at the stream of tears flowing down her cheeks and bit her lip to try to gain control.

"She makes me macaroni and cheese, and I like it when she smiles. And that's the end of my song." Siena bowed, and Gus put his head to the floor with his hind end in the air. His stub wagged furiously.

Erica cried freely, and she wasn't the only one. She clapped wildly.

Siena rose and started to walk away, then turned suddenly. "Oh…and…" She looked at Erica. "I love you, Mommy."

Erica gasped, then choked on a sob.

"I couldn't put that in the song because it didn't rhyme." She smiled.

Erica laughed through her tears. "I love you, too, Siena."

Siena looked at her curiously. "Are you sad?"

Erica shook her head vehemently. "No, sweetie, these are happy tears."

Siena squinted, clearly confused.

"Your singing and your song were amazing. That's the best birthday present I've ever gotten." Erica began to clap again, a wide smile spreading across her face.

Siena beamed and took another bow to the applause rising once more in the room.

Erica had never seen her so animated and happy—the change Leslie had brought.

After chocolate cake with chocolate icing—Siena's favorite—their friends started saying their good-byes. They all agreed they needed to get together more often, not wait for birthdays.

Later, when everyone was gone, Siena's eyelids drooped.

"I think someone might be ready for an early bedtime," Leslie said, picking up the flags. "A party is a lot of excitement. It can wear you out."

Siena yawned and nodded.

Erica watched Leslie. "Would you like to come over and do the honor of the bedtime story?" Leslie hadn't been around at bedtime all week, because, Erica knew, she hadn't felt welcome.

Leslie arched an eyebrow. "Really?"

Erica gave her a small, sheepish smile. "Really."

Siena dropped off quickly—no surprise—and Erica was grateful. She had a lot of making up to do to Leslie and some important things to say. It was time to take that risk.

"Would you like something to drink?" Erica asked, when they were downstairs.

"No, that's okay," Leslie said. "I should probably get home." She held Erica's gaze a little longer than was necessary for an exit.

"I—" Erica faltered. She cleared her throat. "I have some things I want to say to you. Would you stay?"

"Okay," Leslie said, shifting her weight from one foot to the other.

"First of all, thank you so much for that party. I know it was all you. And for going to all the trouble of getting Giordono's pizza. My God, that was such a treat."

"It was no trouble," Leslie said. "And you're welcome."

They stared at each other.

Emotion threatened Erica's composure. "And for that song." She teared up all over again.

"The song was Siena's idea," Leslie said, breaking in. "I just helped out with rehearsal space and a little on choreography." Humor danced in Leslie's eyes, putting Erica more at ease.

Erica laughed softly. "Well, thank you." She turned and studied a picture of Siena on the wall. "Did you know she's never said I love you to me before? To anyone, that I know of."

"That's because she didn't know what love felt like, so she didn't know if she did." Leslie's voice held a resonance Erica hadn't noticed before, like the quality of truth one might hear in a prayer.

Erica turned to her. "How do you know that?"

"She told me," Leslie said simply. "And now that she knows, she's said it to you and Gus." The spark was back.

"And you helped her know what love feels like?"

"Well." Leslie shrugged. "We talked about it, and the different ways you can tell. Like when someone makes you your favorite meal and you feel special. Or how when you love someone, seeing them smile makes you happy."

A sudden realization struck Erica, but she couldn't say it. Not yet. She turned away again, not to look at the picture this time, but to avoid Leslie's scrutiny when she asked what she knew had to come next. "Becky says I have to let you finish."

"Finish what?" Leslie asked.

"Do you remember when we were dancing at the fundraiser last weekend?" Erica closed her arms around herself, recalling the feel of being in Leslie's embrace.

"I remember it very well." The tremor in Leslie's voice revealed her memory of that moment as well.

"I told you I liked seeing that new side of you with the patrons of the center. That I'd seen you as a friend, and a neighbor, and how wonderful you are with Siena. And I know you now as a lover and how incredible that is."

"I remember." Leslie sounded closer. "You said I was quite a package." She repeated the phrase with a hint of swagger.

A tiny, silent laugh rippled through Erica. "You *are* quite a package."

"What do you want me to finish, Erica?" Closer still.

"You said you didn't want to be my...and then Paula stopped you." Erica steadied herself. "I need you to finish what you were going to say. I need to know. You don't want to be my what?"

Leslie was silent for so long, Erica didn't think she was going to answer. She wondered how a moment like this ended without some kind of response. Would they stay suspended in time for eternity? Then she felt Leslie's hands moving up her arms to her shoulders. Leslie's warm breath feathered across her neck.

Leslie eased Erica back against her. "I don't want to be your friend with benefits, Erica," she whispered into her ear.

A shiver ran down Erica's spine.

"I want more than that. I want it all."

Erica closed her eyes and leaned her head against Leslie's shoulder, letting the words caress her soul. "You've helped me know what love feels like, too." She turned in Leslie's arms. "I'm in love with you."

Leslie smoothed her thumb over Erica's lips. Then she leaned in and kissed her.

It was gentle and hot and passionate and loving all at once. It made Erica burn with desire, ache with need, and hunger for more, at the same time it made her feel warm and safe and loved. This was it, what Leslie had said she wanted. *I want it all*, she'd said. And here she was, giving it all.

Erica twined her arms around Leslie's neck and pulled her closer. She deepened the kiss, probed her mouth, sucked her lower lip between her teeth.

Leslie moaned, sliding her hands beneath Erica's shirt, setting Erica's skin aflame under her touch.

Erica broke the kiss. "Come to bed with me," she said in a hoarse whisper.

Leslie eased back. "Are you sure?" Her eyes were hooded and filled with lust. "What about Siena?"

Erica smiled her best lascivious smile. "I guess you'll have to be quiet."

In her bedroom, they undressed each other, slowly, lingering in the moment.

Leslie trailed her fingers over Erica's nipples, cupped her breasts, sank to her knees, and kissed a languid path over her stomach and abdomen. She slipped her hand between Erica's thighs.

Erica gasped at the brush of Leslie's fingers over her clit and grabbed her shoulders for support. Just when she thought Leslie's tongue might find her throbbing center, Leslie rose and eased her down onto the bed. She lowered herself on top of her. The solid feel of Leslie's body, the press of her weight, anchored Erica like a ship in a safe harbor. The light brush of Leslie's lips on her neck and the caress of Leslie's hands along her sides made Erica feel like she was being lifted into the heavens. She was dizzy with the contrast, delirious with all the sensations.

When Leslie moved off of her, Erica cried out in disappointment. But she wasn't disappointed for long.

"Let me inside you," Leslie whispered, teasing Erica open.

Erica did, drawing up one knee.

Leslie's fingers slipped in. Her touch was so tender, her strokes so gentle, none of it felt as though it could possibly satisfy Erica's need. Until it did. Erica's arousal rose with each pass, with every graze. She shifted to her side and reached for Leslie in kind.

Leslie smiled and granted Erica entrance.

Together, they touched, and stroked, and fondled, and caressed, then rubbed and thrust and pumped, until finally, they both came in the exquisite intimacy of love.

When they crawled under the covers to hold each other through the night, Leslie nestled Erica against her and pressed her lips to her forehead. "I love you, Erica. And I'll always be right at your side. You'll never have to handle anything on your own again. I want you and Siena, and I'll do everything in my power to take care of you both."

Erica felt each word deep in her core and knew the truth of them. More importantly, though, she could trust Leslie to hold to them. She let her mind flash on moments she'd already seen that—that very first day when she'd seen Leslie light a spark of joy in Siena's eyes; her clean kitchen that night when Siena had that meltdown and Leslie had done the dinner dishes; that god-awful morning when she'd realized she was half naked, upchucking in the toilet, and it was Leslie standing behind her. And there was so much more: the babysitting, the jungle, the hospital…The night she'd asked Leslie to stay with her and hold her while they slept, and Leslie had done it, no questions asked.

No, Erica had no doubt at all that she'd never have to face anything on her own again.

Epilogue

Leslie sank into the comfort of the patio swing and slipped her hand over Erica's thigh. She shifted her gaze between Erica's mingled expression of amusement, pride, and pure love to the scene of Siena, blindfolded and swinging a baseball bat at a fat, arm-shaped piñata. One of the techs at Siena's ortho doctor's office had made it out of casting materials, constructing it thinly enough to break open more easily, especially for Siena's I'm-Out-of-My-Cast party. A cluster of kids from the support group and their siblings gathered around, cheering and waiting for either their turns to swing or to dive for the prizes and candy that spilled out. Parents mingled close by, chatting and monitoring behaviors, while Gus crouched just out of stomping range of Siena's feet, barking as though his role was paramount in the activity.

Leslie chuckled at Trent adeptly hopping out of the way of Siena's wild swing as he held the piñata steady by the rope it hung from, allowing Siena a more solid strike. "It's a good thing he's agile."

Erica laughed.

"He's sure come a long way with Siena in the months since he and Cynthia have been here," Paula said from a nearby chair. "He's hardly recognizable from how he was before."

"Yeah." Becky sighed, sounding almost regretful. "I guess I should stop calling him dickwad."

Leslie had to agree. He'd really stepped up, and he and Cynthia were an integral part of Siena's life. A lot of it was due to their involvement with the support group and their decision to rent

Leslie's house, when Leslie moved in with Erica, in order to take part in Siena's daily routine. Leslie played a role, too, though. She and Trent had formed an unexpected bond since that morning ten months earlier when he first came over to talk to her. Ever since, he consulted her on almost everything to do with Siena. She still thought it strange sometimes, until she remembered what he'd told her about why he didn't want to ask Erica anything. *I can't stand seeing my failures in her eyes.*

Initially, Leslie felt that was unfounded. Erica wouldn't hold someone's past against them. But when she considered the night Erica had stormed into Leslie's kitchen, loaded for bear because Leslie had pulled away, or the moment in the hospital when she'd completely shut down, leaving Leslie to think her place in Erica and Siena's life was gone forever, she could understand Trent's trepidation. Erica was formidable on a normal day, but if she was scared or protecting Siena, woe be unto the one who crossed her. "Yeah, I think you should stop holding the past against him," she said to Becky. "He's doing great."

Erica squeezed Leslie's hand and rested her head on her shoulder. "This party was a wonderful idea. Thank you for thinking of it."

"I just figured after two surgeries and nine months of having her arm casted, getting out of that itchy, hard, bumpy thing..." Leslie did her best impression of Siena's whiney voice "is something to celebrate. Besides, every time we have a group of people over, Siena's a little more comfortable with it."

"Burgers, dogs, and veggie patties are done," Nell called from the grill. She stood beside Jack, holding a fork like a weapon. "Is everything else ready?" She looked straight at Leslie.

Leslie smirked. "Yes, everything else is ready." She, Erica, and Paula had set out all the sides, salads, buns, and condiments in the kitchen before they sat down. "You're not the only one working. You're just mad because you wanted to hit the piñata with all the other kids."

As though on cue, there was a loud crack, followed by the squeal of children.

Nell's crestfallen expression told Leslie she'd been right.

"I suppose we know what we're doing for Nell's birthday." Paula laughed softly.

Rachel and Cynthia brought two big trays of cookies from next door, and the feast was on.

Leslie ate, chatted, and cleaned up, but mostly she simply enjoyed the comforting feeling of knowing she was exactly where she wanted to be. Had it only been eleven months ago that she'd returned to California with only Nell and Paula to call her own? And here she was with a family, an extended family, and a relatively large social group. She glanced down at Gus, then broke off a chunk of hotdog and fed it to him. And, of course, a faithful dog. She'd never be able to grasp how life worked.

She gazed across the patio at Erica—took in her long silvery hair, wisps blowing in the evening breeze, and the swell of her hips beneath the thin fabric of her sun dress—and she fell in love all over again. She couldn't wait until they were alone in their bedroom. It'd taken a while to think of Erica's room, her house, as theirs, but having things like the blue couch, the jungle, her Buddha's, and the pictures of her parents and Elijah there had helped. Those were really the only things she cared about. Siena had been ecstatic to have all of her own stuff and all the *cool* stuff from Leslie's in the same place.

Erica caught Leslie's eye and winked. A sure sign they were on the same page for later.

When Nell and Paula had loaded up the extra tables they'd brought from the center and waved good-bye, there was still Siena's bath and bedtime ritual to tackle, but that had been a part of the daily routine that Leslie had loved from the start. The three of them moved through it with practiced ease and a lot of laughter.

Finally, Siena raced into her room and jumped onto the bed, Gus at her heels as always. She bounced. "Today was so much fun." She clapped her hands. "And I can't wait for tomorrow."

"What's tomorrow?" Leslie pulled back the covers and gestured for Siena to get in.

"Siena." There was a warning tone in Erica's voice.

"Mommy's going to make macaroni and cheese, because that's the first dinner we all had together…"

"Siena," Erica said again, this time louder.

"…then we're going to ask you to marry us." Siena finished with a huge smile.

"Siena!" Erica said with evident exasperation.

Siena clamped her hands over her mouth, her eyes wide. She stopped bouncing and stared at Erica.

Erica stared back.

"The words wouldn't stay in." Siena looked stricken.

Leslie looked from one to the other. "Uh…"

Erica glanced at her, an apology in her eyes. She took a deep breath. "Okay, wait here." She left the room.

Leslie and Siena exchanged glances.

"What do you think she's going to do?" Siena whispered.

"I don't know," Leslie said. "But don't worry. She loves you." Leslie had to fight back her laughter.

Erica returned in only a moment with something in her hand. She stopped in front of Leslie and motioned to Siena. "All right, come on. Just like we practiced."

Siena gasped. "Really?"

Erica nodded with a gentle smile on her lips.

Siena scurried off the bed and stood beside Erica, Gus next to her. Erica and Siena went to one knee.

Leslie's throat closed with emotion. Her eyes stung with a sheen of tears.

"Go ahead," Erica whispered.

"Leslie." Siena wiggled in her spot. "You made me smile when you let me water that dry grass when you didn't even know me. And you taught me how to wish on stars, so I could wish that we could keep Gus, and then we got to. Then when my mom was sick, I wished she'd get better, and she did. And you went away and I wished you'd come back, and *you* did. So now I know that if I wish for something really hard and wish it on a star, it can happen…even though Tim Davis didn't move away." She cocked her head. "He said his family only lives here so they won't ever move away, and—"

Erica cleared her throat.

"Oh yeah," Siena said, pursing her lips in thought. "And you always read to me and make the funny voices, and that makes me laugh and my tummy tingles. I didn't think I have tingles in me, but sometimes I do with you. So all that means I love you." She looked into Leslie's eyes. "Right?"

Leslie bit hard into her lower lip to keep from crying, but she couldn't stop the tears from streaking her cheeks. She nodded. "By our test, it certainly does."

Siena grinned. "So I love you, and I want you to be my other mom. But you have to marry my mom to do that, because we're a package." She finished in her imitation of Erica.

Leslie laughed, then sniffled. "Well, I guess—"

"No." Siena held up her hand. "You have to wait because my mom has to por-poze you, too."

Leslie smiled through her tears at the mispronunciation of the word. "Okay, I'll wait." She turned to Erica.

Erica gazed down at Siena another moment, her cheeks as wet as Leslie's.

"How did I do?" Siena whispered, as though if she asked quietly enough, Leslie wouldn't hear.

"You did beautifully," Erica whispered back. Then she turned to Leslie.

When their gazes met, a jolt hit Leslie's chest. She sank her teeth deeper into her bottom lip. She just wanted to blurt out *Yes.*

Erica drew in a long breath and visibly steadied. "Leslie," she said, her eyes focused and serious. "You've taught me what love feels like. You've loved me like no one ever has, and with you, I know I'll never have to face anything alone. I'll have your strength. I'll have your love. I'll have your kind and gentle heart to come home to every night. You've changed me so deeply, and made me smile and tingle, too. I'm so in love with you. And I'm not making any sense. So…" She lifted her hand, then took Siena's, and together they held out a ring. "Will you marry us?" they asked in unison.

Gus rose on his haunches and lifted his paws.

Everything in Leslie broke loose and she dropped to her knees. "Yes," she said, gathering all three of them into a tight hug.

Siena's eyes went wide, but she wrapped her arms around Leslie's neck in return. Gus wriggled away. Erica molded into Leslie's body and cried.

"Are these happy tears?" Siena asked, letting go of Leslie. "Like when my mom cried when I sang her my song?"

Leslie laughed. "Yes, definitely happy tears."

"It's kind of confusing." Siena crinkled her forehead. "How do you know the difference?"

Erica straightened. "*That*, my sweet girl, is a conversation for another time. Let's get you to bed."

Leslie pulled the rocking chair up, as she always did, and began to read.

Erica stood behind her, running her fingers through Leslie's hair.

Leslie could barely concentrate. Between Erica's gentle caress, the high of her emotions from the proposal, and the surreal quality of having an engagement ring on her finger, her mind was spinning and her body thrumming. Mercifully, by the middle of *Where the Wild Things Are*, Siena dropped off to sleep.

"That didn't take long," Erica whispered.

"No," Leslie said, tipping her head into Erica's touch. "But I don't want to move. I don't want you to stop."

Erica leaned down and nuzzled her ear. "I'll start again. I promise."

When they reached their bedroom, Erica crossed to the French doors and opened them. A cool evening breeze drifted in, and she lifted her hair up off her neck.

Leslie moved behind her and kissed her nape.

Erica sighed.

"That was quite the surprise tonight." Leslie rested her hands on Erica's hips and pressed against her backside.

"I can't believe Siena blurted it out like that." Erica turned and draped her arms around Leslie's shoulders. "I had it all planned out for tomorrow night, with mac and cheese to symbolize our first dinner together and everything."

Leslie chuckled and lightly kissed Erica's lips. "Did you really think she wouldn't spill it?"

"She kept my birthday party and her song a secret." Erica tightened her hold and let out a quiet moan when Leslie inched up the skirt of her dress and cupped her ass.

"She was sedated and on pain meds that whole week," Leslie said. Then she lost her train of thought. "I want to make love to you."

Without a word, Erica eased away and slipped the straps of her dress off her shoulders, then let the garment slide down her body to the floor.

Leslie heated, and arousal pooled between her thighs. She took Erica by the hand and led her to their bed. As she lowered herself to the mattress, Erica moved with her. She lay back against the pillows, and Erica cuddled against her. In the months they'd been together, they'd grown to know each other well. They knew each other's thoughts, finished each other's sentences, moved in sync like professional dancers even if, as now, all they were doing was holding one another. And still, Leslie knew there was so much more to learn and to share.

"I'm going to make you happy, Erica." She felt Erica's lips curve into a smile against her neck.

"You already have."

Leslie gazed out at the night sky and reveled in how happy *she* was. She tightened her embrace. "Look outside," she said, tracing a pattern over Erica's back. "There are a lot of stars out tonight. Make a wish?"

Erica smiled. "I have you in my life, in our bed, and in my arms. I have our baby sleeping peacefully down the hall. I have our sweet, amazing dog watching over her while we make love. I think maybe all my wishes have already come true. But you never know. Maybe we can come up with a few together."

About the Author

Jeannie Levig is an award-winning author of lesbian fiction and a proud and happy member of the Bold Strokes Books family. Her debut novel, *Threads of the Heart*, and her romantic intrigue, *Into Thin Air*, both won Goldie Awards from the Golden Crown Literary Society, and her contemporary romance, *Embracing the Dawn*, won a Rainbow Award and was a Goldie finalist.

Raised by an English teacher, Jeannie has always been surrounded by literature and novels and learned to love reading at an early age. She tried her hand at writing fiction for the first time under the loving encouragement of her eighth grade English teacher and graduated from college with a bachelor's degree in English. She is deeply committed to her spiritual path and community, her family and friends, and to writing the best stories possible to share with her readers.

She loves writing, reading, movies and lives in Central California.

Visit Jeannie at her website, JeannieLevig.com, or send her an email to Jeannie@JeannieLevig.com. She'd love to hear from you. You can also find her on Facebook and Twitter.

Books Available from Bold Strokes Books

A Wish Upon a Star by Jeannie Levig. Erica Cooper has learned to depend on only herself, but when her new neighbor, Leslie Raymond, befriends Erica's special needs daughter, the walls protecting her heart threaten to crumble. (978-1-163555-274-4)

Answering the Call by Ali Vali. Detective Sept Savoie returns to the streets of New Orleans, as do the dead bodies from ritualistic killings, and she does everything in her power to bring them to justice while trying to keep her partner, Keegan Blanchard, safe. (978-1-163555-050-4)

Breaking Down Her Walls by Erin Zak. Could a love worth staying for be the key to breaking down Julia Finch's walls? (978-1-63555-369-7)

Exit Plans for Teenage Freaks by 'Nathan Burgoine. Cole always has a plan—especially for escaping his small-town reputation as "that kid who was kidnapped when he was four"—but when he teleports to a museum, it's time to face facts: it's possible he's a total freak after all. (978-1-163555-098-6)

Flight to the Horizon by Julie Tizard. Airline Captain Kerri Sullivan and flight attendant Janine Case struggle to survive an emergency water landing and overcome dark secrets to give love a chance to fly. (978-1-163555-331-4)

Friends Without Benefits by Dena Blake. When Dex Putman gets the woman she thought she always wanted, she soon wonders if it's really love after all. (978-1-163555-349-9)

Invalid Evidence by Stevie Mikayne. Private Investigator Jil Kidd is called away to investigate a possible killer whale, just when her partner Jess needs her most. (978-1-163555-307-9)

Pursuit of Happiness by Carsen Taite. When attorney Stevie Palmer's client reveals a scandal that could derail Senator Meredith Mitchell's presidential bid, their chance at love may be collateral damage. (978-1-163555-044-3)

Seascape by Karis Walsh. Marine biologist Tess Hansen returns to Washington's isolated northern coast where she struggles to adjust to small-town living while courting an endowment for her orca research center from Brittany James. (978-1-163555-079-5)

Second in Command by VK Powell. Jazz Perry's life is disrupted and her career jeopardized when she becomes personally involved with the case of an abandoned child and the child's competent but strict social worker, Emory Blake. (978-1-163555-185-3)

Taking Chances by Erin McKenzie. When Valerie Cruz and Paige Wellington clash over what's in the best interest of the children in Valerie's care, the children may be the ones who teach them it's worth taking chances for love. (978-1-163555-209-6)

All of Me by Emily Smith. When chief surgical resident Galen Burgess meets her new intern, Rowan Duncan, she may finally discover that doing what you've always done will only give you what you've always had. (978-1-163555-321-5)

As the Crow Flies by Karen F. Williams. Romance seems to be blooming all around, but problems arise when a restless ghost emerges from the ether to roam the dark corners of this haunting tale. (978-1-163555-285-0)

Both Ways by Ileandra Young. SPEAR agent Danika Karson races to protect the city from a supernatural threat and must rely on the woman she's trained to despise: Rayne, an achingly beautiful vampire. (978-1-163555-298-0)

Calendar Girl by Georgia Beers. Forced to work together, Addison Fairchild and Kate Cooper discover that opposites really do attract. (978-1-163555-333-8)

Lovebirds by Lisa Moreau. Two women from different worlds collide in a small California mountain town, each with a mission that doesn't include falling in love. (978-1-163555-213-3)

Media Darling by Fiona Riley. Can Hollywood bad girl Emerson and reluctant celebrity gossip reporter Hayley work together to make each other's dreams come true? Or will Emerson's secrets ruin not one career, but two? (978-1-163555-278-2)

Stroke of Fate by Renee Roman. Can Sean Moore live up to her reputation and save Jade Rivers from the stalker determined to end Jade's career and, ultimately, her life? (978-1-163555-162-4)

The Rise of the Resistance by Jackie D. The soul of America has been lost for almost a century. A few people may be the difference between a phoenix rising to save the masses or permanent destruction. (978-1-163555-259-1)

The Sex Therapist Next Door by Meghan O'Brien. At the intersection of sex and intimacy, anything is possible. Even love. (978-1-163555-296-6)

Unexpected Lightning by Cass Sellars. Lightning strikes once more when Sydney and Parker fight a dangerous stranger who threatens the peace they both desperately want. (978-1-163555-276-8)

Unforgettable by Elle Spencer. When one night changes a lifetime… Two romance novellas from best-selling author Elle Spencer. (978-1-63555-429-8)

Against All Odds by Kris Bryant, Maggie Cummings, M. Ullrich. Peyton and Tory escaped death once, but will they survive when Bradley's determined to make his kill rate one hundred percent? (978-1-163555-193-8)

Autumn's Light by Aurora Rey. Casual hookups aren't supposed to include romantic dinners and meeting the family. Can Mat Pero see beyond the heartbreak that led her to keep her worlds so separate, and will Graham Connor be waiting if she does? (978-1-163555-272-0)

Breaking the Rules by Larkin Rose. When Virginia and Carmen are thrown together by an embarrassing mistake they find out their stubborn determination isn't so heroic after all. (978-1-163555-261-4)

Broad Awakening by Mickey Brent. In the sequel to *Underwater Vibes*, Hélène and Sylvie find ruts in their road to eternal bliss. (978-1-163555-270-6)

Broken Vows by MJ Williamz. Sister Mary Margaret must reconcile her divided heart or risk losing a love that just might be heaven sent. (978-1-163555-022-1)

Flesh and Gold by Ann Aptaker. Havana, 1952, where art thief and smuggler Cantor Gold dodges gangland bullets and mobsters' schemes while she searches Havana' s steamy Red Light district for her kidnapped love. (978-1-163555-153-2)

Isle of Broken Years by Jane Fletcher. Spanish noblewoman Catalina de Valasco is in peril, even before the pirates holding her for ransom sail into seas destined to become known as the Bermuda Triangle. (978-1-163555-175-4)

Love Like This by Melissa Brayden. Hadley Cooper and Spencer Adair set out to take the fashion world by storm. If only they knew their hearts were about to be taken. (978-1-163555-018-4)

Secrets On the Clock by Nicole Disney. Jenna and Danielle love their jobs helping endangered children, but that might not be enough to stop them from breaking the rules by falling in love. (978-1-163555-292-8)

Unexpected Partners by Michelle Larkin. Dr. Chloe Maddox tries desperately to deny her attraction for Detective Dana

Blake as they flee from a serial killer who's hunting them both. (978-1-163555-203-4)

A Fighting Chance by T. L. Hayes. Will Lou be able to come to terms with her past to give love a fighting chance? (978-1-163555-257-7)

Chosen by Brey Willows. When the choice is adapt or die, can love save us all? (978-1-163555-110-5)

Death Checks In by David S. Pederson. Despite Heath's promises to Alan to not get involved, Heath can't resist investigating a shopkeeper's murder in Chicago, which dashes their plans for a romantic weekend getaway. (978-1-163555-329-1)

Gnarled Hollow by Charlotte Greene. After they are invited to study a secluded nineteenth-century estate, a former English professor and a group of historians discover that they will have to fight against the unknown if they have any hope of staying alive. (978-1-163555-235-5)

Jacob's Grace by C.P. Rowlands. Captain Tag Becket wants to keep her head down and her past behind her, but her feelings for AJ's second-in-command, Grace Fields, makes keeping secrets next to impossible. (978-1-163555-187-7)

On the Fly by PJ Trebelhorn. Hockey player Courtney Abbott is content with her solitary life until visiting concert violinist Lana Caruso makes her second-guess everything she always thought she wanted. (978-1-163555-255-3)

Passionate Rivals by Radclyffe. Professional rivalry and long-simmering passions create a combustible combination when Emmett McCabe and Sydney Stevens are forced to work together, especially when past attractions won't stay buried. (978-1-163555-231-7)

Proxima Five by Missouri Vaun. When geologist Leah Warren crash-lands on a preindustrial planet and is claimed by its tyrant, Tiago, will clan warrior Keegan's love for Leah give her the strength to defeat him? (978-1-163555-122-8)

Racing Hearts by Dena Blake. When you cross a hot-tempered race car mechanic with a reckless cop, the result can only be spontaneous combustion. (978-1-163555-251-5)

Shadowboxer by Jessica L. Webb. Jordan McAddie is prepared to keep her street kids safe from a dangerous underground protest group, but she isn't prepared for her first love to walk back into her life. (978-1-163555-267-6)

The Tattered Lands by Barbara Ann Wright. As Vandra and Lilani strive to make peace, they slowly fall in love. With mistrust and murder surrounding them, only their faith in each other can keep their plan to save the world from falling apart. (978-1-163555-108-2)

Captive by Donna K. Ford. To escape a human trafficking ring, Greyson Cooper and Olivia Danner become players in a game of deceit and violence. Will their love stand a chance? (978-1-63555-215-7)

Crossing the Line by CF Frizzell. The Mob discovers a nemesis within its ranks, and in the ultimate retaliation, draws Stick McLaughlin from anonymity by threatening everything she holds dear. (978-1-63555-161-7)

Love's Verdict by Carsen Taite. Attorneys Landon Holt and Carly Pachett want the exact same thing: the only open partnership spot at their prestigious criminal defense firm. But will they compromise their careers for love? (978-1-63555-042-9)

Precipice of Doubt by Mardi Alexander & Laurie Eichler. Can Cole Jameson resist her attraction to her boss, veterinarian Jodi Bowman, or will she risk a workplace romance and her heart? (978-1-63555-128-0)

Savage Horizons by CJ Birch. Captain Jordan Kellow's feelings for Lt. Ali Ash have her past and future colliding, setting in motion a series of events that strands her crew in an unknown galaxy thousands of light years from home. (978-1-63555-250-8)

Secrets of the Last Castle by A. Rose Mathieu. When Elizabeth Campbell represents a young man accused of murdering an elderly woman, her investigation leads to an abandoned plantation that reveals many dark Southern secrets. (978-1-63555-240-9)

Take Your Time by VK Powell. A neurotic parrot brings police officer Grace Booker and temporary veterinarian Dr. Dani Wingate together in the tiny town of Pine Cone, but their unexpected attraction keeps the sparks flying. (978-1-63555-130-3)

The Last Seduction by Ronica Black. When you allow true love to elude you once and you desperately regret it, are you brave enough to grab it when it comes around again? (978-1-63555-211-9)

The Shape of You by Georgia Beers. Rebecca McCall doesn't play it safe, but when sexy Spencer Thompson joins her workout class, their non-stop sparring forces her to face her ultimate challenge—a chance at love. (978-1-63555-217-1)